'Epic in sheer size and scope'   *SFX*

'Weaves multiple threads of the plot together with consider-able skill . . . readers fond of open-ended epic fantasies set in vivid, and occasionally lurid, worlds will find it right up their alley'   *Publishers Weekly*

'*Leviathan's Blood* is one of the most unique and enthralling epic fantasies that I have read in recent years. Peek's vision and exe-cution are wonderful, and his deft and creative touch with this series a joy to behold. If Peek continues to write to this standard he will go down in history as a master of the genre'

Smash Dragons

'An enthralling story . . . thrills, blood, intrigue, excitement and an original world populated with compelling characters'

Book Bag

'A fast-paced page-turner set in an enthralling new world'

Speculative Book Review

'The first in a crackling, unputdownable new epic fantasy series, introducing a fascinating, original new world and an incredible heroine'   *Rising Shadow*

'I'm not overstating things when I say that Ben Peek is one of the most accomplished writers of richly detailed and intricate-ly plotted epic fantasy working in Australia today'

Newtown Review of Books

LEVIATHAN'S BLOOD

Ben Peek is the critically acclaimed author of *The Godless*, *Leviathan's Blood* and three previous novels, *Black Sheep*, *Twenty-Six Lies/One Truth*, and *Above/Below*, co-written with Stephanie Campisi. He has also written a short story collection, *Dead Americans*. In addition to this, Peek is the creator of the psycho-geography pamphlet, *The Urban Sprawl Project*. With the artist Anna Brown, he created the autobiographical comic *Nowhere Near Savannah*. He lives in Sydney with his partner, the photographer Nikilyn Nevins, and their cat, Lily.

www.benpeek.livejournal.com
@nosubstance

By Ben Peek

THE CHILDREN TRILOGY

The Godless
Leviathan's Blood

LEVIATHAN'S BLOOD

Book Two of the Children Trilogy

BEN PEEK

PAN BOOKS

First published 2016 by Macmillan

This paperback edition published 2016 by Pan Books
an imprint of Pan Macmillan
20 New Wharf Road, London N1 9RR
Associated companies throughout the world
www.panmacmillan.com

ISBN 978-1-4472-5186-6

1 3 5 7 9 8 6 4 2

A CIP catalogue record for this book is available from the British Library.

Map artwork © David Atkinson 2014: handmademaps.com

Typeset in Spectrum MT by Palimpsest Book Production Ltd, Falkirk, Stirlingshire
Printed and bound by CPI Group (UK) Ltd, Croydon, CR0 4YY

For my mother who, like a spy, keeps two first names,
Karen and Elaine Peek

Acknowledgements

My partner, Nikilyn Nevins, was the first reader of _Leviathan's Blood_, but more importantly, she was the first listener and the first sufferer. No book is made in silence, sadly.

Tessa Kum and Kyla Ward were, once again, the fabulous first readers who took me to task for all the things I should have done but didn't. Thanks also to Jessica Cuthbert-Smith and Joy Chamberlain who helped its final shape emerge.

My agent, John Jarrold, is a fine human, generous with both his time and experience.

A whole lot of thanks must go to Julie Crisp, primarily. She is the ghost in the machine that makes a book a book. In particular, she is the ghost of this particular book. In the USA, Pete Wolverton is the ghost that haunts his empire — and this book — similarly. Thanks to Sam Eades for organizing me and the publicity stuff. Huge thanks to David Atkinson from Handmade Maps for the superb maps in _The Godless_. And to Irene Holickit who translated _The Godless_ into German. It was my first piece of work ever translated. Similarly, thanks must go to Laura Carr and Louise Buckley for their work on the book. And to Bella Pagan who, if for nothing else, was willing to give up a table to an Irishman and an Australian because they had beer.

To everyone else who supported the book – to the readers, reviewers, bloggers – a huge thanks as well.

LEVIATHAN'S BLOOD

The White Tree Daily

• Speaking to You Since 1032 •

On the Fiftieth Anniversary of the Siege of Mireea

by VYRA RIEMAL

Once, the gods lived among us.

My mother told me that. My father, as well. Both were born thousands of years after the War of the Gods took place, and neither would see a living god, not before their deaths in 1023, the year the Leerans laid siege to Mireea.

They lived their lives in the aftermath of the War of the Gods. The remains of the gods lay around them, as familiar as the tree in their yard, as the bedsheets they slept beneath. Just as we do, my parents awoke in a world that was lit by the first part of the shattered sun rising. Throughout the day they would watch another two parts rise and fall. Outside the doors of their house, they lived on a mountain range that had been built around a god's corpse. It was normal to them, as normal as the coast that turned all living creatures mad, as normal as the ocean that smelt of blood. They

lived – as we all still do – among the remains of the divine beings who created our world. Beings who were dead, but also alive. Beings who were so alien to us that we can only theorize how they saw the world that they created. We suggest, now, that the gods experienced time as a whole, that their consciousness was so complex and large that none of them experienced time in the linear way that we mortal beings do. We believe that their holy bodies are being torn apart by time, by the collapse of their sense of self, so that the past, the present and the future have an effect on them. It is why their very essence and power seeps into our world and changes it.

Neither my mother nor my father could explain to me why the gods went to war. In the same way, they could not explain to me why the Leerans laid siege to Mireea.

My parents did not have the chance to understand it. They died, not by sword or arrow, not from any violent act by the Leerans, but from the plague that came to the city. It was through the kindness of others that I was cared for, but even those survivors of the siege did not understand, either, why they had been attacked. That understanding was months away, while a complete understanding would not be available for years, not until the diaries of those who were principal figures were found, or until they themselves spoke about what happened.

From them, we (and by we, I mean historians like myself) have been able to make great strides into the lives of those who were important in the days before and after the siege. The work is not complete, of course: there are years that are poorly documented, months that are not spoken of, and days that have, strangely, ceased to exist in any recorded form. But we have made great advances in regards to our knowledge of Ayae and Zaifyr, two 'cursed' individuals, and the mercenary Bueralan Le.

Ayae was one of the many children displaced during the Innocent's seven-hundred-year war in Sooia.

She arrived at the Mother's Orphanage in Mireea at the age of five. Like others who grew up in state-run care, she did not speak in depth about her childhood. Many who met her noted that she did not refer to the name of the orphanage itself, or the matron who died, tragically, in a fire shortly after her arrival. (Her name was Germaine Tislr and she was, it seems, an unpleasant woman, but that is neither here nor there.) Still, conditions were not oppressive within the orphanage, and Ayae and the other children who were cared for within it were given an education. Shortly after completing it, she won a cartographer's apprenticeship with the eighty-second Samuel Orlan. She was, by all accounts, an excellent apprentice, but there is no suggestion that Orlan considered her a successor to his name – though we do not know if he would have changed his mind, for history intervened before she finished her apprenticeship.

Shortly before the Leerans laid siege to Mireea, Ayae was attacked in Samuel Orlan's shop. A fire started while she was inside, but afterwards it was revealed that Ayae suffered not a single burn. Within days, she was identified by the Keepers of the Divine as a child of the gods; or, to use the more common term in Mireea at the time, Ayae was 'cursed'. She was infected by the power of a god, by Ger, who lay beneath her feet. Many believed that the power would soon take hold of her and consume her, as it had done to others in the past, but it did not. Instead, the two Keepers, Fo and Bau, who had been sent to Mireea by the 'cursed' who ruled Yeflam, took it upon themselves to educate her. During that time, Ayae discovered that the two immortals planned to release a plague in Mireea, which would result in the deaths of thousands. This went against the orders that Fo and Bau had been given in Yeflam, and the deaths of the two Keepers allowed for Ayae and the survivors of the siege of Mireea to flee to Yeflam.

Bueralan Le was originally born in Ooila, into a family of privilege and wealth. When he arrived in Mireea in 1023, however, he was the Captain of Dark, a small mercenary unit of saboteurs. He had been exiled from his homeland seventeen years earlier after taking part in a failed revolution.

Bueralan and Dark came to Mireea upon the request of the Captain of the Spine, Aned Heast. They arrived on the day that Ayae was revealed to be 'cursed' and, indeed, the two met before she was attacked. Bueralan and Dark, however, would not remain in Mireea. The ruler of Mireea, the Lady of the Spine, Muriel Wagan, ordered Dark into Leera, to learn as much about the force that was

approaching her as possible. In a last-minute addition, the famous cartographer Samuel Orlan joined them on the journey.

Orlan had his own motivations for joining Dark, but it was not until they had entered Leera that his intentions were revealed. Orlan betrayed Bueralan in a town called Dirtwater, and the saboteur was taken captive. Shortly after, he was delivered to the Leeran general Ekar Waalstan.

It was there that Bueralan learned that the Leerans had discovered a new god. Or, that she had discovered them. It is more likely the latter than the former, in truth. The new god had no name, but she inspired a fanaticism in her soldiers that Bueralan had not seen before. While imprisoned, he witnessed a number of blood rituals. During one such ritual, he discovered that Samuel Orlan had returned to Dark and had convinced his soldiers that they should continue with him to Ranan, the capital of Leera. He wanted them to help him kill the new god.

Unable to free himself, Bueralan found himself back on the Mountain of Ger as the Leerans laid siege to Mireea. He was forced to lead the head of the Leeran priests into the lost city beneath Mireea, to a temple that had been built over the body of the god Ger. The priests planned to take the last essence of the god's power and put it into Bueralan's body to return it to their god. In a series of events that is not yet fully understood, a part of Ger intervened. Bueralan killed his captors and then rode to Ranan, only to discover that he was too late to save Dark. The child god within the temple had already killed his soldiers. However, she did not kill him, and neither did she kill the cartographer Samuel Orlan. Instead, she declared both 'god-touched', and released them with a terrible gift.

In the long, complicated history of our world since the War of the Gods, readers will be familiar with **Zaifyr** by another name, that of **Qian**.

Qian was one of the first 'children of the gods', one of five men and women who believed that they were gods. History would reveal that all five were simply 'cursed', as Ayae would be called, ten thousand years later. Yet, with the four other men and women, whom he called his brothers and sisters, he would conquer much of the world and begin the age known to us as the Five Kingdoms. That age would end with the publication of a book by Qian entitled *The Godless*. In it, he said that he was not a god. It is a difficult book to find now – it suffered, as did so much in terms

of books and art, in the wars that followed after the Five Kingdoms ended – but *The Godless* laid much of the base from which we form our current understanding of the gods, and the men and women who are infected by their essence. Unfortunately, at the time of his writing the book, Qian had reportedly succumbed to madness, a result of having heard and seen the dead for so long. His brothers and sisters were forced to imprison him for a thousand years in a tower that they built in Eakar.

Upon his release from his prison, Qian took the new name Zaifyr. He became something of a wanderer in that time. There are stories of him appearing in Gogair, Faer, even as far away as the White Empire. It is said that he came to Mireea at the behest of his brother Jae'le, who had been watching the Leerans' god for years. It was here that Zaifyr met Ayae and helped her better understand her own powers. In doing so, however, he came into conflict with the two Keepers, Fo and Bau. When the former released a plague in Mireea, Zaifyr was brought to death's door. In such a state, he met the Leeran god in the soul of a dead soldier. She offered Zaifyr the opportunity to join her. However, in doing so, she revealed that she was responsible for the purgatory in which the dead found themselves. She said that the dead, and the living, were hers to do with as she pleased. Furious, Zaifyr vowed to destroy her and, when he awoke, he killed Fo and Bau to set into motion the events that led the Mireeans to Yeflam.

Imagine yourself there. As we pause to remember the Siege of Mireea this weekend, imagine how it felt to stand beside these three people. As you sit down to eat beside your family, or to walk through the displays, or read the histories that will be published, imagine yourself beside these three people who carried so many of our hopes unknowingly.

Imagine:

It is the year 1023. The calendar — a relatively new one, considering the world's long history — is edging towards a new year.

Mireea has fallen. Time has acknowledged Ger's death. The mountain that he lay beneath is crumbling as his divine body rots. Lady Muriel Wagan and her captain, Aned Heast, have taken the survivors of their city to Yeflam, where they now must enter the deadly game of politics between the Keepers of the Enclave and the Traders' Union. On the other side of the Spine of Ger, the Leeran forces are preparing to invade the Kingdoms of Faaisha. Betrayal awaits there. And in Leera, two men leave a cathedral, a terrible item in their grasp.

The world I knew is being unmade; the world you know is awakening.

Vyra Riemal is the noted historian and author of the Chronicles of Refuge. *Originally born in the city of Mireea, she now makes her home in the city of Lumu in Yeflam and has done so for the last thirty-two years. She is the owner of the famous bookshop Surfacing at the End of the World, the only bookstore to have seen two sword fights, one knife fight, a friendly ghost, and an inordinate amount of romance. (Which was possibly the reason for both sword fights, but, she assures you, not the knife fight.) She shares the space with her husband, her granddaughter, and a pair of black cats who are 'cursed'. Well. Most likely.*

She began with the words,
'Do you know who is lying to you?'
   —Tinh Tu, *Private Diary*

Prologue

Leviathan's Blood was what Ja Nuural's mother had always called the ocean.

He grew up a day's walk from the coast and, in the early years of his life, his mother and he would make a pilgrimage to the empty beach each summer. They would leave in the evening, after the bright, broken shard of the afternoon's sun had sunk, but the heat remained. In the dark his mother would hold his hand as she walked silently beside her brothers and sisters to the beach. In the morning's light, his extended family would build a bonfire on the sand – often in the remains of the previous year's – and they would eat and drink through the day and the next night. They would tell the story of how, on the day the Leviathan died, the blood from her body filled the ocean, raising the sea-level and turning the ocean black. For her part, his mother would tell the story of what happened to everything that had lived in the ocean. All the creatures in its depths, she said, were changed. Some were deformed. Some were turned violent when they had not previously been. But all had become poisonous to the men and women who ate them.

The stories were laments from the ancestors of fishermen.

The Nuural family had nurtured the words for generations and, on those long nights, Ja had lain beneath the smeared stars and dull shape of the moon and seen visions of men and women striding beneath the waves. He tried to hold his breath as they had – to hold it longer than any other person – and he imagined holding a spear made from the bones of a creature that had died in the intricate coral reefs of red and gold that had been the Leviathan's shrines.

He could still hear his mother's stories, two decades after her death, when he walked across the sand as the father of his own adult child. He could still hear her voice clearly on the afternoon that he saw the ship *Glafanr*.

He had come to check the rods that leant out into the black ocean. The remains of the day's butterflies were beneath his feet, their corpses cracking in the sand and on the stone as he reached the rods and the nets that lay between. The lines had been set in the morning, shortly before the first of the broken suns rose, but the day had yielded little. The heavy lines were slack in the water; he was not terribly surprised. The night was a better time to catch and he hoped that by the morning the lines would be taut with an inedible creature.

The heavy wooden rods had been attached to steel settings sunk deep into the rocks at the end of the beach. The coloured corpses of butterflies lay in wet circles at the ends of the poles but were mostly clustered around the spools of the catgut lines. The lines had enough length for most of the black ocean's large creatures to tire themselves out on, but he knew that in the depths of Leviathan's Blood were creatures that could break the line, even tear the rod from its setting and drag it away as if it were a twig.

The rising tide had washed the catgut lines and butterfly corpses into the rock pool between the poles, tangling the lines of both rods. The pool – twice his size in length and easily his height in depth – had been cut by hand before a net was settled into its base. It was there that the men and women of the village would pull what they caught from the ocean and hold them for examination. There, the caught beast would be marked and, occasionally, transported elsewhere. The last thing Ja needed was for the lines and rope to be entangled by the morning, so he bent down to free the lines and carefully pull it out of the pool.

It was when he stood that he saw the ship.

A single ship, far out on the black waves, yet so large, so imposing, that in the fading light of the afternoon's sun, he could see the red of its sails.

Glafanr. He did not speak the word aloud. *Aela Ren.* He would not say the name of its captain, either. He— 'The Innocent,' he said in a voice that was not yet a whisper.

Ja's daughter, Iz, had been the first to tell him the rumours about the ship. Her dark, sharp eyes had pierced him to his chair when, two weeks earlier, she had burst into his hut, trailing dirt and bright midday sun through the door. She stood in the middle of the room and spoke rapidly, but quietly, like his mother had. There was little other resemblance: Iz was tall and lean, her skin a deep dark black, not the dark brown, heavy woman his mother had been. In his mid-forties, Ja had more in common with his mother than with his daughter. She took after *her* mother, his wife, who had died a dozen years ago.

'The wreckage of a ship has washed up on shore,' she had said. 'The crew had been nailed to parts of the ship: to the hull, to the deck, to the mast, to the chairs. Nothing had been stolen: they wore their jewellery and their payrolls had been left intact. They were returning from Gogair—'

'Some people,' he said to her, 'do not like slavers. They think their money is tainted.'

'The deaths – they are *his*.'

He told her that every wreckage, every lost ship, was attributed to Aela Ren. If it was not the man himself, it was *Glafanr*, his huge, stationary ship that had been moored on the coast of Sooia for seven hundred years. She knew that, just as he did. She knew better than to repeat the stories she heard. He had been pleased when she had nodded, when she had agreed with him and had promised not to repeat it in the village.

The next morning, two young families, nine people in total, left the village. It was nine that he could not afford to lose, but he had not been surprised by who left. Both families had come down to the coast, lured by the gold in his work, by the Fifth Queen's financial support for what he did; but neither had believed in the task. They had not understood why the witches did not do the work, why they did not work with the blood in the ocean, why they did not accelerate the process of breeding out the poison and disease in fish. He had told them the stories of what had happened to the witches and warlocks who had tried just that, but he did not believe that they accepted what he said. They had never stopped asking him why it was necessary to breed the fish the way they did, why they needed to breed both the large and the small, the dangerous and the sedate, and why all must have the poison of the ocean removed from their flesh.

But they had not left because of the work.

'It is him.' The oldest of the women, Un Daleem, had been the one to tell him. A large, raw-boned woman with black skin, she wore a small dark stone around her neck like a blind third eye. 'Aela Ren. He is coming here, to the Fifth Province. To Ooila.'

'You do not know that,' he said.

'I hear the stories.'

'There are always stories.'

'It is different this time.'

Her gaze never left the empty black waves and the long lines of sunlight that ran towards the village like blades made from the morning's sun.

'I have never believed the rumours of his arrival,' she said, after a moment. 'Not before this. My mother told them to me the day I was born and every day until her death. Aela Ren will come. The Innocent is coming. But I would tell her that Aela Ren has had his war on Sooia for seven hundred years. He will not leave that land. That is why no other country ever invaded. Why no one has gone to help the poor people there. But now . . . now is different, Ja. *Glafanr* has been seen. More than one sailor, more than one ship – you have heard that as well as I have. And now that wreckage washes up half a day's ride from here? That was not the work of a raider, or a mercenary, or another country. That was him. That was the Innocent and his army and Leviathan's Blood has brought the dead crew as warning to us.'

That had been a week ago, and he recalled Un Daleem's words with a chill as he stood on the wet rocks, staring at *Glafanr*.

It is not the Innocent's ship, he told himself. *Red sails are used by more than one ship on the black ocean. And besides . . .* besides, as he strained his fading eyesight, he could not see movement on deck.

The ship was abandoned, surely. It was derelict and nothing more.

The words felt more like hope than truth, but he repeated them. Ships struck bad weather. Ships tore their sails. Ships broke their keel. Ships were abandoned for many reasons, and Ja Nuural ran through the list as he made his way back along the beach, the afternoon's sun setting in a dark orange light behind him.

In the village he nodded to the few people he passed on the streets, but he did not tell them about the ship. If they noted that there was something strange about him — a tension, perhaps — they did not comment. The empty houses that stared at all of them with blank eyes gave them more than enough reason to think he was troubled.

Three years ago, he had petitioned the Fifth Queen for funding, not just for his work with the fish, but for the village. The old Queen had died and it was said that the new one was sympathetic to what he was doing, so he wrote to her. Originally, he had named the village Stone River, but the name had never taken, and the people who lived in it, and those in the area, simply referred to it as the village. No capitalization, no title. He had used the name Stone River when he had petitioned the Fifth Queen, but when she had approved the funding for more buildings and new wells, she had signed it to Ja Nuural, 'of the village'. Yet, despite her support, he had never been able to grow the village as he wanted, had never been able to attract enough people. Many of the new houses sat like the dark husks of the butterflies, waiting to be crushed and reborn. It was widely believed that the Fifth Queen would not fund him for another year once she found out how little her gold had bought.

The thought entwined with the image of the ship – not *Glafanr*, but *the ship*, he repeated – and he thought of how much he had worked to build the village, how much he had sacrificed of his life, of his youth. He considered that as he walked out the other side of the village.

The woods began shortly past the beach, and it was there that a series of large wide rock pools awaited. There were over twenty, including two large enough to hold five creatures that were twice the size of him. These large beasts had long, ugly teeth. Their grey skin shimmered beneath the surface when they were close, but the light disappeared when they went deeper – and they were often in the depths for days at a time. In the old books, fishermen had called them sharks, but Leviathan's Blood had changed them. Their fins were made from hard bone and their dark eyes wept a black mucus at times of great anger and hunger. They had lost two villagers to the sharks over the last five years, but he still regarded the work as a success: three of the five had only known the clean water of the pool.

In another year, perhaps, they would be able to pull out the original sharks and butcher their bodies for research.

He passed the sharks' placid pool, moving to the others. Each was still and silent. In the last of the pools he stopped at, a soft phosphorescent light had begun to emerge as the afternoon's sun finally disappeared. Pausing, he watched tiny minnows dart back and forth, the light becoming a bloom that lit up the area. They were Ja's favourite – caught not with rods, but long nets they threw out into the ocean from a boat. He would often spend the early hours of the evening watching them, enjoying their delight in the clean water, but he could not do it this night. Seeing the light, he thought of it as a beacon that would lead a single, awful man and his army up the beach from where they landed.

The thought followed him to bed, but the sight of the faceless soldiers did not linger in his dreams. No, his dreams were of the deck of the ship he would not call *Glafanr*, and of its gentle sway and its silence.

He dreamed that he was standing on it.

Slowly, Ja approached the railing of the ship and looked into the ocean. The water's surface was like smoke and he thought he saw shapes beneath it. Tiny shadows at first, like the minnows he had seen earlier. They flickered and flickered until, without any warning, a shape rushed beneath the ship, a beast so huge and of such monstrous, unprecedented, size that Ja could not take it in as a single creature. His mind worked furiously to piece together the shape, the mountain-like head, the sharp ridges of its back, the long, long tail that curved up as the beast turned in a spiral and began to descend into the water. It was like a country, a kingdom spreading out around him and, with a sudden onset of panic, Ja realized that the creature was plunging downwards only in preparation to rise. In his mind he saw it bursting out of the black water, its open mouth a huge, horrific cavern capable of swallowing entire nations in a single bite and plunging him into a world where his very being would be broken down, where it would be consumed by the acid of the beast's stomach as if he were nothing.

A hand touched his shoulder.

'Father.'

His daughter.

'Father, you must wake,' she whispered. 'There is a boat approaching.'

He wanted her words to be another part of the dream, but her hand shook him again, and he groggily opened his eyes.

Outside his house, the light came from the stars and the moon, but by the time Ja had made his way to the beach, lamps had been lit, and the people of the village had begun to form a line that he had to push through. 'I am sorry,' Iz said softly, standing beside him on the start of the beach. 'I saw it just before the two guards did.'

Out in the dark water, a single boat approached, a single figure in it.

A single man, he knew.

'It's okay,' he said, finally.

'What—' His daughter hesitated, aware of the crowd listening to their words. 'The children should be sent away.'

'We do not know it is him,' he said, not believing his words. 'It is a survivor from a ship, that is all. A survivor.'

On Leviathan's Blood, a wave rose, and the small boat rose with it.

'We will greet him,' he said, as the boat rode the wave down, as the oars in it rose and fell in unison. 'We will send three people down to help him pull his boat ashore, to help if the man needs help. We will tell him what we do here. We will be proud. We will tell him that we are trying to change the world.

That we are fixing the damage that was done by the gods. We will tell him that, but we will be cautious. We will give crossbows and bows to others. We will make sure that everyone is armed. We will send the young children into the forest with the older children. We will not flee. We will not be ashamed of what we are doing here.'

'Father,' his daughter said softly. 'We need not approach at all.'

'We will not be afraid,' he said.

The Floating Cities of Yeflam

In Leera, she is known as 'our god' or simply 'the god'; but abroad she is called 'the Leeran God', or 'the child'.

The gods of the past were best described as a belief defined by function, but the child is not like that. The first descriptions of her to emerge were of a blonde-haired white girl, no older than seven; but after Mireea fell and the Spine of Ger began to crumble, other visions of her became known. In some, she was a baby, or a toddler; in others, a young woman, a teenager. While each may have been different, they were linked by her youth, defined by it, in fact, for it is from her youth that she crafts her identity.

—Tinh Tu, *Private Diary*

1.

A thousand years ago, Zaifyr's sister tried to kill him.

She had not been alone. Aelyn had been one of four who had come into his kingdom, drawn by the reports of massacres, by the reports of madness.

By his madness.

In the ruins of Asila, in the city that shared the name of the country he ruled, Zaifyr and his family fought. They fought a day and a night. Yet, he could not remember how it had started. He could remember his family asking him to come with them. Could recall them telling him that they did not want to hurt him. But he could not remember who spoke those words. The dead had been so strong and vocal beside him that it was their words he heard before any others. They stood beside him — a new family, a family forever growing — and for the first time in his life he knew that he had made the dead happy. He had given them not just life, but themselves. He had made them as whole as he could. Oh, he knew that he had done that only through a horrific act; even then he knew that, but he was thankful for their happiness. They were no longer hungry. No longer cold. They could remember their names and who they had once been. In their joy, their bodies lit not just the city, but the whole nation in an unearthly blue glow. It remained until his family began to speak to him. Then the light turned bright and hard with their anger. The dead hurled themselves at his brothers and sisters. They tore at them. They burned all the new life that they had in them. And his brothers and sisters met them. Jae'le. Tinh Tu. Eidan. And Aelyn, the youngest. He did not know how she came to be behind him. He had lost track of her towards the end. That is all he knew. When he became aware of her again she was approaching silently between the broken walls and past the corpses of the men and women and children. She was dirty and bloodied, but she was not weak. She was never weak. Her hands flexed strong fingers. With little effort, she could break his neck. He knew that. As she drew closer, he realized that she no longer fought to subdue him. Perhaps she had been right to put that aside. Perhaps she was still right, even now. Beneath him, a series of thick lines began to split open along the ground, and the head of a massive construction began to emerge. It was Eidan's creation, but it was the moment Aelyn had been waiting for. The rocky head gave way to a body, to thick arms, to huge legs. She rushed forward, she reached out . . . and as she did so, the cold hands of a dozen haunts closed around her, their bodies appearing out of the air as his power flushed through them. Not all the dead had fed on flesh and blood for weeks, not all had become as close to human as they would ever be again, and it was these dead that lifted her, these that wanted her, that *needed*—

'Zaifyr.' A thousand years later his sister Aelyn Meah, the

22

Keeper of the Divine, the Head of the Enclave of Yeflam, stood before him. 'Brother.'

And it did not matter that she thought herself a god.

He offered her half a smile. 'Sister.'

The two stood on a road, the Southern Gate of Yeflam behind her, and the Mountains of Ger behind him. He had not seen her in decades, but now he stood before her, his hands chained, a prisoner for killing two men who had been sent to Mireea on her word.

'There is still time to turn away,' she said quietly. She wore a pale robe of blue and her dark hair ran to her shoulders, grown out since he had last seen her. 'Time to stop this.'

'There isn't,' he said.

'Don't bring this war to Yeflam.'

'I already have.' He raised his manacled hands. 'I killed Fo and Bau.'

From behind her, voices rose. They did not come from the twenty-three men and women who stood near Aelyn and himself. In the centurics after Asila, his sister had remade herself and remade her empire. She drew to herself immortal men and women like herself − like him − and had taken the title Keeper of the Divine. She convinced each of them that they would one day be gods. She allowed them to stand beside her as she created an artificial stone continent across Leviathan's Throat. Of the men and women who stood before him now, Zaifyr knew six. They had been alive before he had been placed in his crooked prison after Asila had crumbled. Before the hungry haunts had lifted Aelyn into the sky and begun to tear at her skin. Before the stone giant had reared to its full height. Before he had been forced to release her to stop the heavy hand coming crashing down on him.

No, the sound of voices did not come from them. To him, the Keepers had nothing to say. But the long, tangled mass of people who lined the bridge into Yeflam, the people who called the artificial nation home, did. They had not liked Fo the Healer and Bau the Disease: the voices that they raised were not for them. The sounds of disapproval were aimed at the men and women who stretched behind Zaifyr, the Mireean people who had fled their home and come here for sanctuary. Most of all they were objecting to the woman who now left the head of the Mireean people and came to stand beside him as he lifted his chained hands.

'Lady Wagan.' Aelyn did not look at the woman who had led the people down the Mountains of Ger to Yeflam. 'You have done me a service,' she said. 'You have done Yeflam a service.'

Muriel Wagan, the Lady of the Spine, replied that she had only been respecting Yeflam law.

Zaifyr smiled at her words.

'I will offer you sanctuary for bringing my brother to me,' his sister replied. 'For bringing him to stand trial for the murder of Fo and Bau.'

'We ask for no more,' Lady Wagan said.

Zaifyr had watched Aelyn try to prevent his arrival during the three-week march down the trembling Mountains of Ger. She had tried through her representative, Faje — a tall, soft-spoken man whose brown skin disintegrated across his body, leaving blotches of pale pink. He had attempted to convince not just Muriel Wagan and her people that they should not come to Yeflam, but Zaifyr as well. He had spoken to them about the need for Yeflam to remain neutral in the war between Mireea and Leera. He did not want war to spread over both sides of the Spine of Ger, he said. He tried to warn Lady Wagan away with dire predictions of how the presses of Yeflam would treat her and her people. He told her that the 'free' presses would be without mercy, that factions within Yeflam would seek to exploit both her and the situation. Those words, Zaifyr knew, were also meant for him. He had smiled when Faje had turned to address him with similar concerns. He had not needed to say a word to the mortal man. Faje's dark eyes had reflected the knowledge that his words were falling flat before the charm-laced man, just as they did before Muriel Wagan.

His companion to the meetings, Benan Le'ta, a fat white man who represented the Traders' Union, had virtually hummed with pleasure in comparison. From what Zaifyr understood, Le'ta represented a political force within Yeflam that threatened the Keepers' power base. Centuries of changing attitudes and new political ideals had given the Traders' Union a hold in the Floating Cities, and the Traders had used it to argue for democracy, free markets and a form of self-determination that had found root in the dreams of the populace. The Traders' Union had not yet been able to break the hold of Aelyn Meah on Yeflam. The merchant Le'ta, who wore long, flowing clothes that hid the extent of his weight, believed that the arrival of the Mireean men and women, along with the trial of Zaifyr, would begin that process in such a way that Aelyn and the Keepers of the Enclave would not be able to maintain their grip on Yeflam.

The man was a fool.

'Lady Wagan.' Aelyn raised her voice so that the people behind her could hear clearly. 'The people of Yeflam are humbled to offer you and your people sanctuary on the island of Wila.'

The people behind Muriel murmured, but the Lady of the Spine inclined her head and accepted the prison she was offered.

Ayae had told Zaifyr a week ago about the offer. The former apprentice cartographer had been invited to the meetings hosted by diplomats on the road to Yeflam. She had gone reluctantly to the tents that the Traders' Union had provided and listened to both factions talk to Muriel Wagan about her welcome in the Floating Cities.

'Fo and Bau's deaths will only get her so far. Bringing you to Yeflam to answer for killing them doesn't give her free rein in Yeflam.' The two of them stood beneath the night's sky, the dimly lit tent she had emerged from behind them. 'They won't let the Mireeans in, either. Faje argued that neutrality is too important politically. He believes that there will be a peace to be negotiated with the Leerans, and that the Keepers will be able to preside over it.'

'Le'ta agreed with him?'

She nodded. 'The people of Yeflam don't fear her.'

Her was the child, the gods' only child, the force behind the Leeran army. 'They will soon enough,' he said.

Her warm brown hand touched his arm. 'The trial will go ahead in Yeflam. Benan Le'ta has insisted and Faje has agreed.'

'Good. When my sister officially calls a trial, it will bring the others to Yeflam.'

'What if they don't come?'

26

'They will.'

None of his brothers and sisters would like it, but that was not the point. Ayae did not like it, either, but Zaifyr had, in the journey down the Spine of Ger, convinced her that it was the only way that they could fight the child. He had persuaded her of the necessity of fighting her, as well. Now he just had to prevail on his sister and his family, and convince the Keepers – and the quickest way to do that, he knew, was to frighten them with the return of Asila if they did not call a trial. To remind them, not just of the ghosts, of the dead, but of what happened after, in the empires that they had ruled.

Zaifyr was led to the Southern Gate of Yeflam by Aelyn. With each step, he could feel the vastness of his sister's power, a sensation akin to the long, clear sky turning its gaze on him. It enveloped him, as it always had, and smothered the powers of the other immortal men and women who moved to take control of the Mireean refugees.

On the bridge, the crowd watched him and Aelyn approach. A carriage without horses waited before the gate and, as the two came closer, small twists of wind began to form around the empty shafts. Within moments, they had taken on the shape of two horses and their pale wind-born bodies had filled the leather harnesses of the carriage.

Behind him, Zaifyr heard a shout, a voice issuing a command, but he did not turn to see who spoke, did not turn to see what was happening to the Mireean people.

He stepped into the carriage and his sister, who followed, closed the door.

2.

The Yeflam Guard led the Mireeans to Wila with their weapons drawn. The refugees were unarmed.

For a moment, Ayae resisted moving as the bodies of men and women pressed against her. The order had been given by one of the Keepers, a man with blue dye in his hair, but she had barely registered him, or any of the others.

She had been against the idea of going to Wila from the moment she heard it mentioned in the small tents where Muriel Wagan held her meetings. It had instantly reminded her of Sooia, of the camp she had been brought up in before she came to Mireea. If she closed her eyes, she could see rough wooden walls, small dirty huts, and fear. Fear on faces. Fear in movements. Fear of every sound that came from beyond the large gate that they lived behind.

One of the blue-armoured guards of Yeflam pressed a mailed hand into her back, but Ayae did not move. The guard pushed at her and then jerked his hand back as if he had been burnt. He met her gaze but, as he did, another hand touched her shoulder, and Caeli said, 'Come on, come on.' The tall blonde guard of Muriel Wagan repeated the words as she pushed Ayae's shoulder, urging her back into the press of men and women who were being led across the bridge. The churning coast of Leviathan's Blood gave way to Yeflam's first city, Neela, but she saw little of the city before she was pushed down the stone ramp to Wila.

'You happy?' Ayae asked, once she was on the island.

'You didn't start a fight, did you?' Caeli rubbed at the palm of her hand, the hand that had held Ayae. 'This is no more than a prison.'

'But without cells.' Ayae followed the other woman's gaze around the island. 'Without walls.'

Wila was a flat piece of barren land made from dirt and sand. Ahead, Ayae could see the farmlands of Yeflam across Leviathan's Blood and, beyond them, the Mountains of Ger.

If she turned, however, Yeflam itself came into view. It stretched along the horizon, marked by huge arching bridges linking a series of circular platforms. The platforms were so large that they were like slabs of earth that a giant had lifted from the ocean's floor before resting them on a series of huge stone pillars. The thick columns were made from blocks of stone and dived into the black water, where they sank deep into the ocean's floor. Around them, islands similar to Wila lay beneath the length of the artificial country, dotting the length of the ocean from horizon to horizon.

It was not a new sight to Ayae. She and her oldest friend, Faise, had driven an ox-drawn cart from Mireea to the cities to buy supplies for the witch Olcea more than once. In those trips, however, the two women had never gone near the stone ramps that ran down to Yeflam's empty islands. Instead, they had travelled into Neela, along its wide streets and past its factories and storage yards.

Depending on which side of Leviathan's Blood you approached Yeflam, Neela was either the first of the nation's twenty-three cities, or the last. It was a Traders' Union city, and you could find presses that were friendly to men and women of wealth and position and critical of people who had held power in Yeflam for a thousand years. There were another five cities that the Traders' Union claimed as its own, the biggest of these being Burata, which connected to the eastern docks. In that city, you could buy anything, and it was there that Ayae and Faise had ridden to buy the supplies Olcea had wanted. In one of the free papers that were available in Burata, Ayae first read full-page articles using the term 'cursed' – the first time she had heard the word outside Mireea.

The word had followed her for the last three weeks as well. After they had left the ghost-filled streets of Mireea behind, people had begun whispering it. At first, Ayae had been able to ignore it, but it had only become worse. The whispers began when she made her way into Lady Wagan's tents and did not stop when she left: they continued when she queued for her rations and it was common whenever she and Zaifyr were seen together. The word was not always used with animosity. At times it was spoken with a neutrality – 'The cursed is over there in the chains' – and at times with a grudging respect – 'They both stood for us' – but more often than not, it was said with anger. By the second week, she had been spat at, she had been blamed for the loss of Mireea – either because she had not done enough, or because she had done too much – and she had heard others tell Zaifyr that he was responsible for the ghosts he had shown them in Mireea and that he kept the dead in their purgatory because he took his power from their pain.

'How can you listen to it?' she asked, one night. 'How do you not get angry at them?'

'I don't know them.' He sat on a piece of grass away from where the Mireeans had made a cold camp, the moon and stars the only light around him. It caught on the charms of copper and silver that had been woven through his auburn hair and around his wrists. He held one of those, one made from bronze, in his white hand. 'But,' he said, 'if I had just seen what happened to my friends and family when they died, I would probably blame the man who showed me as well.'

'You understand them?'

His eyes, green in the daylight but simply dark and depthless in the night, focused on her. 'It is an easy enough thing to do.'

Ayae made a face in disagreement.

'Then they shout at you,' she said. 'It's pointless to blame you for what has happened. Why don't they realize that?'

'Give them time.'

She looked away from him.

'You have time,' he said mildly. 'You will outlive every one of these people by thousands of years. You may outlive them by forever.'

She had dismissed his words because she could not fully understand such a life. She could not imagine standing beside Caeli as the blonde in Caeli's hair gave way to silver, while her own remained dark. She could not imagine Caeli's skin wrinkling while hers remained smooth. She simply could not imagine herself held in time like a painting. Yet she could see in Zaifyr that he could imagine such things – in fact, did not need to imagine them. She could see the length of his life in the way he held himself in conversation with others, in the distance he kept from those who were not like him. She could see it in the way he talked of the world and its future.

'Well,' Caeli said beside her now. 'We'd better start getting these tents put up.'

3.

The horses made from wind pulled the carriage through the streets of Neela, towards the huge stone bridge that led to Mesi, and from there, into Ghaam, where three bridges allowed Yeflam to unfold as if it were a dissected giant, its organs and veins open for all to traverse on.

'I felt Ger die.' Aelyn spoke as if she knew that his thoughts were about dead giants. They were the first words that she had spoken since the carriage door shut. She had sat opposite him, watching him intently, without anger. 'It was a light touch, but I felt it nonetheless.'

'There was little of him left when I arrived,' Zaifyr said. 'He didn't have that burning hatred that the others have.'

'It changed shortly after we had begun to build Yeflam. One day, it simply felt as if he had turned his gaze away.'

'Like he was waiting for something?' Beneath them, the carriage shuddered as its wheels left the ground. 'Or someone?'

'He was not waiting for anything. He was just—'

'Maybe he was waiting for the child in Leera,' Zaifyr interrupted. 'Maybe he knew that long before we did.'

'He was dying, Qian.' She used his name, his old name, the

33

name he had given himself a long time ago. 'He had come to the end of time. What we felt was a dying god coming upon death. Nothing more.'

Zaifyr did not reply. It was not that he disagreed – or that he strongly agreed, for to argue one or the other opened the concept of an awareness more intricate than he had thought the gods now had – but he was not sure how to respond to her. Before, she would have been angry at him simply for interrupting her. She would not have sat there and held his gaze until he had finished speaking, as she had just done. But it had been decades since he had last seen her and perhaps, in that time, she had changed. He had believed that Aelyn stored a lingering anger at him, a fury that had driven her to try to kill him. Since his release from the tower where his siblings had imprisoned him, he had not wanted to fuel it and had tried to show her a small respect by ensuring that he had no real presence in her new world. Now that he was in Yeflam, he expected her anger. He knew that what he was doing to her now was anything but respectful. In truth, he could only have been more disrespectful to her if he had arrived with a pack mule and Fo and Bau's bodies strapped to its back. He deserved her hostility. He knew that, yet . . . yet here he was, sitting opposite his sister, unable to draw a spark of irritation from her by deed or word.

The carriage begin to bank and, outside the shaking window, the clear sky revealed more of the Floating Cities of Yeflam.

The cities did not float, of course, but at night, once the afternoon's sun had sunk, the stone pillars that held the cities aloft blended into the black water and its shadows. Seen from a distance then, Yeflam did indeed look as if it floated.

He had seen it first a dozen years ago from the deck of a ship. The stone docks had stretched across the black ocean like giant petrified fingers, their shape lit by the towers on the islands both before and after. At the top of each tower, massive cauldrons of fire consumed hideous amounts of oil to cast a light across the lanes that the ships used when approaching Yeflam. But it had been the length of the country behind the towers and docks that had caught his attention. There, millions of lamps ran along the bridges and into the cities and, for a moment, Yeflam looked like a giant funeral procession.

Zaifyr had not seen its like before, but he knew, even as the ship drew up to the docks, that Yeflam had not been designed by Aelyn. He knew of only one being who could design such a city and that was his brother, Eidan. The realization had not surprised him. He knew that Eidan and Aelyn would have stood together after Asila. The two would not have been divided from each other, as the others had been. Yet, before Zaifyr had come to Mireea, Jae'le had told him that Eidan was not in Yeflam. He had left years ago, his brother said, and whatever calming influence he had had over Aelyn was long gone. It was one of the reasons, he said, that Zaifyr should not linger in the city.

'Where are you taking me?' Zaifyr asked, turning from the window.

'Nale.' Behind Aelyn the sky stretched in a long empty brightness. 'I have a home there.'

'No cell, then?'

'There is a cell for you in the Broken Mountains.'

'No.' He smiled faintly. 'I'll not go back there. You know that.'

She looked away, turning to the window where Yeflam lay below. There, Nale had come into view. It was easily three times the size of any other settlement in Yeflam and sat at the artificial country's centre, a massive city dominated by huge buildings, with none larger than the Enclave, the white tower where the Keepers of the Divine worked. Yet, as the wind-made horses began their descent, Zaifyr could not see the tower. Instead, he saw a series of sprawling estates, each of them kept behind high stone walls and steel gates. It was before a large, yellow-stone building defined by two towers that the horses landed, bringing the carriage to a halt.

Her home. Aelyn's home.

Yet she did not live there. That was clear from the moment she opened the door and led him inside. Dust coated the long half-filled shelves and still tables and chairs that lay beyond the doorway. The air was musty and dry and tainted by the smell of blood and salt from Leviathan's Blood. In Maewe – in the kingdom his sister once ruled – Aelyn had built a house identical to this, but the inside of it had flowed with air, with life, and with her. This house, Zaifyr thought as he followed her, was but a keepsake of the life she had left behind. It was like the churches he had found in rural communities after the War of the Gods. Each had been made as a place of worship while the gods had been alive, but rather than being a building that men and women and children could enter, the houses had existed as homes for the gods. Inside were items that the communities had associated with the god – books, idols, weapons – and each building had been sealed so that no one could enter. Reportedly, when the gods had been alive, the houses had been pristine inside, but by the time Zaifyr saw them, the remaining ones had been broken open like eggs, their insides scooped out for the sustenance they provided. They looked like Aelyn's house, a monument of a time long gone.

'Before you went to Mireea, Jae'le came to see me.' Aelyn stood in front of a wine rack, her fingers running along the old bottles. 'Not in person, of course. Just in one of his little birds. He told me that you would pass by. He said that he had asked you to come to this part of the world. He said that he was not interested in Yeflam. He was interested only in the war the Leerans had begun. I had already sent Fo and Bau by then, but he promised me that you would be no threat. He said that you had not talked to the dead since he released you.' She pulled a bottle from the middle of the rack, grasping it by the throat. 'Do you plan to keep those manacles on while we drink? Or will you lift a glass with them?'

'I like—'

Her free hand shot out, quicker than he could see. A moment later, he heard the black iron crack beneath her grasp. 'I don't need to pretend that you are a prisoner.' She tossed the remains to the ground. 'I know you're not.'

'No.' Despite her actions, Zaifyr's voice did not rise. 'No, I hadn't talked to the dead. Jae'le was right. But your Keepers did not leave me much of a choice in Mireea. Fo, especially.'

'They were children.'

'None of us is a child.'

'They were, compared to you.' She walked down a hallway to the back of the house, to a room that was flooded with light. A dusty, sun-faded table sat in the middle, a pair of chairs on either side. 'But it does not matter. You're here now,' she said. 'Here to stand trial for both their deaths. Here to abuse laws you do not respect. At least tell me that Jae'le had no idea that this would happen — at least tell me that this is not some plan that the two of you have created.'

'I already told you that what he said was true.' Zaifyr watched as she placed the bottle in the middle of the table. 'He will not be happy, either.'

'When has he ever stayed angry at you? Or you at him?' Aelyn pulled two glasses from beneath the table and blew into each to clean the dust out. Once she had finished, she met his gaze. 'I warned them, you know. Fo and Bau. I sent them a message, telling them that you would be there and that they should avoid you. I told them to treat you like Mireea and keep neutral.'

'They failed Mireea as well.'

'I know.' A note in her voice suggested that the conversation was one that she had had before. 'I do not want war, Qian,' she said. 'Those days are long gone for me. I had my fill in Asila. I had my fill before that and after that. Yeflam is a neutral country. I fought to make it so. I spent the last bit of fighting in me bringing it about. Now, instead, I am interested in education, in philosophy. I want to write about the nature of gods and how they influence our world. I want to prepare for the day that I will be a god — and I want to prepare the people for that as well.'

'You've made a treaty with the Leerans, haven't you?' The realization occurred to him with a faint surprise. 'With the child god?'

'The Leerans call her that, not I,' Aelyn said. 'I imagine that the child is like you or me, and I expect this will prove true when I meet her. When the Enclave met the Leerans, it was through a woman named Estalia.'

'Why would—'

It was she who interrupted him this time. 'Take a look around you. Yeflam is a nation that will number four million people within the decade. On Ger's back, Mireea is nothing compared to us. Even to call it a nation is to believe it is something that it is not. If some other nation — and Leera is a nation — wishes to go to war with the Lady of the Spine to control her lucrative trade route, what is it to me? I own the oceans in this part of the world. Any treaty I have with Muriel Wagan is easily put aside to keep war from coming to my country and my people.'

'Except now,' Zaifyr said.

'Except now.' Aelyn's hand did not tremble as she unstoppered the bottle. 'Now Muriel Wagan brings me the killer of two of my brothers and I must offer her sanctuary.' The wine that began to fill the two glasses was so dark that the afternoon's sun could not lighten it. 'The Leerans will ask me why I allow that and I will say that it is so my brother can stand trial for crimes for which he will never be punished.'

'The Leeran Army is no threat to you.'

'I did not say that.'

'Then what are you saying?' He picked up one of the glasses, one of his silver charms hitting the side of the glass as he did so. When she did not answer, he said, 'The child is a real god. I met her.' In the dusty room around them, haunts of dead men and women began to fill the room. 'I met her, Aelyn,' he repeated, 'and she is not like us. She is not a piece of divinity lost in a mortal. She *is* divinity. She was pulled out of the earth in Eakar. Ask Jae'le, if you do not believe me. He saw it happen and did not tell us about it. But it does not matter. What matters is that she is not a complete god. She does not have a name and she relies upon the dead for her power, much like a witch, or a warlock. Only, unlike them, it is she who keeps the dead in our world. She who has locked them away from salvation or oblivion. It is she who creates the misery you see around you. If we do not strike at her, if we do not kill her *now*, she will visit that misery on us, and on everyone else in this world.'

'When I met you,' she said, after a moment. 'The first time, so long ago now. When I met you then, you sounded like this. You and Jae'le both.'

'He is not here.' The ghosts around them began to fade, their shape disintegrating beneath the afternoon sun's light, until nothing remained that she could see, or hear. 'And I am not that man any more,' he said.

'I truly hope so, brother.' In her hand the glass was still, the red wine untouched. 'For that man left nothing in his wake.'

4.

By the time the last of the tents had been erected, pamphlets and newspapers had begun to fall onto Wila.

The afternoon's sun had sunk behind the black ocean when the pieces of paper began to settle on the dirt and sand. For a while, they went unnoticed: Lieutenant Mills, white and grey-haired, had finished recording who would share with whom when a piece of paper came snaking along the narrow lanes. It stuck on the cloth of a freshly staked tent, where it was picked up by a guard. Ayae was one of the next to pick up a piece. It was a single sheet of Yeflam's dirt-coloured recycled paper, with the words GO BACK HOME written in big, block letters on it. When she showed it to Caeli, who stood next to her, the guard swapped her for one with a drawing of the Mireean people standing on the edge of Yeflam. They were tipping the great stone city as if it were a boat, tipping it into the waiting Leeran forces, which held swords and catapults and stood on the bones of their enemies. Ayae balled up the picture in her hand and turned to the stone platform of Neela behind her, where the city's lamp revealed children throwing the papers over the edge gleefully.

'Lovely,' Caeli said beside her. 'Just lovely. Nothing makes me happier than adults using kids to say what they're afraid to say.'

Ayae did not disagree. 'I thought Neela was a Traders' Union city.'

'It is. Surely you're not surprised?'

She was, a little. On the mountain road to Yeflam, Benan Le'ta had assured Lady Wagan that the Mireeans would be welcomed in Yeflam. They were refugees, he said. He had walked through the crowd, shaking hands, greeting both men and women. *People will be sympathetic to your plight*, he had continued. *They will understand. Aelyn Meah would have no choice but to release all of your people into the cities after a few days.* He said that he would personally advocate it. The other representative, Faje, had made no such promises. Ayae had thought that Faise, who had arrived the same day as Le'ta and Faje, had been unnecessarily pessimistic when she heard what had been said. 'Wila is a prison,' Ayae's oldest friend said to an unsurprised Lady Wagan. 'All the islands are prisons. When you stand on one, you're not standing on Yeflam, and you are not subject to Yeflam law. Basically, you have no rights.'

Faise had arrived with her husband, Zineer. A slender, bespectacled and balding white man, he appeared sombre in comparison to his wife, who was small and plump and brown-skinned. She wore a green and purple silk shirt with black trousers over black boots, each article meticulously kept, unlike her husband, whose laces were frayed and the edges of his white shirt stained with ink. The two had been forced to wait until Le'ta and Faje had left the next day before they could speak to Lady Wagan. Ayae had been surprised when they told her that the Lady of the Spine had sent a letter requesting their presence. Still, she had been pleased to see Faise, happier than she had thought possible to spend a night beside a woman whose companionship was unconditional and who, in the face of the animosity that some Mireean people held, responded in a much less complex way than Zaifyr.

'There is no excuse,' Faise said, when Ayae told her why people were acting that way towards her, after she had told Faise that she had changed. 'I mean, what if you decided to set their hair on fire?'

'I'm not going to set their hair on fire.' *Though I'd like to.* 'I'm trying to be understanding. It is a difficult time.'

'How about her?' Faise pointed at Keallis, the dark-haired white woman who had been a city planner. 'A hair-burning would teach her not to stare.'

Despite herself, Ayae laughed. 'Maybe,' she admitted.

Keallis was before her now, one of a handful of people who had been assigned the job of collecting the paper by the lieutenant. The tents were so tightly pegged next to each other that there was no room to avoid the woman as she and Caeli made their way past. Keallis regarded Ayae coldly, but if Muriel Wagan's guard noticed, she gave no indication. They continued to the tent that the Lady of the Spine had taken for her own. It sat on the northern side of the island and was the largest in the makeshift city, though Ayae would not have said that that meant much. The tents that it was compared to were no more than narrow dirty pieces of cloth on a triangle of wood; Muriel Wagan's tent was simply square and nearly normal sized.

The Lady of the Spine had a collection of pamphlets laid out in front of her when the two women entered. Two had drawings of Lady Wagan on them. She pointed at the one furthest from her and said, 'That one isn't a bad likeness of me – if I was to be holding a knife at your throat and had an army of ghosts behind me, that is. It even calls me the Lady of the Ghosts.'

In the guttering light in the tent, Ayae could see where the responsibilities of the last three weeks – perhaps the last year – had left its mark on the woman. Her solid middle-aged body slid more easily into fat and her red-dyed hair revealed grey roots, while the bags under her eyes had darkened considerably. 'The presses must have been printing these for at least a week before we arrived,' she continued, the humour leaving her voice. 'Preparing to drop this on us. How are people taking it?'

'In their stride,' Caeli replied. 'A few will probably blame Ayae, either because she didn't stop it, or because she's here, but any excuse for those people.'

She had noticed, then. Ayae offered a half-shrug to Lady Wagan. 'It's not important.'

'You're showing more dignity than they deserve.' The older woman waved for them to sit on her cloth floor. 'You'd think that they wouldn't so easily forget what you and Steel did for them. Or that the cure for Fo's disease came from Zaifyr.'

'Some people haven't forgotten,' Ayae said, taking a seat.

'Good.' The Lady of the Spine began to pull the pamphlets together. 'But still: when you get an offer to leave, take it.'

That surprised her and she said so.

'The Keepers won't leave you here,' Lady Wagan explained. 'You may not be part of their Enclave, but you are one of their kin – you're an inheritor of a god's power. They won't leave you here. They won't be able to stomach it politically.'

Ayae thought about leaving Wila, about stepping off the island that reminded her so much of her youth. 'I couldn't do that,' she said, despite her thoughts.

'You could,' Lady Wagan said bluntly. 'And you will. They may have allowed Aned to stay in Yeflam, but he won't be able to do everything for us alone.' She lifted the pamphlets. 'And I doubt he'll have any chance to advocate for us with the Keepers and stop these papers, either.'

Ayae did not want to agree. Leaving Wila would be taking a step away from the shared responsibility of life on the island and the collective experience of pain that it held. She had not understood that when she had been a child in Sooia, when she had lived behind the walls, with adults fearful of the Innocent's army, but in the years that had followed, she recalled fragments of the words that the adults had spoken and the importance of community. She understood the idea of a shared burden now and recognized the responsibility that people had to each other. It was something, even with people like Keallis, that Ayae felt was important, especially now, when she felt that she knew intimately what other Mireean people would feel in the coming months. She was about to tell Lady Wagan that when the tent flap was pulled back and the silver-haired white healer Reila led two men inside. A stretcher lay between them, and on it lay Lord Elan Wagan, a thick bandage tied around his face to hide the damaged sockets where his eyes had once been.

'They would not take him?' Lady Wagan stood, her body releasing a sigh as she did. 'Not even for mercy?'

'Le'ta said that he would be better here,' the healer replied. 'With people who loved him.'

Ayae let her words go unsaid. With a brief nod, she and Caeli left the tent, leaving Muriel Wagan with her husband, with the burden that she had to shoulder alone, in the absence of her daughter. Ayae remembered that when Lord Wagan began screaming on the first night that they were on Wila. The sound, brief though it was, did not spare a single man or woman on the island, but they could return to a sleep that Lady Wagan would not find.

Ayae lay in the tent she shared with Caeli. In the quiet that followed the screams, the guard said, 'The sedatives are doing less and less.'

'If ever there was a cause for mercy . . .' Ayae said, staring up at the fabric roof. 'But to spare him his pain . . .'

'Is to deliver him to more.' Caeli was silent for such a long time that Ayae thought that she had fallen back to sleep. But then, 'I had the plague in Mireea,' she said, 'the first signs of it.'

'You got the shot, though?' Ayae asked.

'Yes,' Caeli said. 'A day before you went into the tower.'

'Good.'

'I used to be like that planner, Keallis,' she continued. 'Well, not as bad. But I had my doubts. Cursed people were a problem. That was my opinion. My mother and father used to say it all the time. It's not right to blame my parents, but when I think about where it came from, I guess it is them. Lady Wagan wouldn't tolerate me saying it, so I kept it to myself, but still, it was there. I thought it.'

'It's okay.' Ayae didn't know what else to say. 'Really.'

'No, it's not. You have to admit when you're wrong. Maybe you don't have to say it aloud, but you have to admit it.'

'You don't have to say it.'

'But I am.' Caeli fell silent, but this time, Ayae knew that she hadn't fallen asleep. She knew that she lay on her back, staring at the low ceiling. 'You know that she is right, don't you?' Caeli said, after a minute. 'About leaving, that is.'

'Yes,' Ayae said softly. 'I know.'

5.

The Captain of the Spine, Aned Heast, was not with Muriel Wagan and the Mireean people when they were led down to Wila.

He had been sent into Yeflam two days before. On the night he left the mountain camp, he did so alone, on foot, and with no fanfare. He was, once all descriptions of him were reduced, a man who wore the decades he had lived beneath the broken sun with a sword at his side and a hand out for coin. Upon first sitting opposite him, many felt that his weathered features and pale-blue eyes belonged to a man who had little pity, who weighed their worth against the money he was being paid and little else. People had always said that of him: in his youth, men and women said that it was because he had suffered the loss of a young love; in the decades after he had lost his leg, people who met Heast said that something had broken in him, that a kindness that existed in the hearts of other men had left him with the limb. Neither version was the complete truth, but he did little to convince people otherwise. When he first lost his leg, enough men and women had known what else he had lost that their words had an echo of truth, but the words were now repeated by those who knew nothing about it. He was thinking of that when, an hour outside the camp, he discovered Benan Le'ta waiting for him at the side of the moonlit road.

The merchant had not impressed Heast. A short white man, Le'ta's weight rolled down him as if he was a pear, but with a square and stubby head atop his shoulders. It was he who, once the siege had been laid in Mireea, had sent the letters demanding that the two Keepers, Fo and Bau, be put in chains and brought to him, if the Mireeans wanted his help. It was an impossible request, but then, in Heast's mind, Le'ta had planned an impossible scenario. The merchant imagined a public hearing of the two Keepers' crimes in Mireea and he believed that such a hearing would provide him with leverage, if not against the Keepers, then against his own political enemies in the Traders' Union. The sharp letters in Le'ta's handwriting had admitted that to Muriel Wagan in the first week after Mireea fell. Indeed, when Le'ta first rode into the camp, Heast thought he was going to throw a tantrum and stamp his feet. If it had not been for the presence of Faje, and Aelyn Meah's desire to keep Zaifyr away from the Floating Cities, he might very well have done so.

'Le'ta will turn on us once we are welcomed into the city by the Keepers,' Lady Wagan had said, hours before Heast left the camp. He had gone to her tent to bid her goodbye, to tell her of the orders he had given to his soldiers and to Lieutenant Mills, who would assume command while Heast was gone. 'He is an idiot.'

'You agree with what Faise said, then?' Faise had arrived on the same day as the ambassadors and Heast had done everything he could to lose her and her husband in the camp while Le'ta and Faje were there. 'That it will be nothing but a prison?'

'It was plain to see before.' Muriel looked tired. She had not been sleeping well, but he could not blame her for that. 'Le'ta will try and use us as political leverage rather than work with us. It almost makes me wish that Lian Alahn had remained in power. It would have been a different situation if he had – but we will have to make do with what we have.' She handed him a folded piece of paper. 'Faise and Zineer will meet you at this location the day after we arrive.'

He took the paper, pushed it beneath his old, worn leather armour. 'Essa sent a note. He and the Brotherhood are in Yeflam.'

'Good.'

'He is not happy about it.'

'The only person happy to go to Yeflam is Zaifyr.'

Heast had not disagreed and, in the carriage that took him into the Floating Cities, Benan Le'ta echoed the Lady of the Spine's words.

He had shrugged off the merchant's comment. The charm-laced man had made it clear that he had little concern with what was unfolding around him. He had shown the same lack of interest to the Mireean people who had thrown insults and spat at him after they left Mireea and the streets full of ghosts. The girl, Ayae, who had stood against Fo and Bau, had not fared as well beneath the insults: Heast had watched her move between patience and anger and, fearing that she might justifiably lash out, he had quietly told guards to shadow her. He hadn't ordered Caeli to do it – she had other duties – but he had been pleased to see the former with her. He had ordered guards to shadow Zaifyr as well, but Zaifyr had seen them within an hour and, in a move that terrified his soldiers, Zaifyr approached the guards and told them that it wasn't necessary. Heast related that to Le'ta in the carriage, while it took them over the bridge into Neela, as the morning's sun began to etch across the black ocean, into Mesi.

'They say he is a powerful man,' the merchant said, 'more powerful perhaps than the Breath of Yeflam.'

'Aelyn Meah?' He hadn't heard that title in a long time.

'Who can say? If he is her brother, then he ruled beside her long ago with three others.'

'With a brother, a sister, and — ' Le'ta smiled unpleasantly — 'a lover.'

'A lot was burned back then,' Heast said with a hint of distaste at the other man's comment. 'A lot to hide who was who and what was what.'

The smile slithered away. 'Yes,' Le'ta replied. 'It makes it difficult to know anything for certain.'

Shortly after, the merchant dropped him off before a small two-storey inn made from stone and wood. It was called The Minotaur's Lost Eyes and the sign showed, beneath the words, a pair of eyes spiked through the centre. Le'ta said that it was a good establishment, a fine building of sturdy beds and discreet staff, and Heast assumed that he owned them. Just before he tapped the roof of his carriage to signal that it should leave, Le'ta said that he would come and visit him when everyone was safely on Wila. 'We will discuss what we can do for the Mireean people,' he said. 'What kindness can be given to them in their time of need.'

The next day, after the Mireeans had been led to Wila, Le'ta found Heast in the common room of the inn. Heast had a collection of newspapers and pamphlets laid before him, having flipped through most of them already.

'You were there, I trust?' Le'ta asked as he bobbed through the tables in the mostly empty room. He did not wait for the Captain of the Spine's response before he began to claim how well it had gone, how he had seen fear in Aelyn Meah's face, how the crowds showed that she did not have their support. Heast, for his part, had seen the Keeper's face in the carriage as it drove by. From that brief glimpse, fear was not the word he would have used. Resigned, perhaps. But the horses made from wind had drawn the carriage away and, by then, his attention was on the other Keepers and the Yeflam Guard. They had barely contained a riot as the Mireeans were led to the island with Muriel Wagan at their head. The pamphlets and papers before him had been given out in that crowd by men and women for free. Le'ta, upon seeing them, said, 'Ah those disgusting rags. Printed by presses not on Neela, I assure you.'

'Is that right?' Heast said, leaning back in his chair. 'You're all innocence, are you?'

'Captain, now is not the time to question our trust.' The merchant sat and, in doing so, revealed the man a handful of paces behind him. 'May I introduce you to Commander Bnid Gaerl of the Empty Sky?' he said.

'We've met before.'

He was a tall white man a handful of years younger than Heast. Yet he appeared older, the lines in his long face leaving him with a craggy, liver-stained visage in which dark eyes sat deeply. He wore expensive armour that was mostly a light chain mail, and over his shoulder, beneath the cloak of dark blue, he bore a heavy two-handed sword.

'Well,' Le'ta said, turning back to Heast. 'I trust that it was in favourable conditions.'

'He was the Captain of Refuge then,' Gaerl said, his voice deep and heavy. 'But he shed that title like a snake sheds a skin. He'll shed the title he has now the same way.'

'Refuge no longer exists,' Heast said evenly. 'The rank no longer has meaning when there are no soldiers.'

'Your witch still wears the title.'

'By all means, tell Anemone to stop.'

'Commander. Captain.' Le'ta appeared surprised by the animosity, but he must have known of it before he entered the inn. Over a decade ago, Gaerl – Heast refused to use the self-appointed rank of commander – had tried to use the name Refuge for his own mercenaries. 'We are not here to talk about old difficulties or, indeed, the men and women that you have known in your service to the world of coin. Instead, we are here to ensure that all that can be done is done for the Mireean people.' He tapped one of the papers on the table. On the cover was a picture of Muriel Wagan and, around her, an ocean of bones. 'It is a difficult task when stories like the ones here are being printed. We can all agree on that, I'm sure. It will be difficult to do anything for Lady Wagan and her people if they are linked to this monster.'

'They need blankets and food,' Heast said, turning back to the merchant. 'Lady Wagan has given me access to Mireea's finances to provide for them on Wila. I would like to begin with that as soon as I can.'

'Of course, of course.' Le'ta frowned slightly as he said the words. 'But I warn you, it may not be as easy as simply buying and shipping goods. We will be required to petition the Keepers to allow us access.'

'I will speak to Xrie,' he said. 'We should be able to avoid that.'

'The Soldier?' Gaerl frowned. 'The Captain of the Yeflam Guard is not an easy man to get an audience with.'

'It can be done.' He did not look away from Le'ta. 'I'd also like to request a personal favour, if I could?'

'Of course,' Le'ta said, just once, this time. 'What is it?'

'I'd like to meet with Lian Alahn – privately.'

'He has fallen considerably from favour with the Traders' Union,' the merchant replied. 'He is not even currently in the country. I am afraid he will be able to do little for you.'

'It is a personal matter concerning his son,' the Captain of the Spine said. 'That is all.'

6.

Bueralan Le sat in the shell of a building, the moon's light seeping through trees to fall through a broken roof, where it offered little solace to a man in grief.

He had been unable to save Dark. *Kae. Liaya. Ruk. Aerala. Zean.* He repeated the names to himself each night, an act of punishment in his suffering. He saw them again, each of them fallen in the cathedral. Saw the candles flicker along the walls, the light wavering over the dead. He heard the sound, a shifting mass, in the rafters. Then he saw Kae first. Saw Liaya and Ruk together. And after them, Aerala. Next, he saw the blonde-haired child at the end of the cathedral. She stood at the top of a small dais in a simple dress of white. She was but a handful of steps from Zean's body, as if his oldest friend, his blood brother, did not matter. Bueralan could close his eyes and remember the green eyes of the child. He had been ready to die. Then the child had stepped towards him and said, 'I have a gift for you.'

A soul.

Zean's soul.

After, the child had called him god-touched, had said that

he could call on her — *only when what is at stake is innocence*, she said — and she released Samuel Orlan into his care, but those words, those actions, were like shadows around him. She spoke but he felt only the crystal she had given him. A chill had begun to settle into the black skin of his hand as he held it, had begun to numb it to where his white ink tattoos began on his wrist. Outside the cathedral, he placed it in a dark leather pouch, but he could still feel the cold. Even so, he threaded a piece of leather through the end of the pouch and tied it around his neck and let the chill settle against his chest. It would lie there until he returned home.

He knew instantly that he would be returning to Ooila, to where the witches of his childhood blew dark expensive glass bottles from which pieces of glass were taken for the living to wear around their necks. To where the bottle was whole once again after the death of the man or woman who had worn that piece. To where the family took the unearthly remains of their loved ones and entered into a long-established network of barter and purchase to ensure that the bottle would sit on the nightstand of a pregnant woman in a good family. The soul would be leached into her womb with every sip she took from the bottle, drawn down into the foetus, to search for a perch in the newly created child, to find life again.

The Mother's Gift, they called it.

'Break the damn thing.' The rough voice belonged to Samuel Orlan. The old white-haired cartographer had almost had his throat crushed by a creature made from shadows in the cathedral and it had not yet healed. 'Don't sit there with it in your hands all night again,' Orlan muttered from where he lay.

56

'Break it. Smash it. I'll get a stone from outside for you to do it. Better than what she has planned.'

'Your conscience has no place beside me, old man.' Above him, the swamp crows that lined the rafters shifted, awoken by the sound of his voice. 'Zean is dead because of you. They're all dead because of you.'

'You would be too, if you'd come with them.'

'But not you.'

The cartographer grunted sourly as he pushed himself into a sitting position.

'Why didn't she kill you?' Bueralan asked. 'You're not worth a thing compared to the people who died.'

'She didn't kill you, either.' He coughed, rubbed at his throat. 'She's not a god yet.'

The answer offered little. In truth, little made much sense after the cathedral. Outside, Ranan had been empty, and though Bueralan had felt as if he was being watched, he had not seen a single person on the streets, or in the broken buildings. Both his horses were gone too. The tracks led off down the main street, and then disappeared into the thick sweltering marshes of Leera, but only for a step or two. The tracks stopped suddenly and neither Bueralan nor Orlan had been able to pick them up again. With one sword between them, they had been left to walk through the marshes and swamps, their direction mostly eastwards. The nearest port was Jeil in the Kingdoms of Faaisha, though Bueralan knew that it was not truly near. It would take weeks to walk there. Weeks, he had told himself, without food or water.

On the first night out of Ranan, they had been found by eight Leeran raiders. Both men had slunk into a line of trees that offered some protection, and they had collapsed, exhausted. Bueralan had meant to split a night's watch with Orlan, but the old man had stumbled into a deep sleep, and his own grief had swamped him and kept him awake. He had not heard the raiders approaching until all eight were around him.

He did not reach for his sword, did not stand. 'Go on,' he said. 'I should never have walked out of that cathedral anyway.'

A man stepped forward. His teeth had been filed down and his white skin was sunk against his bones, as if he was being consumed by a disease. 'She sent this for you.' The raider dropped a heavy sack on the ground. 'To reach Jeil.'

He didn't reach for it. 'I don't want it.'

'You'll starve before you reach the border,' he said. 'The old man before you. She has seen it.'

'Then why would I take it?'

'Because she has seen it.'

He asked another question, an angry question, because on those nights his grief gave way to anger, but the Leeran raider did not respond. A moment later, he and the seven men and women who had stood around Bueralan disappeared.

Beneath the green-tinted light of the morning's sun, Bueralan and Orlan had tipped the sack open, scattering fruit, bread, and water across the ground. It had been the meat that had given them pause. It was a square, cured, and as the cartographer picked it up, Bueralan said, 'I don't think we should eat that.' Despite having not eaten for two days, he felt repulsed by the shape of it. 'No telling what it is. Could be human.'

'Smells like pig,' Orlan said.

They had left it there without further conversation.

It had been the only time that the two of them had agreed

on anything. Since then, they had niggled at each other, prodded and probed. Bueralan's anger had been the source of his antagonism. Orlan's was guilt, he assumed. The old man had not apologized for what he had done – not that it would have meant much if he had. Orlan hadn't given much away, either. He hadn't explained why the child had called him god-touched. Why she had not killed him. Or why, in his words, she was not quite a god yet.

7.

Kal Essa was a man easily remembered. In the final days of Qaaina, in the days when the Oolian Queens were burning not just lives, but an entire nation, a heavy, spiked mace had struck Essa across the left side of his head, tearing open his skin. It had been a glancing blow and the skin had been stitched back together in the field, but as often with such makeshift work, it left scars. In the Captain of the Brotherhood's case, it left a series of heavy, spider-webbed lines that ran from eye to ear in white scar tissue.

'By the time the paperwork was done, two men were waiting for me outside the office,' Essa said, after Heast had stepped through the back door of the building he had bought. The expanse of empty floor waited to be filled with produce, with blankets, with whatever Heast could buy to fill it. 'They followed me across Neela and into Maala. It was nearly a whole day's ride in those carriages. They've set up a rotation outside the hostel we rented – about eight of them – but they're easy enough to lose and find again when we need them.'

'I had two following me before I came here, as well.' At the far end of the room were two people, a man and a woman, who were doing a lap of the emptiness. 'Did any follow those two?'

'No.' Essa turned to Heast. 'I told them to be careful with Gaerl, though.'

'But they ignored you,' he said.

'They shrugged it off.' The mercenary spat on the floor. 'They don't know him the way we do, Captain.'

Faise and Zineer drew closer. They carried leather satchels full of paper, full of orders and statements and purchasing plans. Already, in the week since the two had met Muriel on the mountain, they had begun to set up a series of false names and long paper trails to hide the details of the majority of what they bought. They had helped Essa with his purchase and, Heast knew, it had been reported to Benan Le'ta, but the act, much like the purchase of the factory they stood in, was one of misdirection. He wanted the merchant to be watching Essa and him. That way, the majority of what Faise and Zineer would soon be buying would be kept from view, the paper trail lost while the Mireeans gained their leverage over the Traders' Union.

'We'll start buying farmland next week,' Faise said, after they had greeted Heast and then crossed the stone floor to stand next to him and Essa. 'We're going to start on the northern side, on farms that are near to Mireea. Some of that is already owned by Muriel Wagan, and the loss of Mireea will make the sellers a little easier to shift.'

Heast took the map she handed him. She had circled the lots of land. 'Who do you plan to use as a buyer?' he asked.

'A Zoum banker,' Zineer said. 'A lot of the world's coin routes through there and the bankers are often used to represent buyers. We were lucky that one was in Yeflam when we needed her.'

'How long until it becomes public, do you think?' He passed the map back to Faise. 'Before the Traders' Union and the Keepers realize?'

'A pattern will start to emerge after a month or two,' Faise said. 'Lady Wagan wanted us to run an aggressive purchasing campaign, so they'll be alerted to the loss of their assets reasonably quickly.'

'Then it'll be the money they follow.' Zineer gave a slight shrug. 'That could stretch on for years.'

'Don't plan on that,' Heast said. 'Captain Essa and I have soldiers tailing us. If you aren't being followed already, it won't be long until you are.'

'We understand that.'

'Get a guard,' Essa said bluntly. 'Some of my boys and girls will do well by you.'

'That will draw attention to us straight away.' Zineer pushed his glasses up his nose, smiling ruefully. 'The work we did for you here is very easily explained by anyone watching. My wife is Mireean. She has friends who are being kept on Wila. We're helping with the clothing and food. But if we are seen to do more than that, I am afraid something will look wrong very quickly. Benan Le'ta is well aware that we are completely broke and in a lot of debt.'

'He was the one who ruined us, after all,' Faise said.

After they had gone, Essa called them foolish children. Heast responded by telling the other man that they had a point.

'And when things get up and running?' the mercenary captain asked. 'In a couple of months, my boys and girls are going to be spread out across these farms that those two will be buying, ready for the crop season. There's not going to be much we can do to help Faise and Zineer then.' He made his way to the edge of the factory floor, where a leather backpack lay. There, he pulled out a long silver container. 'Cold coffee.' He shook it. 'You tried it?'

'No,' Heast replied. 'I saw the Soldier yesterday, by the way.'

Essa held out a tin cup to him. 'How did that go?'

'He agreed to send the tents and food down to Wila. He wants to look through what we send first, but we can start buying now.'

Yet, as he tasted the not-quite-chilled coffee, Heast admitted to himself that the meeting had been a strange one. He had ridden one of the large, sixteen-horse carriages to Nale two days earlier. He had not seen one that size before — it was essentially two carriages joined together — but the driver managed it much like the carriages that were of one piece and pulled by four or eight horses. From the latter half of the day, after the carriages left Ghaam, the Keepers' Enclave had become the lodestone by which the journey was made. It sat on the horizon like an artificial mountain on an artificial land, a building formed from long white tunnels of stone, built to mirror a large spiral that rose into the sky. The walls were lined with windows and, even from a distance, it gave the appearance of a thousand glass eyes that watched you.

The roads of Nale were swollen with congestion and, beneath the gaze of the Enclave, the carriage made its way past the tall, thick buildings that struggled to match the elegance of the white tower. By the time the carriage came to stop at a huge depot on the edge of the city, the afternoon's sun had set and

Heast had spent a whole day travelling. He had left Mesi just as the morning's sun had begun to rise without warmth. Throughout the day, he had seen fellow passengers come and go, and bits and pieces of their conversation had sifted around him. Some of it had been about the Mireeans: 'They bring the Leerans here,' one old man had said. 'But we should not be afraid of that,' another old man had said in reply. 'The Yeflam Guard—' 'Gogair is unhappy,' a young woman said. She held up a paper. 'It says right here: "The ambassador met with the Enclave to discuss what could be a violation of important agreements."' He heard a young man, not realizing that Heast was there, refer to him as the Captain of the Ghosts, even. But mostly, he heard men and women arguing whether it was their fight or not. Some said that they had heard that there were priests in the Leeran army, in the Faithful, and that made it Yeflam's fight. Very few people mentioned Zaifyr, or the deaths of Fo and Bau; beneath the multi-eyed gaze of the Enclave, it did not surprise Heast.

The Keeper of the Divine, Xrie, had greeted Heast at the front door of the barracks. The building was a huge four-storey complex, and the Captain of the Yeflam Guard had led him up the floors without a hint of pride in the building itself. He was a handsome brown-skinned man, and his handshake was firm and confident, but when he paused to point something out to Heast, he seemed to be a soldier at practice, a soldier in training. Xrie looked no older than twenty-two or -three, but Heast knew that he had been the Captain of the Yeflam Guard for over forty years, and when he stopped to point out the men and women around him, to speak to them by name and rank, they responded to him crisply and loyally, as to a figure clearly beloved by his soldiers.

Heast had met Xrie only a handful of times since he himself had become the Captain of the Spine. He had sent a prisoner, and picked up two, and they had met when the last treaty between the two states had been signed. Still, they had an easy formality that, once the two were in Xrie's office on the top floor, allowed for an agreement to be reached that new tents, new clothes and food and water had to be taken down to Wila. 'In its current state, the island is entirely unacceptable,' Xrie had said, at the end. 'You have my apologies. I was told by Faje that the Traders' Union was going to supply the shelter. What is down there is what they provided.'

'The politics of kindness,' Heast had said drily. 'We'll have a warehouse soon that we'll send items from.'

'I'll be honest, Captain, I am not a fan of the current pacifism that is in vogue with my kin,' the other man continued. 'It is hardly surprising, given who I am, but what happened in Mireea was a message for all of us. That was its point. We were to pay attention to it. The stalemate that you reached between Mireea and Leera diluted the message a little, but it still remains true that one day Leera's General Waalstan will bring his army to Yeflam. His new god will demand that.' *Or*, Heast thought, *your old gods will demand that*. 'But on a personal level, it greatly disappoints me that I cannot tell the Captain of Refuge that we will stand beside him on the field.'

'Refuge appears to be a popular topic,' Heast had answered. 'I expected it from Bnid Gaerl, but from you? My duty is not to Refuge any more.'

'You will have to forgive me, Captain. I am well aware of

your duty to Lady Wagan.' In the narrow windows behind him, the last of the afternoon's sun had begun to fade. 'But I am not a man who forgets war's loyal servants. I would be a poor man if I did. However, I should say, it is not just myself who remembers. Your history was raised with me this morning by a writer from one of the papers in the city. Despite my reluctance, I am afraid that you will soon be well known in Yeflam.'

'Unlike Zaifyr.'

'We call him Qian, but your point is taken,' Xrie had said. 'My kin have kept him out of most of the print shops. It is part of the politics of pacifism.'

Heast was, by his nature, rarely surprised by what happened in the corridors of power, be it by a crown, a sword, or an immortal hand. A good soldier, he once heard it said, accepted what was laid before him. He thought of the thousands of eyes from the Enclave and added to himself that a good captain learned to anticipate.

Holding the tin cup in his hand, Heast took another sip of the not quite cold coffee.

'This is really awful,' he said to Kal Essa. 'Did you pay for this?'

'It was better before the ice melted,' the other man replied sourly, before he tipped it on the ground. 'There's a bar around here. I'll stand you a drink there.'

8.

On the fifth morning Ayae spent on Wila, the morning's sun rose in a dull, flat light, but the smell of blood and salt rose strongly off the ocean. She sat in the opening of her small tent. Unable to sleep well – she felt stifled and restless in the fabric – she had eased herself quietly into position to watch the first sun rise. With one foot pushed out of the flap of the tent and the other drawn up against her chest, Ayae gazed at the grainy edge of the island, at the black ocean that soaked the light and the stone ramp that led up to the flat base of Neela. There, a line of sky blue cloaks revealed the guards. Usually, half of them faced the island, and the other half out into the city, but this morning all were facing away from the island. Ayae could not make out why they were turned but, she admitted to herself, it did not matter. Yesterday, before the third sun sank, the guards had stopped children who had arrived. They had been loaded with papers to throw over the edge, and the boxes had sat there beneath a lamp all night. This morning was probably no different, she thought – until the guards parted. They moved apart to reveal a single man leading a horse and cart down to Wila.

A man whom she knew.

'Caeli.' The guard lay behind her, wrapped in her cloak. 'Caeli,' Ayae said again and squeezed the guard's naked foot. 'The Soldier is here.'

'Is he alone?' She did not sound asleep, even though she had been. 'Is he armed?'

'No, but he leads a cart.' Ayae pushed herself up. 'I'll get Lieutenant Mills.'

'He's here for you.' There was a rustle as Caeli pulled on her trousers and grabbed a shirt. 'You go and meet him. I'll get Lady Wagan and the Lieutenant.'

At the edge of the camp, in the thin folds of fabric nearest Leviathan's Blood, Ayae could hear whispers from men and women woken by the steady step of the horse and the rattle of the cart. In the snippets she heard, the Captain of the Yeflam Guard was not referred to by name, or even by title, and Ayae suspected that none of the people she passed had realized that it was him. It did not surprise her. At the sight of him, she had felt keenly a sensation of steel, a balanced, tempered sword that lay not against her skin, but beneath it. She had finally begun to recognize people like herself, just as Fo and Bau had said she would, but what she did not yet understand was why she had known immediately that it was the Soldier.

'Ayae.' Xrie greeted her from the bottom of the ramp. 'Lady Aelyn Meah bids you a kind welcome to our nation.'

He was taller than Ayae, but she was not a tall woman by any standard, and to another, the Captain of the Yeflam Guard would have been only average in height. His skin was brown, lighter than hers, as if it had been mixed with desert sand and diluted. He had dyed the tips of his hair blue, and wore a blue sash around his waist. He took her hand, and she was surprised when he made no remark on the warmth of her touch and did not seek to withdraw from her grasp quickly. Instead, he held her hand, and inclined his head slightly in further greeting.

'The Lady of the Spine,' Ayae said awkwardly, 'welcomes you to Wila.'

'Her captain has organized tents and clothes and food.' He released her hand to indicate the horse-drawn cart on the ramp. 'But my business is mostly here with you.'

Behind her, people began to gather. Some, she knew, would be those who did not like her. Even though she did not believe them to be a majority, she had begun to be acutely aware of their presence after Zaifyr had left — after the sensation of eternal patience and calm she had associated with him had been withdrawn — and the focus of those who hated 'cursed' people was no longer split between the two of them. In the last few days, she had felt their animosity building towards her, fuelled not just by bigotry, but by their grief, their frustration and their boredom. Thus far, nothing had come to a head, and Ayae had not had to defend herself, but she knew that it would not be long before she was forced to do so.

'You are not required to stay on Wila,' the Captain of the Yeflam Guard continued. 'You are a person of unique qualities and the Keepers of Yeflam do not believe that it is right for you to be constrained by the negotiations that Lady Wagan made on behalf of her subjects.'

'I'm no different to any of the people here,' she said, a hint of reproach in her voice. 'None of us should be here.'

'But you are different. You are not a mortal woman, Ayae.

You have left that behind. You are a god – or you will, one day, be a god.' He said the words in a simple, matter-of-fact tone. 'One day soon you will understand that and the Keepers will aid you in that education. All of Yeflam will. An entire nation waits for you to explore the power that is in you.'

'She knows that and she will go with you.' Muriel Wagan stepped from the crowd behind her, her feet bare. 'The offer is greatly appreciated by all of us.'

Despite herself, Ayae wanted to tell her no. She wanted to tell him no, as well. She wanted to deny the authority of the Keepers, to reject the words that echoed so closely the ones that Fo had said to her after she survived the fire in Samuel Orlan's shop. She was not a god. She would not be a god. Nor did she want to be a god, not if Zaifyr was right. If a god was a being that kept the dead in cages and bled their souls for her own power, then she did not think that anyone should be a god. Another part of her knew that the Lady Wagan was right, that what she had said to her on the first day on Wila was still true: she did have to accept the offer. She did have to leave Wila.

After she agreed, after the horse was unhitched from the cart, after Xrie pulled it out onto the sand with one hand, the Captain of the Yeflam Guard said, 'They are taking careful note of you.'

They were halfway up the ramp when he said that. 'They want to leave as well,' she said.

'I do not mean the Mireeans. I mean the men and women and children who stand on the edge of Neela and look down.'

She looked up and, this close to them, she noticed them properly for the first time. She thought that most looked poor.

The two left the ramp and stepped through the small ring of soldiers. Beyond them, streets ran in straight lines towards square buildings of discoloured stone. 'The Yeflam Guard is mine,' Xrie said, in relation to his earlier comment. 'But we are a large nation and the twenty thousand soldiers who serve beneath me are sometimes not enough to keep everyone safe.'

He was leading her to a pair of horses hitched to a small carriage that had been painted blue.

'Some of those people watching you will be employed by papers, some by politicians, and some will not be employed at all. They will try and sell what they have seen today.' On a seat near the top sat the carriage driver, an elderly grey-haired man in a blue cloak. 'The ones whom you should be concerned about mainly belong to the Empty Sky. They are led by Bnid Gaerl and he is primarily employed by the Traders' Union. By Benan Le'ta, in fact. The Empty Sky,' Xrie said, as if it were an afterthought, 'is a reference to atheism.'

He opened the door, but Ayae did not step into the carriage. 'I've no interest in the politics,' she said. 'I just want to help everyone get off Wila.'

'That is politics,' he said.

Inside the carriage, a sword waited for her.

9.

The first person to visit Zaifyr was Kaqua, the Pauper.

The charm-laced man had not left Aelyn's house. He knew that he was being watched, but he was content to wait, to think about his arguments, and to rest. In the dusty rooms, he had laid his boots with burnt soles on the table near the doorway. He pulled out his clothes from his pack — a man made from wind had brought it on the second day — and cleaned his rank-smelling clothes. On the day that Kaqua arrived, Zaifyr had taken his charms off, one by one, and set them on the table in front of his boots. He checked each for scratches and dents, aware as he did so that not one of the pieces had the spells and prayers that his family had put into his charms, so long ago. Those pieces had been taken from him and he supposed that, even if they had survived the rough treatment of the soldiers who had taken them, then time would have destroyed them anyway. No, it did not matter if the new charms he wore had scratches or dents: nothing would change if they had them. But for Zaifyr, the charms — made from copper and bronze and brass and silver — were about his connection to the man he had once been, the man who had been born in a small village in the mountains and who, at a young age, had been told he would die young.

He had nearly died in Mireea. The thought returned to him as he checked the links of chain, as he cleaned blemishes on a charm. It had been recurring to him for weeks, in truth. In moments of quiet. When he was alone. He would think, *I almost died.* Fo had nearly killed him. Zaifyr could not remember another time when he had come that close to joining the haunts that were trapped around him. For a while, he had asked himself if he *had* died. Over his long, long life, he had been attacked by living and the dead, by mortals and immortals, but he had never been detached from his body in the way he had been in Mireea. Not even when he reached out to the dead as a massive whole — as he had done to bring the ghosts into view — had he felt like that. He was always aware of his body, of himself. So, the question remained, had he died? Had there been no cord to lead him back, would he have found his way back? Was this his death?

He had no answer.

He polished and cleaned his charms. They had no answers, either.

Around him, the haunts whispered to him of their cold and their hunger. They knew as much as the guards made from wind at the gate knew.

'They are not to keep you safe, but to keep the people of Yeflam safe,' Aelyn said to him. On either side of her, swirling, squat figures waited patiently. It was the day that she had delivered him to the house — he had not seen her since. 'I cannot force you to leave,' she continued. 'But I can stop people visiting you. I can stop the newspapers, the Traders' Union, and whoever else will seek to find you. The Enclave will meet to discuss what is to be done with you tomorrow. We have been meeting all week, and I am afraid I cannot dissuade them from a trial. Just as I cannot convince you to leave.'

'You truly want me to leave?' he asked. 'It is your law I broke when I killed Fo and Bau.'

'Take your war elsewhere, brother.'

My war.

The bitterness in her voice gave him pause, even now. He picked up a long copper chain and began to run his fingers along each link. He had wanted to tell her that there would be no war, but even to say the words would be foolish. The child would not fall easily. She would not step out from behind the shield of her army for him to strike at her. He would have to go through it. *Lives* would be lost when he attacked her.

'The girl you came with?' Aelyn said, in her final conversation with him. 'The one from Mireea?'

'Ayae.'

'Do you lay claim to her?'

'Is that what you do here to ensure loyalty?' His tone was mild, but he could not hide the reproach. 'She is her own person.'

'She is—'

'—my friend.'

Aelyn's smile was cool, humourless. 'You do not have friends, brother.'

I have family, instead, he had begun to say, but bit back the reply. Instead, he had watched her leave, watched the carriage and horses made from wind rise into the sky.

He did not have the right to ask his family to go to war for him. He knew that. In Aelyn's house — in her replica of the house she had once lived in — he could not escape the sense of loss that she held for Maewe. It surprised him that she still had the wound. Yet that had defined her reaction to him here, in Yeflam. Aelyn feared that she would lose Yeflam.

Would Zaifyr's other siblings be any different? Eidan had lost the twisting mines of Mahga. The wealth and beauty he had drawn from the ground had been melted and buried by the volcanoes and earthquakes he had caused to destroy his own empire. After his release, Zaifyr had spoken to Eidan on two different occasions and both had been defined by their brevity. But Yeflam was Eidan's construction. Anything Zaifyr could say about Aelyn could be just as easily said about Eidan.

There was no trace of Tinh Tu in Yeflam, however. She had retreated to the lost library of Salar after Asila and, from all that Zaifyr understood, rarely left it. The library lay in the marshes of Faer, in an area where the trees and swamps moved, where a person could go mad trying to navigate to the centre. But, whereas Aelyn and Eidan had chosen a new piece of land for their country, Tinh Tu had built her library in the land that had held her empire. She even used the same name, leading Zaifyr to believe that she, like Aelyn, still carried the wound of what she had lost.

And Jae'le . . .?

His eldest brother was not like the others. He had not rebuilt a kingdom. He had not begun to give animals voices again. He had left his previous life behind and he would come to Yeflam, Zaifyr was sure of that. Jae'le would not have to be asked. He would arrive out of loyalty, out of concern, and out of a sense of responsibility. He would come, also, because he knew what was taking place in Leera. He knew about the child. Zaifyr was not convinced that Jae'le had known that she was a god, but he had known that she was something different. If he had known she was a god, his brother would have surely killed her. For all the power that Zaifyr had, for all that Aelyn, Eidan and Tinh Tu had, they lived in Jae'le's shadow.

When Kaqua arrived, Zaifyr had almost finished cleaning and repairing his charms.

The Pauper was one of the oldest beings in Yeflam. A tall, lean man with a serious face, he had midnight-black skin and appeared to be anywhere between the ages of forty and sixty. His black hair was cut short and touched with grey, because of which Zaifyr had always thought of him as an older man. Before Zaifyr's arrival in Yeflam, Kaqua would have in fact been second to Aelyn in terms of age: he had been born in the centuries after the War of the Gods, in the period when Zaifyr and his family had been creating the Five Kingdoms. In those years, however, he had remained hidden; he had not challenged Zaifyr's family as so many others had, or offered to join them, as had those whose power was weaker or less well formed than the family's. He had simply lived on what would later become Illate until Aelyn found him.

He was a man who was preceded by a sense of humbleness. It was not uncommon for people to believe that he had only simple and honest advice to give, that he cared only for what was fair, and Zaifyr was not surprised that Aelyn had sent him. The Pauper had long spoken for her with his deep, sonorous voice, and he had used that voice to convince others that what they wanted was not for the best.

Zaifyr met him at the door.

'Qian.' Kaqua wore a faded multicoloured robe of brown and white and grey, the colours entwining in the folds around his shoulders and waist. He carried an old leather satchel. 'I am here to discuss your trial.'

10.

'It is a gift,' Xrie said to her, after she had picked up the sword. 'Nothing more.'

It was a short-bladed weapon, simple in its design, but well weighted. Seated across from the Soldier, Ayae turned the blade over in her hand, then returned it into its leather sheath. 'You need to bring better gifts,' she said, holding out the sword back to him. 'I can make you a list of all that you could give me, if you would like. It only has names on it.'

'You will find that I can do very little for the people of Wila beyond what I have just done,' he said, not taking the sword. 'I am but one voice in the Enclave.'

'But you have a voice.'

'So will you, if you wish. But, like mine, it will not be a voice of seniority.' Outside the carriage, huge factories slid past. All but a handful were made from the same stone that the ground of Neela was made from, leaving them with an impression of being scars on a giant's body.

'You must understand that I am not very old, at least, not in the way our kin measures time. I have not yet seen a century, and only four decades of my life have been spent here,' the

Captain of the Yeflam Guard said. 'Before that, I lived in the Saan, where, like here, youth is a condition that you must grow out of before you have authority. It is a point that will be very clear to you when you sit in the Enclave with the other Keepers.'

'Why would I go, then?' Ayae laid the sword on the floor of the carriage. 'That's twice now that you've made it clear to me that I would have no voice.'

'Because if you do not, the only person arguing for the Mireean people will be me,' he said evenly. 'I support their release from Wila. It is unnecessary to keep them there. Much is said about their safety, about the safety of the Yeflam people, and about how Leera will react, but the truth is, locking them on Wila makes neither them nor us safe. It is not something that I am saying to you because I think you need to hear it. It is something I am saying because I am the Captain of the Yeflam Guard. And before I came to Yeflam I was the Blade Prince of the Saan. In duels alone, I have killed one hundred and fourteen men and women. In combat, more. I have led small forces to victory over large ones. If I thought that there was a real military threat to Yeflam from the Mireean people, I would not dismiss it. But Aned Heast and Muriel Wagan are not a risk to us. There is no danger to us here but the one Qian brings.'

'There is nothing to—'

'—fear from him?' Outside the carriage, the factories of Neela began to fall away. 'Ayae,' Xrie said, his voice still even and measured. 'Qian is responsible for the fall of the Five Kingdoms. He is responsible for centuries of war, for kingdoms breaking and empires failing. The history of that time is incomplete, at best, but there are a few who lived it. There are even some here who saw what was done when those kingdoms were made. He is as close to a god as this world has. One day you and I will follow in his steps in that regard, but it does not mean that we must remain blind about what he has done.'

'I am not here to apologize for Zaifyr.' A breeze picked up off the black ocean, but Ayae did not feel its chill. 'But what happened after the destruction of Asila took place while he was imprisoned.'

'It began in Asila.'

Outside, the bridge to Mesi appeared. It was made from thick stone and lined with lamps and long poles that ended in a simple sky-blue flag.

'Fo and Bau,' Ayae said, after a moment. 'They tried to kill him. They tried to kill everyone in Mireea.'

'I know what they planned. They had not been given orders to do what they did. The Enclave sent them there to watch. That was all.'

'To watch as a nation was sacrificed.' She heard the anger in her voice and was not surprised by it. 'If you focus on Zaifyr, as you seem intent on doing, you can be as sympathetic as you want about Mireea, but you'll do just the same thing.'

'They were my brothers, but do not make the mistake of thinking that I am made from their follies.'

'It's their words I am hearing.'

'Then you are not listening properly,' he said, a hint of frustration breaking through the even measure of his tone. 'There will be war and Qian will be its catalyst. That is what I am telling you. His every action brings disruption and volatility. It is not just to Yeflam that he does this, but to the world. All of us need to recognize that. We also need to see that it is highlighting our own faults. For Yeflam to be neutral now is folly. The Leeran threat is a real one that is aimed squarely at the people of Yeflam. It is following Qian and he allows it to do so. He wants us to stand beside him and in this regard he is right to seek our support.'

'You don't support a trial, then?'

'I mourn Fo and Bau. They were my kin. But I am also well aware of the fact that Fo, on any day, would have broken the law to kill Qian. He was born in Asila, after all.' Xrie nodded out of the window to her left. 'This is Mesi. Nearly five thousand people live here.'

A sprawl of close-knit buildings had begun to appear around them. Most were residential, and built next to each other, with the buildings sharing walls and fences. Some of the houses were made from stone and others brick and still others wood. Some were painted red and orange and brown; occasionally, there was one of green, or one of blue.

'I've been to Mesi before,' Ayae said, the anger in her voice not quite gone; but neither was it threatening, as it had been before. 'I know the people who live here.'

'You know two,' Xrie said, his frustration either gone, or well masked. 'Two who are part of Muriel Wagan's plan to gain leverage to get her people off Wila.'

The carriage came to a stop outside a stone house painted red. It had a sun-faded black roof and a door to match it. A small garden of potted plants reached down to a wrought-iron fence.

'Faise and Zineer Kanar,' Xrie went on. 'They are both involved in the plan to purchase Yeflam factories, businesses and farmlands for Lady Wagan. So far, the two are mostly planning to target businesses and lands owned by the Traders' Union. Benan Le'ta is not yet aware of that and will probably not be for a while. But eventually, he will know. By then, Muriel Wagan may have purchased enough capital to gain access to the Traders' Union. Maybe not. Either way, once the plan is well known, Le'ta's response will not be friendly. Not that this will bother Muriel Wagan. The Lady of the Spine did not run Mireea on kindness and sympathy, after all. For our part – for the Enclave's part, that is – we think it will keep the Traders' Union busy while we deal with Qian. Aelyn hopes that she will be able to convince him to leave, but few agree with her. Still, both she and I are well aware that once Benan Le'ta realizes who is behind his losses, he will let Bnid Gaerl deal with them.'

Xrie reached over and opened the carriage door.

'As I said, I do not fear Mireea,' he said. 'But more importantly, neither does Aelyn Meah. In the Enclave, she will be very open to your advocacy for your people, just as she will listen to what you say about Qian. She asked me to tell you that, when I brought you here today.'

'Is the sword a gift from her as well?' she asked.

'No, that gift is from me. You will need it when Benan Le'ta learns the truth.'

When Ayae stepped from the carriage, she did so with the sheathed sword he had given her.

11.

The Pauper did not shake Zaifyr's hand. Instead, he entered the quiet house and looked around the room. His gaze finally settled on the long table, on the boots in the centre and charms spread across it. Without a word, he took a seat opposite Zaifyr's chair. Wordlessly, he picked up one of the boots and turned it over. He revealed a burnt, black sole. 'You will need a new pair,' he said finally. 'It would be unseemly to hold a trial while you wore such boots.'

'I'm happy to see you, as well, Kaqua.' Zaifyr returned to his seat and let the chain he had been holding slide to the table. 'Did my sister send you?'

'The Enclave thought that I would be the best choice.' He returned the boot to where it had stood. 'Aelyn is in a difficult position, thanks to you. She does not want a trial. She has been very public about it — and that is undermining her authority on the situation.'

'Do you want a trial?'

'No,' Kaqua admitted. 'But I understand why others do.'

'She is a child of the gods.' Zaifyr reached for a long piece

of copper, a *haut-ai*. His mother had said that it was for luck.
'If that helps.'

'It is for that reason that I do not want a trial.' A sigh, a
long-suffering, parental sigh escaped the Pauper's lips. 'For the
other Keepers, for my *kin*, Qian, a trial is about the law you
broke. It is about the two men you murdered. It is about justice
– but how can justice be brought to one such as you?' He
shook his head. 'You do not even care that Fo and Bau are
dead.'

He was not wrong, Zaifyr admitted. The two men had been
nothing to him. After their deaths, during their deaths, even,
he had thought only of what he would say to his sister, of how
he would force her to listen to him. 'I know what happens to
people when they die,' he said. 'I know what happens to
someone when they die. I know with more intimacy than you
do. I long ago made peace with the responsibility I bear when
I kill another person. Both of us are too old to sit here and
pretend otherwise.'

'I have killed very few people,' Kaqua said, not yet finished
with his parental tone. 'Murder is very rarely a selfless act.'

'That won't work.'

'I'm sorry?'

'That push in your voice.' Zaifyr tapped the copper charm
against his left index finger. 'It was clumsy.'

'I am not here to influence you, Qian.' He spoke without
the tone now. He reached for the satchel that lay beside him.
'I am here merely as an arbitrator for the trial.'

'If you insist.' He had felt the rough edge of Kaqua's suggestion, of his power, poorly hidden behind the tone he had used.
It felt rushed, either because it had been a decision made at

the last moment, or because he faltered before Zaifyr. Either way, Zaifyr had not missed it. 'You should know,' he said, laying the charm on the table, 'that my name is not Qian, not any more.'

The Pauper unbuckled the satchel. 'If we could focus on your trial,' he said, his voice cold. From the satchel, he withdrew a single book and a pencil. 'There are three kinds of trial: combat, ordeal, or by jury. I am sure that you agree that the third option is the only one available to us.'

Zaifyr did. Trials of combat and ordeal were trials by divinity. It was not uncommon to see them taking place, even now; while the gods lay dead in the world, there was still an acceptance that fate predetermined the outcome. In the days when all seventy-eight gods strode the earth, it had not been hard to imagine that your fate did lie in the hands of a god. After all, your life *was* in the strands of fate that the gods saw, the strands that they themselves could reach out and touch. It was easy to believe that a man's speed with the blade in a trial of combat was the gift of a god. Failure was also seen as an admission of guilt. In his youth, Zaifyr had been told countless stories of a god's fury at being called to defend a man or woman who was guilty. Even though the gods themselves were no longer part of such trials, it was still believed by many that surviving or failing such trials signified guilt or innocence.

'I would expect a jury,' he said. 'Indeed, I would demand nothing less for a public trial.'

'A public trial?' Kaqua repeated, clearly shocked. 'Qian, we cannot—such a trial would do nothing but frighten the people of Yeflam. They would think — rightly — that a tragedy similar to Asila was within them, waiting to hatch. There would be hysteria. Already we have struggled to keep the full knowledge of what happened in Mireea out of the papers. If they knew that you were responsible for the ghosts in the Mountains of Ger, I hesitate to think what would be the response.'

'I will speak to the public.' He smiled half a smile. 'I will not negotiate on that.'

'You will not negotiate at all.' The sense of shock was still in his voice. 'It is you who has committed a crime here. You who is on trial. This is not being held for you so that you can have a public platform. There must be reparation — and it must be to the people you have damaged through your act.'

'Your kin? They're free to judge me.' He picked up another charm, this one a brass disc, with two holes in it. *Karami*: a wish for strength. 'Like everyone else, they can judge me after they have heard everyone speak.'

'And who will speak for you? Your brothers, your sisters?' Kaqua shook his head. 'You will need more to convince people that you were in danger. That you struck against Fo and Bau because of fear.'

'I was not afraid,' he said. 'I killed them because they threatened someone else. But I did not come here because of that. I came here to convince people that the gods' child must be killed. That you join me and march against her.'

'No one will speak for you on that.'

'The dead will.'

This time, the Pauper had no response.

'The dead have always spoken true.' Zaifyr let the coin settle into the palm of his hand. 'In Asila, that is how all murders were judged. I would call upon the dead, and I would allow them to have a voice. Now I will do the same. I will give the dead a voice to name their tormentor. I will let them name this new god for us. I will let them tell everyone about how they have been kept in a grey life for thousands and thousands of years. I will let them tell how their essence is pulled apart. How it is used by this child god as power. I will let the dead speak as they have never spoken before.' He closed his hand around the coin and met Kaqua's gaze. 'Then we will go to war.'

The White Trees of Leviathan's End

She makes her choice because we are obsessed with youth. We see in youth a life unmarked by failure, tragedy, and debt.

The first priests to emerge from Leera were young, like their god. There was colour in their hair and their skin was unlined. They spoke strongly. They spoke well. They would buy you food if you asked, as I did, and sit across from you and share a meal, as one did with me. Miseu was her name. She was slim, red haired and pale. Beside her she kept a book entitled *The Eternal Kingdom*. It was newly printed, but she knew every word, because each word was her god's word. She would not allow me to read it, but she would quote it to me, and when I asked her a question, just one or two, she knew the answers it told her.

I am glad I have left my youth long behind. It was unmarked by failure, tragedy, and debt. It was, in a word, shallow.

—Tinh Tu, *Private Diary*

1.

When the priests appeared in Yeflam, Heast had moved to Zanan, to a small room above a modest bar inappropriately called The Engorged Whale.

He saw the first priest on the night Benan Le'ta visited. The merchant was not happy that Heast had moved again – the fourth time in two months – and he was not pleased that it had taken members of the Empty Sky a week to find him. He was frustrated by Heast's ability to drop the watchers Bnid Gaerl had set on him and the conversation the two would soon have, where the merchant delivered a series of thinly veiled threats, was partly fuelled by that. But before Heast pushed open the door to The Engorged Whale, before he sat across from Le'ta, he saw the Leeran priest.

He was handsome, darkly bearded, tanned, and no older than twenty. He wore a brown robe and stood in the street before the bar on a wooden crate, calling out to people, and reading from a book in his hand. Zanan had a healthy crowd for him to work: it was a small city in the arc that circled Nale on the south-eastern side and was defined by blocks of bars, brothels, bedsits, cheap halls, and trade shops worked by men and women who sweated long days. It was one of three cities in Yeflam where gambling was legal, and the purses of mercenaries, merchants and other travellers there became slimmer each day. Because of that, Heast was surprised that he had not seen the priest before. Surely, among the transients who had lost their wealth, 'open' minds would be found, but no, just as the priests in Mesi, Ghaam, Fiys and Maala had failed to find an audience, so was the priest in Zanan struggling. The young man could not convince a single person to stop and listen. It did not matter if he spoke of healing the body or the soul; it did not matter if he lifted his hands to the sky and claimed that the remains of the afternoon's sun could be fixed as well. No one stopped. No one but Heast, who stood at the corner of the inn, out of the priest's sight. One woman, upon passing him, said drily, 'Get enough of that shit from Keepers,' before she walked up the stairs of The Engorged Whale. Heast had seen her running card games and roulette. Once the door closed behind her, a pair of bouncers crossed the road and moved the priest on. His reaction to the two surprised Heast more than anything else did: the young man smiled and thanked the guards for their time. Then he picked up his small wooden stool and left calmly.

Inside the smoky stomach of The Engorged Whale, Heast made his way to Benan Le'ta. The merchant was watching a card game across from him and, after Heast had sat, Le'ta said, 'I spent a lot of time in places like this.' He had a tall glass of beer next to him, half full. 'You could lose a fortune here. I did, in fact. More than once.'

'Have you waited long?' he asked.

'Enough to count the cards.' The merchant picked up his

beer. 'A message arrived from Lian Alahn today. He has returned to Yeflam and is in Enir at the moment. He has agreed to meet you, if you still wish to do so.' When Heast extended his hand for the note, the merchant shook his head. 'I'm afraid I left it in the office. His home is on Burata. You should be able to find him there within a few days.'

'Thanks.'

'In his letter,' Le'ta continued, 'he mentions a girl by the name of Ayae. She was his son's partner, if I am to believe right?'

'She's in Yeflam,' Heast said, the sound of the crowd allowing him to keep the surprise from his voice easily. 'I'm not sure where. She was on Wila briefly.'

'Ah, so she *is* the one the Keepers have taken interest in. It is said that she cannot be burnt. An interesting talent for a cursed woman.' He finished his beer in one long gulp and rose, his clothes shifting around him like the feathers of a giant preening animal. 'Just a short visit, Captain,' he said, before he left. 'I thought I would deliver Alahn's message personally. You should know that it arrived three days ago. I could have given it to you earlier if I had known where you were staying. If you move again, please let me know. I would hate to send Commander Gaerl to find you next time.' An open threat, then, after a series of veiled ones.

Heast watched the merchant leave, unsurprised. The relationship with the Traders' Union had deteriorated more quickly than he had expected, but he was not particularly concerned. For his next move, he had already decided to slip out of Yeflam and drop Gaerl's men cold. He had reached the conclusion after reading the seventh — or was it eighth? — article that promised to expose the failures of the Captain of the Spine and how they made Mireea's defeat inevitable. Like the other pieces, it had spent most of its time exploring Refuge's defeat in Ilatte. Bnid Gaerl was quoted in this one as well. There were another two sources that Heast did not know the names of, but he suspected that they were Gaerl himself. What separated this last article from the others was the suggestion that the Leeran priests were here because of the Mireeans. It was a small postscript, not much, but he suspected there would be more later. It was the final push by Gaerl to have him moved to Wila, his attempt – short of killing Heast – to have revenge for the slight he had suffered in Leviathan's End.

It had happened over a decade ago. Heast had finished a month of uninspired work in Wisal when Onaedo's letter summoning him arrived. He remembered that on the day it was brought to him, he had been standing on the docks, ready to leave for Gogair. He had not considered ignoring it – no mercenary denied a summons to Leviathan's End.

It sat in the warm, dark waters of the north, past Kakar, a town built into the exposed bone of the Leviathan's skull. Like an iceberg, Leviathan's End showed but the smallest fraction of itself to any who approached. The Leviathan's great skull revealed itself first in the splintered front of her great jaw, where a ship passed to enter the town, and then again in the two great, cavernous eye sockets that were stripped of flesh and vein on the top of her skull. It was through those holes that the light was allowed to shine over the town of Leviathan's End, for it was in there, held high off the black water, that it had been built and linked together by rope bridges that swayed dangerously in the wind.

Heast had struggled along the bridges. He could still remember the men and women, most of them young mercenaries, who watched him after he had been hauled up from the docks in one of the pulleys. They observed him not with sympathy, or revulsion, but with a cold patience. Onaedo had built Leviathan's End and she had built it for soldiers. It was where business was done, where no nation ruled, and where no man or woman was subject to any rule but her own.

Onaedo's house was in the centre of Leviathan's End. Rumour had it that it was the central piece of the town and that all structures were inevitably tied to it. Heast had always believed that to be true, and years later, as he climbed the stairs to his room in The Engorged Whale, he thought how the construction of Leviathan's End was echoed in Nale and Yeflam. Yet, unlike Nale, the centre of Leviathan's End was not something that had been built at the same time as the city: rather, it was a great ship, the biggest Heast had ever seen. Raised from the floor of Leviathan's Blood, the ship was suspended in the centre of Leviathan's End like the carcass of a great animal that had been hunted and killed.

Only one person lived on it, however, and it was across the vast deck, beyond the door of the captain's cabin that Heast found Onaedo. The cabin was unchanged from when he had seen it last: the walls were lined with weapons and tapestries of war, while before them was armour on stands, the insignias of mercenary units that had risen to prominence laid across the front of each.

Onaedo was a tall muscular woman whose skin was a solid brown. Her hair was cut short, black with no hint of grey, and she wore a series of silver studs in her right ear and nose. When she greeted him, she was unarmed, but she was always so in Leviathan's End. On that day, she had worn dark leather trousers, thick black boots and a simple shirt of red.

'Captain.' She shook his hand. 'It is a pleasure.'

'Is he still here?' Heast asked, after he had shaken her hand, after he had greeted her.

'Bnid Gaerl has waited the entire four months.' Onaedo did not offer him a seat and did not take one for herself. 'As I said in my letter, he is making claim for the name Refuge. It is a claim that the Captain must answer.'

'He cannot have it.'

'He makes an argument that because it is no longer in use, it should be free to whoever wishes to use it.'

'It is still in use.'

'Is it?' she said. 'Your leg has begun to bleed, by the by.'

He did not turn away from her dark gaze. 'The name is still in use,' he repeated. 'It has not fallen back to you.'

'On that, we can both agree. However, Bnid Gaerl has said that if it is only Anemone who stands in the way of his ownership of the name, then he will gladly offer her a place in the new Refuge.' To gaze into her eyes for a long time was to see scenes of battle, to see swords, pikes and axes, to see muddy fields and bloody rivers. Very few could hold her gaze for an entire conversation. 'You and I both know that it would make his new Refuge a legitimate group if she was with it,' Onaedo finished.

'You should ask Anemone, then,' he said. 'She has never been one to hide her opinion.'

A faint smile broke across her face and she turned her gaze away from him. 'I already have,' she said. 'Both she and Baeh Lok have been here for two weeks.'

'Then you already know the answer.'

'It was upon my honour to ask.' She shrugged, as if all the ceremony that she created, all the formalities she maintained, were pointless. 'Besides, you are right. Gaerl cannot have the name Refuge. Even if it was not in use, even if it was on a piece of armour around me and it was mine to bestow on another, he would not be allowed it. He does not understand what the name is. He only wishes to use its fame to gain the interest of readers in the new fictions that are being written.'

Until then, Heast had not seen much of the cheaply printed mercenary novels that had begun to emerge. But when Onaedo turned from him and revealed the shelves that lined the back of her cabin, he saw the stacks that she had piled at the front. She told him that mercenary captains from around the world had begun to send them to her after Wayan Meina, the Captain of Steel, had sent her his. 'At least,' the ruler of Leviathan's End said, 'Meina has a sense of humour about it. He knows that I hate them, so he sends them with flowers that have died by the time they reach me. But the others wish for quotes for book jackets — endorsements that no one but a mercenary would care to read.' She had stared at them as if they were a bug she could squash. 'Such a fate is not for Refuge, Captain. You and I are in agreement that Bnid Gaerl cannot have the title.'

2.

When Bueralan Le and Samuel Orlan entered the port of Jeil, they had not eaten for two days.

The food had run out two days after they crossed into the Kingdoms of Faaisha. On the day that it did, a score of Faaishan soldiers on patrol caught them. After Orlan identified himself and his fame had won the soldiers' trust and loosened their tongues, they had been warned that the towns up to Jeil had been evacuated. The Leeran army had invaded and the Lords of Faaisha, the soldiers said, had cleared out the small towns. If that had not been the case, Bueralan and Orlan would have been able to buy a meal, a bath, a shave and a bed; but instead they walked along the empty streets hungry, past the taverns and shops with boards across the windows and doors, and out onto the flat, empty roads without seeing a single person. Orlan muttered complaints, but Bueralan was less bothered. If Orlan had asked, Bueralan would have told him that he did not feel the hunger. He would have said that grief had stolen his appetite. Orlan did not ask. He did not say much and what he did say was not to Bueralan. Even when he had detoured towards the north three days before they crossed the border into the

Kingdoms of Faaisha, he did it without a word of warning. Bueralan had considered continuing on without him, but he was emotionally exhausted and thought it easier to follow the old man until he stopped before a long, empty run of marshland.

'He is not here,' Orlan said, after a while.

'No one is here.' Ahead, the faint, dark outline of Leviathan's Blood marked the horizon. 'You keep going this way and you end up on the Mad Coast.'

'It is not the coast that interests me,' Orlan said, speaking in short sentences, his throat not yet completely healed. 'It is here. Here, where the god Maika fell to the ground. Where the goddess Taane killed him. Since then, he has lain beneath the water, flickering. As if he were caught between two worlds. Which, of course, he was. It was he who ruled the City of the Dead with his—'

'—with his sisters Maita and Maiza,' Bueralan finished. 'I know the lineage. I didn't realize he was here. I thought he was further out in the marsh.'

'No.'

'But now he is gone?'

'Now he is dead.' Orlan's words were raw and guttural. 'But for how long has he been dead? Fifty, sixty years? Did she bleed his life from him in those first days, or later?'

He meant the child. Bueralan ran his hand through the growing hair on his head. 'What do you care, old man?'

'You have a dead man around your neck.' On the marsh, a long-legged bird with white-and-grey feathers rose suddenly from the water, as if startled. 'How do you think she did that? Do you think that all the gods can grab a man's soul?' he asked. 'No, only the Wanderer and the gods that were taken from his body could do that. But the child is not the Wanderer. Nor the others. She is incomplete. I do not say that because she is not yet fully grown. How she looks is meaningless. But how she identifies herself is not — and she does not yet identify herself at all.'

Bueralan could feel the cold crystal on his skin. 'You're such an expert on the gods — you tell me why it is so important.'

'No god is everything.' The cartographer turned to him angrily. 'There were once seventy-eight gods in our world, *Baron*. It was not an arbitrary number. It was how many bodies could hold the divinity of our world. Have you not stopped to think why there are so many powerful people in the world now when there were so few gods in comparison? Human bodies can contain even less of that power. That is why we see so many tragic men and women. Humans such as you and I are not made for divinity.'

'But a god is?'

'Just not all of it.'

'Until now.'

'You'd best hope that that is not true.'

'I don't care, old man.' Out in the marsh, the bird leapt into the air, huge and ugly. Bueralan tapped on the stone around his neck. 'I'm going back home.'

'You were exiled from there!'

He turned, but Orlan continued to talk to him, his voice rising in a ragged shout that carried over the marshes. 'She knows you were! Why is she sending you back there? Think! You are god-touched now. She said it herself! She is building herself into a god and you are the newest god-touched soldier! This is not a coincidence! A god-touched man is the servant of a god! He is not a priest! He is not a believer! He is not faithful! He is the mortal instrument of a god! Damn you! Don't walk to Ooila in ignorance!'

They barely spoke another word until Jeil.

The port sat on the northern tip of the Kingdoms of Faaisha, its white stone walls lined with mould and cracks. A decade ago, its population had been decimated by a series of plagues that had run up and down the dirt streets and wooden docks with abandon. In the years since, its leaders had rebuilt its population with people from around the word and, consequently, of all the Faaishan ports, Jeil was the most multicultural. Along the streets, Bueralan and Orlan saw stalls with goods in a variety of languages, past cooking odours from the north, the west, the south and east, and past men and women with dark black skin, dust brown, white, and the dark olive skin that was more prominent in those born in the country. Among them, Bueralan felt the lassitude that he had been feeling since Leera began to give way, and his anger returned. He split it between himself and Orlan, for the deaths of Dark and for the role each of them had played. With half an ear, he listened to the postscript of that last mission as men and women talked about the loss of Mireea, about the Lady of the Spine's retreat to Yeflam, and General Waalstan's push into Faaisha. Celp had fallen, they said. That caught Bueralan's professional attention with a touch of surprise. Marshal Faet Cohn held the east before the Plateau. He was an old fighter from an old family. Yet he had been forced to limp back to Vaeasa with half his forces in tatters — how small the surviving army was changed as the story went from person to person — and that corner of Faaisha was said to be in the hands of the Leerans.

But the war — *this* war — was over for Bueralan. He owed a little to Heast, he knew, but it was not more than what he owed to the memory of his own soldiers, and certainly not more than what he owed his blood brother, Zean. In Ooila, he could hand the crystal to a witch and undo one of the wrongs that had happened in Ranan. A part of his mind nagged him when he thought about that, repeated Orlan's questions, and asked if indeed the Mother's Gift was the right thing for Zean, but Bueralan ignored it. On the docks there was a ship that waited to take him to Ooila, to another port and a series of roads that would wind their way through the First Queen's Province. To roads that would end in Cynama, where he had been born, and from where he had been exiled.

He would pay for that ship with the small pouch of gold that Orlan had obtained from a moneylender who owed him on one of the streets of Jeil. Maintaining the silence that he had treated Bueralan to since the marshes, the cartographer found the pair two rooms and paid for a week outright. Half of what he had left he gave wordlessly to Bueralan, though the saboteur had had no plans to ask for it. In fact, he considered tossing it back and walking out of the inn. But his own coin was long gone, lost in the fall of Mireea and in the cage where the Leerans had kept him. He knew that if he wanted to return to Ooila, he needed the coin.

In a separate room, alone for the first time since Ranan, Bueralan also knew that the time to cut Samuel Orlan loose had come.

3.

Zaifyr was sitting on the front steps of Aelyn's house, enjoying the last warmth of the afternoon's sun, when Ayae and her two friends arrived. He held a slim book in his hand – a diary, he would tell her later – but he put it down as he rose to greet her.

'I'm pleased to see you,' he said.

She hugged him. 'It's as if you haven't seen anyone for two months.'

'Only Kaqua.'

The Pauper came once a week. He claimed other responsibilities limited the time he could spend with Zaifyr, but mostly he was drawing out the formation of a trial as long as he could. Each time he visited, he did so with another detail to debate. He struggled with Zaifyr's insistence that he was not on trial for the murder of Fo and Bau and, no doubt, the Enclave's belief that he was. Zaifyr figured that Kaqua and Aelyn were chiefly hoping to frustrate him, to push him into action of his own accord, or simply to force him out of Yeflam. With that in mind, Zaifyr had listened patiently to Kaqua's idea of drawing a jury from the population of the Floating Cities. 'We cannot have everyone on Nale,' he said. 'But five hundred, a thousand people. We could manage that. It would be quite a sight, actually. We have yet to figure out a way for them to vote once everyone has spoken, but assuming we could do that, it is the way we should proceed. Unless, that is, you have a problem with it.' He promised that next week he would bring over one of the ideas they had for registering guilty and innocent votes.

For his part, Zaifyr was untroubled by any of the delays. He had written to the remaining three members of his family — to Jae'le, Tinh Tu and Eidan — to request their presence. He sent the letters in the claws of small haunts. He gave each of the birds' spirits enough power to make the journey across Leviathan's Blood to his siblings' homes. For Jae'le, that was a house in the dense forested edges of Gogair; for Tinh Tu, it was in the swamps of Faer; but for his last sibling, for Eidan, Zaifyr admitted that he did not know where his brother was. He had placed in the mind of the dead bird an image of him, of his stout body, his plain features, his strength, then sent it off. Eidan's home, Zaifyr suspected, was Yeflam, but that was when his brother had a home. Eidan liked nothing more than to find ruins, to find pieces of the world that were thought to be lost, and rebuild them. If it took him thirty years, if it took him a hundred, he did not mind. He would live in those ruins until he was finished. If the bird could not find him, Aelyn would know where he was and, once Jae'le and Tinh Tu arrived, she would have little choice but to contact him.

That left Zaifyr with only one thing to do while he waited for his family.

'The diary belonged to an old pirate,' he said to Ayae, after she asked. The four of them were inside, then. They had walked through the dusty rooms, to the back room where piles of books had begun to form. 'Captain Dlar was his name. He lived in the middle era of the Five Kingdoms, but what I remember about him mostly was that he claimed to be descended from priests of the Leviathan. He wanted to be a king of the sea and his lineage was the claim to it. The Leviathan's priests lived in giant ships as big as small nations. I was hoping – if it was true – that he named some of the priests in the War of the Gods.'

'Was it true?' she asked.

'No,' he said. 'Like so many others, he lied about where he had come from.'

'But you're searching for dead people to speak for you?' The idea made Ayae uncomfortable, he knew. 'Is there no other way?'

'I could always rely upon my sister, I suppose,' he said blandly. 'It's her law, after all. I'm sure she'll defend me with it.'

'Why do you need a name?' Ayae's two friends were a couple, Zineer and Faise. It was the former who asked the question. He was flipping through a heavy book, looking at the old black and white drawings. 'I mean, I thought you could just see the dead.'

'I don't want to see all of them,' Zaifyr said, his hand falling to the charm beneath his left wrist. 'They stop being distinct if you look at them all. They're just a huge mass: generations upon generations pushed against each other, fallen in on each other, until you cannot see where it begins and ends. It is not just people, either. Everything that has lived and died since the War of the Gods is still here. Birds, whales, dogs. If it has been alive, it is there, trapped in the afterlife. If I want to navigate that, I need a name to focus on. Less-common names are better. You'd be surprised how many Zineers are out there.'

'It was my father's name.'

'And your father's father's name?'

He smiled ruefully. 'I'm afraid so.' Zaifyr liked both Faise and Zineer, but it was only later, after Ayae had told him why they were with her, that he had reservations about their presence. 'They are my friends,' she said, when Faise and Zineer had gone upstairs to sleep. 'My oldest friends. It does not matter what they are doing; I would stand by them. I would not let them be hurt.'

'Muriel Wagan is not a foolish woman,' he said. 'She uses them to bind you to her as well. If not them, she'll find someone else.'

'Mireea is still my home.'

He did not push it. With a shrug, he said, 'I am too old for homes.'

'For new shoes as well.' She sat across from him, her slim face lit by the candles. When she smiled, he was struck by her youth, by the things she had not seen. 'Do you think Aelyn will treat me well when I see her tomorrow?' she asked, as if she sensed his moment of introspection. 'The people of Mireea don't deserve to be on Wila.' He hoped so, he told her.

In the morning, with Faise and Zineer, he walked with Ayae to the Enclave, but did not go in with her. She had protested at his company, but after he had pulled on his burnt-soled boots, he told her that no one noticed him in the streets. The Enclave had done its best to keep information about him out of the public eye. He was not sure that she believed him, but not a single person stopped and stared at him, or asked him a question as they walked through the streets. Nor did they when he, Faise and Zineer continued on afterwards. He did, however, see two men in dark-blue cloaks obviously shadowing their steps. He was thinking about pointing them out to Faise, when he saw his first Leeran priest.

She was a young white woman, tall and long-limbed, with dark hair and dark, serious eyes that searched across the faces of the people who passed her. She held a book in her left hand and she used it like a pointer when she indicated to the crowd, when she asked if 'sir' or 'ma'am' had any desire to see the world fixed. She had little luck with either sex, but that did not stop her from preaching to the people around her.

'The Faithful,' Faise said, standing beside him. 'It's the name of the Leeran army, the name of the Leeran priests.'

'This is allowed?' he asked.

'You hear of some being picked up by the Yeflam Guard, but most are polite. They move when you ask them to do so. I don't think the Keepers are too happy about it, but rumour has it that this was a deal struck with the Leerans after the Mireeans were offered sanctuary.'

Zaifyr was genuinely surprised. He could not imagine Aelyn agreeing to that. 'The book in her hand?'

'It's called *The Eternal Kingdom*,' Zineer said. 'At least that's what they say.'

'No one has read it?'

He shook his head. 'Each one of them says that they would rather die than let a faithless man or woman read it. If you ask, they will read out excerpts, however.'

Zaifyr had another question, but it was then that the Faithful saw him. She stared at him for a moment, then scooped up her stool and quickly disappeared into the crowd.

'I think she likes you,' Faise said.

4.

From the window in Aelyn Meah's office, Ayae watched Faje lead a small group of workers into the garden beside the Enclave, where long-branched white trees grew. The workers carried shovels, axes and long-bladed saws, and behind them, as if aware of the weight it would soon carry out, a brown ox pulled an empty cart at a slow, steady pace.

'There are twenty-five trees in the garden,' Aelyn Meah said. After she had greeted Ayae at the door, she had led her to the window in silence, much as Faje led the men below. 'They grow from the bones of the Leviathan. Most grow in Leviathan's End, but there are others throughout the world. If you have ever heard sailors talking about islands of bone, that is where they come from. Some sailors will tell you that they move, but they don't. When a man or woman like you and me becomes a Keeper of the Divine, they are required to travel to one of these islands and bring back a tree for themselves. It is a test of endurance, more than anything else. To stand on a part of the Leviathan is to feel a pain you have never felt before.' She was silent for a moment, then: 'Today Faje is having the two that belonged to Fo and Bau dug up.'

The workers and ox continued into the heart of the garden. 'Do they ever have leaves?' Ayae asked. 'Do they ever have flowers?'

'They will bloom when we are gods.'

No, then.

Since her release from Wila, Ayae had requested to see Aelyn and the Enclave, but until now, her requests had been denied. Xrie had told her, when she asked him, that she simply had to wait. 'Fo and Bau were family,' he said. 'You will have to respect the time it takes for our grief to wane.'

A part of her did not believe that there was any real grief. She had heard no love for either Fo or Bau from the people she spoke with. Indeed, the funeral for the two had been a private affair. But no matter what Ayae thought, it remained true that she could not gain an audience with Aelyn Meah, not until today. *Today* she had been led through the twisting halls of the Enclave and given a private audience. It did not surprise her that on the same day Fo and Bau's barren trees were to be torn out of the ground. Over the last two months, she had come to believe that every act of the Enclave was one that also had to be an act of symbolism. The scene she was witness to now was like the pillar of white stone that Nale rested upon. Eight times the size of any of the pillars that descended into the black ocean, it was a singular, unnatural presence, and the Keepers said that, should the pillar begin to crack, then the end of the nation would begin.

In the garden, the cart stopped and the men with the axes and saws began to circle a pair of trees. 'When do you plan to allow the Mireeans to leave Wila?' Ayae asked.

'For the moment,' Aelyn Meah said, 'I have no plans.'

'For the moment?'

She smiled, but there was no friendship in it. 'I hear you talk to my brother,' she said. 'My guards tell me you are a regular visitor.'

'No one has said that I shouldn't be,' Ayae said.

'Nor will anyone.' The sound of an axe hitting a tree trunk reached them dully. 'You know what he did in Asila, don't you?'

'He has told me. He has also told me that he is not the man he once was.'

'He is not that man, at least.' Aelyn turned from the garden to her crowded office. It was not a large room. Ayae suspected that it was the smallest room in the Enclave. It nestled in the highest, but shortest spiral of the building and the roof and walls of the room curved steeply inwards. The majority of the space was taken up by books and papers, filling the walls in double and triple stacks, leaving only two doors unblocked. The first was the dark wooden door through which Ayae had entered. The second – lighter than the first – led to a sleeping chamber. 'But he reveals an important fact about the nature of atrocities.'

'Which is?'

'The further you are from them, the easier they are to forgive and forget. Take a seat.' Aelyn indicated a cushioned chair, barely visible between books. 'You have killed, haven't you?'

Ayae left the window. 'In the siege.'

'When your blood was up.' The other woman smoothed her gown, eased into her own chair. 'That is how I killed my first man. I was young then. No different from so many others at that time. I had a job in an inn pouring drinks. I was learning to read. I had to work for the money to go to school because not everyone was taught, then. The man I killed came into the bar with four others. They thought that they could rob the inn. They thought that they could take what they wanted. They were not very imaginative, so what they wanted was money and flesh. I drove a knife into the first man's stomach when he came close. I spent days afterwards washing my hands.'

Ayae thought of the first man she had killed. She remembered the filed teeth and the ruined eye socket. 'Do you still remember what he looked like?'

'Not now,' Aelyn replied. 'Once, I did, quite vividly. I stopped dreaming of him months after I had killed him, but I only stopped looking for him when years had passed. I have not even thought of him until now for . . . it must be two thousand years, at least.'

'I'll not forget,' Ayae said. 'I don't think I'll be able to.'

'You will.' She was matter of fact. 'You will be glad to, soon enough. If you do not, you will be like Qian. You'll hear the voice of every man and woman and child who has died and it will distort the world for you. I do not think any of us fully comprehended that until Asila. We had heard him talk about what he saw, but it was not until the Five Kingdoms had to be destroyed that we understood it, I think. I was wary that he would still have that view when he was released, but he has mostly preached a form of inaction much like what Yeflam is built on — or he did, until very recently.'

'He has a reason,' Ayae said. 'You yourself just said that you understood it.'

'I do. But you and I are not like him. Neither are the people of Yeflam. It is not difficult to forget. It just takes time. In truth, we overlook deaths every day. We must, for our sanity. Our minds cannot comprehend the fact that hundreds and thousands of people die in war, poverty and disease. They die every day from these things. It is for our own survival that we have such callous disregard. Some of that needs to come to Yeflam in respect of the Mireeans. They need to forget Fo and Bau's deaths. At the moment, with the presses printing what they are, it is difficult.'

'You own those presses,' Ayae said. 'You could stop them writing about Captain Heast and Lady Wagan. You could stop them reporting on Leera's threat – which is *not* tied to Fo and Bau.'

'I do not own all of them,' Aelyn said. 'In fact, I do not personally own any. Other Keepers own them – as do wealthy individuals throughout the cities. Not all of them are happy and they are letting it be known. For myself, I do not want the Mireeans to be on Wila. The sooner I have them out of there, the sooner I can get rid of the priests who are in my streets. I'm hoping that you will help with this. Indeed, I have made sure that there is an office on the lower levels for you.'

Ayae began to speak, to reject the offer.

'You should take it,' Aelyn said. 'I am not your enemy, Ayae,' she added, tiredly. 'I am not my brother's enemy, either. I just want to maintain peace.'

Had there ever really been peace? Ayae thought it was a naive thing for Aelyn to have said, much less believe. The thought remained, long after she had left the Enclave, after she had returned to the streets of Nale. There, the ox plodded past her, the cart full of white wood. None of the men who had cut it down spared her much of a glance, but Faje, who came last, offered her a polite, if impersonal nod.

Later, when she had returned to Zaifyr's lonely estate, when she had told him what Aelyn had said, he dismissed her words. 'War has already come to Yeflam,' he said. 'She knows that. That is why the priests are here. They're the scouts, the first wave, like the raiders in Mireea. But the child knows that she cannot send cannibals here. You don't ride into Yeflam with steel and flesh and bend it to your will. You do it by attacking the Keepers' right to godhood. You talk about the things they cannot fix.'

Ayae had heard the priests speak on the streets. 'The sun and the ocean,' she said. 'But Faise tells me that that is what the Keepers say they will do all the time.'

'That was always Aelyn's goal,' he agreed. 'But she will not share it with them, I assure you.'

5.

At the gates, one of the guards made from wind turned to Zaifyr. 'Lady Aelyn requests that you do not leave.' Its voice sounded like a thousand whispers spoken upon each other. 'There is nothing in the night for you, she says.'

'There are priests,' he said, walking past the guard. 'You can tell her, but she knows that already.'

The night-lit streets of Nale ran ahead of him. On the corners and intersections stood the cold and frail figures of haunts to direct him towards the priest. Unseen by others, they led him through late-night crowds; they ushered him into streets that passed dull bars and nearly empty restaurants; they took him to the sound of waves, to the edge of Nale and the sight of the bridge that crossed into the Spires of Alati, where the tall universities and schools lay. The haunts did not lead him across the bridge. The woman he was searching for had not left Nale. She had turned down a narrow alley, just as he did. She had gone to the small hotel that sat at the end, the hotel that was lit by two lamps; the third, high up on the building, had gone out.

The priest stood outside the front, but she was not alone. A male priest was beside her, but what surprised Zaifyr was that the two were in the company of three other men, who did not wear the brown priestly robes of the priests.

All five were in deep conversation and Zaifyr could hear their voices, the sound carried by the night-silence of the city and the narrowness of the alley, but magnified in such a way that the voices overlapped and cut across each other:

'No, we're not here for—'

'—we hate to see people in pain.'

'It will be winter soon—'

'—hard to find work—'

'—years in Gogair sleeping in snow—'

'No, just campaigns of dead men and frostbite—'

'—you shouldn't have to carry the shame of amputation—'

'—a small bit of magic, a gift from our god—'

'—for our friends.'

Zaifyr had still not identified all the speakers when a haunt beside the female priest cried out in a voice that only Zaifyr could hear. With a small knife in her hand, the priest cut into her thumb, and used her blood to draw power from the dead, to take from it so she could regrow the fingers of one of the men before her.

His power answered without thought: suddenly the haunt appeared among the five, the image of a young woman sketched into shape by broken white lines. She might have once been pretty, but her face was distorted by streaks of pain and by the piercing scream that came from her throat. She snatched the man's hand and tore his new, half-grown fingers from it. His scream matched hers and his two friends grabbed him by the shirt in an attempt to pull him away. One even cried out to the two priests to help.

But they had run into the hotel.

Zaifyr sprinted past the haunt, whose scream turned into a horrible high-pitched wail as the man was pulled from her by his two friends, but she was on the three of them again moments later, just as Zaifyr shouldered the hotel door open.

He moved quickly across the dull wooden floors to the stairs. A haunt waited there, pointing upwards, indicating the direction the priests had taken. As he put his foot on the first step, a guard appeared before him. Even as she reached for her sword, the haunt that had directed him leapt forward and snatched the blade from her scabbard in a small burst of Zaifyr's power. It was enough to give a glimpse of the child that appeared and disappeared and no more.

In the narrow hall of the next floor, a pair of haunts waited. Both directed him down the hall, where the doorway at the end slammed.

Inside – the door had not been locked – the two priests stood on opposite ends of the room. The male was by the window, the glass punched out by his robe-covered arm, while the female was at the other side with two leather packs in her hands. Neither bag looked particularly full, but Zaifyr's glance at both packs was enough to cause the man to punch out the remaining glass and step towards the window. At the same time, the woman shouted, '*Go!*' and hurled one of the bags at him. Her arm was halfway through the motion before the haunt of a middle-aged man wrapped his arms around her, and his lover, a younger man, took hold of the other priest in the window.

'You two.' Zaifyr closed the door gently behind him. 'You two are in trouble.'

'We know who you are,' spat the woman. 'I saw you earlier, Madman! We are not afraid of you!'

The pack she had attempted to throw had landed on the floor. He picked it up and upturned it onto the first of the two beds in the room.

A few coins, a knife and a book fell out.

'Those are not for you!' the man cried. '*She* will not allow it.'

'*She* is not here.' It was a mid-sized book, the cover made from leather, but without a title or author printed on it. With the tips of his fingers, Zaifyr reached for it, intending to flip it open to see if it was *The Eternal Kingdom*, but as he touched it—

—it broke apart and disintegrated.

The male priest laughed. 'She will not allow it,' he repeated. 'She will not allow you to read her words.'

'You wanted to go out of the window, didn't you?' The man's shout was lost as the haunt thrust him through the broken glass and out onto the street below. It was not a long enough fall to kill him, but it was enough that he landed painfully, that he broke his leg, that he could not rise quickly – certainly not quickly enough to outrun the haunt that Zaifyr had left on the street.

'Do you have one in your bag?' he asked the other priest, after the screams began. 'Do you both have a book?'

'You—' The screams ended suddenly, causing her voice to stop. 'You're a monster,' she said. 'You didn't have to kill him.'

'What is it that you think you did outside?' Zaifyr asked, approaching her. 'Do you think that your blood has power? That you take from yourself? Do you not know that you use it to steal from the souls of the dead?' The haunt that held her tightened his grip and whispered to Zaifyr that he was hungry. 'No, you know. You know what you do. For nearly three thousand years, I outlawed blood magic because of what you do. I made witches and warlocks the rarest of creatures. I did to them what I did to your friend. But they at least did not hide what they did. They admitted that it was born in pain and suffering and that they themselves would share that fate.'

'We will not,' the priest hissed. 'We are *hers*. She is the last god, the only god. She owns us. If you believed, you would understand that.'

'I do.' The second pack lay at her feet. He picked it up as a white light filled the room, as it caught the edges of his charms. 'Of all the people in Yeflam, I am probably the only one who knows as you do.'

The white light of the haunt from the street fell over the priest's face. 'You are not Faithful,' she whispered. 'To know is not enough.' The haunt was stained in blood and horrific to look at, but at least her screams had stopped.

'Take the book out for me,' Zaifyr said.

The priest shook her head.

'The blood on her face is not yours,' Zaifyr said. 'Not yet.'

Slowly, her terror of the cold, dead woman settled through her and the priest reached into the pack and took out the book.

He tossed the bag aside. 'Open it for me.'

She hesitated, then flipped it open. The pages were blank.

'You cannot read it, you cannot touch it,' she whispered. 'But my god knows that I hold it. She knows that my life is hers. She knows that I give it freely.'

And, without sound, without evident injury, the Leeran priest slumped to the ground.

He reached out for her, intent on grabbing her haunt, on pushing into her mind; but as he reached for her, as his power took hold, the priest was drawn away from him. He felt her – then, suddenly, he did not.

In her place, he saw for a moment a large dark shape, a shadow that was so huge and encompassing that it left him powerless.

6.

Another two articles about Heast and Refuge were printed during the week and he read both while still in his room in The Engorged Whale. The authors wrote about how Refuge broke in Illate: they related how two hundred soldiers died in a battle that ran through two villages, but the details of individuals were never clear and never consistent with the day itself. There were hints of betrayals that hadn't happened, cowardice that never eventuated. It left Heast unmoved, but he kept reading. He read the descriptions of the Ooilan armies and knew they were twice the size of those mentioned; neither author discussed the slave trade that had ruined generations in Illate; nor did they mention the desire of Illate to be free; the destruction of the Illate armies was barely touched upon, the mass graves no more than a couple of sentences. But both pieces mentioned that it was in these battles that Heast lost his leg. They said that, because of it, he had been spirited away in the final days of the battle. He had heard that before: it was one of the strongest rumours in the months after Refuge's defeat. It meant nothing to him compared to the other lies in the articles, but he knew that the point of both was not Refuge,

Illate or Ooila, but to circle back to Mireea. The authors wanted further to reason that the retreat from the Spine of Ger and the arrival of the Mireeans on Wila were failures of his. More than that: it was a portent of worse to come. Neither article did it well, but the combination of Gaerl's disinformation and the memories of Refuge's final days succeeded in returning Heast to his memory of Leviathan's End, to the judgement that Onaedo delivered to Bnid Gaerl upon the smooth deck of the ship that she made her home.

Onaedo had ruled Leviathan's End since the first mercenary had climbed the rope bridges, long before Heast was born. It was said that she had raised the ship out of the ocean herself, and that on that day, as she pulled the chains that would lift it to its place in Leviathan's End, the ship had had a name upon its hull. The name, when repeated nowadays, bled with the name of other ships – with the infamous like *Glafanr* and the famous like *Cilea* – but it was never repeated by Onaedo. To her, the ship's name was long gone. Now it was her home, now it was Leviathan's End. In its depths she had built cells for those who disobeyed her rule and it was there that she told Bnid Gaerl he would go if he did not accept her judgement.

'I have been patient while I waited. I have gone through our *formal* channels.' Gaerl turned to the crowd that lined the deck, turned away from her to appeal to others. 'My request is a simple one.'

'And it has been denied,' she said.

'*Denied.*' He repeated the word to the crowd lit by the morning's sun, their heads crowned with bright light. 'Denied a word. A *word*! We are soldiers. Warriors. It is we who give words their strength, their meaning. It is we who dictate what they mean. But you hear what is being said. You hear as I do. Ask yourself, how can she deny any warrior a single word?'

The mercenaries on the deck did not reply, but it was clear to Heast that they did not support him. Gaerl had his supporters, of course. Every man did. But the new mercenary unit that he wanted to make would be his third, and the previous two had been notorious for their cruelty and their brutality. Gaerl took easy jobs and he had earned a reputation for taking contracts that allowed him to run roughshod over other units that were trying to make their mark. That had caused the end of his last unit — Beaz, if Heast remembered right. Gaerl's own soldiers, when faced with the prospect of marching against young, poorly trained troops, had instead removed him from command. It was said that even his hardened veterans had been unable to stomach the battle against what Gaerl had called 'kids with rusted knives'.

'When did we become a weak nation?' He had thrown his hand out in disgust. 'A nation of killers. That is us! We take what we want! We leave nothing that we do not want! We should not follow a Queen of Words.'

'Captain Gaerl.' Onaedo's voice rang out. Its authority spun the man back to her. 'I make the rules in Leviathan's End because it is I who saw Baar, the God of War, fall. It is I who saw the folly in his actions, who saw the magnitude of his failure. It is I who have given us a code so that we do not repeat his acts.'

He screwed his long face into a snarl but said nothing.

'If you wish to challenge my decision,' she said, her voice conjuring the images of swords and battlefields that were in her eyes, 'then by all means, draw your sword.'

'I would not challenge you.' Gaerl would not raise a sword against her. Both he and Heast had seen what happened to young mercenaries who rose to her challenge. 'But I would challenge for the name Refuge. I would challenge the infirm –' he waved his hand at Heast – 'and the old –' and then at Baeh Lok, a stocky, olive-skinned man in his sixties on Heast's left – 'though both are clearly not capable of meeting it.'

'Anemone answers all the challenges for Refuge,' Onaedo said.

'You would give a witch that privilege?' he asked angrily.

'Yes.'

'Why am I to be treated so poorly? What conspiracy is this? No witch has ever had that right!'

'The witch of Refuge has always had the privilege,' Anemone said, standing on the right side of Heast, 'as she has for each incarnation of Refuge.'

She was old, but Anemone had always been old. When Heast had first met her, when he was no older than ten, she had been small and fat and old. Her iron-grey hair was cut short and her olive skin, when not lost beneath the folds of her black and white robes and beneath the discoloured strips of white linen she wrapped around her hands, was mapped with lines, as if half a dozen lives had left their mark. But it was her voice that people often remembered, for when she spoke, she did so with a tone that left you in no doubt that she considered you a fool.

'You stand here before us and ask to become the custodian of Refuge's reputation and name but you do not even know what is entailed in that,' the witch said. 'You think it is about money and fame, but that is only because you are a greedy fool. No one in Refuge has ever made money. Why do you think that our Captain moves from job to job working for people who are beneath him? Why do you think Baeh Lok is a sergeant for a Faaishan marshal who has seen fewer battles than Lok has teeth? Refuge does not work for money. Refuge provides safety where there is none. Refuge goes where no other soldier will. Refuge provides a sword for those who do not have one.'

'I've heard you, in the bars, in the inns,' Baeh Lok said. His heavy hand rubbed at his nose. 'I've heard you say that we were wasted in Illate. That we should have never gone into there. But they wanted freedom. They wanted to be slaves no longer.'

'That is why the name is not yours,' Heast said, speaking for the first time. 'Because you are not a man who understands that simple principle.'

Gaerl spat on the deck. 'Only a fool dies for free.'

'*Enough!*' Onaedo said. She seemed to grow, then, though of course she did not; but a part of her filled the deck, and the town. Before her, Bnid Gaerl fell to his knees, pushed down by a force that was raw and primal. 'You are no longer welcome in Leviathan's End,' she said, her voice the only sound to be heard. 'You are stripped of your rank, stripped of your connections, and you are banished from my sight. Make your new unit your last, and fill it with the disgraced soldiers of our world, for no mercenary who wishes to grace Leviathan's End will ever serve you.'

Like smoke, the words followed Heast now as he left The Engorged Whale. Gaerl's passage from the deck to the docks wisped around Heast in the streets of Zanan, each moment a prologue to the articles he had read. Not that 'Commander' Gaerl needed to explain himself in Yeflam. Onaedo did not police her proclamations outside Leviathan's End and, indeed, was not well known beyond the bone borders.

It was later in the day that Heast first noticed a change in the way people around him acted.

He was at a street stall on Zanan. He had ordered a meal that never came and when he questioned it, the young man behind the counter shrugged in a surly manner. He had served it eventually, but while Heast waited, he felt the eyes of everyone on him. It was not until he returned to his small room that he understood. There, pushed under the door, was an article about him. A single sheet, it had text on one side and a caricature on the other. The drawing exposed his steel leg and elongated it, leaving it ugly and violent. From it ran a chain of bone that led to the ankles of faceless soldiers who had served under him. The chains ran into a background sketch of the Mountains of Ger, where the title 'Captain of the Ghosts' was written.

The ease with which he was noticed after that publication was the final mental affirmation that he had overstayed his time in Yeflam. Two nights later, he picked up the pack he had carried into Yeflam and went into the streets, intent on being beyond Yeflam before the morning's sun rose. He planned to make his way to Ghaam, and to a brothel called Sin's Hand, from where he would slip out of Yeflam in the carriage of a well-known prostitute.

But before he left, Heast visited the house of Faise and Zineer Kanar in Mesi.

7.

He arrived in the late hours of the evening. He had made the journey in one of the long, and at this time of the night, near-empty carriages that were pulled by four horses. His company for the length of it was a pair of drunk young soldiers and a member of the Empty Sky. The latter had enough sense to look embarrassed at being so exposed, sitting resolutely a handful of seats behind Heast. The carriage stopped in Ghaam and there he slipped away from her and boarded a new carriage to Mesi, alone.

At the door of Faise and Zineer's house, he was greeted by Ayae. She offered him half a smile when she recognized him – a smile he had seen in Zaifyr – before she let him inside.

'Has it come to that?' he asked, once he saw the sword she held in her hand. 'You answer the door armed?'

'Just recently,' she said. 'Someone splashed red paint out at the front this morning.'

He hadn't seen it in the dark, but he acknowledged the threat and her need for caution. 'How are they holding up?'

'Better than I am,' she said. 'You can see for yourself.'

Faise and Zineer sat at a small table in the kitchen. It was lit by a series of candles and both had drinks in front of them. They rose to greet Heast. If he had not seen Ayae and her sword at the door, he would not have thought that anything was wrong. They were polite, friendly, and at times, drily funny. 'There is less and less I can do in Yeflam,' he said, after he had sat, declining a glass of wine, having chatted for a few minutes. 'It's time to check on the farms we've bought. I want to see what they have in terms of produce and seeds. There are a few people I can contact from there as well. But mostly, I figure it is time to let Le'ta and Gaerl spend some time chasing me.'

'We still have a lot we can do,' Zineer said. 'It's not enough to just own land and buildings. You have to use them wisely in the markets.'

'I have been trying to convince them,' Ayae said, 'to step back a bit.'

'Might be a good idea,' Heast agreed. 'Muriel has enough for the leverage she wants. The goal was to allow her to begin gaining sway and control in the Traders' Union — or at least to threaten that she could. Once she has that, she is more than capable of getting what she wants, with a little help from Ayae. The two of you should remember what Essa and I told you about Gaerl.'

'We haven't been found,' Faise said. She smiled at the other woman. 'Ayae just brought it up because she thinks every bit of paint is a knife in disguise.'

'You have to ask yourself why it was done.'

'Lian Alahn returned to Yeflam this week,' Zineer said. 'It was done because of that. Le'ta is afraid that we'll work with him again.'

'Alahn really has returned?' Heast had thought that the fat

merchant was lying to him. 'Have you been in contact with him?'

The accountant began to answer, but he swallowed his words when he realized that they had not been addressed to him.

'Alahn and I have nothing to discuss,' Ayae said flatly. 'All the bile that was ever said by Illaan came from his father.'

Heast was not surprised by her tone. In truth, he thought Illaan deserved it, for the way that he had treated her. 'Don't get over-confident,' he said, turning his attention back to Zineer and Faise. 'You want to be alive at the end of this. We all want to be alive at the end of this. If you need me, if things get bad, however, you can reach me through Sinae Al'tor.'

'Of Sin's Hand?' Faise asked. 'The infamous brothel in Ghaam?'

'Where everything has a price but Al'tor himself.' Heast rose and, with a brief nod, made his way to the door with Ayae beside him. 'You're right to be careful,' he said quietly. 'If it reaches a point where both of them have to leave Yeflam, Al'tor can help you with that. I'll make sure he knows that when I see him tonight.'

She thanked him and, when he shook her hand, it was warm, but not painful to touch her.

Ayae stayed in Heast's thoughts as he rode a carriage back to Ghaam. The lamps along the roads and along the bridge burned as if in a procession, and he saw a lonely lamplighter making his rounds through the streets to keep them lit. As he passed the man, Heast reflected on how Ayae had grown since he had first seen her in Samuel Orlan's shop. He did not mean as a woman, but rather in confidence. When he had first met her, she had smiled nervously, unsure how to react to the people around her. Her apprenticeship had caused a small squall of gossip in Mireea and beyond, because she had no family, but Orlan, for all that he was a difficult man to read, had shielded her from most of the storm. After the fire in the shop, and after her power — Heast did not call it a curse — revealed itself, Orlan had, however, left Ayae to the mercy of those around her. After Illaan had rejected her, Heast had thought it likely that Ayae would retreat within herself, though Muriel had argued that it needn't happen, and assured him that she would make sure it didn't. In this, he had thought she would fail. He had seen that retreat before in stronger women: Onaedo had built walls around her, for example. She had retreated from the failure of the gods, of her god, and when her own power emerged, she had isolated herself and fortified her world. Since then, she had never left the bone walls of Leviathan's End. But in Ayae's case, Heast had been wrong. She had not retreated in the same way and Muriel had been right, no matter what part she had played.

Faise and Zineer Kanar, he thought, ought to be thankful for that.

8.

'Do you know what I always want to say to him?' Faise said, after Ayae had seen Heast out, after she had shut the door, after she had returned to the small dining room. 'I want to tell him how much I love the mercenary novels. How he reminds me of Captain Cahelo, the main character in one of my favourite series. He even has a steel eye! I swear the character is based on him. I want to ask if it is, but I know he won't tell me.'

'You should listen to him,' Ayae said, returning to her seat, 'when he tells you to be careful — when he tells both of you that you have done enough.'

Next to his wife, Zineer laughed good-naturedly. 'I told you,' he said to Faise. 'You owe me now.'

She slumped in her seat and gave an exaggerated sigh. 'You could have said something else first,' she said. 'You could have said, "I've not read those books, can I borrow them?"'

'I have enough to read,' Ayae said.

'They're making you humourless.'

'Life is making me humourless.' She reached for her glass of wine. 'You two aren't helping,' she said, using it to point at them.

They laughed again, but she wasn't surprised. Since she had

knocked on the door it had been difficult to make Faise and Zineer recognize the danger around them. To a degree, she understood: the soldiers who shadowed them, who splashed red paint over the stones outside their house, were a threat who had, as yet, done nothing more than be a nuisance. Nothing that they had done equalled what the couple had been exposed to only months before.

Ayae had been surprised to learn that, before Muriel Wagan's letter arrived, Faise and Zineer had been broke. Worse: Faise told her that they had no food, that they were weeks away from losing the small house they owned and that they were looking at a future where they would be living in a shelter. Ayae had begun to tell her that she would have given them money, that Samuel Orlan would have helped, that Olcea might have as well, but Faise only smiled: 'Would that have been before or after the Faithful laid siege to Mireea?' The worst of it had come after Mireea had fallen, she added. Benan Le'ta had pushed the creditors and, the night before Lady Wagan's letter arrived, a pair had visited them to give them two weeks' notice.

Faise still spoke with anger, but Zineer, when he talked of it, did so with shame. He told her how he had been working for Lian Alahn before the problems began. He had been keeping accounts for a handful of small businesses on Mesi and Neela. 'Nothing much,' he said, and Ayae nodded when he told her that. Illaan had helped him get the work by recommending him to his father and, according to him, it had been a reluctant favour. 'It went well,' Zineer admitted, 'until Le'ta made his push to take control of the Traders' Union.' He broke into the office that Zineer and Faise kept in Neela and stole the details of a dozen merchants. Within a week, the men and women were killed by 'unknown' assassins and, in the public fallout that saw Lian Alahn stripped of his powers for not vetting his workers properly — Zineer was accused of selling the details — he was ruined. 'It was less than what happened to those poor merchants, but I couldn't get a job at all afterwards,' he said to her. 'Faise and I made an official complaint to the Traders' Union about defamation, but it did nothing but bring Le'ta's angry eyes on us.'

Then Lady Wagan's offer arrived.

They had come so close to ruin, Ayae suspected, that they did not see the new threats around them. They ignored what Xrie said to her, even after they agreed that he had been right about what they were doing. She had watched Captain Essa tell them that the Empty Sky would have more and more people on them, soon enough. They had told him not to worry. At least, after the Brotherhood left Yeflam and Essa's prediction proved true, Ayae had been able to insist that the two accompany her to Nale when she visited Zaifyr.

The whole situation left her, as Faise said, humourless. She felt confined by her responsibilities and, worse, overwhelmed by them. She was not a political person. After she had returned from her meeting with Aelyn Meah, she said that she had gained nothing from it, and Zaifyr, Zineer and Faise had spent the evening telling her otherwise. It was they who made her realize that the office she had been given was a positive sign. 'She has done it so you'll be able to talk to the other Keepers, to sound them out,' Faise said. 'She has basically said that you have to build support for what you want and is giving you the opportunity to do so.'

Zaifyr had agreed. He had then added, his smile threatening to become a smile at her expense, that she could also begin researching Ger. 'Some of his final words still survive,' he said to her. 'A lot was lost, but it's a place to start.'

She had visited the Enclave's library the next day and it was there, in a room that ran the length of the entire building, that she saw Aelyn Meah. The Keeper floated gently in front of the highest shelves, a point so high that it left her a smeared dot; but when Ayae entered, Aelyn drifted to the ground, a pair of books in her hands. 'The Five Kingdoms were not kind to history,' she said to Ayae, after she had led her to the empty seats and table in the middle. 'We are slowly putting back what we can, but it is not easy. We have to rely upon historians, scholars, memories and, more often than not, my sister, Tinh Tu. In relation to Ger, the Cities of Ger have made it especially hard because they had an oral history. They taught a specific few how to read and it was they who told the stories. But what remains here is yours if it will help. I will also help you if I can.'

'Thank you, but—' She was unsettled that Aelyn knew what information she was looking for. She thought of the woman floating up the shelves, the woman who still had that eerie calm about her. 'But it is fine.'

'Ger was the Warden of the Elements,' Aelyn said, as if she had not spoken. 'His chains kept them subdued: there were no fires, no floods, no earthquakes, no storms unless Ger agreed to them. But he did not rule the sky or the sea. Those were the domains of others. Jul was the god of the sky. It was he who gave the gift of flight to the world. It is he who I will, one day, replace. If I can help you use the air currents in the way I can, I am happy to do so.'

Ayae remembered falling from the tower in Mireea. She remembered the wind tearing at her. 'I . . .' She stumbled over the words. '. . . thank you,' she said, finally.

'One last thing,' Aelyn said, as she stood. 'A small piece of advice. On Ghaam, there is a printer run by Eira, one of the Keepers of the Divine. She is one of the more vocal elements of us who are against the Mireeans leaving Wila. You would do well to visit her before the next Enclave meeting.'

'She is called the Cold Witch,' Faise told her, later. 'You can imagine what they call her on the streets. Everyone loves a rhyme. But — well, I don't think she will be very sympathetic to you. She was Fo's partner. She had been for nearly two centuries.'

Alone at the table, Faise and Zineer having long gone to bed, Ayae stared at her glass, at the remains of wine within. If she held the glass tightly, she could make bubbles emerge, but she could not control it.

The thought was still there in the morning.

9.

When Kaqua brought up the dead priests, he did not mention Aelyn or the child. 'Five people are dead and there are half a dozen witnesses,' he said. Zaifyr sat in the first room, at the table where he always sat, a collection of red-and-white stones in front of him. 'It took a lot of work to keep the story out of the print shops. A lot of requests. A lot of promises.'

'You needn't do that.' Zaifyr picked up a red stone. The Pauper had poured them from his satchel wordlessly before he sat. 'You do not have to hide anything.'

'We are trying to ensure that peace is kept,' he said. 'It is not about you. Nor, I should add, is it about Leera and Yeflam. It is about ensuring that the streets in our cities are safe. That our rule of law is obeyed. Surely you can agree with that?'

'Your streets are no safer than they were before.' The rock was not naturally formed. It was smooth and circular and constructed, but its colour did not come from paint. He curled his fingers around it and met Kaqua's gaze. 'Why has Aelyn allowed the Leeran priests in?'

'Your sister does not rule Yeflam,' he said. 'You seem not to understand that, Qian. Yeflam is ruled by the Enclave.'

He smiled faintly. 'Then why would the Enclave let them in?'

'Because we wish to make peace a priority,' he said. 'I keep repeating this to you, but I feel that you do not believe me, or that you do not agree.'

'I never met any of the priests that existed after the War of the Gods,' Zaifyr said, after a moment of pause, letting Kaqua's words pass without comment. 'There was a shaman in the village where I was born, but she was not the same. She lost her faith. Aelyn, Eidan, Tinh Tu: they are all the same as me, because they were born after the war, after the priests had died. But Jae'le — my brother — saw them. He knew them. When I first met him, he told me stories about them. He told me about an old priest who had served the Leviathan. He said that after the ocean turned black, after the last god died, after the Leviathan died, the priest beached his ship on the edge of what would become Sooia. His ship was huge, Jae'le said. One of the largest that he had ever seen, if not the largest. But when he came upon the ship, it was not lying on the edge of the ocean and spread across the ground. No, it was floating in the sky. Because he is my brother, he climbed up to it. Once he pulled himself over the rail, he came face to face with absolute carnage, with thousands of bodies lying on the decks and in the rooms of the ship. Men, women, children: they were all dead. Jae'le told me that what struck him was that no one had died violently. It was as if they had been walking, or eating, or sleeping, and their life had just been drawn away. He said that it was like a tide around him. He followed it until he reached the captain's cabin. Inside, he found the priest. He was sitting in a chair, his hair grey and long and twisting into his beard. His flesh had sunk into his bones and it was clear that he had not moved for some time. Jae'le thought that he had been sitting there for about twenty, thirty years. Since the Leviathan died, he said. When he approached him, the priest opened his eyes. He was not afraid. He said, *The land and ocean are impure, just as the air is. All that is pure is the life of those who believed and I shall be sustained by them.*'

'Did he kill him?' Kaqua asked.

'Of course.'. Zaifyr tossed the red stone on the table. It thudded, then rolled up against the others. 'What story of my brother does not end in death?'

'Yours.' Before he could answer, the Pauper picked up one of the white stones. 'He did not kill you. He merely imprisoned you. Do you think he would be pleased by what you are doing now?'

'You haven't listened,' Zaifyr said. 'You let priests in here. Priests who are not interested in keeping any kind of peace, just like their god.'

'You are so sure that they want war.'

'War is how faith is spread. You are old enough to know that.'

'War spreads many things,' Kaqua said. 'I saw that when the Five Kingdoms were made. I am not interested in seeing that return.'

'Who is?'

He spread his hands: the white rock lay in his left palm, his right empty.

Zaifyr grunted. 'Are the rocks for the trial?' he asked, changing the subject.

'Yes,' Kaqua replied. 'We have been making them. The colour

comes from a dye we mix into the mud before they're put into a kiln. I have them here today as a sign of intention to have a trial, but after the deaths of those priests and those men . . . it may be that they are not used at all. I assure you that they will not be handed out if there is panic in the streets.'

'You told me you kept it from being printed.'

'Yes, but you cannot treat Yeflam as if it is yours, to abuse and to treat as you will,' he said. 'There are laws. There is a society. You have to understand that, Qian.'

'That's not my name.'

'Do you understand what I am saying?'

Zaifyr *did* understand. After he had returned to Aelyn's house, after he had walked past the guards made from wind, he prowled through the rooms, he walked up the stairs, he walked until he ended up in one of the towers. There he had stood in the cool night air and watched the morning's sun rise, angry at himself. He could hear the whisper of the haunt he had empowered, her plea as he drew the power out of her, as he rendered her powerless, as he returned her to the horror of her death. He had seen the three men she killed on the street when he left the hotel. He had heard their whispers. But what made him angry with himself was the absolute failure of what he had done. He had killed those people and used the haunt for nothing. *Oh, not nothing*, he thought with self-disgust. He had reminded the child that he was here, that he stood against her, that he was moving against her.

'I understand,' he said, finally.

10.

Cold Press, Eira's printer, was located at the heart of Ghaam, in a beautiful two-storey building made from brown stone and dark, polished wood. Tall windows of frosted glass had been installed on the top floor and, from a distance, its reflection guided you through the streets — streets that contained half a dozen bookstores, two additional presses, and a series of restaurants and cafes — as if it were the only real business in the area.

A chill drew Ayae down the street, a chill that only she could feel. She made no mention of it to either Faise or Zineer, but when the three had stopped across the road from Cold Press, Faise offered to go in with her. Zineer offered a moment later. Ayae declined both. She knew they had agreed to come with her today to provide moral support and, for a moment, as the carriage they rode in on crossed the bridge from Mesi to Ghaam, she had been tempted to ask them to accompany her. But, a handful of steps away from the wood-and-glass door, she knew otherwise. 'You'll be all right here without me?' she asked.

'It's a very popular cafe,' Faise said.

'We'll be fine,' Zineer added. 'Unless you want us to come with you.'

She shook her head and walked across the road.

A bell on the door rang when she entered Cold Press and rang again when the door closed. Inside, a simple and elegant office waited.

Ayae had expected a printing press, but what she found instead was a series of dark-mauve lounges and polished coffee tables. On the one closest to her was a collection of papers, the top one bearing a caricature of Aned Heast and Lady Wagan on the front. The former was defined by his steel leg, while the latter was defined by weight and, Ayae thought, age. Both stood in a whale's carcass, a sail made from the tattered remains of swords and a flag that was stitched together from cloaks – Yeflam cloaks, Ayae suspected. A caption beneath said, 'How the Captain and the Lady of the Ghosts left the Floating Cities'.

'One of the papers we printed today,' said Eira, her pronunciation clipped and precise. 'It is called the *Ghaam Daily*. Quite popular.'

She descended the stairs from the first floor, the palest person Ayae had ever seen. It was not just her skin, which was smooth, but the long, simple white dress she wore. She had pale-blonde hair, almost white, and she wore no jewellery but a simple silver bracelet that sat loosely around her left wrist. She was, to Ayae's eye, a beautiful woman, her body a collection of slim long limbs and, for a moment, as Eira left the stairs, as she drew closer to her, Ayae was conscious of her own leather trousers, her black shirt, her scuffed leather boots and, of course, her sword.

'Ayae, I presume?' Eira smiled, but there was no warmth in

it. 'I had heard your name before you arrived here. You were Samuel Orlan's apprentice, not so long ago. It was quite an honour for someone with no last name.'

That's how it would be, then. 'You don't have one either,' she said without pause.

'Santano. My family originated from Nmia. They are still there, actually. But I stopped using it when I became a Keeper of the Divine four hundred years ago.'

Ayae turned, reached for the door.

'You're leaving already?' Eira asked.

'Maybe you mistook me for someone else,' Ayae said, her hand on the handle. 'But I did not come here for this.'

'No, you came to petition for the Mireean people.'

She released the door handle and, despite herself, turned back. 'I did.'

'Tsk. You should have walked out,' Eira said. She stood next to a glass case a handful of steps from the door. 'I might have respected you for that.'

'They don't deserve to be there,' she said, saying the words, but knowing—

'Of course they do.'

—that they would be ignored.

'What I would like to hear from you,' Eira said, 'is what my beloved's final moments were like. I hear you were there. In fact, I hear that you were the reason he died. He and Bau.'

'Why don't you ask Zaifyr?' Ayae said. 'He was the reason they died, not me.'

'I am forbidden to talk to Qian. We all are.' Her pale hand fell to the top of the case she stood beside. In it were two large books, lying open. Between them lay heavy curved wooden blocks with handles on one end and holes for typeface on the other. The typeface, made from big pieces of metal, was set out before them. 'He is a little like this press here. A relic that is being kept beneath glass. But he will be broken out soon. He will stand trial.'

'He wants to,' she said. 'But the Mireean people aren't on trial.'

'They will stay on Wila or they will swim to shore,' the other woman said. 'They have said a number of things about Fo that simply are not true. He was not so foolish that he would let a plague out that he had designed. And he would not ignore the Enclave's orders, not now. Not when we had so much to learn.'

'Yet he did.'

Eira stared at her, the room growing colder as she did.

'You want to know how he died?' Ayae said. 'The dead tore him open.' The glass beneath Eira's hand cracked. 'The dead are everywhere, do you know that? Generations upon generations packed upon each other. Each day you and I walk through a thousand, unawares. Everyone does. Everyone except Zaifyr. He sees them. And all he did was give them enough life so that they could appear before Fo and Bau and rip open their skin. Enough life so that they could devour what was there. Be sure to print that in one of your papers so everyone can read it.'

A moment later, she was out of the door, and halfway across the street, her hands feeling as if they might ignite in anger.

Faise and Zineer were there immediately, but it was not until later, when she had gained control of her anger, that she could tell them coherently what had happened. By then, they had returned to Mesi, to the small house, and the afternoon's sun had set. 'There's a meeting of the Enclave next month that I'm invited to,' Ayae said, once she had finished. 'I had hoped – I thought that I might be able to make some headway into getting them off that island.'

'I'm sorry,' Faise said, sitting opposite her.

'It's not your fault.'

'Not, but – you know what I miss?' she said. 'I miss being a witch's apprentice. I had no stomach for that blood magic, but no one said anything bad to me when I worked for Olcea. If I'd been like that war witch, I could have done what she would have and walked into that shop with you. I could have told that cold bitch what was what.'

Despite herself, Ayae laughed. 'It wouldn't have made a difference.'

'Then I could have slapped Benan Le'ta and his paid soldiers around.'

That caught Ayae's attention. 'I'm glad that you've noticed that they're there.'

'There were at least five today.' Faise shrugged. 'It doesn't bother me. We're pretty safe, I know that. But it'd be nice to . . . well, to be powerful,' she said, after a small hesitation. 'To be safe because everyone was afraid of you.'

11.

On the morning that Bueralan boarded a ship to Ooila, he had not seen Samuel Orlan for over two weeks. He had changed inns twice after the time in his first room expired, and once again, a day before he walked up *Bounty*'s wooden plank.

It had taken just under three weeks to organize a passage to Ooila. It had been hard to find a direct passage to the country, partly because of the fighting in the east, and partly because of the rumours that were beginning to emerge from Ooila. Aela Ren's ship, *Glafanr*, had been seen in the waters, it was said. The Innocent had landed. His army was preparing to follow him. The rumours were not new, but combined with the child, with Waalstan, and with some of the stories about ghosts in the Spine of Ger that had begun to emerge, it became another one of the world's problems. He was told by a number of captains that he could book a passage to Gogair or Nmia, but Bueralan did not want to pay for half a voyage. Financially, he needed to make the trip in one booking. Eventually, after a week, the Ooilan spice trader *Bounty* pulled into harbour, and the young captain on it took Bueralan's coin without a second question. He would have to wait nine days before the ship set sail, but that did not bother him. He used that time to pull himself further and further from Samuel Orlan. Indeed, the old man appeared to have made the same decision: after a few nights he stopped knocking on Bueralan's door and when he changed inns, Orlan seemed not to know and not to care.

It was with some surprise, then, that Bueralan found the cartographer on the deck of the ship, waiting for him.

'You're not welcome here,' said Bueralan bluntly. 'I have had more than enough of your company.'

'I sympathize with that, truly I do.' The marks around Orlan's throat were faint and he spoke in the voice he had had when Bueralan first met him. In fact, the weeks in Jeil had been kinder to Orlan than him, and the old man appeared before him with a neatly trimmed beard, cut hair and new clothes. Expensive, black-dyed wool trousers, a black vest over a red silk shirt and brand-new boots gave him the appearance of what he was: a rich man of considerable fame. 'But it is a mistake to return home,' he said.

'It's not your home.'

'Neither is it yours. Do you think Zean would truly appreciate this?'

'Don't speak as if you know him,' Bueralan said softly. *Bounty* shuddered as it pushed away from the quay. 'You don't know a thing.'

'I know what a blood brother is,' the cartographer replied. 'I know what it means to own another man.'

'Nobody owned Zean.'

'It is not so dissimilar to the situation in which you find yourself.'

'Nobody owns me.' He took a step closer to the other man. 'You certainly don't.'

'I don't mean me.' Orlan did not move back. 'I mean what you are now. What it means to be god-touched.'

'Ger helped me to help save himself, that was all.' It would take but one push, one swift movement to force the old man into Leviathan's Blood, to be free of him. 'You and the child can say it all you want but it doesn't mean a thing.'

'It does.' *Bounty* began to turn in the water, the smooth blackness broken by the dip and pull of oars. 'You have heard the word, I'm sure. It is used in Yeflam. In Gogair. It used to be a popular term for those who we now call cursed. But the child did not say it to you as if you were one of those men and women. She used it as it was originally intended, as it was spoken by the gods so long ago. She used it with respect.'

'She had no respect for either of us in Ranan.'

'And then she sent you to another god-touched man,' Orlan finished.

Bueralan frowned. 'She didn't—'

'*When innocence is at stake.*'

His skin crawled suddenly. 'Aela Ren,' he whispered.

'The Innocent.'

'She said the same thing to you.'

'She would,' Samuel Orlan said, 'but it is not true. She says it because she knows that the very first Samuel Orlan declined the offer of immortality when the goddess Aeisha offered it to him.'

'Why?'

'It was an offer of chains. He killed himself a day later, believing that it was the only way he could be free.' Orlan reached up and touched the pouch around Bueralan's neck. 'All the other god-touched men and women were made that offer, but you weren't. You and your blood brother have more in common now than you think. You have no freedom. Your mortality is pinned to a moment ten years from now, maybe fifty, maybe a thousand – to where Ger has decided that your death will be meaningful.'

'Ger is dead,' Bueralan said. 'He has been dead for over ten thousand years. What happened beneath Mireea – I can't explain that, but it isn't what you just said. There was no time for that.'

'The world of a god is not our world,' he said, taking a step away from the saboteur. 'The first Samuel Orlan knew that. He has made sure that every Orlan has known that since. Whatever they think, whatever they want, they think and want. To them, we are just cattle to that end. The very thought of one returning . . .' He shook his head. 'Why do you think I gambled on going into Ranan to kill one that was half made?'

'What makes you think you should go to Ooila instead?' he asked. 'That god you tried to kill is back the other way.'

'But you are here,' he said. 'Soon enough, it will be clear what happened to you. Perhaps it will start to make sense, then.'

He walked away then, walked beneath the deck, to his cabin. He left Bueralan on the deck, Leviathan's Blood growing around him.

12.

The midday's sun rose over five hundred acres of recently ploughed land. Heast, his pale blue gaze on the dirt road, watched the riders approach.

He stood on the deck of a small farmhouse, alone. Behind him, through the doorway, past the rectangular table, beyond a second door, his sword lay on a narrow single bed. Yet, as the riders drew closer and closer, he made no move towards it: it would not help him against the flashes of blue that he saw, against the two score of the Empty Sky that Bnid Gaerl had sent. He knew that by the time the head of the column thundered into the yard before the farmhouse, the leader pulling heavily on the reins of his black horse.

He was young, probably a little over thirty, and he had thick brown hair cut short around a tanned, handsome and dishonest face.

'Captain of the Ghosts.' If he expected Heast to react to his new unofficial title, he gave no indication of disappointment when he did not. 'It was some work to find you.'

'I have been here for a month, Sergeant—'

'Menan.' He dismounted; the rest of the guards in dark-blue

armour followed him in unison. 'Is there no one here to help my men?' Menan held the reins of his horse in his left hand; his right held the sword he had slung from the saddle. 'You surely haven't been out here by yourself, Captain?'

'I am afraid,' Heast lied, 'there's just me.'

The other man's humourless smile revealed straight white teeth. He handed the reins to one of his men and walked slowly up the stairs, the spurs in his boots clicking with each step. 'I do not want to get off to the wrong start,' he said, 'but you don't seem particularly disturbed that forty well-trained and well-armed soldiers are before you.'

'That's not how I would describe anyone who served under Gaerl,' Heast said.

The response stopped Menan, two steps before him. 'Captain, there is no need to be anything but civil. Let us both talk.' He pointed to the open door to a room with a long wooden table. 'Surely we can act like professionals?'

'You're the one with forty soldiers.'

'Exactly.' Confidence returned, he brushed past Heast. Inside, the sergeant waited for Heast to enter, his hand on the chair closest to the door. 'Please, take a seat.' Menan laid the sword across the table. 'It must hurt to stand for long periods of time.'

You've never been to Leviathan's End. Wordlessly, Heast made his way to the chair at the end of the room. The sword blade pointed to him.

'Aned Heast. Captain of the Ghosts, Captain of the Spine, Captain of the Wisal Guard and the Behani Guard. But most famously, the last Captain of Refuge. I must admit, when I was young, my father told me endless stories of Refuge and its soldiers. He had been a soldier himself and, I think, if he had not had a family, would have served in Refuge. If he could, that is. But after all his stories, I used to imagine myself in Refuge's battles. In yours, actually. I would always imagine that I was one of the sacrificing tragic heroes.' He seated himself in the chair in a swift, fluid motion, a contrast to Heast. 'Youth. Nowadays, few even know the name Refuge, and even fewer know the names of the men and women who served in it. Only men like my father, who sit in bars and drink away what pittance they have, remember.'

'It can be a cruel life for a man who seeks fame,' Heast said.

'Indeed, it can. Still, in your final years, you must be content that you have seen nearly all the world.'

'There are places I have not been.' At the mention of *final*, he rested his hands on the top of the table, above the ugly dagger he had hidden beneath. 'They are not many, though.'

'Sooia?'

'No, I have been there.'

An honest curiosity – the first honest expression Heast had seen on Menan's broad face – saw him lean forward. 'What is it like?'

'Awful.'

'That is all you will say?'

'The land is both drowned and burnt, the soil sown with bones and salt.' Through the door, he watched the dark-blue armoured soldiers spread out, watched them begin to search the farmhouse and the empty fields. 'The things that Aela Ren and his army have done will not be easily undone.'

Menan's fingers touched the hilt of his sword. 'It will require cooperation. As you and Muriel Wagan have been cooperating with the Traders' Union for the last three months. Helping each other send food and clothing to Wila. Keeping your people safe. Standing up not just to the Leerans, but to the animosity in Yeflam. An increasingly difficult task now that the priests have begun to arrive in the cities and give sermons on the very topic. Sometimes it feels as if not a day goes by without a new fear expressed about Leera and Mireea. Yet we have stood beside you. We have maintained our defence of you. Even as you and Lady Wagan have been purchasing Yeflam land.' Outside, Heast heard the sharp stamp of a horse's hoof, the snort of another. The low voices of the Empty Sky grew as they returned to the front of the building empty-handed.

'I must admit, it took the Traders' Union a long time to uncover your deception,' Menan continued. 'From what I understand, they were aware of the purchases two months ago. It was the two hundred acres from the Galan family that tipped them off. Galan was unable to keep secret the sum that was offered. The banker from Zoum revealed little, and you cannot harm those bastards, not if you want to keep your accounts. But the trail could be followed. And it was, across Leviathan's Blood and back.' Menan smiled sourly. 'Zineer and Faise Kanar. Benan Le'ta had a fit when he heard, but not enough of one to do as I suggested, and cut both their throats and toss them into the ocean.'

'A sound plan,' said Heast, turning his focus back to the soldier. 'What stopped Le'ta?'

'The two live with another woman.' His hand tapped the straight blade of the sword in front of him. 'A cursed girl.'

The Captain of the Ghost's hands remained on the table,

above the hidden dagger. 'Are forty soldiers not enough to kill her?'

'A cold suggestion.'

'You did not answer my question.'

'You can never tell.' Menan flashed his dishonest smile. 'Cursed — they're always a problem. But she's not a soldier. She can be made to run. She can be made to take her friends into hiding. To force them to give up everything.'

'So you kill me, instead?'

'I do admire how casually you are approaching it.'

Outside, far out on the vacant fields, a member of the Empty Sky toppled to the ground, the first in a violent ripple.

'I think you misunderstand the situation,' Heast said.

'I am not a fool,' Menan replied evenly. 'It won't be easy. Even Benan Le'ta knows that. He knows that what has been taken won't fall back into his hands straight away. He knows he'll have to kill Muriel Wagan as well.'

'Greed is always very reliable, isn't it? Muriel told me that years ago and I have not doubted it since. She told me because I asked why she was not wealthier.' Heast had sat in her disorganized office after he had returned with Lord Wagan from Balana. His report had been short and simple, the trip uneventful. The only note of interest was his opinion that Elan Wagan had left a number of financial opportunities on the floor, discarded for no reason other than lack of interest. 'She said to me that a fortune is an empty goal. Wealth is much like a sword, she said. It is a tool to be used for an end, nothing more. The moment you begin to value it for itself, it becomes blunt and can hurt no one. I think those words will mean something to you very shortly.'

'They won't.' Menan rose from the chair, his sword in his grasp. 'Wealth is power, Captain. You and my father and Muriel Wagan, you are all the same. You all refuse to see that our world is made by wealth.'

Behind him, through the door, a short, stocky man in plate and chain mail appeared on the field. In his hand he held an ugly spiked mace, a weapon that might well have torn open the side of his face, if he had been struck with it then, if the blood that stained it was his.

A shout erupted from the soldiers who stood around the farmhouse. The cry forced Menan to turn and, as he did, men and women in heavy armour and weapons began to surge around the house, as if a dam had broken.

'What is happening to my men?' he demanded.

'They're dying.' Heast's hand reached beneath the table, grabbed the hilt of the dagger.

An anguished cry drew Menan to the open door of the farmhouse, ready to give an order. But it was useless. More and more Brotherhood soldiers appeared before him, each of them holding heavy crossbows that began and ended a short and ugly battle. Already, the forty soldiers who had arrived had been cut down to a dozen. The survivors were throwing down their weapons to the ground and surrendering with loud shouts.

The sword slipped from Menan's fingers. 'I do not wish to die,' he said. 'I surrender, we all su—'

His words cut off wetly as Heast's dagger cut deep and hard across his neck.

There would be no prisoners. The Captain of the Ghosts could afford none, and did not, in truth, wish for any.

'A lot of bodies today.' Essa used a rag to wipe his mace clean as he climbed the two steps. 'Be hard to keep them buried for long.'

'I know.' Heast cleaned his dagger against his leg. 'We'll have to prepare for when they are dug up.'

A Bird Preceded Him

No one knows where the first copies of *The Eternal Kingdom* were printed, but in Gogair there is a story told by the locals in Xanoure. They tell of a small house, which if you were to visit now, you would find barren. They say that once it had been filled with print machines, filled with ink, filled with paper and leather and stitching. Then, one morning, it was empty.

The story goes that a ship left Xanoure that night. A ship, the locals said, that went to a port in Leera, a port that was slowly becoming infamous for its misery and sadness. It is not an uncommon story — it is simply a story of theft and there are other thefts in Xanoure — but it is a story, nonetheless. What commends it to memory is that the locals will tell you that the theft was not of the printing presses, or of the inks, or the papers, but of the ship. And that it was the printer and his family who stole the ship.

—Tinh Tu, *Private Diary*

1.

On the slick deck of *Bounty*, Bueralan Le watched the port of Dyanos approach, a rain-dark shape lit by flickering lanterns.

The small town stood on the eastern edge of Ooila, protected by jagged rocks and steep ash-stained cliffs, both partly obscured in the drizzling night. The crew of *Bounty* navigated the choppy black water that led to it by standing at the bow with long poles to gauge the depth. They did so because stone riddled this part of the ocean's floor and it had torn through the bottom of more than one ship. In fact, a long history of wrecks had ensured that Dyanos remained not just a small port, but a stop for desperate men and women, for merchants who ran contraband, for poor families wanting cheap fares, for runaway slaves, for hard-luck mercenaries and, of course, for exiled barons.

Bueralan was not ready to return home. The reluctance did not surprise him as the wet docks drew closer. He had never considered himself a man of nationalist identification: the hereditary title of baron had stuck to him after his exile as half an insult, and though he had embraced it, he had kept nothing of the Ooilan traditions implied with it. He had not sought out the clothes that he had once worn, nor the meals he had once eaten. He had not contacted old friends, had not tried to re-establish old relationships. Few knew just how much he had distanced himself from his former life in exile, and of those who did appreciate the length, only Zean had known the exact distance. The other man had never made mention of it, however. To do so would have been to discuss how much he himself had left behind. To do so would have been to remind each other of Zean's blood-bonded slavery, of the long hard road that had delivered him independence, but only after he had left Ooila.

Bueralan had spent most of the journey on *Bounty* running through what would happen once he stepped ashore in Ooila. He knew that he would not be able to stay hidden. He was too distinct a man for that: with his smooth, shaved head and his white tattoos he would not be able to hide for long. The point had been made to him halfway through the journey, in fact. *Bounty* had just passed between Gogair and Kakar when the captain asked him if he was the exiled baron his first mate said he was. He had been in his cabin when the young man had asked, the afternoon's sun illuminating the room as if it were the inside of a jewel.

'I am,' Bueralan said.

'You don't want no trouble. I know that.' The captain of *Bounty*, Po Danal, had inherited his ship from his father, and he was intent on returning it to its glory. 'And I don't want no trouble,' he said bluntly. 'I have cargo I don't want looked at too hard.'

'That's why we're going to Dyanos, both of us.'

'Yeah, but the Eyes of the Queen are known to be there as well. I don't need them on me when we dock.'

'Pueral?' He remembered the last time he had seen her, the ease with which she had found him. 'I'll be careful,' he said.

'Maybe you'll be lucky,' the captain said, before he left. 'Maybe she'll be too busy with the Innocent.'

Bueralan did not think he could bank on that, but it was true enough that Aela Ren had stopped the men and women on *Bounty* talking about him. There was no time for an exiled baron, not when they could be drifting into a nation at war with the feared warlord. Not that what they said was new to Bueralan: he had heard stories of the Innocent regularly when he had lived in Ooila. But the crew spoke as if it was the first time they had heard them, despite being natives themselves. They talked about the Innocent at dinner and at breakfast; they talked about him on the deck and below it; they even talked about him in storms. They speculated about him as a person. About his martial ability. About his swords. And about his army. About the size of it and its capabilities. Bueralan listened with half an ear because there was little else to do. The only consistent thing the crew of *Bounty* could agree upon was that a man named Aela Ren existed. That the man that existed had an army and a ship – a huge, hulking beast with red sails that could carry all his army, no matter its number. *Glafanr*, they said.

For all that Bueralan gave the words no credence, it was one of the few topics that Samuel Orlan felt he had to discuss with him. At first, Bueralan had shrugged him off, had told him that he did not care, but the child's words – *call only when what is at stake is innocence* – kept returning to him. It could mean anything, he knew. It could refer to a threatened person. A child, even. It did not have to refer to Aela Ren.

'He calls himself the Innocent,' Orlan said, after Bueralan finally asked, after the fever that gripped *Bounty* finally rubbed off on him. 'He calls himself that because there are no gods. He says that there is nothing to judge him, no rules for him to obey. In this world we live in, he believes that he cannot be guilty of any sin.'

He had said this when the two of them were standing on the deck, weeks before the sight of rain-slicked Dyanos appeared before Bueralan. Yet the words and the empty, dark night mingled in the saboteur's mind as *Bounty* made its slow way through the dangerous waters.

'His army is the same,' the cartographer had continued, a memory's ghost beside him. 'They don't wear the name that he does, but they might as well. They are all like him. They are all god-touched. They all stood beside a god, once. They heard the words of their god and it was bliss, I imagine. After all, of all the mortals in the world, they were the most beloved. They were the mortal hand of their god, even if their mortality was a thousand years away. I cannot imagine how they felt after the War of the Gods, when all of that was taken away.'

'You said that each god had a servant,' Bueralan said. 'That they were each only allowed one. That would mean that the Innocent's army has only seventy-eight soldiers.'

'Seventy-four, including him.'

'Are some dead?'

'No.'

'Then where are the others?'

'Not with him.'

'Does that include you, old man?'

Orlan sighed. 'I keep telling you,' he said, 'I am not god-touched. I die like most people in our world die.'

Painfully, stupidly, quickly and, upon occasion, happily. Bueralan finished the line internally. His mother had first said it to him, when he had been a child. He had not known it then, but she had been quoting from a famous play that criticized the Mother's Gift. When he saw it performed, years later in Yeflam, he had not laughed, as most of the audience did; he had nodded. In his life he had seen more than his share of people die, and they had, in one way or another, died as the playwright said.

'*Glafanr* was once the ship of the dead,' Samuel Orlan continued. 'It was said that it drifted on the rivers of fate, that it took men and women to the City of the Dead. After the Wanderer died, Ai Sela, his servant, found the ship in the ocean. She was in nearly a wreck herself. Great cyclones and tsunamis had been throughout the ocean during the War of the Gods and Ai Sela was caught in one. She thought that her time to die had come, but instead, *Glafanr* appeared before her. She did not know why. She had never stepped on it. Some said it was sentient, but no one knows for sure. All that is known is that Ai found herself the captain of it. She found in it a new home and offered it to all who were like her. For thousands of years, the servants of the gods lived in it. They let *Glafanr* drift in the oceans with them. They did not care where it went. They did not believe they had a place, or a purpose, until Aela Ren found them. That was seven hundred years ago, before they began their horror in Sooia.'

'You sure know a lot about them,' Bueralan said. 'For a man who is not one of them, that is.'

'I read, baron.'

Since then the cartographer had never been far from him. It was as if, in the words that the two had said, an unspoken truce had been called. Bueralan had not agreed to it and did not like the assumption that had been made by the other man, but if he was god-touched — *if* Ger had done something to him beneath Mireea — it was better to have the old man around than to leave him and his words as a niggling doubt in his mind. Besides, and this Bueralan admitted to himself as the rain-slicked docks drew closer, he could do nothing to stop Orlan. The cartographer had proved that to him since he had first met him. Better instead to keep the old man close and focus on what he had come to do.

The leather pouch that held the crystal against his skin was cold. For his whole life he had stood outside the Mother's Gift, but he would not turn away now. He would hold the dark cold bottle that the witches created and he would feel the thick blood move sluggishly inside. His mother had called it a barbaric practice and he did not doubt her. What concerned him now was how he would achieve it.

When *Bounty* touched the docks and the ropes were uncoiled, Bueralan Le prepared himself to step onto shore, unable to do otherwise.

2.

The Keepers met in a large curved room in the middle of the Enclave's twisting shape. Dark, heavy oak doors enclosed the long room from west to east and between those doors, beneath white walls and their narrow windows, lay a long table. It was held aloft by six pairs of stout legs larger than Ayae. It had been crafted from a wood darker than the doors, and the polish added another layer of darkness to it, leaving it a deep mix of black and brown, the combination of which bordered on red when the afternoon's sun came through the windows, as it did now. Around the table were twenty-five high-backed chairs, similar in their colouring.

Ayae had arrived early in the company of Xrie. The last had been accidental: she had met him as she walked to the Enclave. He had asked her how Faise and Zineer were, told her that a new shipment was due to go to Wila at the end of the week and, before they entered the Enclave, told her that she was being followed by two Empty Sky soldiers. She told him politely that she knew. The two soldiers had not bothered to hide themselves. None of them did, any more. They appeared on streets next to her, passed her and Faise and

Zineer in markets, and rode in carriages when one or all three of them were in them. In fact, it had become so prominent that Faise and Zineer no longer went anywhere without her.

She did not tell Xrie that, however. It was likely that the Soldier already knew — he knew about her meeting with Eira, for example — and after they entered the meeting room, Ayae put the thoughts of her friends aside. The Empty Sky were not important for her right now. Now, she had to see if there were others who would support her in having the Mireeans released. The Cold Witch clearly would not. With that in mind, she watched the Keepers who entered.

For their part, the Keepers did not spare her much of a glance. Instead, each of them stared at the vacant chair beside her. It looked much like the others in shape and design, from the high back to the grey cushion on it, but it was not until Xrie leant over and told her that it was intended for another new arrival to Yeflam that she understood the curiosity. Her immediate thought was that the chair was for Zaifyr, but by the time Aelyn Meah and the remaining Keepers had filed into the room and Zaifyr had not appeared, Ayae had reached the conclusion that it wasn't.

'We have a full schedule today.' Aelyn sat at the head of the table. Beside her was Kaqua, the Pauper, a tall, dark-skinned man. Ayae had not met him, but she knew he was the one who was organizing Zaifyr's trial. 'There is a lot of news and a lot of information to cover,' she continued. 'The month has been busy.'

'I want to discuss Qian.' It was Eira who spoke. She sat four or five seats away from Ayae, but had not looked at her since she entered the room. 'His trial should be first on our agenda.'

'We will discuss my brother in time.'

'Why must we wait? It is the only topic that we have to discuss.'

'Eira,' Kaqua said, his voice soft and calm. 'It will be done. But you know as well as I do that there are other interests to address first. Paelor, if you would please begin.'

A white man in trapper's leathers who smelt of forest damp rose from beside Eira. He had dark hair and a beard streaked with grey. His hand, as he spoke, never left it. 'General Waalstan has had success in the Kingdoms of Faaisha,' he began reluctantly. 'His Faithful have torn through the eastern side of the kingdoms. Their most emphatic victory was in Celp, the largest city in that part of the kingdoms. It was protected by Marshal Faet Cohn. I would have thought that he would give Waalstan more of a fight, but he lasted no more than five days. By the time I arrived, the battle was over and little remained of the city. The insides of Celp were awful. The stories we have heard about cannibalism and slavery are very evident, I am afraid.'

'The priests here deny that,' Kaqua said. 'They say that they are Mireean lies.'

The other man pulled at his beard uncomfortably. 'The bones tell no lies about the first. As for the fact that they're selling their prisoners as slaves, well, I saw one chain being led down to Leera myself. It's possible that they could be used for something else, but from what I heard being said by the soldiers and prisoners, I'd easily believe that they were being sold. It is true that the Faithful are not slavers in their blood, not like the people of Ooila or Gogair, but they need the coin. Their army is made from what they had. They have no trade to fall back on, no resources. They have spoils — spoils to pay for supplies for their soldiers' food and weapons and supplies for the priests who travel, but the spoils will not be enough. I think we will also begin to hear soon that they have gone into the Plateau to take Tribesmen to sell as well. That's why Waalstan struck so hard at the east before he broke up his force.' He shook his head and pulled his hand free. 'General Waalstan is not a fool. We shouldn't underestimate him. He knows that if he keeps a single force, the marshals will force him into a siege and starve him out. He has already divided up his forces—'

'That is enough, Paelor.' Eira laid her hand on his arm. 'I will not sit here and listen to what is a farce of news. We have reached our truce with Leera. We have allowed their priests and their propaganda into our streets. We have all agreed on that, so there is no point in debating whether or not the Leerans have our morals. Especially not when we could be discussing a man who threatens all of us.'

'The world around us is our concern,' Kaqua said evenly. 'We are all aware of your loss, Eira, but it does not mean we can ignore the rest of the world and our place in it.'

'What is to say he will not do the same to us?'

'He will not.'

'I do not believe you. More than that, I have heard how my love died!' She rose from her seat angrily. 'Have you? Have you asked this tiny flame what he did?'

'I know what he did. Have you forgotten that I speak with him every week?'

'Have you forgotten who you are?'

'Eira,' Kaqua said. 'Surely you do not question my loyalty?'

'Why is there no trial?' She almost shouted the words across the table. It caused the other Keepers to flinch back, as if her fury was a physical force. 'Why do we delay his execution?'

'Eira.' Aelyn, now. 'You do not know what you ask.'

'I ask for justice and I think I deserve it. We all do. We have all been patient while you and Kaqua have asked Qian what kind of trial he would like. We have watched you bow and scrape to him so that he is not upset. We have been patient but our patience is at an end. He is guilty of murder. He *must* be punished for what he has done.'

'Don't be foolish, child.' For all that Aelyn claimed she did not rule the Enclave, Ayae could not help but note that her words left Eira chastised. 'My brother will not allow you to kill him,' she continued. 'I know you want justice for Fo and Bau and I know it frustrates you not to have it. But you must understand that he is not here to be tried. He, in fact, cannot be tried. Perhaps Kaqua and I have made a mistake in not letting you all meet him, not letting you see what he is. Perhaps it is my own fault for how I conduct myself. You have all decided that he is your equal, but he is not. He is beyond your rule.'

'You once imprisoned him,' Eira said.

'I did not do that alone.'

'You could do it again,' Eira insisted. 'We could do that. For his crimes, we could at the very least return him to his crooked tower.'

'He'll not go there,' Ayae said. She did not know why she spoke. She should have remained silent and let the argument between the two finish, if it could. 'He'll never go back there. But why don't you just listen to what he has to say? He is only interested in telling you about the child. That is why he wants his trial. He wants you to hear what she is. He wants you to stand with him against her. He has even written to the rest of his family.'

'Which brings us to the chair you have all been staring at,' Aelyn said. 'You talk about Qian as if he is a single being, but he is not. He has brothers and sisters. I am one, but you will find I am the only one who will support you. The others — well, the others will not, no matter their relationship to me. The one who has arrived today will definitely not. In truth, he has been here for days already, listening to each of you, drawing his own conclusions, making his own plans. His little birds have fluttered around the Enclave. A dog has walked into the Yeflam Guard's barracks. An ox-drawn cart sat alone on a road near here for hours. Yes, I can see that you are all suddenly aware who has arrived.'

The silence that fell around the table surprised Ayae. Many, she saw, glanced at the chair with apprehension, as if, suddenly, a terrible fear had been made real.

'I want you all to listen to me,' Aelyn said, her voice without pity. 'I want to be very clear to all of you. You must all accept that we are not equal. I want there to be no misunderstanding in this regard. Jae'le is here. He is in Yeflam. You know the names he has. You have heard the stories about what he has done in his life. Not a single one of them is a lie. Not a single one is an exaggeration. And neither is this: Jae'le will never allow you to execute Qian.'

3.

'Who wrote this one?' Faise asked as he entered the room. 'I can't read the name — I don't know the language.'

Zaifyr paused in the doorway and stared at the old, thin book she had picked up. It had been sitting on the pile near the windows at the back of Aelyn's estate and the afternoon's sun fell strongly over it. For a moment, the glare hid the title of the book, the print on its leather cover faded even more than usual beneath the glare. 'Sister Meliana,' he said, when he could make it out. 'She was a priestess for the goddess Linae before the War of the Gods. This is an Ooilan translation of her diary.'

'Do you want to keep it?'

'No.' He indicated the pile by the door he had just passed, the pile of books that had failed to provide him with useful names. 'The diary was damaged when it was originally found,' he said to her, picking up another book. 'It was just weather damage, but the villages in the Broken Mountains were considered cursed after Linae's death and it was centuries before someone entered the area. I thought maybe a name I could use would be there, but it is mostly a list of births and deaths and the number of eggs that the chickens laid.'

'Meliana herself is not useful?'

'No, she died before the Wanderer fell.'

'She could have been reborn,' Faise said, returning the book to the pile. 'Could you not look for her, then?'

'If she was reborn, it would not be identically. She would be shaped by what she was born into in a new life – and it would be that life that her spirit remembered, nothing else.'

He continued towards the piles by the walls, on the other side of Faise. Since he had killed the priests, Zaifyr had not left Aelyn's house. Instead, he had spent the weeks gathering books from libraries and stores and focusing on his search, which had so far, he admitted, revealed little. He relied on Ayae and her friends – and to a lesser extent Kaqua – to tell him what was happening outside, a task that only Ayae took to the most. She looked at the piles he had made, the research he had sunk into, and he knew she saw the search as a retreat because of what had happened with the priests. He had not been surprised yesterday when she suggested cleaning up the books, a task that Faise and Zineer had taken to after Ayae had left earlier.

'By the way,' Faise said, taking another book. 'Do you have children of your own?'

'No.' It was not the first question she had asked like that. Indeed, before he entered the back room where Faise was, Zaifyr had been upstairs in the piles he kept strewn through the room he slept in. There, Zineer had asked how many wives he had had. He took both of their questions good humouredly, for he enjoyed Faise and Zineer's company. He found them sharp and capable and, in the days after he had killed the priests, he found them, more than anyone else, to be the antidote to what he was feeling. 'I have never heard of any of us having children,' he said. 'Even gods didn't have children. When they had a child, it was just an aspect that split from themselves, a metaphor from the original, I suppose. Most of us assume that we can't.'

'Does everything still work? You're not, y'know—' she made a dangling finger motion.

He looked up at the ceiling. 'Aren't you supposed to be more modest or something?'

'No. In fact, I am writing a book on the juiciest details of immortality,' she said blandly. 'Zin and I plan to sell it at the trial.'

'We'll make our fortune out of you,' Zineer said, entering the room. He carried a stack of books and on his shoulder was a bird. 'This ugly little guy knocked on the window to come in, if you can believe that.'

It was a storm petrel, a small grey-and-black seabird found throughout Yeflam. It was one of the few seabirds that had adapted to the poisoned flesh of fish in the ocean, but just as its diet had changed, so had its form. Its beak had sharpened to a pair of hard blades and its black eyes were rimmed with blood. To eat it was just as fatal as eating the fish from the ocean.

They were not considered tame birds, but at the sight of Zaifyr, it left its perch on Zineer and glided casually around the room before drifting lazily to the table in front of him.

'Cute,' Faise said, after it landed. 'Do you think it does tricks?'

'Well?' Zaifyr asked the bird. 'Can a distrustful bird do tricks to amuse us?'

'One or two.' Jae'le's voice sounded inhumane and cruel when it emerged. 'I greet you, brother.'

'This is Faise.' The charms on his wrist flashed as he indicated. 'You have already met her husband, Zineer. For both of you, this is Jae'le, my oldest brother. He sent me to Mireea without once warning me that there was a god there.'

The bird's dark eyes ignored the silver. 'You are angry at me?'

Zaifyr crossed his arms. 'You could have warned me.'

'You would have ignored me. After the tower, you had no time for these mysteries. What did you call them? Childish puzzle boxes.' The bird fluttered onto the leather cover of Sister Meliana's diary, near Faise. Involuntarily, she took a step back. 'Disaffected. That's how you were, brother. You agreed to come to Mireea because you had nothing else to do. You agreed to anything because it gave you something to do, something to pass the time. You did not care for the reasons.'

'I hope you don't plan to have him defend you in your trial,' Faise said. 'They would have a gallows ready before he'd finished.'

'Yes, your trial.' The bird's vocal cords stretched out the end of the word painfully. 'Did you really need to kill Fo and Bau?'

'I told you I did,' Zaifyr said. 'I was left with little choice in the matter. It was either them or Ayae and me. If you want to lecture me, you'll have to come here in person. I know you are sitting on a bench, somewhere in Yeflam. You don't have to hide. Besides, a trial will draw all of you here and I will be able to explain what this child god is responsible for. I will be able to show all of you – even Aelyn's Keepers – the horror she has created.'

'I am in Yeflam, as you said.' A silence stretched out between all three, long and taut. 'But you should understand, it will not be as you think. A trial—'

'—is the only way.'

'Brother.' He could hear the concern, the pain in the bird's voice. 'Brother, you have made a mistake. A trial will not draw all of us here. It cannot. Aelyn and myself are here, true, and Tinh Tu may come. But Eidan . . .'

The pause stretched out before the bird spoke again.

'Brother, Eidan is with the child.'

4.

Zaifyr took a breath. For the first time in months, it tasted of salt and blood, of Leviathan's Blood. 'When—' The ocean taste was not a portent; he could not think of it as that. 'When did you learn this?'

'When I was in Mireea.' The storm petrel's inhuman voice struggled with the name, drawing out the centre of the word in a screech. 'I found him when I went in search of the priests. He was in Ranan. I remember that I was not surprised when I felt him. Ranan was in ruins. You could see that from high up — and you know as I do that our brother has always been drawn to ruins. But these were not the ruins that a battle made. The destruction of it was much more deliberate, much more studied. To my eye, it had been stripped. Stripped by the army to build siege machines and fuel their war, I imagine. But they had left one building, a huge cathedral. It was unlike any I had seen before. None of the priests I saw could have possibly dreamed of it, nor could they have begun its construction. Yet I was wary of going down to the city. There was a presence there that I could not contend with, but I tempted it. I circled, lower and lower until I saw a man. A single, solitary man, who cut blocks of stone from the earth and dragged them into the city.'

'Eidan,' he whispered.

'That is why I am here. Our brother—'

'Sided with *her*.'

'—needs us,' Jae'le finished. 'He will know what she is, just as you and I do. He may very well be trapped there.'

'Aelyn must know,' he said.

'She must,' he agreed. 'They never hid from each other.'

Zaifyr thought about the things she had said, about the treaties with the Leerans, about the need for peace. He thought about the priests in the streets. Aelyn knew about the child before he arrived. She would not have been surprised by what he said. 'Do you . . .' he began, then stopped. He was not sure what he had meant to say. Was Eidan a prisoner? Was this the reason that Aelyn had been so intent on peace? What if Eidan was not? Zaifyr was arguing for war. He had no army, but he meant to make one. He intended to gather his family, to gather everyone with any power, and he meant to march them on the child. His cause was just. The ruined haunts that followed him were an endless parade of victims who gave him the right to seek a bloody end. Zaifyr did not believe that anyone would deny him that in the face of the tragedy that the dead found themselves in. Yet if his family was compromised – if Eidan was a prisoner, or if he had sided with the child – then their unity would be broken. His ability to form an army would be lost. Aelyn would not side against Eidan. The Keepers of the Divine would not follow his plan. They would instead be guided by their own desires, their own needs, their own loves.

'You okay?'

Ayae's warm hand fell to his shoulder.

'Faise tells me you've been sitting here all day.' The afternoon's sun had set. Zaifyr was surprised to realize that he was alone in a dark room. 'You had a bird that visited, she said.'

'Jae'le.' He touched a charm beneath his left wrist. 'When did he leave?'

'He wasn't here when I arrived.' She knelt before him, her hands on his legs. 'The Enclave knows he is in Yeflam, though. Aelyn has told them that he will not let them find you guilty of killing Fo and Bau. They seemed genuinely frightened of him.'

'They should.' He took a breath, but could taste nothing. 'Ayae,' he said, after a moment, 'Eidan is with the child.'

She frowned. 'Your brother?'

After Asila, Eidan had carried him to the crooked tower. Zaifyr had learned of it from haunts who had watched his brothers and sisters arrive, who had lingered as they built the tower. Eidan was a large man, stronger than any of the others. He had held Zaifyr while he instructed the others in the mix of the bricks and the laying of them. Jae'le had, years later, told him that Eidan had despaired at the design of the tower. He had been an engineer, before, a builder of bridges and siege equipment, and the tower had been an offence to his cold, methodical mind.

'Yes,' he said. 'He is Aelyn's lover.'

'But—'

'He has always been. A hundred years may part them, but only in the flesh. In the mind, in the soul, they are never separated.'

Her hand tightened on his leg. 'Talk to her.'

'I can't step back,' he said, aware that a note of desperation had settled into his voice. 'I can't step back. I can't let this new god continue to exist. I will not tell her that I will do that.'

He felt as if the ground he had been standing on had shifted. The pillar that held Nale had, in his mind, cracked, and he could not bring himself to stand straight. Ayae repeated that he should go to the Enclave, but he shook his head. 'If I go there,' he said, 'if I walk up all those floors and I knock on the door of her office, what will we say? She might say that Eidan is with the child. She might say that he is a prisoner. She might say that he is an envoy. She might say that, on his advice, she sent Fo and Bau to Mireea to see what kind of force General Waalstan led. But in the end, she would say to me, "This is why we need peace." She would say to me, "We are not going to war now because we are planning, we are learning." She would ask me to leave, then. She would tell me that I have made things difficult. That I continue to do so.' He took Ayae's hand into his. 'And I would not say to her, "You are right." I would not say to her that the dead did not matter. I would not say to her that we could wait. I would not say that I would go away and plan from afar and return with an army later. I would tell her that I can stare at the dead, knowing what has kept them here, what has trapped them in our world, and she would not expect me to say that.'

She tried to talk to him some more, but he would return to the same point again and again; eventually she left him alone. He heard her and Faise and Zineer in other parts of Aelyn's estate, but each time he heard them, his mind returned to Eidan, to Aelyn, to the child.

They left in the early hours of the morning and, after he

had seen them to a carriage pulled by a pair of oxen, he walked back to Aelyn's estate. The cool, salt-stained streets unravelled around him. They plunged into a momentary darkness as the morning's sun had not risen, but the flickering lamps that populated the Floating Cities began to die in expectation that it would.

A block from the estate, a shadow shifted in the sky and a storm petrel settled lightly onto his shoulder.

'Where have you been?' Zaifyr asked.

'This body was hungry and you were not talking,' his brother replied. 'Now, are you ready to begin?'

'Begin?'

'Explaining how you will win your trial.'

'I don't know,' he said, staring out into the darkness, able to see only the outline of the estate gates and the solid shapes of the guards made from wind. 'Maybe it is a mistake.'

'It is.'

He gave a hollow laugh.

'But if we are to save Eidan,' Jae'le said, 'we must also win it.'

5.

Bounty faded behind Bueralan, lost in the deepening dark of the night and the hardening of the rain.

Both he and Samuel Orlan were soaked before they left the docks of Dyanos and entered its dimly lit tumble of streets. The cartographer led the way sourly, muttering complaints about the weight of his coat and the fact that it did little to protect him from the elements. He did not appear to expect a reply from Bueralan, and the saboteur, who held both their long duffel bags, made no attempt to engage him. If he had replied, he would have said that he was glad for the poor visibility to hide them.

If he had been able, Bueralan would have entered Ooila much as he had left it, crossing over the border between it and Qaaina. Covering nearly all the northern quarter of the continent, Qaaina had been conquered eight years ago by the Five Queens, and the deep mines that lay at its heart had been divided up among the five provinces. When he had heard the news years before, he had felt a touch of sadness for the memory of him and Zean making their way along the highway on slavers' horses, riding to freedom. They had had very little money or food and had sold the horses at a port to buy a ticket to anywhere.

Beyond the fleeting emotion of memory, however, Bueralan had not been surprised. The Five Queens had long looked to their neighbour with an eye of expansion, and the quick peace that Qaaina sued for revealed that it, too, had been but waiting.

Neither helped him now, though.

'There is an inn a block to our left, if I remember correctly,' Orlan said. 'It will be adequate for us.'

'How long ago were you last here?'

'Eight years.' As if he knew Bueralan's thoughts, he elaborated. 'The First Queen invited me after the conquest of Qaaina.'

He grunted, but said nothing else.

The Mocking Quarrel was a block and a half through rain that came down so hard that the distance felt twice that. It was a two-storey inn with a jester's hat pierced by an arrow on the board outside. Inside, it was well lit, warm and with a good-sized crowd. The owner, a large middle-aged woman whose hair had been shaved down to the scalp, recognized Orlan almost instantly. As she rose from behind the bar, the eyes of men and women turned to them, and Bueralan, his hands digging into the sodden bags he held, waited for the cartographer to introduce him. *Stupid*, he thought. *I've not thought this right . . .* but Orlan, after a few words, begged off from much conversation due to being wet and cold, and soon Bueralan found himself upstairs in a room with two beds and a square table with two chairs.

'You'll have me in chains before I even reach Cynama,' he said, closing the door. 'There must have been thirty people there.'

'It has been . . .' Orlan hesitated. 'What? Fifteen years?'

'Seventeen.'

'Did you even have those tattoos seventeen years ago?'

The small man peeled his jacket off. 'You should have more trust, Baron.'

In myself, Bueralan thought. 'Orlan—'

A knock at the door interrupted him.

Bueralan's hand dropped to the wet leather hilt of his sword.

'It will be for me,' Orlan said disapprovingly. 'In all parts of the world, there are men and women whom I pay to listen for me. They listen for politics, for news, for gossip, anything that might be interesting. You may find this hard to believe, but a good map is not the work of one man, or one woman, but many. The lines in the world are made by us all.'

Wordlessly, he cracked the door open: in the hallway stood a thin, elderly man. He would have been taller than Bueralan if not for his stoop and the long, yellowed cane he leant heavily upon. Yet his gaze did not show any of the age that afflicted his body. Among crow's feet and a silvered stubble, his awareness and intelligence was clear, and Bueralan's hand tightened.

'My name is Tawain.' His voice was deep, another body's voice. 'I'm here to see Samuel Orlan.' Entering, the old man smiled and shook the cartographer's hand firmly. If he was disturbed by the sword Bueralan held, or the soft click of the door being locked behind him, he did not show it. 'Look at you,' Tawain said to Orlan. 'If I didn't know your hair was black in your forties, I'd swear you hadn't aged in a decade.'

'I think I have become more handsome,' the other said. 'Which is more than I can say for you.'

'That's harsh.'

'You *had* hair, once.'

'Lice.' He moved awkwardly to the chairs in the room, his

cane falling like a heavy third foot. 'It has been all over the docks for the last month. You avoided that, at least.'

'It is often said that I am quite lucky.'

He grunted sourly. 'Not this time.'

'Oh?'

'Surely you have heard that the Innocent is here? They say that there is a fleet off the coast of the Fifth Province that is his.'

'He does not have a fleet,' Orlan said, mildly. 'He has one ship.'

Tawain's grin revealed crooked, discoloured teeth. 'You're right, but it's not the truth of it, it's the politics of it. That's where you're unlucky.'

'The Queen of Cynama is still the First Queen, is she not?'

'Yeah, but she grows old, as do we all. Her children grow bolder.' He paused. 'Why are you taking off your clothes?'

'It's not a new level of our friendship, I assure you.' Orlan picked up a towel from beside his bed, began to dry his soft, pale chest. 'I am simply cold. What else is going on?'

'Be happy. Tomorrow it'll be nothing but humidity.' Tawain turned to Bueralan. 'Whether or not the Innocent is off the coast doesn't matter. People are leaving Ooila. It's not a mass exodus yet, but it is enough to be noticed. It's not just in the Fifth Province, either. It's all across. There are spies across every dock and port, listening for every desperate whisper. Do you know who you travel with, Samuel?'

Bueralan met the other man's gaze, but said nothing.

'He is just a man,' Orlan said, after a moment. 'A man without history, or title, or land.'

The old man held his gaze. 'Is that right?'

'Yes,' Bueralan replied. 'You will remember that, won't you?'

6.

Heast rode across the stone bridge to Ghaam alone.

It would not be long before the corpses of Menan and his soldiers were found. No matter what Heast thought of Bnid Gaerl, he knew that the man would not ascribe any delay in reporting to a dereliction of duty. When they failed to return, he would dig them up by question and by shovel. Heast had dug up friends, family and soldiers similarly. He suspected that he had had little more than three days to prepare for Gaerl's response.

Sin's Hand appeared from the cold lamp-lit dark: a large, sprawling building of discoloured stone decorated by a single red hand above the door. Beneath the sign stood two men: one black and one white, both twice the size of Heast. They acknowledged him with a nod and he gave the guards a weary nod in return before he turned into the narrow alley and let his horse move slowly to the stables at the back of the brothel. An elderly woman sat on a stool rolling a thin cigarette from stained paper. On her left hand she had three fingers, but she held the reins of Heast's horse tightly as he leant forward and awkwardly swung his good leg over the horse, dismounting.

Inside the stable, two children were cleaning stalls and laying down hay. The tired beast was led to them to be unsaddled.

Sin's Hand was not nearly as quiet, or orderly. As he unlaced the leather ties to his scabbard, a dull thud of noise leaked through the door and collected at the feet of another two imposing men. Heast had just passed his sword to the man on the left when the door opened and the sound burst out. Revealed was a narrow path lit by a series of red candles. Scented smoke lurked in the ceiling. Yet, rather than enter, Heast waited, allowing a tall grey-haired man in expensive greens and reds to pass him.

'Captain Heast,' said the man, remaining in the door. He was a white man, his face verging on longness, as if a particularly dour expression had lengthened it over the years. 'It has been some time since I last saw you. You have been busy, if I am to believe the rumours.'

Lian Alahn. 'I am sure the Traders' Union realizes that Muriel Wagan has people to look after,' Heast said, hiding his surprise.

'Indeed it does.' He stepped out. Behind him, a young man, dark-haired and wearing light leather armour, followed. One of Sin's guards handed a long straight sword to the younger man. An expensive blade, Heast noted. Alahn said, 'I tried to reach you when I returned to Yeflam a few months ago. I had heard you were looking for me, but I had no luck finding you. May I enquire what it was about?'

'It was about your son,' he said.

The other man nodded. 'Of course. Please, let us step aside for a moment.' With Heast beside him, Alahn moved out of earshot of the others, leaving his guard beside the two that Sin's Hand employed. 'I had heard that Illaan did not return from Mireea. You have my apologies, Captain. It is unthinkable that my own flesh would fail at his duty.'

Heast – who believed he had seen every way a parent could respond to the loss of a child – was taken aback. 'He fell, just as many do,' he said. 'I thought to tell you how it happened, if it would provide you closure. I do that for all who fall under my command.'

'That he fell is enough, Captain. Failure is not something I wish to dwell on. However, if you could do me a favour,' the merchant added, 'could you pass on a message for me? It is to the girl with whom my son had a relationship. Ayae, I believe her name is. I met her but once, and I am afraid I do not know her last name.'

'She's an orphan,' Heast said, a coldness emerging in his voice. 'She arrived from Sooia without a family name and I do not believe she intends to purchase one.'

'Except by marriage.' If Lian Alahn noticed the change in Heast's voice, he heard it only as a confirmation of his opinion of Ayae, and nothing more. 'At any rate, I mention her only because I thought that she might like to visit me, to pay respect at the tomb we have purchased for my son. I do not want her to feel ostracized by our family. After all, if anyone is to blame for Illaan's death, it is me. It is I who organized his commission under you. I thought it would be good for him. I thought it would give him structure, purpose. I do not blame the girl he stayed for.'

Illaan had been spoilt and arrogant, yet Heast had thought he saw the flicker of something in him: a glimmer that had been trying to escape his father. 'There was a difficulty between the two of them before he died,' he said. 'I believe that will keep her absent from your family.'

'Yes, I had heard that she was cursed.'

'I do not use that term myself.'

'My apologies.' Alahn smiled. 'I have heard she has taken up residency with the Keepers.'

Heast did not correct him.

'Still, if I may impose, Captain?' he continued, as if, like Heast's coldness earlier, the silence was not in response to Alahn himself. 'I would appreciate it if you could pass on the message for me? To let her know I would like to meet her. I have much I would like to discuss with her and I do not want bad blood between us in the future.'

7.

After Lian Alahn left, Heast entered the red-lit smoky hallway of the brothel unarmed. The music was a dull beat as he followed it to a large open room. Thick candles lined the walls and stood on the tables, but did so in a way to cultivate a sense of shadows and anonymity, leaving only the centre stage brightly lit in reds and oranges. There, the band, made up of three different drum kits and an assortment of cellos and wind instruments, let their sound out to an audience who largely ignored it, and whose time was for the women who wandered from shadowed booth to corner in various states of undress, drinks and smiles in hand. At the bar, the man behind it caught Heast's eye and pointed up, pointed through the ceiling, to the single room above.

The music followed Heast to the seemingly unguarded door of an office, but it was muffled once he entered. Inside, a long semicircle of a dark couch dominated the centre of the room, facing a thick glass wall that looked out over the stage Heast had passed. Two people were sitting there. The first, a man in his mid-twenties, was the owner of Sin's Hand, Sinae Al'tor: long and lean and darkly olive-skinned, he sat against the cushion in a mix of black and orange, every inch the well-moneyed, well-made man of illegality he wished to be. A slim, pretty white girl lay against him, her pale blonde hair falling over her shoulders and back, but stopping long before her slim legs and bare, ringed feet. Every inch of her pose and clothing was designed to heighten a sensation of languid sexuality, and did so, until you met her deep, dark-green eyes.

Her feet shifted up for Heast as he eased awkwardly onto the couch. 'You mind?' he asked, pointing to the bottle and glasses on the low table before the couch. 'Unless Lian Alahn drank from it?'

'Clean glasses,' Sinae replied. 'Clean hands?'

'Are yours clean?'

The girl smiled.

'You want some?' Heast reached for the whisky. Beneath it were two overturned papers.

She shook her head, but Sinae nodded. 'If I had known you were coming tonight,' he said, 'I would have made sure you were here for my fascinating conversation with Mister Alahn.'

'I've spoken with him enough.'

'He does create a certain disgust, doesn't he?' He took the glass that Heast pushed to him. 'I should add that he told me that Bnid Gaerl's men are looking for you. I already knew, of course. By your clean hands, I see that you have avoided them.'

The Captain of the Ghosts — he would own the insult, as he knew Muriel would — raised his glass in salute. Five years ago, Sinae had been working in a brothel in Mireea. A thin strip of a cheap prostitute, he had sold pieces of information to Heast for small amounts of gold, but they had not had a real conversation until after Sinae was found, bruised and beaten, in the house of a wealthy man. He had been chained to the wall and used for close to a month. The young Sinae had strangled the man one night a week before, but it wasn't until the smell of the merchant's corpse worked its way out that the neighbours had thought to investigate. Heast had not given Sinae much consideration after that, but in the months he had spent recovering, the young man had come to Muriel Wagan's interest. She had found an intelligent man, lost and without direction.

'Did Alahn ask for anything for that?' Heast asked. 'Or did he just provide it as a favour before he asked if you could take a message to Muriel?'

Sinae's smile was lazy. 'It was rather obvious.'

'He's not very subtle.' When Sinae had recovered, Muriel had offered him a job in Yeflam, not to learn the business he already knew, but the business he didn't. A year later, she had financed Sin's Hand and Sinae Al'tor's independence. 'He's also as cold as fuck,' Heast said, leaning back into the cushions. 'You should have heard what he said about his son.'

'His third son,' Sinae replied. 'They're always the least cared for.' After Heast grunted in reply, the spy pointed to the table. 'He also delivered these papers. They are from a Keeper-run press here on Ghaam, and a Traders' Union one on Burata.'

Heast didn't reach for them. 'I've read enough of those things,' he said flatly.

'Not these,' Sinae said. 'These are the first papers that are breaking the official embargo on a man named Qian. He was the prisoner, and I use that term very loosely, whom Lady Wagan traded for her place on that forsaken island.'

Intrigued, Heast leant across the table and flipped the papers over. On the front of the first, huge black letters said, *JUSTICE DENIED.* The second had a picture of Zaifyr, thin and, to Heast's mind, much more evil than he was in real life, standing over a grave. *KILLER AMONG US*, read the title beneath. He opened both and saw huge blocks of text inside. 'They have a lot to say,' he said, leaning back. 'Are they up to the usual standard of propaganda?'

'According to Alahn, they are trying to force the matter of a trial. The second paper – the one with the picture – is owned by him. He said that the Keeper Eira, who is known as the Cold Witch or Bitch, depending on your experiences with her, told him personally that they were to make the public aware of what has happened since Qian's arrival. She said he stands in the way of Yeflam being an independent power in the area. She told Alahn that once the trial is finished, the Leeran threat will be dealt with. It is not the official line from the Enclave, but Alahn ate it as if it was a treat. He is of the opinion that that is where the real threat lies, though others in the Traders' Union do not agree with that.' Sinae swirled the remains of his whisky around. 'In fact, rumour has it that Benan Le'ta has been pushing for an alliance with the Leerans. That is more in keeping with the stance of the Enclave, but Le'ta claims that *The Eternal Kingdom* is an anti-Keeper book that will ultimately see Leera side with the Traders' Union in control of Yeflam.'

'How could a man be so stupid?' Heast did not expect any answer. 'He'll be bitten by a snake before this is all over.'

'The snake already hunts him. Unkind whispers suggest he may be a believer of the new god. People are trying to connect him with the printing of *The Eternal Kingdom*, but with little luck. At any rate, Lian Alahn senses weakness and has begun to fill sacks of snakes for Benan Le'ta.'

'Muriel will want to hear that. Did he give you a letter to take to her?'

From within his clothes, Sinae pulled out the folded note. 'He had his guard write it. Just in case it fell into someone else's hands.' The girl passed the letter to Heast. 'This trial,' he said, after the Captain of the Ghosts had taken it, opened it and read it. 'Alahn believes the Keepers are seeking Qian's death.'

The letter said no more than that Lian Alahn would like to extend his welcome. 'Only because they don't know better.'

The girl's naked toes touched Heast's side. 'Everyone dies,' she said softly.

'You and I, yeah,' he said, but did not touch her. 'I used to ride with a witch called Anemone. This was before either of you were born. She was a Faaishan witch. You don't see many these days; not many witches are willing to be bonded to their kin, much less go through the ritual. A Faaishan witch — a true Faaishan witch, a woman who sits with generations of her kin around her — feeds her kin with her own blood. Anemone was an old witch, from a long line. She liked to say that there had always been a witch in Refuge, and Refuge stretched back — well, some of the soldiers in it said it stretched back to before the War of the Gods. Anemone never claimed to keep her kin from back in those days, but she kept enough that she was frightening. Truly frightening. And she feared no one. But Zaifyr — the man called Qian in Yeflam — she was frightened of him. When I met him, we were both in Faaisha, and she offered us a small job. I won't say it was anything special. It went how it went, and at the end of it we were all alive. But at the end of it, she told me that standing next to him was the most terrifying experience she had ever had. I had seen her stand before warlords. I had seen her kill swordsmen as if it was nothing. I even stood on Sooia with her. I had known Anemone since I was ten and had never before heard the fear she had in her voice then. It was not something that I understood until I heard him refer to Aelyn Meah as his sister.'

Sinae pushed his glass back to Heast, empty. 'Yet you led him here in chains?'

'He let us.' He took the glass. 'My advice is to keep a low profile while this plays out. But at any rate, I have a request, if you don't mind?'

'I don't dance.'

Heast poured another two glasses. 'I want you to tell Bnid Gaerl where I am.'

'Your hands are not that clean, Captain.'

'They never have been.' He handed a glass back. 'But I want you to tell the Captain of the Yeflam Guard where I am as well.'

'Would you like a small army too?'

'No,' he said. 'But I would like you to move Faise and Zineer Kanar to somewhere safe after you've done that.'

8.

A soft patter against the window woke him.

'It is still beautiful to watch,' Samuel Orlan said. The old cartographer stood at the window between their beds, the morning's shadow-speckled sun falling over him. 'I remember the first time I saw it. I had been told, of course. Everyone who is not born here is told of the mornings of Ooila. But it does not prepare you for the sight. Before I arrived, I was told the story of how the goddess Maita died and broke against the ground, falling to pieces. Thousands, millions: each piece was so tiny that cracks and holes and slivers in the ground took her deep beneath the soil, to lava, to the hearts of the volcanoes, to where it was said she bathed while alive. It was said that after she fell, the bottles that the witches held turned cold. They had been warm until then, but now they froze to the touch. So did the volcanoes. For a night, all of Ooila mourned, thinking that they had lost not just a god, but the souls of their brothers and sisters, mothers and fathers, lovers and friends. They wept until the morning, until the butterflies emerged. Then they watched them die throughout the day. A few at first, until there was more, and the tread of men and women broke their bodies. They wept again that night, until the morning, when more rose. Only this time, they noticed that lava in the volcanoes rose with them.'

'And cooled only when all were dead.' Bueralan had been told the same as a child. 'Until I was ten, I thought it a myth.'

Orlan's laugh was touched with bitterness. 'Ooilans live near death every day, and think not to blame the gods, not once.'

'Why blame the dead?' He pushed back the bedcovers, the hits against the window continuing as he pulled the chamber pot out from beneath the bed. 'I'm going to find us a pair of horses this morning.'

'Are we in a rush?'

After a moment, he nudged the chamber pot back and began to lace his breeches. 'Tawain has surely sold our whereabouts to the Eyes of the Queen by now,' he said, reaching for his jerkin, and his sword.

'You truly have nothing to fear in relation to that.'

Bueralan grunted in reply, pushed open the door, and left.

Out on the street, the humidity was already starting to rise. Butterflies scattered around him, bursting into the air with each step he took. They were reds and oranges, greens and blues, black and white, and with so many patterns that no two seemed alike. It was impossible to count. Bueralan suspected that thousands upon thousands were around him, but not all were in the air. Many rested on the walls of buildings, lying against glass and wood and brick without distinction, while others already lay on the muddy road, their colour nought but brown in death.

He had seen more, deeper into Ooila, but it was only around the volcanoes that one had to be careful of their mass. The faint outline of Karaanas lurked on the horizon, the biggest peak in the range of mountains that divided the First and Third Provinces. There the sky would remain dark until the midday's sun reached its zenith and the clouds of sulphur lifted free.

You could die in the morning there, if you were not careful.

The horses he bought were both grey, speckled with black. The merchant – a middle-aged woman whose head had been shaved – said that they were military mounts, at nine and ten too old for service, but still strong. Both were scarred from front to end from bit and whip and sword, and the taller of the two had a mean eye that Bueralan responded to. The merchant said that they were a deal: 'They came together, they leave together,' she said. For that inconvenience, she had given new shoes to both and offered saddles cheap.

'You don't want them that much?'

She already knew that she had made a sale. 'The tall one tried to take a chunk out of a little girl the other day,' she said. 'The smaller has kicked two stable boys.'

He dropped two of Mireea's circular, hole-punched essr gold coins into her hand.

'I'll have to melt these down.' One of the Ooilan golden raqs held the weight of two essr. 'But we're good. I hope they serve you well.'

He led the horses back to the inn without incident, but at the narrow entrance, his stomach tightened. The stable boy was nowhere to be seen and, inside, many of the stalls had been filled with hay and saddles, leaving only one empty pair of stalls in the middle. With a rub on the nose of the smaller horse, he led them both in, his boots sounding a lonely beat as he did.

He had tied both horses in the stalls when new steps sounded. Heavy, booted steps, coming from opposite ends of the stable, slow and cautious.

Dropping his hand to his sword, Bueralan stepped into the middle of the stable and looked to his left, then his right.

Three: two first, one last.

He did not recognize any of the shaven men, but there was no mistaking their intent. From the left, the two men held short swords, while the one on the right had a heavy staff. They were not soldiers, he knew: the rust on their blades was old, and the way they held them in both hands was similar to an axe. The man with the staff was different in that respect: he held his weapon lightly, the balance of it letting Bueralan know that it had not been simply picked up off the road.

'Lice really made you all very ugly.' He drew his sword, felt his stomach settle. 'I say that as a man who is bald by choice.'

He met the left pair first.

He stepped into them quickly, catching the man with the staff off-guard and leaving him a handful of steps behind. The two men in front of him stepped back, and Bueralan parried a clumsy thrust from one, using his momentum to carry him past the other. Then, with a quick slash that pushed them back, he spun around, placing the pair neatly before the man with the staff.

One of the sword-wielders spat. Steel-clad hooves lashed out.

The hooves caught the two men with swords first, the back legs of both horses crashing out, uncaring of blade or armour, catching each man in chest and shoulder, before a second kick caught both in the skull. Only the man with the staff escaped the sudden burst, but his step back — the start of a run — did not have a second as Bueralan shouldered forwards, his sword plunging into the chest of the man, punching through to the other side. Placing his foot on the man's chest to withdraw his sword, the saboteur turned back to the two other men, one still alive, but struggling to rise — a desire never fulfilled, as Bueralan's sword struck down.

Their bodies had a few coins, little more, but it didn't matter. Bueralan knew how they had found him — and if Tawain was not responsible, then it was merely someone else who had noticed him last night — and he dragged the corpses into one of the stalls and hid them behind the hay. He tossed some sawdust down over the blood outside the stalls. It would not fool anyone who looked hard, but it would do for the time that he needed.

Upstairs, he found Orlan packing. 'How did it go?' the cartographer asked, as the door fell shut.

'Just how I thought it would,' he replied.

Stone Divisions

Yet, what of its contents?

You cannot hold *The Eternal Kingdom* unless you have pledged yourself to this new, nameless god. But you can hear it spoken — in parts, though, and never whole. The entirety of the book is kept for those who are faithful.

What is read aloud is curious, for it is not so much a religious treaty as a treaty on history. It claims to clarify the events that led to the War of the Gods and, like a cheap stage magician, it raises the curtain of a show that insists that the gods killed each other in an act of love. That what they did for thousands of years was, in fact, a form of ritual suicide that blessed their only child. That what they were doing was making the world a better place.

—Tinh Tu, *Private Diary*

1.

Zaifyr had left a trail of books that Faise and Zineer had attempted to consolidate. They succeeded with the books he had read and did not want, but failed with those he had not and those he had and wanted to keep. Those remained throughout the estate, lying like a line of his thoughts, left near the front door, or on the table, in the wine rack, on stairs — all of them seemingly dropped at random. They lay face-down, or on their spines, open at a page he had stopped at, at times with a second book laid over the top. They were old, made from cracked leather, thin parchment; and they were new, made in clean, straight lines from heavy paper produced in Yeflam. They were originals, copies of originals, translations of originals, written in languages he knew well, in others he struggled with. Faise had asked him — as she picked up one that looked as if it had fallen beneath a chair — if he remembered any of the ones he still needed and he said that he knew what they all were.

Most had come from the Enclave's library. Kaqua borrowed some for him and so did Ayae. But he had gone outside the library as well. An elderly woman who owned an antique bookstore in Nale had received a number of orders from him, orders that sent her deep into her stacks of books, into narrow heavy-titled lanes that her cane tapped against, where he, gazing through the eyes of a dead scholar, had isolated a hidden set of expensive treasures.

'I borrowed the money off Faise to buy them,' Zaifyr said. He led Jae'le deep into the dark house, letting the shadows of the stacks guide him. 'They have given me a couple of names that I can use in the trial, but none is a witness to the War of the Gods. I'm still struggling to find those.'

'Our own fault.' The storm petrel drifted from stack to stack, shifting from half-read, to read, to unread titles. 'We left the mountains after imprisoning you and returned to riots and revolutions.'

'The real damage was done before that.' He entered the back room and struck a match. 'We burnt much of what was lost.'

'I know. For our crimes, Tinh Tu spends her days trying to recreate what we destroyed. She may well ask you again to help her recreate those lost books after all this is finished.'

He remembered the day she had asked in person: a sticky, warm day in the twisting limbs of Jae'le's house. 'It is a cruel thing to do to the dead,' Zaifyr had said to her. He repeated the same words to his brother now. 'It is still cruel,' he added as the wick on the first candle caught light.

'Is it any less cruel than what you are doing now?'

'It is for them that I do it.'

'I have heard those words before.' The flame reflected in the bird's dark eyes. 'They remind me of old times in Asila, brother.'

'Then do not listen.'

'I already have that regret.'

'I thought you wanted to help me, not lecture me.' He smothered the match's flame with his thumb, felt the sharp pain. 'It was you who sent me to Mireea.'

The petrel's wings fluttered in irritation. 'I am only concerned for you.'

'There is plenty to be concerned with.' Zaifyr picked up the candle, placed its flame next to a second. 'That is why there are so many books.'

'What do you search for, exactly?'

'Mentions of the child, of the gods' division, of Linae's death.' Another candle lit. 'The latter is proving the hardest, simply because most of it is rereading. We searched for why the gods went to war a long time ago, but there was no specific evidence for it then, and there is none now. We put it down to the fact that they were alien to us and that we would never know. Whatever divisions lay between each god we thought would never be known. But what if it was? What if a story that we thought was about someone like you or me was really a story about the child?' He shrugged. 'The rereading hasn't amounted to much.'

'Have you considered using recent evidence?' the storm petrel said. 'You could argue Ger's reaction to you.'

'Using a god as the base of my argument will not make it strong.'

'All your evidence will be argued against.'

'Not if I find the right dead.'

'They will still question, brother.'

'I watched her destroy a soul.' Zaifyr finished lighting the last candle, the seventh in the room. 'I could not do that. Flesh and bone has its limitation, it is true, but there is more to it.

The power she had, the casual cruelty of it. The way it meant nothing to her. She viewed the soul as an object she owned. Once that is shown, no one will question it.'

'We were no different at one stage,' Jae'le said quietly. 'Souls, minds, flesh, land and air, we once believed that it was all ours. How did we respond to those who argued against us?'

He met the bird's gaze. 'No one spoke against us.'

'Not until your book, that is.'

Zaifyr did not respond to the barb. With Jae'le's inhuman gaze on him, he approached one of the unread piles before him and began to flip through the books. 'Do you plan to help?' he asked, pulling a large volume from the bottom. *Against Darkness:* a biography of Sir Alric Caloise, the religious knight, written by his squire.

'Birds cannot read.' The petrel shifted to the back of the chair. 'It's difficult for me to read more than a title like this.'

'That is not what I meant.'

'I will, but I am in Enilr. It will take me a day to reach you. I may even stop to enjoy this country our brother and sister made.'

The joke – even from a bird – fell flat on Zaifyr. His brother had not left the huge branches of his home since the construction of the tower where Zaifyr had been held captive. He had hidden his flesh away, put his body into exile and travelled only by animal, speaking to his brothers and sisters through the voices of others. It was a sign of how worried he was that he had come to Yeflam himself.

'You followed the child to Leera,' Zaifyr said. 'She told me that.'

'I did.' He was silent for a moment. 'But I simply thought

that she was one like us. I did not suspect what she was. Not once.'

Zaifyr had felt it immediately, a quality like him, yet not. He found it hard to believe that Jae'le could not have known, not even suspected.

'I will speak to Aelyn before I get here,' the storm petrel said. 'It would be respectful to do so, but it will also let me ask about our brother. After Asila, Eidan became a vagabond of sorts. He would travel to ruins and rebuild them, then leave them empty. But he would always send letters to Aelyn each week. She will know more than she admits.'

Zaifyr touched the charm beneath his wrist. 'She may not tell you.'

'She may not.' A ragged noise — a sigh, perhaps — escaped Jae'le. 'Our meetings are always difficult. This used to be my land. I do not lay claim to it now, but it has always been between us that she took it. We were meant to disappear, to slide into history, and let everyone forget what we had done so terribly. She was not meant to build a city as the surviving ruler of the Five Kingdoms, yet she did.'

'Why did people not drive her away?'

'There had been dark years after us, and new tyrants,' he said. 'And there were some who wanted to worship us, still. The call was difficult for her to deny.'

'I do not miss it,' Zaifyr said. 'Not at all.'

The storm petrel ruffled its feathers and flicked its wings, but said nothing.

2.

The ride back from Nale to Mesi was long, even longer when Ayae, Faise and Zineer arrived at their small house and found the front yard plastered with caricatures of Muriel Wagan and Aned Heast. Yet, even after little rest the night before, after the cleaning of the yard, Ayae could only sleep for five hours. Like most nights, her dreams were terrible: images of her fight along the Spine of Ger lingered on in the visions of men and women she killed. She saw Illaan in his hospital bed, saw Fo and Bau again and again. She dreamed of the fight in the tower. Of Queila Meina's frail hand on her shoulder as she died, followed by her rise as a ghost. And she dreamed of the tents on Wila, of how they merged into the rough walls of a nameless camp in Sooia. Each night she awoke to find herself twisted in her sheets, so hot to the touch when she awoke that she was afraid she would set the bedding alight.

Most nights, she would read by pale candlelight until the morning's sun rose. Occasionally, she would practise with the warmth in her, trying to draw it out, but without reward. No matter how much she tried, she was unable to recreate much of what she had done in Mireea. Her dreams may show her swords alight with flames, but she could cause nothing to move along steel. She could heat herself and boil water and move faster than she would normally be able to do so, but that was all. Ayae had begun to suspect that to do more she needed to give way to her emotions – an idea that she was not comfortable with.

Caught up in her thoughts, Ayae did not realize that there was a light downstairs until she was in the kitchen. At the table sat Faise. She wore a dark-orange robe, loosely belted. At the sight of Ayae, she offered a faint, tired smile. 'I did not mean to wake you,' she said.

'You didn't.' On the table were the papers and pamphlets that had been in the yard when they returned. 'And don't apologize. It is not your fault.'

'Would you like something to drink?' Faise asked. 'I was trying to tell myself it was okay to drink alone. Now you're here, I don't have to lie about that.'

She smiled faintly. 'Sure.'

A squat amber bottle of waer and two glasses dropped onto the table. The cheap spirit smelt horrible when the wooden lid came off, but Ayae took a glass and settled into the chair across from her friend.

'One day I will have to give up this awful drink,' Faise said. 'But I'll start another day.'

'Regrets?'

'Once we finish this, yes.'

'I meant for what you're doing.'

'I know.' Faise lifted the glass. 'There are more every day, I guess. I don't know if I'll have the nerve for it much longer.'

'You won't be hurt.' Ayae swallowed the sour drink of her teenage years. 'I will make sure of that.'

'I should have said no to Lady Wagan.' She poured for both of them again. 'But we had lost so much. Zineer was right. It was a chance for us to rebuild. We could get everything back that we had lost. We could help everyone on Wila get back what they lost.'

'And you could get revenge.'

'*And* I could get revenge.' Her smile was stained orange in the candlelight. 'That was icing. To think that I could show that fat bastard what I thought of him. That I could hurt him like he hurt Zineer and me.'

'Is Zineer not concerned?'

'Only when I'm awake.' Wearing loose trousers, Zineer reached for the chair beside Faise, his hand lingering on her arm. 'When I am asleep, my dreams think for me.'

'I'm sorry,' Ayae said softly.

'For what?' He leant across for the drink. 'For Benan Le'ta? He was born long before any of us, and the Traders movement before him.'

'I'm sorry for all of it.'

'We're not children,' Faise said. 'Sometimes, I wish I was. I could claim that I did not know what would happen when we agreed to Lady Wagan's plan. I could say that you convinced me to do something that I did not want to do. I could say that Zineer did not know, either. That we were completely innocent. But we're not children. We have to take responsibility for everything we have done. We made choices. Adult choices. We can't come home and pretend that we did not.'

'I wish I could go home and pretend.' The remains of Ayae's drink caught the dim light as she swirled the glass. 'I miss my home. I knew who I was inside that house. I could close the doors and shut everything out. Now, it feels so far away. In the morning, I look up and see—'

'—the mountain crumbling,' the other woman finished. 'Do you draw any more?'

'No.' She placed the empty glass on the table. 'I have tried a few times, both here and in the Enclave. I sit down with a pencil and paper, but I do not have the patience for it. I barely have the patience to read the books I have found – when I open them, I think of everyone on Wila and how I haven't been able to help them. It doesn't help that all that has survived of Ger's words are poetry and fiction, all of it allegorical, all of it about how he asserted control over the elements to stop their destruction.'

'Being here doesn't help,' Zineer said.

'It's not that.'

'You have so much to do,' Faise said, continuing, giving voice to concerns that the two must have shared with each other when they were alone. 'You shouldn't have to worry about us.'

'I would worry wherever I was. Maybe we should go somewhere else.'

'Somewhere safe?'

'Leviathan's End.' Zineer refilled their drinks. 'I would feel safe there.'

Faise took her glass back. 'I suppose we have become mercenaries,' she said. 'Accountants for hire. Maybe we need swords.'

'Sinae Al'tor would help,' Ayae said.

'I doubt that.'

'Captain Heast said he would. He said he could get you out of Yeflam.'

'Out?' Faise repeated. 'Out to where?'

'He didn't say.' Ayae lifted her glass. 'I can't believe we still drink this.'

'We started because it was cheap and got you drunk quick.'

'Well, there's that. At least we learned something in our childhood.'

3.

Approached from the coast's road, Cynama appeared fractured, as if it had been shattered across the land. Built to sprawl over the flat plain beneath, it was cut by five thick stone-lined canals that ran throughout. Laid to funnel rain water into a large low-tided lake, the canals fulfilled that purpose while also – inevitably – dividing the city symbolically.

The long muddy road on which Bueralan and Orlan approached Cynama held few travellers. The first they had passed had been as the morning's sun reached its peak and the humidity left lines of sweat down their backs. An elderly man, seemingly unaffected by the oppressive conditions, walked past with a large backpack. Shortly after, two women with a loaded mule and cart followed. They had said nothing, and after that, Bueralan and Orlan had watched the butterflies that fluttered across tall grass and trees before falling into the muddy ground. At midday, they passed a father and a son at the front of a wagon, the back filled with men and women and animals. Again, none of the people had spoken, or made eye contact with them. As the afternoon's sun began to rise, and the humidity started to wane, the largest group of men and women they had seen walked past, their belongings bagged and strung between the shafts of wood they carried.

'They're fleeing,' Bueralan said, once they had past. The final six men and women had had chains around their ankles. 'The rich and the poor.'

'That they do,' Samuel Orlan agreed. 'Not many countries will recognize their right to the ownership of slaves, however. Assuming they survive the journey, or are not sold at Dyanos, the prospects of those men and women will improve greatly. Much better, perhaps, than ours.'

'The road goes back, if you want to leave.'

'*We* have more than enough reason to turn around.'

He grunted sourly. 'You speak as if you know how it will end.'

'There are enough refugees from Sooia to tell that story to both of us.'

Bueralan nudged the tall grey forwards but did not reply. He had heard the stories. At their core was a man and his army laying waste to a continent and its people. There were atrocities, always. There were seven hundred years of horror stories, but he never felt as if they particularly affected him. By Aela Ren's own inarticulate reasons, and by the distance between Sooia and him, he had been unmoved by what he heard. As a child, it had been a violent fable that his parents had threatened him with. He had maintained that state of disinterest, through no real intention of his own, well into adulthood. Regardless of which story was told to him about the Innocent – either by refugees or by those who worked the charity ships out of Sooia – the words were elusive and intangible, a child's horror.

'Do you feel as if you have come home yet?' Samuel Orlan asked.

'No.' He did not hesitate. 'I do not know that I have a home anywhere these days, but if I do, this is not it. We'll have to find a place to stay.'

'I have a shop in there, across from Pereeth Canal.'

An expensive part of the city. 'How many shops do you have?' Bueralan asked.

'A number.' Orlan shifted on the smaller of the two horses, stroking its neck as he did. 'Did you have somewhere else planned?'

He had not. His mother's estate had been claimed by the First Queen, part of the price of his exile. Even if he had still owned it, he was not sure that he would have gone there. Ignoring the neglect that it would have come to over seventeen years, it was located an hour's ride outside the city, one of the many estates that populated the flat plains before the rocky, jagged, excavated land that led to Karaanas opened up.

'How far is your shop from the palace?' he asked.

'Three or four blocks, if I remember right.' Orlan regarded him curiously. 'Do you still plan to present yourself at first light?'

'You saw the blood in the stables.'

'I did, yes,' he agreed. 'Do you hope for mercy?'

'I'll get none if I am caught in the city.' He shifted the tall grey's reins from his right to left hand. He had replayed the fight in his head as he rode. It was the first fight he had had since he had stood above Ger, and the god had used him. He would not say he felt stronger, or faster, not as he had in the submerged temple, but he would not say, either, that he felt the same. He had briefly thought about bringing it up with Orlan, and thought of it again now, but he dismissed the thought. He did not need to encourage the cartographer to talk about gods. He said, 'Besides, a man in exile has no chance of receiving the Mother's Gift.'

'Neither does a dead man. We can still turn around and put this folly away.'

'As I said, the road goes back if you need it.'

The last of the day's butterflies lay on the ground before him. Ahead, the afternoon's sun had fallen and, slowly, one at a time, Cynama's lights began to emerge, as if the city had seen them and stirred awake.

4.

Beneath the early light of the morning's sun, Ayae, Faise and Zineer walked through the crowded lanes of Mesi's Farmers' Market.

It reminded Ayae of Mireea, though she knew there was very little to compare the two. The number of stalls in Mesi was only a fraction of those that had lined the cobbled roads of Mireea, the total probably further reduced by the deepening cold of winter and the ocean's brittle winds. Most of what the market sold came from across the ocean, from the trade lanes that Yeflam owned, and it halved as the produce they brought from Gogair and Faer fell quiet with the winter. The Mesi market sold only food: there were no toys to tempt children, no games of any kind, and no card, palm, or psychic readings by men and women with no power. In addition, while music could be heard from Mesi, it was at the midday mark, and was characterized by the simple, stripped-back instruments of musicians at an early stage of their career. In general, the Mesi market also lacked the hard hustle and long barter that had been an integral part of the Mireean markets. Ayae supposed that this was because the stalls were constrained by prices set by the Traders' Union, prices that increased the further away from Burata your stall was.

'One day, you won't have to come here,' Faise said as they made their way along one of the wide lanes, wooden crates of green, yellow and orange fruits and vegetables on either side of them. She was the only one of the three who held a canvas bag, the bottom of it already sagging with fruit. 'One day we'll be able to come here without you.'

She shrugged. 'I won't get apples that day.'

'They're sour, awful things – and you'll thank me that day.'

In the past, Ayae had laughed, or stuck out her tongue, or responded quickly, but today, she managed a slight smile, her attention on the people around her.

She was nervous. She had been on edge since they had stepped out of the house. Both Faise and Zineer were anxious as well. Halfway to the market, Ayae had thought that they should turn back, but she told herself that she shouldn't. In the final hours of the night, Faise and Zineer had rejected the idea of going to Sinae Al'tor. They shouldn't have to hide, Zineer said and Ayae agreed with him. She agreed with Faise as well when she said that they still had to help the Mireeans. None of them should have to hide because of that. But Ayae knew that her movements were quicker than they would normally be. She knew her skin was warmer than usual. And she knew that she was searching for anyone out of place, anyone who paid too much attention to her or Faise or Zineer, anyone who held a cloak strangely across them. Yet all she had spotted was a Leeran priest at the back of the market, speaking to the largely unresponsive crowd. His hand rose occasionally over the heads of people, a book in his hand.

Faise touched her shoulder.

Startled, Ayae said, 'Sorry?'

'You're not paying attention.'

She grimaced. To the left of Faise, Zineer was buying large thick-skinned oranges. 'I just — it doesn't matter. What did you say?'

'I asked if you wanted one of those books for Zaifyr.' The other woman turned in the direction of the priest. His arm had dropped and Ayae could no longer see him. A wave had washed over him and he had sunk beneath the black sea. 'He'd probably appreciate it.'

'He would,' she said. 'But those — only the priests can touch those books. He told me that.'

Zineer turned, a twine sack of fruit in his hands. 'Who do you think is paying for the books?' he asked. 'I mean, the printing of them, that is.'

'Why not the priests?' Faise replied.

'They claim not to have any money.' Slowly, the three began to pick their way through the crowd. Zineer took the bag from Faise and placed the fruit in it as he continued to speak. 'They are arriving without artifice. I heard one claim that the other day. We are but flesh and blood, were the exact words, I believe. They offer nothing but the truth of that.'

'The Enclave thinks it is Benan Le'ta,' Ayae said. 'They haven't come right out and said it, but he has been seen meeting with the priests, so the accusation follows.'

'There aren't that many presses capable of printing books in Yeflam.' Zineer pushed the bag up his arm. 'Most do papers, pamphlets — only five, by memory, can do actual books.'

'One is owned by Le'ta,' Faise added.

'Leaving four . . .'

Ayae's voice trailed off. Before her stood Commander Bnid Gaerl. He was a tall man with a heavily lined face. He had dark flat eyes almost lost in the lines of his face. Over his back he carried a large two-handed sword, and when he stepped into the path the three had been taking with casual ease, he did so without evidence of the weapon's weight.

'Leaving only four.' His voice was rough, as if his throat had been damaged at some time. 'Rather inauspicious, don't you think?'

'You're only one.' Ayae moved in front of Faise and Zineer. 'I would say the odds are not in your favour.'

'They say you don't burn, girl.' Gaerl's tone sharpened the last word. 'But do you bleed? I bet you do. All you cursed bleed.'

She took a step forwards.

'You think I'm here to fight?' He laughed unpleasantly. 'I'm here to see you panic. To hear you plead.'

'You haven't enough life left for that.'

'You'll plead,' he said. 'You'll plead once you hear that the Captain of the Ghosts was arrested.'

'He isn't even in Yeflam.'

'Oh, he is. He told me where he was. He told the Soldier as well. He thinks he'll be able to play us against each other and get some safety.' Around the mercenary, the market crowd became still, his words capturing those closest first and then spreading. 'But he's just going to go to Wila and rot.'

'You're lying.'

'Little girl.' He laughed again. 'Do you want me to tell you your fortune? I do that for girls I find special sometimes.'

'There's no need.' The anger in her voice did not surprise her. She took another step towards him. 'I know how it goes.'

'Then you know about the two people I got behind your friends.'

Ayae stopped.

'You are no soldier, girl.' Gaerl's voice was hard. 'When Heast is on that island, he won't be able to help you. He won't be able to begin no miracle, no twist, no turn. He'll just have to watch you bleed from Wila. He'll know it's his fault as well. He'll know he failed. He'll know 'cause I'll drop your traitorous heads down to him before I start working my way through his spies and paid-for soldiers.'

He stepped back into the still crowd, ending the conversation suddenly. The crowd rippled as he did, the stillness evaporating as he presented the long, well-oiled leather scabbard of his sword to Ayae and Faise and Zineer before he disappeared.

'I think you made a friend,' Faise said, finally.

'I'm using my charm.'

'I can tell.'

'I'm s—'

'If you say sorry,' Faise said, suddenly angry, 'I will not buy you apples.'

Ayae laughed, but there was little humour in the sound. She heard again Gaerl's words, *the Captain of the Ghosts was arrested*, and knew that she should have killed him then and there, before he walked away.

5.

'Do you always sleep with trousers on?'

He did not open his eyes. 'Only in brothels.'

'That's funny.' She did not laugh. Instead, her hand touched lightly the leg of his trousers — the left leg, the bad leg. 'There is a man outside for you,' she said.

'A fat man?' The Captain of the Ghosts opened his eyes: the morning's sun slanted through the small window at the top of the room. The girl, her pale blonde hair almost lost in the light, murmured 'yes' as she traced the ring of blood around his leg. 'There is a Keeper, as well,' she said. 'The Soldier.'

'Good.'

Slowly, he rose, his steel leg falling heavily to the wooden floor.

'Does it hurt?'

She had fallen forward, onto the warm, rumpled sheets he had lain on. Her bare feet stretched down to where his head had lain. 'You get used to it,' Heast replied, picking up his jerkin. 'Like all pain.'

Her smile was slight. 'Do you want a knife?'

He ran a hand through his grey hair, shook his head.

'I have two.'

'They're not a threat to me.'

'What if you are a threat to them?'

'You don't need a knife for that,' he said. 'Do you plan to come down?'

She shook her head and he left her there, wrapping herself in the unmade sheets of his bed.

Sin's Hand was quiet, the morning's light illuminating the black stains left from candles, the sooty remains of the evening and its transgressions and transactions. Downstairs, he passed a man cleaning the bar, a woman sweeping the floor, and a pair of large guards waiting at the front door for him. They were unarmed, but for one, who held Heast's sheathed sword. He handed it wordlessly to him as he approached.

Outside, Sinae Al'tor and two more unarmed guards stood before Benan Le'ta and Xrie. Half a dozen blue-mailed guards stood on either side of the two men, but Le'ta stood easily between them in an expensive mix of browns and blacks, and a heavy cloak to shield him from the ocean's cold wind. Yet it was the other man who drew Heast's attention.

'Captain Heast.' The Soldier's voice was strong, assertive. 'I am afraid I must return you to Wila.'

'For what reason?'

'Your safety, of course,' Le'ta interjected smoothly. 'Commander Bnid Gaerl and I are duly concerned that some of his men have not reported back. We fear the worst and we are afraid that people will blame the Mireeans.'

It was not what he expected to hear. 'What does that have to do with me?'

'We are merely concerned that the law will be taken into another's hands.'

He tossed the sheathed sword to the Soldier. 'You're welcome to check it for blood,' he said. 'There's none there. I just buy things now.'

'Yes,' Le'ta replied blandly. 'I've heard.'

'Enough.' Xrie did not check the blade, but did not return it, either. 'I have not the time, nor the inclination for this. Captain Heast, it is not exactly as Benan Le'ta is explaining. Bnid Gaerl has accused you of being responsible for the loss of his men. You must know this because you let me know you were in Ghaam.'

'I expected Gaerl to be here with his accusations.'

'*Commander* Gaerl —' Benan Le'ta was the first to emphasize his title — 'is a law-abiding citizen. He believes in allowing justice to take its course. The soldiers who disappeared were part of an investigation by the Traders' Union into land purchases that have threatened Yeflam's economic stability.'

'I don't own any land,' Heast said. 'I never have.'

'Captain—'

'The Captain,' Xrie cut in, 'surely understands that going to Wila is as much for his own safety as it is a response to the charges.'

He told them that of course he did, and let himself be led to a carriage. At the door, Heast waited for Benan Le'ta to seat himself. He glanced behind him to Sinae, who gave a slight nod of his head, before Heast stepped into the carriage. The Soldier followed, closing the door to the carriage behind him. A whip cracked and the carriage shuddered into movement. Around it, blue-armoured riders spread out and fell into orbit for the slow journey to the island.

After a while, Benan Le'ta said, 'You seem quiet, Captain. Could it be that the extent of your situation is dawning on you?'

'I was thinking of a young woman I know,' he said. 'I thought that the Soldier might know her.'

'There are many people in Yeflam,' Xrie replied. 'But I think I know the one you mean.'

'Might you pass on a few words for me, then?'

Across from him, the merchant's smile strained, but he said nothing else, not even after the two had finished talking. He did not even bid Heast farewell once he arrived at the ramp that led down to Wila.

6.

Seventeen years had passed since Ce Pueral had last held an official rank, a captaincy. She had just past two and forty at the time and her body had begun to struggle to carry the weight of the heavy gold-edged armour of the First Queen's Guard. Two years later, she was one of many to convince the Queen to replace it, to have the gold rims melted down with the steel, and a lighter, but darker plate and chain used. She did not like the weight of it, either, but she bore that uncomfortable fit in stoic silence when she wore it. It was not the fault of the armourer: it was the fault of the body, of the woman who, as she aged, preferred the weight of fabric to leather, leather to chain, and chain to plate, and whose unofficial rank led to an unofficial uniform that supported the first best.

She had been called the Queen's Justice, the Queen's Fist and the Queen's Teeth: there were more, new titles every year – as many flattering as insulting – but she had always thought of herself as the Eyes of the Queen.

The First Queen herself had given her that title after the death of the exiled Hundredth Prince, Jehinar Meih. He had returned to Cynama unexpectedly and Pueral had moved quickly to correct the mistake she had made. After all, it had been she who had delivered him and his followers to the slaver. She had not thought he would escape, but the story of it, when it was told, had drawn a smile from her. A blood slave had rescued the Hundredth Prince. Meih had been immune to that irony – indeed, all irony – which perhaps explained why it had been so easy for Pueral to convince the men loyal to him to turn on the promise of an ill-defined forgiveness for them.

'You are wasted in your position.' The First Queen had stood over the bodies of the Prince and his followers, frail even then. 'You have been told that before, Captain.'

'Your Highness,' Pueral had said, 'I am but a humble woman, of no notable past.'

The Queen's hand had reached out, brushing the gold edges of her armour. 'I have need for eyes like yours. In the morning, you will begin to earn a different birth if you wish, one in which this – this will not be ornament.'

She had not lied.

Seventeen years later, in dark red trousers, a shirt of crimson and black, and soft leather boots of the darkest red, Ce Pueral came to the door of the First Queen's chamber. She knocked twice before entering.

The door opened into a large room, filled with chairs and tables and books. Of the latter, the majority were thick volumes of a leather-bound diary, the recollections of the First Queen over three hundred years, written in a hand that had been reborn. Yet it was always her hand: the shape of it might change, the length of the fingers might alter, but the Queen, just like all of the five Queens, was forever. She would be reborn after her death. As would her children. They would rule until she could do so again. Until she was able to open the books in the room. Pueral had never read any of the volumes: they were for the Queen herself to read, but she had often wondered how the words were, within. Did her hand waver in its prose, going from thick, to thin, to cursive to printed? Did the First Queen look back at her own words and wonder who had written them, or did she remember the circumstances of all that was contained?

The First Queen had not said, but Zeala Fe would not. At five and sixty, she once said that she had long ago learned the cost of intellectual weakness.

She had paid the price of physical weakness, as well, but she had paid that without ease for decades. At the back of the chamber, the First Queen sat in a deep red-cushioned chair, a fire beside her, and a thick blanket across her thin knees. The chamber felt warm the moment Pueral stepped in, uncomfortably so by the time she drew before the Queen. There, the fire highlighted the thinness of her washed-out black skin, revealed the shape of her skull, and the lightness of her hair, white and frail with age.

'Ce Pueral.' Her voice was soft, not yet a whisper, but soon. 'You are late.'

'Forgive me, Highness. There was a matter that required my attention. Would you like to hear of it, or shall we begin as usual?'

'As usual.' In her lap, the First Queen held a collection of jewels. As a young woman, she had loved heavy works of silver and gold, but the weight was now too much, and she had taken to holding them instead. 'How have my daughters plotted against me today?'

Pueral eased into the chair across from her, embarrassed still by her use of it. For most of her time as the Eyes of the First Queen, she had delivered her reports while standing, but in the last few years, her ability to do so for three, four hours straight had begun to fail her. She had been forced to ask the Queen if she could sit, to which the woman across from her had nodded, and said, 'If you had made it another year standing for three hours, I might have had you executed.'

'Your daughters continue with their preparations,' Pueral said. 'The captain of a ship by the name of *Mercy* has been to see your eldest, Geena. I have yet to locate the ship itself, but I suspect it is in one of the bays off the coast, and will sit there for as long as your daughter pays the captain and his crew to do so. Given the captain's reputed port of home, I believe she is planning to flee to Zoum soon.' She paused for a moment, but when the Queen did not speak, she continued. 'Hiala continues to try and treat with the Second and Third Queens, but as yet, neither has seen fit to hear her.'

'They do not think she will survive succession,' the Queen said sadly. 'They are not wrong, but a mother should not think it. What of my youngest?'

'She plans a party.'

'Will I be invited?'

'No,' Pueral said evenly. 'But Usa Dvir, war scout for the Saan family Dvir, will.'

'She is as ambitious as she has always been.' On her lap, the First Queen twisted a dark-blue butterfly between her thin fingers. 'What do you think she is offering after they kill me and her sisters? Marriage, land, money?'

'All of that, and slaves.'

'It would not be surprising,' she conceded. 'Now, to important matters: what do you hear of Aela Ren?'

'More rumours that he has arrived, of course.' There had been stories for years. As a child, she had heard her father's friends, from morning to evening, sober and drunk, claim that it was only a matter of days before he arrived. 'Very few have any credibility, but there is a letter from the Fifth Queen, Dalau Vi, that may interest you. She talks of an attack on the coast, of a village that was destroyed. It is notable only from the point that it was a village that worked the black ocean across from where the Innocent's ships had been sighted.'

The Queen took the letter, gently unrolling the seal Pueral had broken. 'She sent these to all the Queens,' she murmured.

'Do you wish to ignore it?'

'No.' She placed a silver locket at one end, to weigh the fold down. 'You will go to the coast and see these ships. Dalau reports having a man here who saw the Innocent, and if that is true, then the time will be well spent. If he is lying, then you will have seen how the Fifth Province is doing. Already we have seen a marked increase in the number of people crossing the border from there to here, and the men and women who are leaving here for various docks have also increased. Dalau's generals have been reluctant to listen to her, which is no doubt helping that. She is young, and shows very little of herself in her office so far, but it will be good to know for certain how much control she has over her kingdom.'

Pueral tilted her head. 'Of course, Highness.'

'Do not thank me,' the First Queen said. 'We are both too old for such a long time in the saddle. Now, what of this last piece of news?'

'Bueralan Le has returned.' Even now, she could not believe that she was saying the words. 'He is in the company of Samuel Orlan.'

The First Queen's laugh was a whisper of sound. 'Now that is truly interesting. Do you think Samuel has brought him for me?'

7.

Despite the fact that Sir Deran Caloise's *Against Darkness* was written in the final years of Caloise's life, a life that ended well after the War of the Gods, Zaifyr was drawn to it because of the years the author had spent as the squire of Sir Alric Caloise, also known as the Beloved. In its entirety, the book was a drawn-out final letter of loyalty to a knight who died weeks before Jae'le conquered Kuinia, the name his brother would give to the land that stretched across Gogair, the Saan and the continents that Yeflam spanned.

The Beloved was a minor figure in history, if truth be told. Indeed, Sir Alric Caloise was not the first, nor the last to bear the title. It had been worn by at least seven men and two women and it still waited, Zaifyr believed, for someone to own it in a fashion that no one else could. But that did not matter to him. As the morning's sun rose, he scanned for a section of *Against Darkness* where Alric Caloise rode into the Broken Mountains. The story of his expedition was detailed well by Sir Deran, but it was a story of death, of a force unprepared for the poisoned land that they would travel on. Yet Sir Alric — as Zaifyr had read in another book, Batiano's *Lost Knights*

– was one of the few men to have claimed to have spoken to the last of the goddess Linae's priests. It was well after the War of the Gods, but the conversation, as recorded by Deran Caloise, had little to recommend it. Deran retold the tale secondhand, repeating Alric's words: he described an old woman riddled with disease, a hut that was barely big enough for her, and a promise she made to him. His squire did not know exactly what that promise was, but it was clear that after the meeting Alric was in the grip of an obsession. On more than one occasion, he was said to have claimed that it was a divine command that drove him. Whatever that command was, it saw the knight waste the remains of his considerable wealth in a campaign against those he called False Gods.

That campaign brought him into conflict with Zaifyr and his family, but only momentarily. Within a year, the armies that Alric had been part of – as either a leader or a companion – had been broken. The remains of them were pushed into the mountains that divided the Saan from Gogair and there, in rugged, wormed-out tunnels, Alric Caloise had tried to take the remnants of his army to the Saan. He told his squire that he could begin an extended campaign of rebellion from there.

Zaifyr remembered that well, but not because of anything the Beloved had done. A fatigue had started to creep into his brothers and sisters then, a fatigue that would eventually lead to a larger weariness that would result in the end of their wars before they conquered all the continents of the world. For the Beloved, however, the tiredness of Jae'le and Eidan, who had chased the knight's small force, resulted only in an ugly death that Deran Caloise's book recounted:

We did not face an opponent of flesh and blood in those tunnels. Such a man would have been met by the straight steel that Sir Alric wielded. The finest swordsman of us, he would have stridden into the tunnels and he would have wrought a horrible toll on them from the dark corners and the hidden passages. He was one of the few men to know the paths that led up the awful mountains, to the daylight of the Saan, and the culmination of his superior knowledge and skill would have been the death of ordinary men. But we did not face such mortality. Instead, we faced a continual shuddering of the earth, as if it were being broken by fists around us. The ground split, the walls cracked, the roof fell. I could not count the number of times we were forced to move due to death, to leave tunnels we knew for those we did not.

There was no respite, ever. We could not sleep, could not find water, or food. We starved. We were forced into behaviour unfitting men of our stature. We drank our own wastes, we ate the flesh of those who fell. After a week, the ground awoke creatures — those that you know to live deep within a cave and those that you do not — and they threatened to swarm us. We stomped and swatted, but against such enemies, no sword could cleave, no armour protect. We could not light fires. We consumed our ill-gotten fare raw, standing. To sit, or to lie down, was to be attacked, to be bitten. In my own weakness, this is how my arm became swollen, how the delirium that separated me from Sir Alric and the others came upon me, and how I do not remember my escape from the mountains.

According to his own maths, Sir Deran Caloise had lived into his late seventies, his swollen arm cut off and the rest of his body the inheritor of the pitiful unsold estates that bore Sir Alric's name.

Still, the book had provided Zaifyr with Alric's final resting place, even if it was in the tunnels that led to the Saan. Jae'le would not thank him for that, when Zaifyr told him. Once Zaifyr found the haunt, his brother would have to enter the tunnels to bring Alric's bones to Yeflam. But the tunnels that led to the Saan were the first problem. Many ended in dead ends and strange creatures. A lost man or woman could spend decades in the tunnels before they stepped out into the light of one of the suns again. Finding Alric's haunt first would cut the time down considerably, but he could almost hear his brother's curse, his disgust at the idea—

'Qian,' Kaqua said from behind him. 'It is time for you to leave Yeflam.'

8.

'Your hands move too fast,' Xrie said. 'That's your problem.'

'I have been told that before.' Ayae caught the three bruised apples she had been attempting to juggle. A fourth and fifth lay in soggy remains on the ground, while another two waited on the small stool behind her. She had been given them when the three had returned silently from the Mesi Market, after Zineer had closed the door behind them and said, 'We could go to Wila.'

'Become refugees?' Faise asked. 'In our own home?'

'It would be safe.'

'Zin—'

'It *would*,' he insisted. 'What could Sinae Al'tor offer us? Nothing. *Nothing*. Heast is on Wila. He knows it is safe.'

'Honey.'

'This has — is — Faise, they're in the *streets*.'

'Honey.' Faise took Zineer in her arms, drew him against her. 'Honey, we would just endanger them. The people there are unarmed. Gaerl lied. The Captain isn't going there.'

Ayae stepped outside. She eased herself into the chair, the weight of what she had just witnessed — in both the market

236

and the house – settling onto her heavily. She did not know what she would do next, or how she should react; the threat had been clear, and she did not want to wait for it to be fulfilled – but before her mind could unravel what choices she had, she was startled by Faise, who placed the bag of apples in her lap. 'We need just a moment,' she whispered and Ayae had nodded. The door closed and she heard them talking, heard their movements, and she heard the pair of them slowly rebuild themselves, their strength and tenacity. Knowing that she could do nothing for that, Ayae had opened the bag and began, unsuccessfully, to juggle.

She had been doing that when the Soldier arrived.

He stood with his hand on the gate that led to the house. His other hand rested on the hilt of his sword.

'I am trying to control them,' she said. 'I want to control the air around the fruit and use that to move them. Aelyn told me that I had to trust the currents, that I had to feel their texture, much as I did the fruit itself, and I am trying to use my hands for that, but always compensate by movement and they get faster and faster. It is as if I cannot stop myself.'

'Aelyn told you that?'

'Yes.'

'She rarely speaks about what is inside her.'

'It was just something she said in passing, nothing more. But I need to be more . . . disciplined, I think,' she said. 'What brings you here, Xrie?'

'Captain Heast, I am afraid.'

She felt her stomach tighten. 'Is he——?'

'He is on Wila.' He nudged the gate open. 'He sent me a message in the evening, telling me that Bnid Gaerl would soon be attacking him. Shortly after that, one of my men told me that Gaerl was awakening his forces, that he had heard that Captain Heast had murdered a number of Gaerl's men. It wasn't too much longer before Le'ta was at my door, promising that he had stopped Gaerl's bloodshed, but we had best both take Heast to Wila for his own safety.' Xrie grimaced. 'I did not like it. Heast did not either when I showed up at Sin's Hand without Gaerl. He asked that I come and see you – in fact, that I come and warn you and your friends that you are in considerable danger from that man.'

'I met Gaerl in the market today,' she said.

'Delightful, isn't he? Your friends would be best served if they left Yeflam. Do they have any plans?'

He stopped, his attention drawn, like her own, to the man who made his way across the road. At first, she did not understand why he had caught her attention. Men and women passed her often, and only those who lingered, or wore the brown robes of the priests – an increasingly vocal presence in Yeflam – caught her attention. None were like this man: there was a roughness to him, a sense that his thin frame had emerged from the ground, his dark skin so heavily sunk against his bones that he appeared emaciated, with only the long, twisting beard he had giving shape to his face. He was without wealth, that was obvious, but the leather he wore had once been purchased by a man who had been otherwise. If she had not thought that about the well-cared-for leather, then the simple but well-made sword he wore and the cloak of thick green feathers the like of which she had never seen on any animal, would have suggested it was so.

She had never seen the man before, but she knew him, *knew*—

'Jae'le.'

The word was a whisper, but he heard. 'I knew you would not forget me.' His smile revealed filed teeth. 'You look different to my own eyes.'

'I can barely sense you,' Xrie said. 'It is no wonder I have never felt you in Yeflam.'

'Yet I have been here many times.'

'What do you want, Jae'le?' Ayae turned the apple over in her hand, gripping it like a stone. 'Have you come to help me and my friends? I know you heard our conversation.'

'No.' His smile faded. 'No, child, I fear I have come to ask for your help. I will see my sister by the end of the day. I do not look forward to the conversation, but it is one that we need to have. We will need to ensure peace is among us if we are to help my brothers.'

'Aelyn is not your problem.' Her fingers sank into the fruit's flesh, bruising it. 'She does not want a trial.'

'Others in the Enclave push for it,' Xrie said.

'They do so in error.' As Jae'le spoke, juice began to run down Ayae's fingers. 'Zaifyr does not care for your justice – but even that is not important. Not now.'

'Why not?'

'Because of Eidan.'

'He is in Leera,' she said. 'You told him that.'

'I told him our brother was with the child,' he said. 'And he is. But he is not in Leera. I had meant to tell Zaifyr that, but the knowledge that Eidan was with the child was enough to disturb him in such a way that I held back. That I was afraid.

For he has begun to descend into what he was in Asila. He looks just as Samuel Orlan described to me in a letter he wrote before he died. He told me of rooms filled with books and ghosts. Rooms so similar to the one that my brother sits in now, turning pages, and looking for dead men and women to defend him. How do you think he will react when he discovers that Eidan and the child are on their way to Yeflam?'

'She is coming?' Ayae's apple cracked in her grasp as she spoke. 'Why is she coming here?'

'Zaifyr wrote to his brother.' Jae'le moved his fingers gently as if they flapped. 'A dead bird searched for him and told both of them of the trial.'

'She would not come for that.' Ayae dropped the remains on the ground. 'That is madness. That is—' Her words failed her.

'Trouble,' he said. 'It is trouble.'

9.

'I have tried to be patient with you,' Kaqua said, his voice low and tense. It matched the stiffness in his limbs, the rigidity in his walk that, as he entered the room, spoke of fear. At first, Zaifyr was not sure why he would be afraid; for the first few moments that the Pauper spoke to him, he was lost by what was happening. It was not until he saw the long, dark-bladed knife in his hand that it dawned on him that the Keeper had come here to threaten him. To kill him, even. 'I have sat here for weeks talking to you. I have laced my words with all my power. I have suggested that you cannot have the public stage you want. That Yeflam is not yours to launch a war from. I have tried repeatedly to lead you back to the path of peace.'

'And now you think to threaten me with a knife?' Zaifyr asked. 'You and I are much too old for that.'

'It is not how I would prefer things to be done.'

'Then put it down.'

'It should be your sister who is here,' he said. 'You are Aelyn's responsibility. You are your beloved family's responsibility and it should be she who stands before you now and demands that you leave.'

'Does she know you are here?'

'No, she would tell me it was foolish. She would tell me that to push you is a mistake. But I cannot step away as she does every time the topic is raised.'

'You should do as she does.' Zaifyr did not feel threatened, not yet. He talked calmly, kept his gaze level with the other man. 'She is giving you advice,' he added. 'You should listen to it.'

'I have listened to her for nearly all of my life.' The Pauper stopped. Only a chair separated the two of them. 'Of all your family, she is the best. She has kept her humanity where you have all lost yours. None of the horrors that any of you are responsible for touches her. She has always known what it meant to be a god. In Maewe we had created such a society – one of peace and intellectual debate. There was no discrimination, no hatred, no violence. She was worshipped. She *was* a god to those people. So was I. But when Maewe fell after Asila, all of it was lost. All that beauty, all that progress, all of it because you could not see in yourself the solution to your problems. Because you could not give the dead the peace that you believed they deserved.'

'It is not what I think they deserve,' Zaifyr said, still calm. 'Or do you not ask why your power – to influence minds, to control intent – does nothing to me?'

'My power.' His hand tightened on the hilt of the knife and he raised the blade. 'My power is words. It is justice. It is rarely used to hurt.' Suddenly, he tossed the knife into the air. '*Catch*,' he said.

Zaifyr's hand snatched out involuntarily.

'I do not stitch my lips together because my words are

poison,' Kaqua said, his voice soft but compelling. 'I do not use my power like a knife – I do not march into the streets and command as you and your family do. But you, Qian, you have driven me to extremes. You have forced me to raise your arm, to have you rest the knife against your chest. You have forced me to this.'

The blade had sunk through Zaifyr's shirt, had come to rest against his chest. 'You do not want to do this,' he said, raising his gaze from the steel. 'You do not want to begin this with me, Kaqua.'

'She comes here.'

'She?'

'Your child god,' he said. 'This being you wish to go to war with. But you will not do so in *this* nation.'

'Kaqua—'

'*Push the blade*,' he hissed. 'If you will not leave Yeflam, push it into your chest, push it into what you have left of a heart!'

The dagger did not move.

As if she stepped out of a shadow, a young woman appeared, her cold hands wrapped around Zaifyr's arm; she was joined by another, a woman who looked just like her, whose hands had closed around the hilt, stopping it from moving.

'You will not deny me,' Kaqua hissed. 'You will *push* that knife into you. You will bleed out like a mortal man, you will—'

A haunt grabbed him by the throat.

'A mortal man,' Zaifyr repeated. 'The mortal man who holds you now killed both those two women. He was obsessed with them. He could not bear the idea of another having them. After he killed them, he killed himself. He wanted to be with them for ever.' Slowly, the two sisters drew the dagger away from his chest, and as it left him, his hands released it to them. 'He did not know that he would be, of course. He was just obsessed.'

Around him, haunts began to appear, the faint outlines of the dead who had been his company as he read, as he moved from room to room. Their awful, hollow voices began to sound, the whispers of hunger and cold joining the crash of waves against the foundations of Yeflam, not one singular, not one isolated. Like a tide, their words filled the room; his power, his *will*, flushed through them, awakening the dead throughout the house of Aelyn Meah, awakening the dead down the long path to the gate and past the two guards and out into the streets of Nale, out into the people there.

'But he shares them with all the others who have died.' Zaifyr stepped through the haunts, parting their insubstantial bodies, feeling the faintest hint of their touches against him. 'Now, you want me to leave, is that right?'

The dead lined the northern bridge to Burata, the eastern bridge to Rje, the western to Fiys, and the southern that led into Quo'Theme.

They appeared in pieces, a hand first, a leg, a torso, clothed and naked, the palest outline of a person long and recently dead.

They appeared beside men in broad daylight, beside women in shadows, beside children in bed.

They appeared beside the white-branched trees of the Keepers' Enclave, in the occupied and empty houses, in the factories, in the offices, in the tiniest and largest confines.

'But I think it is you who should leave. You who should take your knife and go back to my sister. You who should tell her that the gods' child is here.'

They appeared with their mouths open in anguish, as if they would scream.

'Tell her that she is here for the trial.'

And then they were gone.

10.

As the morning's sun rose above Cynama, the exiled baron, Bueralan Le, presented himself at the First Queen's palace unarmed.

It lay in the centre of the city, the Pareeth and Battar Canals on either side. Built from heavy blocks of ash-coloured stone, the design of the palace was dominated by two wings that stretched out like the arms of a giant, leaving a huge courtyard of paved stone for any visitor to cross before he reached the gate of the palace. Awash with the morning's butterflies, the square was populated by merchants setting up their stalls, their titles and wares half obscured by coloured wings, the cleaners already present to sweep the wet stone, to scoop the three fountains that were filled with the brightly coloured corpses.

The night before, Bueralan and Orlan had arrived to find his shop door chained shut. The building, a slim, two-storey creature made from stone and indistinguishable in a series of narrow streets similarly filled, had boarded-up windows and a lock showing rust. Muttering to himself about the failure of paid employees, Orlan had pulled out lock picks and worked it open, only to enter to a building of stale air and mouldering maps. There were mice droppings on the floor, long strands of grey webs from shelf to shelf, and a huge table covered in a discoloured drop cloth. More cloths had been used to protect the tables, chairs and desks that were further into the building, each hard with age and heavy to lift.

'Are you sure it's been eight years?' Bueralan asked. 'It feels as if it has been a century since this place was opened.'

'I had a well-paid woman living here.' The elderly man was pulling maps from shelves, dropping most to the floor. 'She put in an order for new material every four months.'

'Not to sell here.'

Upstairs revealed three rooms, the largest one a workshop dominated by a long table covered in a sheet. Of the two bedrooms, one held a bed made of linen and dust and a wardrobe of moth-eaten clothes. The second had an empty bed and wardrobe and no sign of the woman whom Orlan had paid to work his shop. The thought brought a sad smile to Bueralan's face: at least someone had betrayed the cartographer.

In the morning, Orlan was absent from the shop. Bueralan had heard him moving from shelf to shelf, muttering to himself, opening cupboards, creeping up the stairs, the steps and words fading as the saboteur drifted to sleep in the early hours of the morning, and had been concerned when he had awoken to silence. That anxiety had continued, slowly building, ignoring the parts of him that said that the old man had headed out to replace what had been lost, to learn what had happened to the woman who worked here: arguments that all but died away when he reached the end of the butterfly-filled courtyard and the dozen guards in black-and-red armour that lined the entrance to the palace.

From the centre, a man stepped forward. His face – like all the faces around him – was hidden beneath the flat face plate he wore.

'You are expected, Bueralan Le.'

He almost laughed bitterly.

Instead, he nodded and was led along a series of empty hallways beautifully tiled with black quartz. Shortly, a door of heavy onyx appeared, flanked by two guards.

It opened into a large, tiled room. The black quartz was laid out in a huge expanse, with the speckles through it like the night's deepest sky. Around the room, in the silent corners, between the armoured guards, was the First Queen's full court, or so it appeared to Bueralan. Always a busy chamber, it was one that flowed with the entrance of men and women, reaching a peak during the middle of the day. It was rare for it to be filled earlier; that was only the case when the First Queen had summoned the court, a thought that made him close his eyes briefly.

When he opened them, the court was still silent, and the First Queen awaited him in her large throne of dark stone. In it, she was a frail figure, more so than when he had last seen her, but he did not feel sympathy for her. To feel sorry for the Queen was a mistake, he knew. Pity led to the belief that she was, somehow, not fit to rule, that she could not do so properly, and it was from there that others had begun a descent into rebellion and revolt, though he himself had not done so, no. He had begun from a much uglier place.

On either side of her stood two women. To her left, but just behind the First Queen, was Captain Pueral. She stood tall and straight in the black armour of the guards around him, and had changed little from when he had last seen her. She remained upright and muscular, her skin dark and lined from the sun, and her grey hair cut close to her skull.

'The last of the Hundredth Prince's men returns.' It was the second woman who spoke, the one to the First Queen's right. A young, beautiful woman with skin darker than his own, she stood on a lowered step so that the First Queen could whisper into her ear, and she wore a gown of orange and red, with gold jewels about her wrists and ankles. The Voice of the First Queen said, 'What brings the last traitor of those men to me?'

Aware of the eyes of the court on him, of the eyes of guards, he fell to his knees, his head bowed. 'I arrive to beg forgiveness.' The rehearsed words tasted like ash in his mouth. He knew now that they were pointless, but he spoke them anyhow. 'I arrive to beg that my exile be lifted, that my name, my titles and my lands, be restored at your will.'

The First Queen whispered.

'Such favours you ask for. Tell me, why should I grant you such a boon?' the Voice said.

'A private matter.' He hesitated. 'A death in the family.'

'Did you have children in exile, Mister Le? Or take a wife?'

'I have neither, Your Highness.'

Silence.

'Rise,' the Voice said.

Slowly, he pushed himself to his feet, the court silent around him.

'You have neither parents, nor wife, nor child,' the Voice said. 'The only family to remain is the family that is not a family.'

'It is for my blood brother I return, for him that I ask for my exile to be lifted.'

'For a slave?'

'For my brother,' he corrected.

The gasp in the court was slight, but audible. You did not correct the Queen, not if she was the Fifth, or the Second, not if her court was here, or on the other side of Ooila. You did not stand in the court of a Queen and tell her she was wrong, not on a subject such as this, but Bueralan did not regret his words. If he was betrayed — and he was, he knew, and he felt that bitterness deep in his being — he would not betray Zean, or any of the others. Beside him, he heard the rasp of steel being drawn, and readied himself to be struck, to turn with the blow, and did not understand why the First Queen's frail hand rose, halting the soldiers on either side of him.

'Are there any who can vouch for you?' the Voice asked.

'No.'

'I will.'

Samuel Orlan's voice emerged from the left of the court, from behind a clump of men and women. He walked slowly onto the floor, smiling at the court, at the First Queen, and at Bueralan. The cartographer was richly dressed, his beard and hair neatly trimmed, and he held in his hand a tall, delicate crystal glass in which a dark-red wine sat untouched.

'You would vouch for this exiled man?' the Voice of the First Queen asked, devoid of any of the surprise that the First Queen must have felt. 'Do you know what this entails, what this risks?'

'Of course.' He raised the glass in toast. 'I will vouch for him knowingly. I will support him, I will share all punishment, all success.'

The silence of the court stretched, thin, tense, waiting to be broken.

'Why,' asked the Voice, 'would you do that?'

'I have a debt that cannot be repaid,' Samuel Orlan replied.

Your Brother, Your Sister

The Eternal Kingdom implies that Mireea was attacked because it violated the final resting place of the Warden of the Elements, the god Ger, who she calls her father. One, I might add, of many.

Yet it does not explain why, once the Spine of Ger fell, she turned her army — her Faithful — on the Kingdoms of Faaisha, where the remains of no god lie.

—Tinh Tu, *Private Diary*

1.

Aelyn arrived after Zaifyr delivered Kaqua to the Enclave. The two sisters marched him through Nale, their bodies lit with his power, the pair of them a new creature born into the world, a cold flame that walked along the streets. At the door of the Enclave, Zaifyr drained his power from them and, to the crowd that gathered, to the crowd that watched Aelyn's wind-made horses rise to the window of her office later, it appeared as if the two girls ceased to exist. But they walked with the crowd back to the estate. They drifted, cold and alone, two women among another crowd that could not be seen. At the gate of the estate, they drifted past the six members of Yeflam Guard who had taken up a position alongside the wind-made guards. They walked up the path, up past the empty carriage that Aelyn had arrived in, walked through the open door and into the house, where Zaifyr stood with his sister.

'Brother,' she said. 'Qian. What have you done?' She spoke slowly, cautiously, her emotions calm, a centre against the fears around her. 'You cannot drag Kaqua through the streets. You cannot line them with the dead. Yeflam is in—'

'I was attacked,' he said. 'Your Pauper attacked me.'

'He would not . . .'

'He said that the gods' child was coming.'

Aelyn's emotions flickered across her face, a kaleidoscope of resignation, disappointment and fear. 'She does,' his sister said finally. 'And it appears that I must apologize for Kaqua. He has made a mistake, but he has not done it out of animosity. He understands that Yeflam is already at breaking point. He has been moved by the fear of what will happen when the two of you meet in our streets.' The calm in her voice began to strain. 'Understand, if I had known that he would do this, I would have told him no. But you should understand that we have known about this child god of yours for nearly a year. Eidan is there beside her. He has been our eyes in Leera.'

'Is he why you let her priests in here?'

'They are no threat to us. They allow Eidan to continue at her side. It is a scheme that you have endangered from the moment you arrived at our gates.'

'The child is not to be negotiated with.'

'We cannot make those judgements any more,' she said. 'We are not gods. We are not yet allowed that privilege.'

He did not reply.

'Qian.' The calm broke and defeat entered her voice. 'Consider what is at stake here. Yeflam is not Asila. The people here are my responsibility. They are *my* world.'

'What has Eidan told you?' There was no sympathy in his voice, no give. 'What is it that you know about her that frightens you?'

'It is not *her*.' A sigh broke through the defeated threads in her voice. 'It is *you*. You threaten the very thing which you rage against. You will trap us all in the horror that you see.'

When the afternoon's sun sank at the end of the day, the Yeflam Guard had been deployed throughout all twenty-three Floating Cities of Yeflam. Jae'le, who arrived at first by storm petrel after Aelyn left, later came in person once the night had set. He told Zaifyr that a curfew had been put in place. He said that there had been panic in the streets. A group of people on Neela had tried to storm Wila, believing that the Mireeans were responsible. The Soldier himself had quelled that, Jae'le said. By morning, the Yeflam Guard had dispersed the crowd that had gathered at the front of Aelyn's estate. They returned and they were driven away. When Ayae, Faise and Zineer visited, he heard that the papers had begun to call the day the haunts appeared over Yeflam 'the Day of a Million Ghosts'. He was shown some of the pictures that were printed of him, and read half of one of the stories, but he had little time for the description of himself as a madman who needed to be brought to justice. He tore up the papers and used them as bookmarks in his research.

Then, after a fortnight, the trial was announced.

It was Jae'le who told him. His brother returned from the Enclave in the early hours one morning with the news.

'Six days,' Zaifyr repeated after he spoke. 'It is not enough time. I need more time. One of the dead I want is in the caves that lead to the Saan. Six days is not enough to get him.'

'It is what you have. In six days the child will be here.'

'She will have the child attend the trial?'

'It is what you wanted, is it not?' Outside the window, the world stretched darkly, filled with the smell of salt and blood. 'But you should know, there was a condition attached to that. A condition I agreed with.'

'Why was I not asked about this?'

'Because it is about you,' he said. 'If at the end of the trial you are found guilty, you will be returned to the tower in Eakar.'

He saw that small space again. Saw it closing around him. 'I will not return there,' he said.

'Not willingly,' Jae'le agreed. 'But nonetheless, it will be your punishment. I will stand by Aelyn and her Keepers of the Divine to enact it, if I am required to do so.'

'I'll not fail,' Zaifyr insisted. 'You know I won't. You can feel the child approach as well as I can. You can feel the pull at your skin, as if she could consume you.'

'I feel it,' his brother said. 'Like the first row of teeth in a giant maw.'

'She cannot be allowed to exist.' There was no doubt in his voice. 'No matter what else is said, she must be destroyed. You must be able to see that, at least.'

The shadows of the night had left his brother gaunt, more so than in reality. The light of the lamps faltered around the edges of him, alternately revealing and hiding his expression. 'Yes,' he said, finally, 'I believe I do.'

2.

With the afternoon's sun behind his back, Bueralan led the tall grey through the stone entrance to his mother's estate. The top of it resembled broken teeth and the rusted gate no longer locked. His boots and the horse's hooves trod rock, weed and the hollow corpses of butterflies in slow discord to the main house and no one appeared in greeting or warning. The once well-kept gardens stretched on either side of him, a thick, tangled mess of green shot through with bright wild-flowers muted by ash.

'Why was it not sold?'

He had asked the question of Ce Pueral two weeks ago. She was no longer a captain, he knew, and her visit to Samuel Orlan's shop the morning after his appearance in court had not been unexpected. She appeared in her black-and-red armour, her long sword comfortable at her side, a group of men and women out on the street waiting for her.

'The Queen was close friends with your mother.' Pueral was coldly indifferent to him. 'She spent time out there when she was younger.'

'She kept it out of sentimentality?'

'Occasionally, Mister Le, the answer is a simple one.' His title did not go unnoticed. 'Since your exile, no one has lived there. Not officially, anyway. No caretakers were given the land but I imagine there have been squatters. You may find that you have to clean out more than weeds.'

The main house was huge. It had been made from heavy blocks dug out of the ground years before the Five Queens came to rule. His mother had extended the house carefully, drawing up plans, consulting with builders and expending a fortune to have similar stone dug out of the ground. Much of his childhood had been spent listening to her plans for the house, which was the main reason why he considered the sprawling building his mother's, and not his parents'.

'Why am I being offered this?' he asked Pueral.

'It is a gift from the First Queen.' Her gloved hand finally left her sword, her fingers flexing. 'Another one. What you won yesterday is something few have.'

'I am grateful.'

'No, you are not,' she said, no trace of malice or bitterness apparent in her voice. 'You were a rash man in your youth, Bueralan. You wielded your blade with considerable skill, held your own in politics and took risks. In the case of the Hundredth Prince, you made a poor choice. Others had previously done you well and I always viewed that as a mistake of youth, I believe. You must have understood that on a certain level as well. After your exile, you kept your confidence, your ability to take risks, your flair. I haven't paid too much attention to what you have done in the last decade, but for a while I watched you closely. You wore your exiled title openly and you worked for rich and connected men and women – so of course I watched you. I even admire some of what you have done.'

'Thank you,' he said.

'Don't thank me.' She had turned to the door, to the soldiers waiting for her outside, and her hand closed into a fist. 'I am not flattering you. I am warning you. The man I remember and the man in my reports is not standing before me. Instead, there is a man without confidence, a man for whom risk is played out. You have the eyes of a dead man, yet you come here to play politics, to stand in the First Queen's court and talk about the Mother's Gift for a dead slave. You will not get what you want with eyes like that. Instead, you will make a mistake. A mistake that will cost you your life – and that of your blood brother as well.'

The lock on the door of his mother's house was broken, the inside littered with the husks of butterflies, glass and animal remains.

Bueralan made his way through the entrance, the afternoon's sun a splotched pattern across the walls showing destruction by shadow and light. In the main room, he found shattered furniture and the ashes of a fire against the far wall. Bueralan's boot nudged the solid cinders, scattered a handful of spiders and animal bones. Nothing suggested that it had been used recently. No tracks had crushed the dead butterflies spread across the tiles. From the main room, the halls were scattered with them and other bugs, with ashes lingering in the corners, while the walls were bare of family paintings. Burnt on the fire, no doubt.

'I like her,' Samuel Orlan had said, after Pueral left.

'You would.' The cartographer had come downstairs, dressed

in old paint- and ink-stained clothes, a large magnifying glass in his hands. He had spent much of the morning at his work table since they had returned from the court and had not bothered to come down until Pueral had left. Bueralan did not doubt that he had heard every word, though. He asked, 'Did you have anything to do with the estate?'

'I had not even considered it.' Orlan shrugged. 'Was the First Queen that good a friend of your mother?'

'They were childhood friends.'

'I had wondered why she did not ask for more of me.'

Bueralan did not reply. Pueral's words returned to him: her judgement and summation of his life. He had not smiled in response, as he might have once. He had not thought that she had made a mistake in relation to him. Wordlessly, he had watched her ride down the road. Around her, Cynama was awakening, and butterflies scattered in colours while people moved out of her way. He remembered the child's words — *call only when what is at stake is innocence* — and thought, once again, of her name, the name that he did not know.

'Do you plan to go out there today?'

'No,' he said.

'You shouldn't delay too long,' the cartographer said, walking back upstairs. 'We must all return to the homes of our childhood eventually.'

3.

Before the morning's sun rose, Lord Elan Wagan began to scream.

Heast lay in the tent he shared with the young baker's apprentice, Jacrc, and awaited the start of it. He had been awoken by the shrieks on the first nights – loud, piercing sounds that had come down the mountain with them – but his body soon remembered the pattern and, like the others on Wila, he awoke before Lord Wagan began to scream. He would lie in the salted dark until the noise turned into a whimper, the ending brought by the healer, Reila. Then, he would listen to the silence that followed with a certain pride in the men and women around him. Not once had he heard any complaint, not once had he stepped from his tent to find anger, or resentment, though he could well have understood it if it did appear. But those around him had nothing but patience for a man driven mad and for whom not even death would provide a release.

That was ultimately why they had that patience, Heast knew. When Lord Wagan had returned from Leera, his face a bloody ruin, his mind clearly lost, and his body held to the back of his horse only by ropes, Heast's nature had urged him to free the man: a simple thrust of his dagger, a human kindness, an end to the cruelty Lord Wagan had endured. He would not have regretted the death: he had provided such kindness to other soldiers, to men and women who clung by a thread to a destroyed life.

Yet he had not done so. Quietly pushing up the flap of the tent he shared, he made his way beside a cold wind through the narrow lane of shadowed tents, unsure if his inaction had proved to be the kindest choice. He had owed Muriel Wagan more than the knowledge that the ghost of her mad husband haunted the ruins of Mireea, yet she deserved better than the sad responsibility she had now. Among the thousands of tents packed tightly across Wila, his sympathy was not isolated, and her plight not singular. Not one man or woman had left Mireea without a member of their family rising from the ruins, without a friend returning whom they had already mourned. Not one person on Wila was spared the awful realization that, for all of them, such a fate awaited. For most, though, that burden was shared. It was shared among themselves and in their families, if they still had them. They were not isolated by leadership and familial estrangement as Muriel was with her position and her daughter.

At the soggy edge of Wila, Heast stared out across the dark ocean and urinated. Far out in it, he could see small dots of light. Navy ships out in the ocean, perhaps, or one of the keeps that sat on islands around Nale and which doubled as lighthouses and barracks. But it was far enough that he could not be sure about either, which pleased him. He had worried originally that the navy would set ships around the island after the mobs had appeared on the day the ghosts did; if he had been the Soldier, he might have done that for safety; and he might have done it because he feared that Gaerl would arrive. But in the weeks that followed, nothing had happened beyond the extra postings of the guards. He learned also – through the few papers and pamphlets that fell to the island, now that the deliberate dropping had ended – that curfews had been enacted on Yeflam and that Zaifyr's trial was going ahead. None of it, though, had anything to do with the Mireeans. It appeared that they had become much like the long ropes next to him, leading out into the water, where heavy bags of waste bobbed.

It was there that he heard the oar, the soft splash of it, and saw the outline of a boat a moment later.

It was a small boat, no more than a dinghy, and it held two figures, one large and one small, to judge by their silhouettes. They came directly from the northern shore, using the night's dark to hide their approach from the guards on the bridge above, and the screams of Lord Wagan had covered the sound of the oars – all except the last few strokes, which were done in nude silence. As the two men became clearer, Heast made out the scarred serious face of Kal Essa from the smaller shadow, and a dust-stained man he did not know as the second.

Splashes echoed as he stepped into the fetid water, raising a hand to grab the edge of the boat and help guide it to the shore.

'Turn it over, lift it,' he whispered. 'We cannot leave it on the beach.'

'Aye,' Essa responded quietly.

It would have looked ridiculous, had any guard glanced

down onto Wila and seen an overturned boat moving quickly and quietly through the packed tents.

'Captain Essa,' he said softly, the front seat against his shoulders. 'I trust that there is a good reason for this risk?'

'The tribesman insisted. I held out against it, but he told us that there would be movement down the mountain. It's been priests, mostly, though some look like soldiers.' Essa had thrust his arms up to the centre seat, unable to carry it on his shoulders. 'The tribesman told us that the Leeran leaders would be with them. I held him until it sure looked like that.'

Heast grunted, unsurprised. 'Do you have a name, tribesman?'

The third man, who was both taller and heavier than Heast and Essa, looked like a brawler, a man who fought with his fists as well as an axe, though the Captain of the Ghosts knew that he did neither. Stained in dirt, he wore heavy brown breeches, a long dark-green tunic and, in the folds around his neck, layers of a black-and-brown scarf that could be wound around his tanned face and heavy brown-red beard and hair. He would do that when he stepped onto the empty plains of the plateau, against the strong winds that circulated the grasslands that the pacifist tribes had lived upon since the War of the Gods.

'My name is Kye Taaira,' the man said. 'And I have come to deliver you a message, Captain Heast.'

4.

Ayae could not sleep.

In the last week, after she and Faise and Zineer had returned to their house, after they had left Zaifyr, her five hours of regular slumber had been drained from her, taken in fitful hours, in twisted minutes, and in the counting of seconds. Now, for the third night in a row, she sat alone long after Faise and Zineer had gone to bed, her hands clasped around a cup and a heated copper kettle beside her while she tried to read. The thin book before her was poetry, written by one of the women who had built the first City of Ger. It focused on the elements and described them as wilful, childish, demure and stubborn. It was awful, but neither it, fatigue nor tea could free her from the strange sensation of teeth pulling at her skin, as if something was trying to consume her.

'It is the Leeran god. She approaches,' Zaifyr had said to her on the day she left. 'The sensation is different to what you will feel before the remains of the gods.'

She frowned. 'Why would she be different?'

'Because we have something she believes is her own.' The two were standing on the right tower of Aelyn's house, the afternoon's sun high above the shifting mass of Leviathan's Blood and a cold wind she barely felt rising from it. The charms in Zaifyr's hair and on his wrists caught the light. 'In that way, she is like all the gods. She feels entitled to the world.'

Ayae did not want to believe that, but after the haunts had filled the city, after she had seen the fear in the eyes of men and women, she had felt the seeds of doubts about Zaifyr's plan to return. When she had heard from Jae'le that, at the end of the trial, Zaifyr could be sent back to his prison, she had begun even to fear for him. What surprised her, however, was Jae'le himself. Since the ghosts had filled the city, Zaifyr's brother had sat in the rooms below, surrounded by books, helping with the research. His long thin fingers turned pages slowly, carefully, as if he was dissecting an animal.

Pushing away the thought, she had said, 'Why doesn't the child have a name?'

'A god's name is chosen by mortals.' Zaifyr shrugged, his charms glinting. 'It is said that when the name is spoken, she will go to that man or woman and bestow on them a gift. At least, that is what was always said.'

Before her, the ocean heaved, its black waves crashing against the pillars that held Yeflam. 'What will happen when she gets here?'

'We will be offered a chance to end this war without building armies and without slaughter.' He did not hesitate in his reply.

'What happens if they don't see the threat you do?'

'I will not go back to the tower.' There was no give in his voice. 'How are Faise and Zineer?'

'It has been quiet since the ghosts,' she said, allowing him to change the topic. 'I think — well, I think everything changed.

I haven't seen anyone follow us for a week now. The papers are full of stories about you, but there are a few stories about Illaan's father and an internal fight within the Traders' Union. Still, they have a passage to Zoum at the end of the week that has been organized for them. They're taking that, at least.'

'Are you going with them?'

'As far as the border,' she said. 'But there's still so much work to be done.'

She had left the tower a short time later and walked down the stairs to where Faise and Zineer waited. They did not want to leave Yeflam. They had, in fact, tried to argue against going to Zoum, but Ayae had reminded them of Bnid Gaerl. He would not forget them. Maybe he would not pursue them now, not with all the other things going on, but he would eventually. And, perhaps selfishly, Ayae admitted, she also feared what would happen once the child arrived. She could not envisage a scenario in which no one was hurt. When she thought of the trial and its aftermath, she saw again Queila Meina's hand touching her, her skin sunken, her life stolen by Fo's diseases as if she were of no consequence.

And it was because of that fear, that danger that she held above all others, that when in the last moments of the night a knock sounded on the door of Faise and Zineer's house, Ayae opened it.

Outside stood a priest.

He was a tall man, middle-aged, white-skinned. She had seen so many priests of late, but even so, there was something different about this one. He was clean-shaven, his salt-and-pepper hair cut in a harsh military fashion. The last – registered briefly, and not analysed until much later – saved Ayae's life.

As she drew back from the door, the priest, his eyes widening, cried out and leapt to his left to reveal a second man, smaller, stockier, and holding a heavy crossbow. The wooden levers let out a loud twang sound and pain ratcheted up Ayae's arm as, in that split second, her free hand — her left hand — snapped down, the fingers latching painfully around the bolt.

She hurled it back, following the poor trajectory with her body, her right hand ripping the spent crossbow from the shorter man's hands while her left, palm up, crashed the heel heavily into the man's forehead.

The man crumpled, his head snapping back at a painful angle. As if in response, she heard the door at the back of the house crack, as it was kicked in. The priest — false, she knew, to judge by the dark-blue armour that the other man wore — leapt at her, crying out wordlessly, but she shifted her weight and turned to use the man's momentum to throw him across the pavers and into the wooden table she had used to hold the soggy, broken apples she had tried to juggle. She heard it crack, heard him land, but in front of her she saw figures, half a dozen, maybe more, flooding through the back door, and she heard a cry from upstairs.

Her first steps took her through the doorway, her next onto the kitchen table, the hot kettle coming to her grasp as she skidded across it.

Her first hit caught a man across the face, the now-boiling water splashing across him. She struck a woman next, her foot cracking down, a spark flying as her bare foot broke the heavy boot, shattered the bone beneath the leather. The woman grunted. Her short sword thrust forward and her free hand tried to grasp Ayae, but the kettle hit her in the jaw. Bone cracked — and Ayae turned, her hand trapping a thrust sword against her side, feeling the blade cutting as it did, while using the straightened arm of the attacker to lean back and wield her scalding kettle against another in heavy red lines. In a hard arc, the kettle came back round and slammed into the head of the man whose arm she held, sending him to the ground and leaving his sword in her grasp.

The shining copper cast a dull light around the room, illuminating four people still standing, one of them the woman with the broken jaw.

'Zineer!'

No reply to her shout.

Louder, she cried, '*Faise!*'

One of the men in front of her smirked.

Ayae's kettle lashed out, catching him in the face, her stolen sword following. It plunged into his belly and she let go of the handle, stepping back as a pair of swords thrust forward at her. Her kettle came up, heavy and dented, and before the two men knew it, she was on them, her feet striking up sparks as she hammered down on heavy boots, as her free hand slammed against mail, feeling it give soggily into a scream while her kettle lashed out, bashing aside a sword and then cracking the bone in another's arm.

The woman with the broken jaw came last, giving an unsure thrust that Ayae stepped from easily, so slow that her hand could close around the woman's wrist and twist—

The sword dropped and the kettle crashed again into her jaw, its copper form finally giving in against its punishment, caving in against the broken bone as it struck.

Scooping the blade up, Ayae took the stairs two at a time,

knowing, *knowing* as she came to the last and felt the ocean's breeze through the shattered window illuminated by the first rays of the morning's sun, that she was much too late.

Both Faise and Zineer were gone.

5.

Zaifyr gently closed the frail covers of *Fallen Pyrates* when the white raven arrived. The bird's blue eyes scanned the room from the open window, looking first at him, then at Jae'le.

It was he, the man who had once been the Animal Lord, who rose to approach it, whose left hand stroked its head, and whose right untied the message attached to its leg. The bird was calm, pleased with the attention, its pleasure one of adoration. The bird's ancestor, a large, heavy and shaggy creature, a monster of a bird, in truth, had been a gift from Jac'le to his sister, Tinh Tu. In Salar, the offspring of the first white raven, the immortal bird, had roosted in the country's fabled libraries, neither male nor female until spring, and then only one gender or the other for two weeks. After the Five Kingdoms, the hunting of the white ravens had begun and those that remained now lived around the fortress Tinh Tu had named after her lost country. The birds were now seen solely when she wished to communicate with family, an event, Zaifyr knew, that was as rare as the birds themselves.

'You do not need to read it.' He rose, hoping that he was

wrong, but knowing — *knowing* — that he was not. 'She is not coming to Yeflam.'

'No,' his brother replied. 'She is not.'

The note, a rolled piece of thin paper, was passed to him.

Brothers,

I will not be coming to Yeflam, not for a trial, not for war. I will not lie and claim that it is with regret that I write this, for I do not.

Family, the fabled Queen of Taln wrote, is the site of love and shame. For our family, no other words hold so much truth: for with our love we shame each other by allowing thoughtless acts. A trial held in Yeflam is one. A call to war in Yeflam is such, again.

As the eldest of us, as the guides to your sisters and brother, you both suffer from the secrecy and arrogance of the eldest siblings. You act in the belief of your right by your superiority of first birth, believing that your younger siblings will fall into line soon enough. You believe that they will recognize that they are wrong, that you are right. After Asila, Jae'le persuaded his sisters to give up their beloved homes and convinced his remaining brother to become a vagabond, and it is because of this that I will not travel to you, not to witness such a choice forced upon our sister again.

In your solitude, brothers, I do not believe you have understood the damage you have done to your siblings, and the damage that you will bring to Aelyn by forcing a trial and act of war upon her. I do acknowledge the need for action, should this child be indeed responsible for what Zaifyr claims, but for as long as we have all lived, we could wait a month, a year, a decade, to ensure that our family is not hurt.

Your sister,
Tinh Tu

Zaifyr folded the note carefully into squares, the curled ends resisting at first, until they were firmly creased.

The letter stung, especially with the growing sense of teeth digging against his skin. He did not believe the words were entirely fair – his sister clearly did not know that Eidan was with the child, did not know the agreement that Jae'le and the Enclave had entered into – but yet, he had to admit that they stung also because there was truth in her words. There was *always* truth to Tinh Tu's words. In them, he heard the echo of Aelyn's accusations that he did not care for her own desires, her wants, and knew that she was not wrong. He did not plan to let the child leave Yeflam. When he relaxed his control, he saw the dense layers of haunts around him, the generations upon generations of dead men and women who whispered for warmth and food and he believed himself right, where Aelyn was not.

At the window, the white raven shook, stretched it wings, and drifted to the copy of *Fallen Pyrates*, its thick beak nudging the cover. The book was the first slim history written by Bele Ferna, an elderly scholar whose academic history had become mixed with the popular style of fiction used in various mercenary novels. Ferna had, Zaifyr knew, done serious work in his youth, but the ugly yellow cover of grand pirate books and quotes from a retired mercenary captain on the cover lent it very little weight. But the author had died in Yeflam, and his body remained in the stone crypts, and Zaifyr had hoped that he would prove useful. Unfortunately, Ferna, who retold his story through the explorations of a young woman who dived for treasure in Leviathan's Blood, wrote mainly about the wrecks around the Eakar, about the fortunes still there, and viewed the stories of a siren who lured vessels to the coast to be nothing but a metaphor for greed.

For a moment, Zaifyr saw Aelyn, caught in the desire of her brother, being pulled to a jagged shoreline that promised only wreckage . . .

6.

Ayae went out of the window.

A trampled garden lay below. Heavy boots had left tracks through the mud, leading to a broken fence and a narrow lane behind Faise and Zineer and their neighbour. From there, heavy boots led out to the empty street, the morning's sun falling through the shadows, illuminating the dirt on the path. *Left.* Ayae moved quickly, her bare feet barely hitting the stones as she ran, her mind throwing up the images of the bedroom: the torn sheets, the broken table, and the blood across floorboards to the window sill.

Ayae ran on the edge of her control, her limbs warm and loose. She did not feel the morning cold and she knew that she could move faster, but fought the urge, afraid of what would happen if she did. Her earlier recognition that her power would manifest only when she lost control lay in the back of her mind, but she pushed it away. She had to stay in control. She had to keep her mind clear. She could not afford to make a mistake, not now. Faise and Zineer were not broken apples she could replace, juice on her fingers that she could wash away, pulp across the ground she could clean. She had to stay in control, had to trust that the speed she moved at was faster than any individual could run, that it was fast enough to catch a group with two prisoners.

As the morning's sun rose higher, Ayae could make out the shapes of carriages ahead.

They were at the bottom of the curved road and she heard the cries as the dark-blue-armoured guards saw her.

She could count fifteen, sixteen. Ten horses, but six of them were not attached to the two carriages.

The sword in her hand straightened and along the steel flames flickered to life. Shouts from the soldiers reached her ears. *Go!* Followed by *She's here!* None wore the pale-blue armour of the Yeflam Guard who enforced the curfew that had kept the streets quiet since the Million Ghosts. Their voices became indistinct, the cries a mix of panic and shouts as she closed in on them. A long whip rose and the crack of it ripped through the morning's quiet, the largest of the carriages shuddering into a run just as four men and two women quickly pulled themselves onto their horses.

Ayae ran through them.

A short charge with her burning sword caused the horses to baulk, but they were too well-trained to throw their riders, too disciplined to flee, and the narrow gap between them that she aimed for was filled with cuts and slashes and she was forced to parry, dodge and drop beneath the attacks while not slowing her run. Her bare feet twisted, the concrete tearing at her skin as she slid beneath the last swing, that of a heavy axe.

Then she came face to face with a line of the unmounted soldiers.

The line crumpled as she hit it, her burning sword battering aside the heavy weapon she met first, slashing deep across the face of the man as she tried to force her way through the soldiers. Her momentum took her up onto the chest of the soldier, using it to rise into the air, to launch herself over the men and women. She blocked a second cut, made a wild slash with her sword and almost — the road leading to the carriage beckoned emptily as she landed — made her way through, but the mounted soldiers came charging and she felt a blade cut into her shoulders.

Her blade swept around impossibly fast and cut the following soldier from his horse. The animal rose on its legs and she dodged back. More riders came and Ayae felt her control slip as she met the thrust of another woman. She twisted the weapon out of the woman's grasp and grabbed her arm to pull her from the horse. She could feel the warmth in her own body, close, so very close to overwhelming her, and saw the woman recoil from the heat in Ayae's hand. The mail sleeve began to melt, burning it into the skin of the soldier as the horse, feeling its coat smoulder, recoiled in fear and reared, throwing the woman across the stone road. Ayae took the woman's fallen blade, longer than her first, and watched as fire immediately ran along its steel.

The next attack that came to her was slow and clumsy, and she side-stepped it, her blades cutting through the unmounted man's face with shocking ease. The following attack felt slower, the charge of a pair of horses at nothing more than a walk; she avoided both and her blades cut quickly, violently through those who had become no more than lethargic, ugly actors around her. Their mouths opened to cough blood. Their gazes betrayed fear, anger. Their arms rose to become stumps. Fire caught on the hems of their cloaks and flickered poorly as if it were deciding whether to burn, now that it was separated from her. She felt a touch of her old fear, that the fire would cover her, a cold shock that sped up the flames on the cloaks, brought the smell of smoke and burning flesh to her nose. A cry for mercy from the desperate rider cradling her twisted arm – the last soldier, *the last* – finally brought Ayae to a stop and she turned to the bridge that had taken Faise and Zineer.

A single figure waited there.

Leaving the weeping woman, she approached the familiar man. It was not until she reached the foot of the bridge that she realized it was the false priest. 'Stop right there.' He had thrown off the robe and wore the same dark-blue mail as the other soldiers. On his right arm was the insignia of an over-turned sky. 'You will not cross this bridge,' he said, the fury in his voice overriding his very real fear, fear that showed each time his eyes glanced at the dead and dying behind Ayae. 'You will stay here in Mesi, Cursed. Should you leave it, the wife of Zineer Kanar will be killed.'

'Where is she?' Ayae demanded.

'I provide you with proof of our intentions.' He ground the words out and raised his hand, revealing a bloody cloth in his clenched hand. 'Commander Gaerl wants you to know that if you do not cross this bridge, no more will be taken from her.'

A flame flickered on his clothes, a single, isolated note on the hem of his trousers.

'Zineer Kanar will be held accountable for his crimes,' the man continued. 'He will be punished by sword or by rope for what he has done, and if his wife is found innocent, then she will be returned—'

The words turned into a scream.

The flame, multiplying with sudden angry speed, raced up his trousers, up his chest and to his hair. He made to run, but found that he could not, the fire having set into the skin of his legs, the skin peeling, bubbling, bursting and turning black. He cried out, but Ayae ignored him and picked up the bloody cloth he had dropped, a cloth that the fire had not even singed.

Inside was a finger.

Ayae made her way to the lone, sobbing survivor of the soldiers who had taken Faise and Zineer.

She had questions.

7.

'You must understand,' said Kye Taaira, 'on the Plateau, to be without violence is strength.' He sat across from Heast at the large table in Lady Wagan's tent, the morning's sun soaking the taut cloth walls, leaving them warm to touch. 'We are taught to live in harmony with the grass of the plains, with the trees, the birds and the insects. We are taught to protect and herd the horses and the buffalo. We are taught that no blood must be spilt. Our women bear the burdens that they are born with and our men carry them on litters during times of bleeding. Our children are born above the ground, delivered in high wooden beds that we must burn after. We grow gardens from dirt that we purchase in the markets of Mireea, the vegetables and fruit planted in the back of carts. We drink from water we catch in towers. We wrap ourselves in cloths made by careful hands. We drain the blood of our dead into jars, our shamans watching that no drop spills. All of this and more we do without violence. Our ancestors demand it of us.'

'We are not on the Plateau.' Heast's steel leg was stretched out before him, the other curled under his chair. On the table between them lay a sparse breakfast. 'Your ancestors have no voice here.'

The tribesman began to pull the old leather gloves he wore off his hands, one finger at a time. 'Yours speak enough for them.'

'Do you mean the ghosts in Mireea?' Muriel Wagan sat beside Heast, her exhaustion clearly evident to him. On the other side of her sat Reila, the healer, quiet and grey-haired. At the door, the lean figure of Caeli stood guard, one ear and eye on what was taking place behind her, the other on the sandy, tent-riddled landscape of Wila. 'I cannot imagine that they would interest the tribes or their ancestors.'

'What happens to you, happens to us, Lady Wagan.' Kye picked up a thin piece of day-old bread. 'The Leeran Army has come to us.'

'How so?'

'A small tribe by the name of Entia first encountered them,' the man said, tearing the bread with his thick fingers. 'They welcomed the soldiers with offers of food and water, but the men and women who arrived were only interested in chattels. They took the Entia captive, though the tribe outnumbered the soldiers three to one. But the tribe responded as they should: they became weights to be dragged, they reacted without violence. In response, the Leerans took the carts that held their food and loaded the prisoners on to the back. It was this that drew the attention of all the tribes, and I do not doubt that the Leerans knew that they were being watched.'

'They did not come looking for slaves, did they?' Muriel Wagan asked. 'They did not come to take prisoners when they marched up the Mountain of Ger.'

'No, they did not,' Kye Taaira agreed. 'However, they did take the Entia with them after they left. We believe they were taken to be sold, an opportunity that presented itself, not design. The design of the Leerans was quite different, their intent dictated by the young woman at their head. From a distance, it was clear that the soldiers followed her in a fashion akin to worship, for though beautiful, she wore no armour and carried no sword.' He dipped the torn bread into salted water and ate a piece. Once he had swallowed, he said, 'Of the forty soldiers with her, only one was but worthy of note, and that was the man who stood by her side, always. In appearance, he was no older than I, but he was much stronger. Across his back he carried iron spears of such a weight that no ordinary man could hold them all as he did. Our shamans said that he was a powerful ancient being, a man our oldest ancestors knew and feared.

'Soon, the man staked forty members of the Entia to the ground with his spears. He did it with ease, even when, in panic, members of the tribe forgot their vows and fought him. But no blow they struck caused the breaking of skin, or the stopping of his actions. He drove spears into the chests of the Entia, plunged the iron through their bodies and into the ground, to carry their life to the spirits of our ancestors.'

In the silence that followed, Heast watched the tribesman dip more torn bread, eat more. He observed the man and his movements, and after a while, he said, 'Your ancestors rose, did they not? They became ghosts, as in Mireea.'

'They did, but it was not as in Mireea, Captain,' Kye Taaira said. 'The beautiful girl led her soldiers to each of the spears. Then, one by one, she tore open the chest of the Entia. She let their blood flow into the land, to awaken our ancestors' spirits, and then drew them out and held them in her hands. The power she wielded made the shamans tremble. According to the oldest and wisest of us, she then had her soldiers consume the parts of the body she held, to bond the ancestor to her soldier. Over the days that followed, after she left the site of her forbidden act, we watched her soldiers change. Some bloated, others shrank, but the melding of our ancestors to flesh could not be denied. Her act was of such horror that, for the first time in a thousand years, all our shamans gathered in one place to discuss how all the tribes would respond. You must understand: our ancestors were not kind men and women. They were warriors when Ger stood tall, when he kept the elements chained, and when an approach to him was one met with steel. They did not take kindly to his death, did not agree with what our wisest knew, that the violence of the world could not mirror the violence of the gods. In life, they were led by a man named Zilt; in death, they are still led by him. They have struggled for life ever since their deaths. They have howled for thousands of years. They are furious because our blood is kept from them, because we cremate our dead. They are furious and they lust for a life they once had, and before our eyes, the girl took forty of the worst, took General Zilt himself and those who served beneath him, and led them from the Plateau.'

'And you've been sent to get them back?' Lady Wagan asked.

'Yes.'

Quietly, Reila said, 'You are Hollow?'

'Yes,' he said.

Heast regarded the man thoughtfully. The Hollow were rare

figures on the Plateau, rumoured to be drained of their own blood at birth by shamans, the fluid stored in a totem. He had heard it described as an animal, a jar, a twin, and more, but had never met a man or woman who claimed to be Hollow to ask them. They were hidden, feared figures, the only defence in a pacifist land against enemies that came to the Plateau. They rarely left to pursue those enemies.

'You did not come here first, did you?' Muriel Wagan asked. 'You would have gone to the Kingdoms of Faaisha. They are closer, and the fighting has moved there.'

'You are correct.' The tribesman placed the bread upon the table, reached into the folds of his clothes, and pulled out a letter. 'After I left the Plateau, I made contact with the Lords of Faaisha. The Leeran Army had made its way over the border, routing Marshal Faet Cohn. The land was torn apart in ways that I could not understand and I was told that the Leeran soldiers were responsible. They had taken full measure of Marshal Cohn's forces, I am afraid to say. Those men who were caught were crucified. Parts of their bodies were eaten, as well. As you might imagine, panic is quite prevalent in the other parts of the country.'

'So they sent you here?' A sharpness entered Muriel's voice. 'Do the Lords of Faaisha truly think I would be sympathetic to their plight?'

'I imagine not.' He passed the letter across the table. 'It was why I was instructed to hand this letter to the captain and not you.'

Heast took the envelope and, across from him, the tribesman returned to the soggy salted bread.

The seal of the letter broke easily. The single page inside

unfolded to reveal a simple image, sketched in the middle of the page. It was a square split into two colours, the top red, the bottom black. Over it was the uncoloured image of a planet, with the continents sketched in black.

Wordlessly, Heast passed the letter to Muriel.

'Do you know what this image is?' she asked the tribesman.

'I am told that it is the insignia of Refuge.' Taaira dipped another piece of bread. 'A man by the name of Baeh Lok told me this. He said that he had drawn it for Lord Tuael.'

'Where is Lok now?' Heast asked.

'He is dead.'

8.

In the dark corners of his mother's rundown estate, Bueralan's childhood still remained.

Earlier, the saboteur had stepped into the overgrown gardens around the house. Beneath the frail cloud-broken light of the afternoon's setting sun, he searched for dried wood, leaves, anything that he could use to restart the fire inside the house. He would need it during the evening to cook and to keep warm, especially once the rain returned. Yet, despite the honest need and the two and more decades that separated him and his mother's death, he felt her disapproval follow him around the yard and back inside, where he placed the pile of kindling on the stone floor. She would have demanded the servants take it outside once she found it and her displeasure when she found him would have been filtered through her resignation that the house, the grounds, and her only son would all be nothing without her.

'*You.*' The fire at her deathbed had been strong — stronger than the one he built now. She had lifted her frail hand when she spoke, pointing to the shadowed doorway, to where Zean stood. 'You make sure he does not do something stupid in sight of the Queen.'

'Yes, ma'am.'

The relationship between his mother and Zean had always been formal. She had shown him little kindness after he had been purchased. Bueralan had no memory of her using his name, not even the night that the two were introduced. He had been no older than four then, and Zean six. His father, whose only defining memory to his grown son now was of a largeness that verged on fat, had spoken the ritual to bind them. It wasn't until years later, after his father's death, that Bueralan learned that his mother was against slavery, against the blood bonding of boys and girls from Ilatte to noble-born Ooilan children.

What his father had said to her to allow the ritual to take place, Bueralan could not imagine. In his first days in the court from which his mother had exiled herself, he had been told by many how much she had loved her husband, and he had puzzled over the grudging respect strangers gave the words and the bitterness with which her friends said them. *She had loved him* was how the sentence began before it tailed off in an awkward silence. Only now did he understand the sacrifice implied, if not the reason for it.

He recalled her face the night that he and Zean were introduced. In the ceiling of the room where he sat now, the lamps had shone, the shadows cast against it by those on the ground a hideous puppetry. The huge form of his father was before him, a small table with a stone bowl and knife on it. But it was his mother's face that he remembered most, as if the flicker of the fire he had built recast it for him: the still mask she wore, the constructed facial features, the downcast eyes: the face of a woman who hated everything taking place before her.

'Until he dies, Bueralan, this boy will be your brother.' He had asked later if his father had had a blood brother, but his mother had told him no. 'You have a great responsibility to him,' his father continued, 'for he will bear your ills and your shame, and suffer where you will not. What happens to him will be your responsibility.'

Before the fire, Bueralan's hand touched the pouch around his neck.

He should have saved them all, he knew. Not just Zean. Kae, Ruk, Liaya and Aerala: they had all been his responsibility.

His mother would disagree with him, if she was here. She would tell him that life is not the responsibility of another. You cannot decide who lives and who dies. She had said that more times than he could remember. She would say it to him now: she would reach out for the cold stone that lay against his chest. She would roll it around in her hand. She would ask him why he thought Zean was his responsibility. He would tell her simply that he had failed him. That he had failed all of his soldiers and if he could bring them all back, he would.

Bueralan picked up a branch and fed it into the fire. His mother would not be moved by the argument. She would tell him that he had lost soldiers before. That he had lost friends as well. She would be right: death was a part of the work he might never return to, a truth that could not be denied.

'What happened to your family?'

He said the words to Zean a week after the ritual, the stitched scar over the palm of his hand leaving it stiff and all but useless, as it would be for another month. Before him sat the older boy, holding his own left hand. Before them, spread out, were toys. He did not remember what they were. Horses, probably.

Or soldiers, the wooden figures parents gave their children. Yet he could remember clearly how Zean had waited very carefully for him to pick first from the toys, how he had followed Bueralan's lead.

'I don't know,' he said, after a moment. 'They gave me up when I was young.'

Both had been too young to understand how parents on Illate gave up their children, but the young Bueralan had said, 'I could help you return home.'

Zean had shrugged, uncomfortable, but unable to say no.

Bueralan had tried to be true to his words, though. With the other's help, he had stolen food from the kitchen, prepared a bag to carry while he sneaked him into the back of his father's carriage, only to be horrified when Zean returned, still hidden. He did not know where to go, he said, and so the pair had made maps, copied them from books in his mother's library and stolen more food. On the third attempt, Bueralan had packed a change of clothes – 'It was cold,' Zean had said after the second failure – and had given him gold, neither stolen, but rather his own.

'Where was I to go?' an older Zean asked him, after they had fled Ooila. 'I had no family outside that carriage, no one to help me. You were the only one I had.'

9.

Zaifyr watched the white raven drift into the morning's sun, quietly, and without a reply attached to its leg. Both Jae'le and himself had tried to compose one, but could not.

Zaifyr had a few names of dead men and women he could call up, but he had yet to bring the remains of one into Yeflam. None was close enough. They were lost, in mountains, or in towns that no longer existed, or in another continent simply too far away. He had to find others, he had to find men and women close to him, though the calm he needed to search both books and the dead for them was difficult to find. When he closed his eyes, he saw the tower where he had been kept, saw the walls that closed in and the dirt that was beneath his feet. The threat of being sent back to that prison had lodged in him a fear, not of what he was doing – he knew that Jae'le had agreed to it because he was afraid that Yeflam would become Asila again – but because he feared that he might not be able to convince the Keepers and his family about the child. Tinh Tu's reply felt like a prophecy, an echo from a future where his trial had finished and he had already been found lacking. Yet, he knew that he had to push beyond that, that he had to continue his search. He must not fail to show Yeflam that the child was responsible for pain and suffering on a scale that they could not imagine.

At the top of the tower stairs, Zaifyr breathed deeply from the cold air and tried to control the frustration he felt. Around him, a splash of haunts drifted: men, women, children, all of them faint silver sketches. Animals blended in: mice, cats, birds and insects, their forms at first a flutter of light that slowly began to meld together as the generations of the dead collaged over each other, threatening to slowly explode into an endless mirror of light and reflection.

He had failed as a brother. He had planned too much around the reliability of his siblings, yet had given them no reason why they should help him. Oh, he could point to the fact that they had made no effort to contact him after he had stepped, half blind, from the crooked tower: he could point to that and note the failure of all of them but Jae'le on a familial level, but he had not tried to correct it. He had listened with less than half an ear to their conversations as the years drifted by, passed less than that in an eye over their letters, a quiet and solitary figure behind Jae'le. He thought little of Aelyn's Yeflam, less of her Keepers. He had not seen Tinh Tu's new library. He had said no to her requests repeatedly, even the one time she left her fortress to speak to him face to face. He kept little track of Eidan and his projects, could not begin to fathom what his plans were now.

He rubbed at his face. He had not slept since Ayae and he had last stood here in the tower, but he was not alone. All who felt the child's approach would be lying awake.

Zaifyr gazed across Yeflam, tracing the bridges and the

circular stone continents, seeing all the roads that led to Nale and nothing beyond it. Only after a moment did he notice the figure on the stone edge of the tower's wall.

It was black, but not in the sense that its skin was like a man or woman's pigmentation. It was, instead, a smooth black, dark as the ocean around him, covering the being so densely that it appeared to have been created without light and formed by the absence of it. It was not tall, or large, and no bigger than his hand, nor wider than his palm. Its eyes were tightly shut and showed no sign of ever being open.

From it came a chill that Zaifyr was familiar with.

'Qian.' Its voice was that of a male, deep and adult. 'I greet you.'

'That's not my name,' he replied. 'Not any more.'

'My apologies.'

'Your apologies? I don't even know what you are to accept that.'

'Perhaps it is I who should ask for an apology, then.' Its smile was a sardonic, inky curl. 'Will you be quick? I have not much time.'

Zaifyr stepped closer to the black figure, a sharp cold biting against his skin. 'Why does a dead man have to worry about time?'

'Ah, but that is how you know me.' Its smile widened. 'I am only sorry that I made such a poor impression in our first meeting.'

'I have never seen you before.'

'You have.'

He reached out his hand, closing in on the still black figure, the cold seeping into his fingers as he touched it. 'No, this I have—' He released his cold hand, suddenly. 'You are the soldier from Mireea. The one the child was in.'

'Yes,' it — no, *he* — whispered.

'She destroyed you.'

'She remade me.'

The implication was not lost on Zaifyr.

'She will be here soon,' the small man continued. 'Once she is here, I will not have the independence to speak to you, so I urge you to listen to me, please.'

A Fear Whispered in Your Heart and Mind is a Real Fear

On the continent that Leera, Mireea, the Kingdoms of Faaisha and the Plateau share, there are three gods: Ger, the Warden of the Elements, Maika, the God of Ascension, and Taane, the Goddess of Memory. The final two lie in Leera. Two hundred years ago, the Kingdoms of Faaisha sought to take the land under which the god Taane lies, but that army turned mad, as all do who travel to the end of the northern marshes, and no other attempt was ever made. It has remained in Leeran hands since.

On the Plateau, however, the lack of gods is balanced by what else lies there. It is best to view the whole part of that land as a prison, if you will, one that is maintained by the people who live on it. Yet it is here, I think, that we begin to a see a more honest depiction of this new god.

—Tinh Tu, *Private Diary*

1.

Before Pueral, the coastline lay under the bone-white light of the moon, the black ocean an empty promise that the shore wound around.

She had arrived at Oetalia, the capital of the Fifth Queen's Province, eight days earlier. Her guard of twenty seasoned soldiers, a tracker and a witch followed her from the dirt trails to the stone streets of the capital, a silent ribbon of un-announced black and red. Oetalia was larger than Cynama: spread across an uneven, rocky ground that turned into a ruined mountain, it was broken by half a dozen huge stone canals, the bottoms of which dropped into a darkness that, even when the fractured suns sat directly above, no end could be seen. Elaborate steel bridges stitched the city together over those fractures and, from the rise of the first, Pueral could see a rocky horizon stretched on either side of her. Originally, Oetalia had been the capital of the First Province, and a certain grandeur haunted its narrow streets, a nobility lingering in its steep roads, its long stairways and tall stone buildings.

It also laid claim to the largest population in Ooila, though Pueral could find no evidence of it as she and her company made their way through the streets. She saw men and women and children, but they were furtive, at the edges of lanes, in the shadows of doorways and windows, silent and sullen. *Fear has done what no army could*, she thought, crossing the third bridge, unconcerned by the new sway it had. *It has broken this city, turned its population into refugees.*

The Fifth Queen's castle was a high, severe fortress built on the top of the mountain. It ill-suited the young, pretty queen within.

After arriving at the huge iron gates, Pueral was led through the corridors still armed (a fact, she noted with approval, met with professional disapproval by all her soldiers) and was presented to Queen Dalau Vi before the afternoon's sun had set, but as the last of the butterflies fell to the ground. As the light began to fade, she was taken from the chamber by the Queen herself, led past narrow windows that watched her, until she reached a door that opened into a private room. Inside were a long and lonely table and a pair of high-backed chairs.

'Please,' the Fifth Queen said, 'sit.'

Pueral unbuckled the belt holding her sword and laid the sheathed blade over the table, next to the silver teapot. She took a seat, grateful for it, and to her surprise, watched as the Queen began to pour tea into two cups. 'Three generations ago,' the pretty woman said, holding the steaming pot lightly, 'I was killed by a friendly envoy from another queen. She is the Third Queen now, but was then the Second to my First. I vowed in the next generation that I would never be so betrayed and so I met with no one. After two lives of talking to no one, I wish for conversation, but find that I have only old generals who order me to hide outside my city and claim it is for my safety.'

'Do you need them?' Pueral asked, after thanking her for the hot tea.

'I do.'

'Kill their children.'

'And if they decide they do not need me?'

'Kill them,' she said, simply.

Dalau, the Fifth Queen, smiled faintly and lowered herself elegantly into the chair opposite Pueral. She was a fine-boned figure, a delicate woman of the darkest skin who, though she had left childhood behind, could not abandon her youth. It was easy to view her as a figure in need of direction or control, as if she had not the experience or intelligence necessary to rule. To hear her speak did not dispel the illusion, for her voice was soft and gentle, a confidante's voice, a lover's voice, unable to be otherwise.

'You have a man who has seen the Innocent?' Pueral blew on her tea, then said, 'That is why my Queen sent me.'

'Of course.' The Fifth Queen clapped twice, sharply. 'The First Queen has been the only one to answer my letter. Please tell her that for me.'

Pueral nodded.

She had almost finished her tea in silence when, after a knock on the door, two guards, both in grey-and-white-edged armour, entered with a man between them. A middle-aged man, he had been dressed in soft clothes, and had tight manacles around his wrists, though he appeared neither agitated nor violent. Yet Pueral, gazing at his damaged face, knew that such was not always the case: she could see that his fingers had torn his cheeks, his chin and lips, while across his face was a thick scar made by a knife, a knife that had clearly and intentionally gouged out the man's eyes.

'Ja Nuural cannot see and cannot talk,' the Fifth Queen said. 'His tongue has been cut out as well as his eyes. But if he could talk, he would tell you that he was in charge of a community down on the coast. He ran a research team dedicated to the cultivation of healthy fish, a scheme I have helped to fund. It aims to breed out the poison and disease that have contaminated the fish in Leviathan's Blood.'

Pueral rose from the table and approached the blind and mute man. Closer, she saw that, in addition to his face, Ja Nuural's feet had been damaged, and blood from dried scabs ran across his sole and toes. 'Did he walk from the coast to here?'

'Yes.' The Fifth Queen stood beside her. 'We have tried to care for him, but the best work of our witches and warlocks has been of little help, because once he is alone, he digs at his wounds. His feet first, then his face, as if he cannot decide which has failed him more. We have taken to keeping him chained as best we can, but after a few hours, he begins screaming. He stops only when we unchain him so he can dig at his wounds.'

It was awful and Pueral felt sympathy for the man. 'What makes you think that the Innocent did this to him?'

'He had a letter.'

Pueral had it now, as she led her horse along the ruined coastline.

For the last two days, she and her soldiers had not passed a living creature. The oldest of her group, a man a few years older than her, a tracker by the name of Ae Lanos, had been the first to tie a black stone around his neck. The stone was flecked with glass, a cheap piece. As if compelled, the others, even the witch who rode silently with them, followed his lead, and by morning, when awoken by the smell of blood and salt and the sound of the ocean, Pueral found herself the only one in her party without a stone hung around her neck to catch her soul.

She did not blame them. Against her breast, between the padded cloth and the black steel of her armour, was the stained, tattered letter that the Fifth Queen had given her. It was written in a firm hand, in ink, and it was unsigned. Yet the letter that the man who had lost both his eyes and his tongue had carried lodged in her a very real, very deep fear.

I am far from innocent, it said

2.

'Tell me,' Heast said, 'how did Lok die?'

'Of course.' The tribesman had finished the bread and water and, as he spoke, began to pull his gloves back on. He said, 'I was not originally given the task of delivering you this message. For the most part, I was kept from the discussions of war in Faaisha. I told the story of the beautiful girl twice in the presence of Lord Tuael. The first time, it was before him and his staff. The second time, it was before the Lords of Faaisha, their marshals and Baeh Lok. I thought it strange that he was there, for he was no more than an old sergeant in Lord Tuael's guard, responsible for the training of young lords and ladies in the art of violence. Yet, it became clear in the middle of my story that I was not speaking to the Lords, but to him. It was to him that a message was being delivered. At the end of it, he told Lord Tuael that he would carry a letter to you. They were the only words he spoke.' The tribesman flexed his left hand, the leather making no sound as he did. 'When Lok began his journey, he was given half a dozen men as an escort. Truthfully, I think most served as a guard to ensure that he did deliver Lord Tuael's message —

I overheard one of the soldiers say that Baeh Lok was not the most loyal of men to Faaisha. Still, that was after I had asked to accompany him. I hoped that I would find further evidence of my ancestors and could begin the task I had been set, though of course I did not say that when I made the request. I simply offered to be a guide through the battle zones and Lord Tuael agreed. Baeh Lok saw through the deception, which is why I relate it now, but we reached an agreement that at the border of Faaisha and Mireea we would part and finish our respective duties.'

Everything Taaira said rang with truth to Heast. Baeh Lok would have been close to seventy now, if not already that, and would have known what Kye Taaira was immediately. He would have heard the story and known, like Heast, how rare it was for a Hollow to leave the Plateau. He would have known that the situation was serious.

'It went wrong from the start,' Kye Taaira continued. 'On our fourth night, we were found.'

'You were betrayed?' Muriel Wagan asked.

'No, just unfortunate. We did not leave much of a trail, but Baeh Lok insisted that we take a wide track up through the east, to skirt the ruins of Celp, and then go down through a few of the towns and cities that still stood. He was particularly interested in Maosa, and though I told him that there was an easier route to the border, he would not be swayed. Still, I thought I had found a way through the Leeran forces that were scattered across the land there. But it was not safe. A simple mistake on my part, I am afraid. We were discovered.'

'Were the girl and her companion there?'

'No, it was just soldiers. Her Faithful.'

'Faithful?' It was Reila who spoke, the elderly healer's voice sharp with her sudden intensity. 'To the girl you described?'

The tribesman nodded. 'The name was in common use by the time I arrived in Faaisha. The Leerans claimed she was their god.'

'We had been told,' Muriel Wagan said carefully, 'that she was younger. A child.'

'No.'

'You could not be mistaken?'

'I saw her again,' he said. 'During our escape, I was separated from Sergeant Lok and the six accompanying him. With some difficulty, I reached the border of Faaisha and Mireea. That was where my agreement with the sergeant ended, but I found myself faced with the moral choice of finding the men who had briefly been my companions or abandoning them. I must admit that I felt some obligation to Baeh Lok and his men, but I also knew that I could combine the search for my ancestors with a search for them and so I set out into the lines and camps of the Leeran Army. I found five of the sergeant's guards without much trouble. They had been killed with arrow and sword and their bodies had been nailed to trees, their blood drained cleanly from their bodies. They had borne no insignia and no uniform, but the message was clear, and I feared that I would find the sergeant in a similar state. When I did discover him, however, he was by a river crossing, a two-man patrol dead beside him. He was alive, but his own stomach was a bloody mess, and he knew that he would not survive. He asked me to bring you the letter that you hold. I thought to deny him — what did I care about his task? I did not believe I would get much help from it. The thought must have shown on my face, for he laughed. It was in the face of that laughter that I agreed. It shamed me that I had considered ignoring a final request, despite my duty. I offered to bear him as far as I could as well, but he asked for mercy instead.'

'You killed him?' Lady Wagan asked. 'I thought such a thing would be forbidden?'

'Even were I not Hollow,' he replied, 'you must not mistake pacifism with cruelty. Baeh Lok was in such pain there was only a single cure available.'

'What of the last soldier?' Heast asked.

'I found him on a trail that led to her.' Taaira's voice turned soft, ominous. 'He had been hanged from a tree and his blood drained, as the others had, but it had been done half a day's walk from her camp. It was a mobile outpost, like much of the rest of the Leeran Army, and it was dominated by a series of well-disguised tents. I was lucky that I had not walked into it by mistake. But it was there that I found my ancestors, as well as the girl and the man who had walked across the Plateau. There were other soldiers too, and men and women whom I would later come to identify as priests. Over the two days that I watched, I saw the latter two mingle, and leave the camp in pairs, heading into the Mountains of Ger and, I assume, Yeflam after.' He held his gloved right hand up, much as he had his left, and flexed it. 'It was this path that she herself took days later, in the company of that same man and many of her priests.'

'Your ancestors?'

'They did not follow.' He looked up at the warm roof of the tent. 'If you listen carefully, you can hear them approach now.'

Silence fell around the room. At first, Heast could hear

nothing but the sound of the waves, and beneath that, the movement of life outside the tent, the men and women who spoke and moved on the dirty sand of Wila. But then, as if it were a heartbeat slowly emerging from the womb of a pregnant woman, he began to make out voices. He could not understand the words as they grew louder, and that confused him until he realized that it was a language he did not know. Worse, the language was one that Heast had never heard, and it slowly dawned on him that the words were completely alien, and that the volume in which they were spoken was one that grew and grew until it filled the tent as it wished to do to the world.

3.

The woman screamed for mercy, but Ayae had none.

She had never considered herself a violent person, either in desire, or intention, but she was aware, as she left the soldier of the Empty Sky trying desperately to pull melted armour from her body, her voice caught in the shrill, awful panic of someone in pain, that she had become capable of shockingly violent acts. The realization felt small as she crossed the bridge, the wet length of Faise's finger in her hand, as if the acknowledgement from her conscience was unnecessary, a concession after the fact. The rest of her had already accepted it, condoned it, moved by the knowledge that she was unable to withstand another loss to a deep, integral part of herself that had been damaged when she had lost Mireea.

Lost her *home*.

But not yet her family.

She had met Faise the night she had arrived in Mireea. Huddled in the back of a cart, she had been one of fifteen children to leave Yeflam, where the aid boat from Sooia had come into port shipping water.

Her arrival in Mireea had signified a new part of her life.

Behind her were men and women who were thin, strained and humourless. Her skyline was dominated by the solid wall that had been the edge of her world, the boundary she was forbidden to step beyond. She had, of course, and she had feared that she would be taken, that she would be killed or, worse, that she would draw *him*, Aela Ren, the Innocent, from the empty, scarred land. Her life behind the wall was one without parents, a life of vulnerability that she would only fully appreciate later. The men and women who had led her and the others onto the ship floating low in the water had appeared so straight, so pure, that a part of her childish self had thought all white people were saviours, even when they gave new names to the children whose names they could not pronounce. The orphanage at the end of that journey had appeared before her like a mansion, huge and extravagant, as a sign for a new life.

Inside, the large, red-faced matron who would come to dislike Ayae had led the aid workers and their found children through the big, high-roofed dormitories in an imposing silence. She spoke only when she separated them by gender, the first floor for boys, the third for the girls. The second was the home of the matron and her staff, physically and morally guarding the virtue of the two groups. It was late when the matron finished assigning beds for them all, and in the big window of the girls' dorm, the stars were laid out so clearly that she could see the wide alien spread of them for miles upon miles. Their strange emptiness was a sudden violence and she stood staring at it, while the other children introduced themselves.

It was only when a hand touched her from behind that she

realized she had been ignoring all attempts at conversation. The hand was pudgy and brown, and it belonged to a girl who had the bed next to her.

Beneath Ayae's bare feet, the hard ground began to pass quickly, her speed increasing, the bridge and the dead soldiers falling further behind her.

Xeq, the woman had told her. *The Commander is on Xeq*.

Around her, the streets of Yeflam were beginning to fill, men and women wandering, some in pale-blue armour, others in the robes of priests, their voices seeking to spark ('Today! She will—' '—our Heavens and Hells will return—') but finding little tinder in most of those stepping out. The houses loomed and dipped and the flags of the approaching bridge slipped into view. She would have to cross through Ghaam to reach Xeq, but the path would take her away from Zaifyr. The morning's sun sat high in the sky and the heat from it began to settle into the stones, but for Ayae, there was no chill to be warmed away.

The carriages she chased had left tracks, from the faeces of the horses, to the hard skid of the wheels as they hit the bridge, but Ayae knew that she would not have to search hard for where Faise and Zineer had been taken. The Empty Sky were not secretive. They were proud. They were open. Ayae would be looking for a compound large enough to house private soldiers and carriages, a compound large enough for a man who, in the absence of true military rank, called himself Commander Bnid Gaerl.

'My name,' the girl had said, long ago at breakfast the first morning, 'is Faise.'

They had sat at long tables in the dining room, everything

around Ayae so large it was cavernous. In front of her were rows and rows of food, and all of it looked and smelt strange, from soft, white bread, spreads in jars with labels she could not understand, and fruits of colour and taste that she had never seen or eaten before. She did not know the name of anything that was before her and she had trouble under-standing the conversation taking place around her. Most of the girls and boys in the room spoke the traders' tongue too quickly for her, proficient with it in ways that she and the others who had learned it in Sooia were not.

Yet, for all the strangeness, and not knowing that soon the matron would single her out and speak so threateningly to her, Ayae felt safe.

She had been given new clothes and the girl who sat beside her, who had spoken her name – *Faise*, she remembered re-peating to herself – was now explaining to her slowly what was good to eat and what was not.

Soon, the streets of Xeq began to unravel around Ayae. She had run faster than she thought she could, run harder than she knew she should have, and pain began to creep into her feet, but she did not stop.

Neither did the men and women of the Empty Sky who appeared on the street.

4.

'She has come to watch you fail,' the inky black figure said. 'That is her only goal, her only desire in Yeflam.'

Zaifyr watched the being's movements across the stone edges of the tower. Before each half-jumped step, the creature cocked and turned his head in the direction of the Northern Gate, the gate that the child would enter through. Then the long, four-fingered hands would press onto the hard surface in caution before he moved, taking two steps before turning around to take another, pacing as if trying to shake and dry himself. Yet, he could not have moved so carefully and slowly when he made his way up the tower to stand before Zaifyr, for that climb required a sure and dexterous grip. 'Are you a deceit?' Zaifyr asked, finally.

'Perhaps.' That curled smile presented itself again. 'She has never known it, if so.'

'You can keep your mind from her?'

'She has no interest in what I think.' He dropped into a crouch. 'I am her eyes, but I have more independence than the others she has made, according to your brother.'

'Eidan?'

'Yes.'

'Jae'le should hear this.'

'Tell your older brother in your own time.' The creature's blind gaze settled on Zaifyr, his expression still, like a statue. 'Already she draws near the gate. Soon, she will force me to open my eyes and see where I am. We will both be in trouble if I am still here.'

'How does she not already know?'

'I have fallen into Leviathan's Blood. She believes it only because her attention is elsewhere and she does not like the ocean. I am not that clumsy.'

'She did not make you clumsy,' he said.

'No, she did not.'

'What else does Eidan say?'

'He has not sided with her,' the creature replied. 'It may be hard to see at first. Many will say that he could walk away if he so desired, but it is not true. He is a powerful man, your brother, and all her creations fear him, but she does not.'

It was difficult to imagine his brother was captive. Zaifyr said, 'I will speak with him when he arrives.'

'He will not be able to speak with you. Neither of us will be able to speak once she is here.'

'Then how do you two conspire in Ranan?'

The inky smile twisted sourly. 'She is still a child.'

The child was not omniscient, then. She could see through the eyes of whoever she had made and could exert her will over those living creatures, but after that, she would struggle. In Leera, there would be corners for his brother to hide in, tunnels he had dug, hidden beneath trap doors, surrounded by hard earth. Eidan was not a man given to fancy: he was methodical, exacting in his thoughts, and by slow process he would have found all the parts of Leera he could rest quietly in away from the sensation of being devoured. It was not impossible for Zaifyr to imagine the large man and the small creature in a cave of stone, deep beneath the sweltering marshland. 'What do the two of you plan?'

'She cannot continue,' the creature replied. 'The pain she inflicts cannot continue. No more like me can be made.'

'I thought she had destroyed you,' the charm-laced man said. 'There was nothing of you left after she had used you.'

'She kept me.' The creature's long arms wrapped around itself, the limbs lost against the smooth black skin. 'I cannot explain it, beyond that. I remember a feeling of being caved in, as if my very own being was being crushed. I saw you, but you were not the cause of it — the cause of that suffocating pain I saw later, when I awoke in a cathedral. I came to awareness on a hard floor, with her face above me, looking much as I did as a child. Beneath her eyes I could not move. It was as if I was pinned to the ground by spikes. As she witnessed my anguish, she told me that that was what she would name me, and try as I might to resist it, I answer to it. But I did not suffer the worst. There was one who killed her favourite. For him, she fashioned a charm of a loved one.'

'Where is this charm?'

Anguish shook his head. 'Gone with the man who killed her favourite, but she is here now because of what he did. She did not wish to come here, but after her favourite died, there was no one to take her place, no one to guide her Faithful. She had no choice. It is why you must not waste this opportunity — for if you do, all of us will suffer.'

'I am trying,' Zaifyr said, a touch of frustration in his voice. 'It is difficult, though. I have too many dead who are close to us now.'

'Your brother gave me a name to pass on to you,' the creature said. 'He said that you would not like it, that you would resist it. It is a name that belongs to the ancient dead.'

Zaifyr blanched, grateful that the expression was lost on Anguish, who had begun to fidget on the stone ledge. He could feel the child, stronger than before, which meant that she had reached the outskirts of Yeflam. She would soon step onto the Northern Bridge and the small being's eyes would open. 'The ancient dead are not like you. They are punished by the gods. Where would Eidan get the name of one?'

'He did not say.' Anguish turned on the ledge of the tower, his fingers spread across the stone, ready to launch himself. 'What your brother did say was that beneath Yeflam there was one of the ancient dead. He said that his name was Lor Jix. He was the Captain of *Wayfair*. That is what he said.'

Then he was gone.

5.

Heast pushed aside the cloth door of the tent and stepped out.

The chanting from the bridge was louder. It drifted over the edges of the stone bridge above Wila and washed ashore between the low waves and cold wind from the black ocean. It had roused the Mireeans and they gathered around their canvas homes, in pairs at the furthest point from the bridge, and then in groups of four and five, growing larger and larger until, at the dirty edge of the island, they stood like half a stained ring. 'Caeli,' he said, not turning to face the woman behind him. 'Find Lieutenant Mills. Tell her to make sure the guard is spread throughout the island as a precaution.'

'Sir.'

After she had left, the Captain of the Ghosts turned to the stone bridge above him.

It had filled so that he could see men and women standing around the thick edges at the end furthest from the gate. As the chant rose and fell, he saw a young boy climb onto the wall of the bridge. He had dark, olive skin and was thin and without a shirt. Timidly, he rose once he was sure of his perch, and stared further up the bridge. As he did so, another boy followed him, this one white. A tall, olive-skinned third followed and then, lastly, a black girl climbed up. Once all four were up, they began to move along the ledge. Heast imagined that they had seen lines of brown-robed men and women on their knees at the gate of the bridge and, drawn by the chant, had decided to make their way there, unaware that beneath the robes, hands clutched knives and swords.

'Do you think the girl is our enemy?' Muriel Wagan said, standing at his side in the door of the tent. 'That she is the child Zaifyr spoke of?'

'Yes.'

'Good.'

Heast turned to her, but she did not meet his gaze. Instead, she watched the bridge, watched the children who were moving slowly but surely along it.

'Since we left Mireea, I have had dreams where I kill a child,' she said quietly. 'It is not every night. Just once a week, maybe twice. I see her playing in an empty room. She has hair like spun gold and is a very pretty child. Each time I see her, I approach with a knife in one hand and a cloth in the other. As I get near, the room she is in falls away, revealing the ruins of Mireea. The ground shakes with earthquakes and giant bones appear suddenly. Through it all, she does not acknowledge me, not until I step on gravel. When that happens, she turns to me and smiles. I reach for her, but my hands are old and bent and it is too late.'

'And now?'

'Beautiful young women have never been in my dreams, Aned.'

He smiled, but his humour was short-lived. 'You know what has been asked of me, don't you?' he said, after a moment.

'Lord Tuael is in a state of desperation and has reached out for you,' she said. 'He wants you to fight for him, even though you have no soldiers.'

'Baeh Lok agreed with him.'

'That is why you will go.' The Lady of the Ghosts stepped out of the doorway. Her feet were pale and bare and the crumpled edge of her red dress trailed in the dirty sand behind her, obscuring the prints that she left. 'You would stay if I asked, I imagine, but it would sit sourly inside you. Soon enough you would hold it against me, and rightly so. That is not who we are,' she said, as he followed her. 'You have done more than enough for Mireea in Yeflam. You have been more than the Captain of the Spine. But what happens now is my responsibility. The trial of Zaifyr is going ahead and Lian Alahn has begun to push for my release for that. He has assured me that within the week I could find myself in the Floating Cities.'

'Le'ta will not easily stand for that. Nor will Gaerl,' Heast said. 'If they find out I am no longer here, they might—'

'—do the same thing they would do if you were here,' she finished. 'I have Caeli to deal with those moments. You have said that more than once to me. But I suspect that our friend Benan Le'ta will be more interested in what Lian Alahn is doing than in what I am. In fact, I am planning on it. While those two push and pull on each other, I plan to see how well aligned Aelyn Meah and I are in terms of the Leerans and their political foothold in the area.'

'You think to turn her to war?' he asked.

'No, that is beyond me.' At the edge of the beach, she stopped. Above her was the length of the stone bridge, solid and immovable, the four children in the middle of it. 'There is no reason for you to stay, Aned,' she said. 'Not after a soldier of Refuge has made a request to his captain. Not after he has died to make it.'

Above, the chant continued without interruption. The first child halted on the bridge, his arms outstretched as he turned his head into the crowd. A voice had called out to him. Heast had not heard it, but the body language of the boy, and of those behind him, was that of guilt, of being caught in the middle of an act that they knew to be dangerous and forbidden.

'The Lords of Faaisha will be reluctant to listen to me,' he said. 'I will have nothing to offer them but myself.'

'You are not there to be a marshal,' Muriel replied.

On the bridge, a pair of blue-armoured guards were emerging from the crowd. They were hidden behind the children and Heast could not make out their features, could not see if they were male or female, but the morning's sun glinted off their armour as they reached up for the children, to lift them down onto the safe path of the bridge.

'Do you hear that?' she asked.

The chanting had begun to fade, the words disappearing into a silence that was soon across Wila as well.

'She is here,' Heast said.

6.

She grabbed the bridle of the first horse to reach her, its rider already raised in the saddle to slash down—

Ayae's weight dropped heavily and, dragging down on the leather reins, she skidded under the horse. Unprepared, the beast rolled and the rider crashed down behind her, the following men and women and horses colliding with the pair. Ayae twisted through the failing legs, her hands and feet finding brief purchase in each turn and tumble, using pieces of metal, skin and fur to push herself through, to fall out into the empty space at the end of the tangle of flesh, her left foot twisting as she landed. The leg of her trousers tore open against the stone before she came to a stop, before she could rise.

Ahead of her was the open gate of a large estate: the carriage that she had seen leaving Mesi with Faise and Zineer was within, its doors open.

Behind her—

'*You.*'

The word was a hard spit of a curse behind her. With flames spluttering to life on her stolen blade, she turned.

She supposed that ten riders had charged her from the gate,

though it was hard to be sure by the mess of horse and dark-blue armour that had collapsed into each other and was still pulling itself apart. The man who stood before her was the rider of the first horse, a tall white-skinned man with short brown hair and a heavy gash down his forehead from where he had landed on the road. He spat out '*You*' again and again, as if by each utterance the word became an insult and an indictment, rather than the violent announcement of his rage.

His heavy sword crashed forward. Easily, Ayae stepped to her right and the soldier swung his blade back in a hard cut that she was forced to catch in a block. He followed, pushing against her, using his weight and anger. She took another step back and flicked her gaze over his shoulder to where the others were rising with swords drawn.

The pressure on her lessened and the soldier drew back his sword in a heavy arc – but Ayae pushed forward, pushed past him, and thrust her sword down through the back of his calf to crack leather and skin and shatter bone.

The others charged as the man screamed. She let them push her back, let the fallen man find protection in his comrades while her burning sword quickly blocked and parried their attacks. The ease with which she fell backwards caught them by surprise. Whether they thought it a ploy, or hurt, or without confidence, it gave them heart and they spread out, thinking to herd her, to push her to the compound.

She offered a faint smile to the one directly before her and then turned her back to them.

Her feet protested against the suddenness of the move, the strain on her ankles resonating up her legs as she sprinted to the compound.

She heard the solid twang of a crossbow from high on the stone, steel-capped walls after she saw the bolt. Her body angled to let it slide past, the trajectory of it slow, a fat length of steel faster only than the dark-blue-armoured soldiers who followed it. For them, however, Ayae did pause. She met the soldiers, her joints burning as she thrust her sword, afraid that her forearms would break on contact, the bones splitting to reveal a hollow, liquid centre; but her sword sank through steel chain and flesh and when she drew her swords back, the aches in her bones had disappeared. She could no longer sense any part of her mortal flesh. She felt as if she had been turned into liquid, as if oil inside her had broken out and ignited beneath her skin. 'When I want to change the air, when I want to alter its currents,' Aelyn had said, before the Million Ghosts, before she had seen her that last time, standing next to Zaifyr, 'I reach for it, I take hold of it.'

'I can't do that.'

'No, you are different. You are Ger's child.' Above her, the ash-white limbs of a tree twisted, thick and ancient and bare. 'For you, it is internal. Since you have walked into my office, there has been a fire inside you, a sense of warmth that emanates from inside you. It rises and falls as a heartbeat does, overwhelming all other elements.'

Her warm fingers had curled against her palm. 'I cannot feel anything else.'

'All four are there,' Aelyn said. 'Perhaps they are not as strong, perhaps the balance inside you is imperfect, but I do not think so. We should not hope that such is the case, at any rate. Without balance, you will be consumed, eaten by the fire inside you, for it was the task for the Warden of the Elements to maintain harmony, not offer allegiances.'

The air around her began to burn now.

It was as if the oil beneath her skin had soaked into the sky and lodged in pockets, secreting itself in hideaways to wait for her fury, to await the fire inside her to flicker not just off her sword, but her clothes, her hair, her skin. Flames popped and burst into the air, living creatures. From her, they found the invisible purchases, the hidden reserves. It was not oil. As she stepped forward, her sword blocking, then thrusting, Ayae admitted that it was she who allowed the fire to leap into the sky. It was *she* who found purchase in the air for her fire to climb high beneath the morning's sun without any physical purchase. She could feel the air cupping flames, nursing it, feeding it to scale higher and higher, until the small flames bursting from her skin had turned into a huge dome that covered, for a brief moment, the entire compound of Commander Bnid Gaerl.

It hung there, a perfect creation of such pure terror that in its wake, only silence remained.

Then it fell.

In tiny slivered droplets, in droplets that fattened and plumped, the fire began to rain from the air as her burning sword led her through it.

The burning rain seared the dirt of the compound, leaving behind pitted holes. It fell onto the wood of the wagon, splattering off the lacquered roof and onto the horses that reared up in fear. It fell on the men and women in dark-blue armour, their screams at times cut short by her sword, at times left to announce their long, inarticulate cries of pain, their hair caught alight, their skin burned, and their armour melted. Beneath it, the line of men and women who had sought to stop her from gaining entry could not remain, and their defence shattered as the soldiers fled and left the door to the estate empty.

The door that would lead Ayae to Commander Bnid Gaerl.

7.

She approached quietly, as if Bueralan had not heard her and her horse, as if the water that spilled from the broken gutters to the ground hid not just her approach, but her as well.

It had been the tall grey who had warned him, the horse's hooves stamping hard on the stone floor of the shelter where he was stabled: once, twice, then silent. In the echo, Bueralan had risen from his place by the fire, his memories the smouldering wood, a fading set of scenes leaving him cold. For that alone, he was glad of the grey's sound and for the approach of the rider. At the door, he looked along the path down the overgrown gardens – bowing beneath the heavy rain – and watched the approach of the two, horse and owner. For a moment, he thought it was Samuel Orlan. The cartographer must have grown tired of his office and set out into the evening to discuss gods and their touch, to once again push Bueralan on the topic, but as the rider drew closer, the saboteur realized that the horse was too tall, too dark and, ultimately, the rider too female.

He remained in the shadows of the doorway as she led her horse beneath the roof where the grey stood, then made her way to the door.

'Don't tell me,' he said as she reached him, 'you pay rent.'

'I don't even live here.'

She wore a dark-green cloak, soaked black by the rain, and she pushed it back to reveal a young, beautiful face.

A face he knew.

'Could we continue to stand in the rain and talk?' The Queen's Voice held little tolerance in its dry sarcasm. 'I do *so* prefer to admire warmth from a distance.'

He stepped aside.

Like much of the court since his return, the Queen's Voice had been created during his exile, another part of the First Queen's reclamation of her body from her illness. Bueralan had first heard of the appointment over a decade ago, sitting in on a bar conversation between two other men who discussed the First Queen's decline, her children, and the woman who walked before him now. She had been little more than a child then, just ten full seasons old, beautiful and beautifully voiced, a girl destined for the operas.

'You'll have to forgive me, I don't usually do this.' Before the fire, she slipped the wet cloak from her shoulders. Beneath it she wore dark-orange leather trousers and matching riding boots, and a light shirt of red-and-yellow silk that left her slender arms free. 'Late-night meetings are usually the work of the Eyes of the Queen.'

'And for a moment I thought it was a social call.'

'Still looking for a mother, I take it?' She lay her cloak on the stones before facing him. 'Will I be wined and dined in the ruins of your youth?'

'Are the ruins of yours better?' He approached the fire. 'Do you have a name?'

'Yes.' Her hands were long-fingered, with a single gold ring on her right pinky from where a chain ran to her wrist. The low flames reflected off them as she leant towards the fire's warmth. 'But to you, I am the Queen's Voice.'

'What does the Queen say, then?'

'She would like you to accompany her to a party a fortnight from now.'

'You rode out here for that?'

'Your control is most admirable, Bueralan.' The Queen's Voice was unchanged in its dryness, but the chill beneath it was a disdain not disguised. 'I did not do nearly as well at controlling my face when the First Queen informed me I would make the journey out here tonight. She told me that her guards were instructed to wait at the front gate while I rode up to deliver you your invitation. She even told me that the guards would expect me back within half an hour.'

In his youth, well-placed mothers had kept spiralled candle holders to watch the time that he was allowed to spend privately with their daughters. A stone was placed into the spirals, and it was wound up and down beneath a candle, each spiral worth ten minutes of time. He wondered if the guards of the Voice had found a shelter beneath the rain for such a candle. 'Whose party?' he asked.

'The Queen's youngest daughter, Yoala.'

Bueralan grunted sourly.

'I see you know of her,' the Queen's Voice said. 'I do not envy either of us this night. You are also to know that the Queen has not been invited to this party.'

'Could I say no?'

She raised a fine eyebrow at that.

'Yeah.' He walked around the fire, picking up some of the branches he had brought in and began to feed them into the simmering flames. 'How have Yoala's ambitions been of late?'

'She still has two sisters.'

'Because she still has a mother.' The First Queen's daughters had, in the opinion of much of Ooila, been born in the wrong order, the spirits of the Queen's aunts and mother swallowed on the wrong nights, the wombs of the right children given the wrong lineage. Safeen Re, the witch who had performed the Gifts, had denied it strongly, and there was some suggestion, in the darkest part of the court, that the bottles had not been used at all. 'Tell me, what is this party for?'

'Officially, I do not know.' Elegantly, the Queen's Voice reached down for her sodden cloak. 'But I have heard rumours of a marriage.'

Bueralan fed another stick into the fire. 'Is this rumour similar to the Innocent being on the shore?'

'I was told you were a spy, a saboteur.' She held her cloak to the fire, water running into the broken tiles. 'Is it true?'

'Yes.'

'It will be apparent to you, if it is not already, that the First Queen's eyesight is not good, her voice frail and her hearing a struggle around loud noises. Her physical strength vanishes quickly,' she continued, 'and you will have to help her from her carriage. She will not take any of her guards with her so that her arrival is not viewed as an act of aggression, but I will be there. However, the position of helping her physically will fall to you. Once out of the carriage, the First Queen has a chair that you will have to push, and it is heavy and awkward.

But do not think of this physical weakness as one of her mind, Bueralan. There is no flaw there, except the flaws that are reported to her – and I will know, should you be the voice of those.'

'I have no desire to do that,' he said.

'I would hope so.' She turned the cloak around to warm the inside. 'I would hate to tell my guards that you were anything but a gentleman.'

8.

Inside Bnid Gaerl's house, soldiers waited for Ayae.

They waited in a large wooden-floored room, the high ceiling pooled with smoke above, obscuring much of the first-floor gallery. The flames came from walls lined with paintings, the oils of which had caught alight as she stepped into the centre of the room. She had seen, before the flames distorted her vision, scenes of military action, of huge battles where foes lay fallen in the horrors of war, the reconstructions events of one man's valour, a man who appeared both youthful and middle-aged in the art, and whose hair in the former was a russet, a colour that repeated itself later in the shine of his sword as he raised it above his vanquished foes.

The same sword that he now held behind a kneeling Zineer and Faise on the first floor.

'*Ayae!*'

The day the matron had died, a five-year old Ayae had run into the streets of Mireea.

She had fled after the children had been taken out of the orphanage, after they had been turned to face the building that had been their home, the middle floor seething a broken, burning smile in their direction. Later, the Mireean Guard would tell the older children how lucky they had been. The flames that had consumed the matron had struggled to spread after they poured free of her broken lamp. Oh, the flames had settled into the bed's linen and occupant with easy violence, the result of which had been a smoking blanket wrapped around the matron's ample frame, carried out of the ruined smile by three men – and the sight of which finally forced her to slip away into the early morning dark, intent on fleeing what she viewed as her responsibility.

'*Ayae!*'

She met the soldiers on the ground floor without words.

They had wrapped wet cloths of dark blue around their faces and they fought in companion to each other. For every cut of her burning sword, one would parry and the second thrust back in response. Even with the moves coming slowly, she found herself pressed, found her burning feet moving backwards, not forwards, found herself turned towards other men and women who fought with a similar, terrible unison. Like the long, uninterrupted peel of an apple, the soldiers took away her space, cutting her freedom further and further back until, in an act of frustration, she stamped one soldier's blade down with her foot and used the blade to push herself up into the solidifying air and land outside the ring. And then plunged her burning sword back into the group.

'You are Cursed,' the matron had said. 'You listen to my words, child. Through no fault of your own, you were born wrong.' Around her, the dining room was silent, the eyes of the other children in the orphanage wide, frightened, not so much by the words, but by the matron's tone, the fury in her face and voice. 'Rooms warm when you step into them. Skin begins to sweat. Clothes begin to stick. If I were to cut you open, I would find flames inside.'

Ayae emerged in the clump of soldiers as a figure of flame, her sword slicing a long, burnt arc through one man, parting chain, skin and bone.

She was aware that she had lost all sense of her body as a mortal fixture that held her in the world. She remained cognizant of her sense of self by only the faintest strands, by only the most primal recognition of herself and her actions. Her senses remained slippery, incorporeal, twisted through her mind by a rage that focused itself on the private soldiers before her. She blocked and parried the attacks that attempted to reel her in as before, but her blade hammered out to kill those in front of her with brutal disregard for their skill.

It was from one of the last that her sword came back with its straight form lost. The metal had yielded beneath the heat inside her, the heat that had begun to pulse with the beat of her heart.

'Ayae!'

All those years ago, it had been Faise who had found her after the matron's death, who had drawn her out of hiding by walking down the streets, screaming her name when no one else would look for her.

'Ayae!'

But it was not Faise who shouted now.

'Look at me, girl, and know that I will not bow to you!'

Bnid Gaerl lifted his fire-stained sword—

—and for all her speed, all her power, she could do nothing

to stop the blade's heavy cut that went cleanly through Zineer's neck.

He lifted his sword again, over Faise's head, and Ayae felt her final strands of consciousness break apart. Her anguish emerged in a scream of such raw emotion that the last thread of control that she had over her body, over the fire inside her, broke. It rushed from her in such a torrent that she felt herself rise off the ground, the centre of an emerging nova. Her gaze found Faise's and she saw the terror in her, the fear of the blade rising above her, the blade that the heat would melt before it came down; she saw the blood from Zineer that had splattered across her right cheek; and she saw Faise's devastation at having seen her husband so cruelly cut down. Ayae wanted desperately to reach out to her, to draw her into her grasp, to hold her safe in the centre of the burning storm that was consuming the room, but she could not. She was not in control. She had lost control. The threat of her bones splitting, her skin bursting, her body erupting in fire had come true and she could do nothing as the fire tore upwards, as it melted the sword of Bnid Gaerl and flesh of his arm, as the wave of fire tore over him and over Faise, the horror announcing itself in the catching of her hair, the splitting of her skin. The scream that emerged from Faise was the only sound that Ayae could hear over her own terrible loss.

9.

From the tower, Zaifyr watched as fire rose in a massive pillar of devastation and loss, the scream in its centre so raw that it pained him to hear it.

As the pillar rose, he stepped back from the edge of the tower. He steadied himself as it tore apart in the sky, reaching higher and higher, carried by Ayae's loss – he knew it was her, knew that it could be no one else – and then watched as the fire broke apart. It fell over Yeflam, raining over the buildings of industry and domesticity, over the streets that ran wide and narrow, over a population of men and women who had looked up to gaze into the storm that they were unprepared for.

He was in the streets of Nale a moment later.

His awareness fell into an old man, a man who had fallen to his knees in the streets, his heart stuttering and shuddering in an attack he would not rise from; a young woman was next, a suicide near the bridge to the north; he slipped into the haunt of a dog next, her body crushed by one of the long carriages pulled by nine horses on the bridge.

In the tower, next to his physical body, he was aware of Jae'le approaching him.

He did not have to explain to his brother what had happened. He could not, at any rate: the further he pushed his consciousness away from himself, the further he stretched the connection with his own body, the less he could do with the part of him that was anchored in reality. Yet that part of him was surprised when his brother did not turn around and return to the books that lay below. He liked Ayae, Zaifyr knew that, but for Jae'le, the divide between being friendly to someone and being family with them was not insubstantial. It grew even wider the closer the child came to Yeflam. As she approached, Jae'le became obsessed with finding names that Zaifyr could call upon. He had explained the reason for it a week ago, when he said, 'The Keepers have created an elaborate trial for you, brother. It will be unlike anything that you have seen before. Unlike anything that the world has seen. You will find it difficult to defend yourself from claims of madness.'

Zaifyr pushed himself into an old man who had died in his home from a knife thrust into his throat. A young boy, the first of his victims, buried beneath the house where the old man died, led him further across Fiys. A thread between the boy and an elderly woman, his mother who had died years later, years after she had found the old man, helped Zaifyr reach the bridge that led to Ghaam.

On Ghaam Zaifyr moved into the haunt of a Yeflam Guard who had been killed by a hammer to the back of his head. An unrelated man followed, a gambler who had run out of luck before he ran out of liquor. His life, like the lives of all the haunts Zaifyr pushed his consciousness through, flickered like the first strike of a match. It flared in his consciousness, a sudden illumination of the dead's final moments, before it faded to the dull sense of loss that the long-term dead shared.

On Xeq, however, it changed dramatically. The recent dead appeared before him as slivers of light, as if the falling rain had been stilled. He pushed his consciousness into an old dead, a boy who had slipped off the edge of the bridge while walking across it years earlier, and as he did, he saw the new dead turn to him. His presence called to them in their pain and confusion, just it called the dead wherever he walked. But the emotions were rawer, more intense, and they forced him to settle into the boy's haunt further. He felt his desperation as he tried to rise above the waves of Leviathan's Blood and felt the pain as the water stung against his flesh. Zaifyr rode the fear until he could move it to one side. Once he had done that, he concentrated on focusing on the drowned boy, and the new dead faded before him. With them gone, he could see the fires that ran throughout Xeq. Fuelled by loss and by grief, they rose unnaturally high and ran from roof to roof and onto the ground, finding life in the stone as he had seen no other fire do. From there, the fire reached for the people around it, as if its limbs were the extremities of a huge submerged animal. It even reached for the haunt that Zaifyr guided down the road, to where the centre of the destruction lay.

The walls of the estate were made of stone and metal, but they had melted beneath such heat that he doubted he would have been able to approach it if he were in his flesh. Yet, once he stepped past it, he realized the walls were in fact acting as a warped barrier that offered a faint protection from a much worse heat, from a furnace in the centre of a once-lavish house. There, parts of the frame were gone, as if it had simply disintegrated. Another part of the frame had been blown clear into the air and the blackened wood and stone lay in a hideous parody of confetti across the ground.

In the centre of it lay Ayae.

She lay curled into a foetal ball, her clothes smouldering, but otherwise unhurt.

Above her stood a familiar haunt.

'Cold,' Faise whispered. 'I'm cold.'

The woman revealed the horror of being caught in the explosion. Her skin had peeled back, had revealed her organs, had allowed them to be melted, to be destroyed as the very bones of her body had been turned brittle and black. The injuries flickered before Zaifyr as she struggled to reform herself in the wake of her trauma.

A part of Zaifyr, the part that was on the tower in Nale, felt tears seep from him.

In the ruins, the haunt he controlled gently lifted Ayae. He was delicate with her touch, careful that the haunt's desire to be warm and to be fed did not overcome his simple actions. He had to exert a stronger control over the drowned boy when the fabric of Ayae's clothes flaked beneath his touch and both he and the haunt's touch saw dried blood and cuts on her.

Outside the destroyed wall, an ox and cart waited. The huge, brown beast was unconcerned by the fires around it, even as they threatened both it and the cart.

'Thank you, brother,' Zaifyr said through the haunt, said to the man who stood beside him.

The ox grunted and, moments later, it set out for Nale, guided by an invisible hand.

10.

A day, years ago, a single day, with the midday's sun high in the clear sky, a single hot day, she had helped Faise load her belongings on to the back of a small cart. It was drawn by an ox Zineer had bought. He was silent that day, a man of slight smiles, of kind but quiet gestures. He took the boxes she carried with a thank you each time, no matter if it held plates or clothes, ornaments or soft toys. Inside the house, her house that she shared with Faise, the other woman asked her if she was sure. 'You need knives. You need forks. You need chairs.' But she had shaken her head and said no, no she did not need them. She said it bravely, though a part of her did want to keep them, keep them all, souvenirs of Faise, talismans she could line her rooms with as the days turned into weeks and months and the journey from Mireea to Yeflam became a difficult one to make due to work and relationships. She would visit, yes, but it would not be the same, it could not be, and the thought was in her mind when she hugged Faise, when she held her tightly.

It was only later that she realized how wrong she had been.

11.

The fire had stopped falling from the sky, but the ash-black clouds still remained, a series of circles that threatened to reignite at any moment.

The scream that tore over Yeflam with the explosion had pierced the people standing on the bridge and island, breaking the heavy silence. Heast, no less affected by the sound than the others, had felt chilled when he lifted his head to the sky and saw the first droplets of fire fall. If the burning rain reached Wila, he knew that the Mireeans would have no shelter from it. The men and women on Wila would have little choice but to run into the black ocean, to use the shallows of the poisoned water as protection, unable to hide in the tents that lined the island. Yet, before he could react, he had seen the figure of Lieutenant Mills giving orders. A dozen of the Mireean Guard raced to the closest tents and began to strip the fabric off their poles, before they ran to the ocean to soak it as a shelter.

The tents lay now on the edge of the beach, not needed now but days, if not weeks, away from being used as shelter again.

Further up, following the stone ramp, up into Yeflam itself and the bridge, were a handful of sky-blue armoured guards.

The child – the Leeran god, Heast corrected himself – had arrived and gone. In the moments before the fire ripped into the sky, Heast had been able to make out a figure on the stone path . . . a vision that had all but disappeared when the woman's scream had sounded and the crowds had burst into panic, a panic that the Yeflam Guard had reacted quickly to by herding everyone on the bridge off it and onto the roads the other side of it.

But the rain had not reached them. It had fallen on one city in Yeflam, on Xeq if Heast was right, and now it smouldered on the horizon.

'Does the sky not remind you of the Keep?' Reila stood beside him and Muriel, the age that had crept onto her face during the battle in Mireea still apparent. Yet she had emerged swiftly from the tent when the scream sounded, leaving the tribesman Kye Taaira behind her. 'You could see ash in it for weeks after Fo and Bau were killed.'

'It is gone now,' he said. 'I watched the last of it fade away months ago.'

'Yes, but I fear that Ayae and her friends are in the heart of this.'

Heast had already reached a certain fatalism about both Faise and Zineer. He did not believe that Ayae was dead, a sentiment that Muriel and Reila shared. Once it became clear that the fire would not rain down upon Wila, the Lady of the Ghosts had said, 'Poor girl,' softly. He was not surprised to see Reila nod in agreement. Both left him shortly after. They headed into the crowds of Mireean people, where Muriel would take their hands, would talk to them and ensure that they were safe.

Left alone, Heast contemplated his role in their deaths. He thought about the failure of Sinae Al'tor to take them to safety, about the failure of the Soldier to alert Ayae properly, but the thoughts did not linger. Heast was not a man who blamed others for his faults and he was not a man who lingered upon death.

Ahead of him, the tribesman stood alone on the beach. He had turned away from Leviathan's Blood, watching the Mireean people gathering around Muriel Wagan.

'We will leave tonight,' Heast said to Kye Taaira once he reached him, once he made his way awkwardly through the sand. 'Kal Essa, myself, and you, if you wish.'

'Thank you,' he said quietly. 'Will your mercenary captain and his men come with you over the mountain?'

'No.' *Kal Essa and the Brotherhood have important work here. Essa will offer, though.* 'I will not hold you in bond as a guide. You have a duty of your own.'

'No, Captain, I will bring you to Faaisha.'

'I appreciate it.'

The tribesman continued to stare at the crowds. Those closest to him stood around the tents that had been stripped. The bare wooden frames exposed the flat beds and meagre belongings of the inhabitants, leaving none with illusions. 'It is horrible to be without a home,' he said, quite suddenly. 'It was a truth that I learned at a young age. The shamans choose you to be Hollow at birth, and you are taken from your parents once you are weaned. It is a great responsibility you are placed under and it turns you into a nomad on the Plateau. For my entire life, I have lived in tents similar to this. I imagine that, if I took each tent that I had pitched and slept in, I would fill this island just as your people have filled it in their loss.'

'I would not have thought you a man given to such thoughts, if it is all you have known.'

'A man knows envy.'

'And you are an envious man?'

'A fault I do not enjoy.' He turned to Heast. 'Do you not value home as well?'

'I have slept in too many tents.'

'Baeh Lok said the same thing to me on one of our nights together.'

'It is the life of a mercenary.'

'Indeed.' The tribesman nodded, thoughtfully. 'You will make an interesting companion, Captain.'

After he had gone, Heast remained on the beach. He watched not the tents, nor the sky with its dark, ashed lines, nor the black water that tasted of blood and salt. Rather, he watched the men, the women, the children. Watched those around Muriel and those who were not. He watched them going through the motions of keeping a community, of ensuring that it still existed, even on a small piece of land that they had been sentenced to for no reason other than survival.

He watched because, by morning, he would no longer be able to.

12.

At the end of the beach, they found thirty-seven crucifixes.

The air was still, as if the wind off Leviathan's Blood knew the horror that it blew towards, that it knew the foul deed that had been done, and held itself guilty for the aid it had given to the men responsible. Pueral slid off her horse without correcting herself. She could not believe that the rough wooden pieces had been constructed while men and women waited beneath the gaze of one man. She would not believe that one man had such power that he could make men and women wait, with patience, for their death.

Yet they had.

The bloated bodies had been nailed with thick iron spikes through their wrists and shins to the crosses. No one was spared, not even children. With her soldiers, Pueral led her horse to stand in front of the empty gazes of eleven children. The youngest would have been no older than five, she estimated. The black-and-red armour felt heavier than before and, beneath their eyes, Pueral told herself that she would pull the children down first, once her soldiers had finished with the area. She promised that she would bury all of them, that she would pull the spikes from each, starting with the children, granting as much mercy as she could to the dead.

Closer to the crucifixes, she saw that the heads of all thirty-seven men and women had been tied in place with wire. There were two thin strips, one across the forehead, one across the jaw, both ensuring that the scavenger-picked faces of the dead were directed out to the sea, a direction that Pueral's gaze followed.

Nothing.

But—

She released the reins of her horse and walked closer to the black water's edge. She had seen something, just. It had caught on the reflection of the ocean, but it was gone, just as quickly, and she could not see—

There.

A speck of light.

A flash, then gone, then back.

A lamp, no more, she decided. But it was a lamp deep in the darkness of the ocean, a single, swaying, half-lidded eye watching her from the deck of a ship. A solitary ship far out in the waves – a massive ship.

Glafanr.

Down the beach to her left, not far from her, sat a dinghy. It had been pushed on to the sand and inside were two oars, the wood pitted and scarred.

'Lady Pueral.'

The tracker, Ae Lanos, emerged from the night beside her.

'Tell me,' she said softly, 'that it was not one man who did this.'

'I wish that I could,' the old man replied, his voice equally low, as if to raise it would signal a reality that neither were prepared, as yet, to accept. 'The light on the ocean must be from the ship that brought him here, but the last part of the journey was made on this. He arrived alone and I can find no other tracks, or boats, that lead from Leviathan's Blood. He was greeted by a man. That man was struck down, almost instantly.

'The man from the boat then walked to the village, carrying the man he had struck down.' As the tracker turned, Pueral saw a flash of the image he had drawn – an unconscious Ja Nuural being slung over a shoulder and carried up the beach. There, a series of wooden huts sat, a line of portly guards who had been stripped of their armour to reveal dark holes in their flesh. 'He was challenged twice – here and here. The fights were quick, brutal, and none of the blood comes from him. It is important, also, to note that he killed both his attackers while still holding the man who greeted him. Then he reached the village. He was not fought here. Instead, he placed the man on the ground and tore out his tongue. It was after that that he had crucifixes built. He ordered the wood taken off the houses and carried out onto the beach.'

'Did you . . .' Around Pueral, her soldiers had gathered, stern and silent. She cleared her throat and said, again, 'Did you find the man's tongue?'

Lanos wordlessly unwrapped a rotting piece of flesh, covered in sand.

'Where did he go, after?' she asked.

'To the north,' the tracker replied. 'He went on foot, with no food or water.'

She nodded and, after a moment, turned to head back to the crucifixes, to where her horse waited.

'My Lady,' Lanos said again.

'If it is him,' she said, not just to him, but to all of her soldiers. 'If it is him, then now is not the time to be afraid. The trail is cold, but it is not dead. We can and we will follow it to scenes that I only imagine will be worse than this.' Going back to her horse, she ran her hand along the neck of the beast, and then began to untie the folded shovel that lay over her saddle bags, bundled in with her tent, her pots, her pans. 'But we will not turn away. We will ride this man down, no matter his history, nor his name. We will kill him, and if we cannot kill him, then we will give an account of ourselves in such a nature that when he speaks of us to his soldiers he is given pause.'

She unfolded the shovel, tightening the bolts to screw it into place. 'First, we will bury our dead,' the Eyes of the Queen said. 'Then we will begin.'

A Cracked Jar

No one had heard of General Waalstan before he laid siege to Mireea. Before the child called upon him, it is said that the General was nothing more than a teacher of linguistics, a man for whom the words on a page, rather than the people before him, battled for dominance. If it is true, Ekar Waalstan has put aside his quill for a heavier weapon, and marked it by going to battle against the infamous Captain of the Spine, Aned Heast. He did not win that battle, but he did not lose either, and for many, that spoke quite forcefully of him.

After Mireea, Waalstan surged into the Kingdoms of Faaisha. After a large, initial success at Celp, he put aside the traditional forms of combat and scattered his Faithful across the Kingdoms. As if he was courting the approval of the man he had just fought, Waalstan began a campaign of savage guerrilla tactics, striking towns and cities suddenly, taking men and women hostage, and leaving behind only devastation. One such survivor, a young woman by the name of Jiqana, was taken into the Leeran camps and, in particular, Waalstan's base, before she was sold into slavery in Gogair.

She had been blinded before she was sold. 'It happened,' she said, 'after I rejected their god a third time.'

—Tinh Tu, *Private Diary*

1.

When Ayae awoke after three days, Zaifyr was waiting beside her.

She was lying on a large square bed in a room that smelt of dust and ash. He was sitting across from her on a sun-faded red-cushioned chair, books lined around his feet, but none in his hands. His eyes were closed, as if he were asleep, or in deep thought. A pitcher of warm water sat in the middle of the room, a glass next to it. Her body was naked and sweaty and stale and heavy and a blanket had been drawn over her. It tangled and twisted in her legs and she could feel the roughness of it against her skin, as well as the soot and dirt and the stitches that had been sewn roughly into her wounds. The sensations were so magnified that, later, when she thought of Faise and Zineer, she would remember the feeling of her body, the used weariness she felt, and the taste of ash, and how her first urge had been to reach for the pitcher of water on the ground, to hurl it or to drink from it, she was not sure. Yet, when she had sat up, Ayae had thought that she would break. Her back was so stiff it felt as if her joints had solidified, and for a moment, in panic, she thought exactly that – that the fire in her had turned her spine liquid and it had cooled into a solid length, but with a series of loud cracks, Ayae rose from the bed, her bare feet touching the ground numbly before failing her.

Zaifyr caught her as she stumbled, returned her to the edge of the bed. Wordlessly, he poured her a glass of water and brought it to her.

She could only taste ash. 'You saw her?' she asked. 'You saw Faise?'

He nodded.

'It was my fault.'

'I know.'

You could have lied to me.

'It will be hard.' He lowered himself into a crouch. His left hand touched her naked knee and she could feel the edge of a silver charm against her skin – but it felt dull, as if someone other than herself was feeling it. He said, 'It will be hard for the next month, the next year, maybe the next decade.'

'What about the next hour?'

'It will be unbearable.'

She had no reply.

'If I could hold the burden for you, I would,' he said quietly.

'No.' Ayae met the fractured green of his gaze and felt, for the first time, that she understood how it had become broken, why within it was disciplined cynicism. 'No,' she repeated. 'It is – this is mine alone.'

'It is.'

Soon, Zaifyr left her. He returned to collect his books, to bring her food and water and to speak to her, but for the most part, he gave her space. Jae'le was similar. He came into her room quietly, spoke softly, but was a reluctant and poor carer, his attention always outside the door that he came through. Ayae understood that. Though she did not leave her room for the first days after she awoke, she was aware of both men in the house below her, aware of their presences as they prepared for Zaifyr's trial, though neither spoke directly of it to her. She was thankful for that. She heard their voices through the floorboards and, in her dreams, Zaifyr's upcoming trial and her guilt would entwine, blending Faise and Zineer with Fo and Bau. She would awake believing that she should be subject to judgement, to the punishment Zaifyr was not seeking.

The thoughts might have lingered had not Aelyn Meah visited Ayae on the fifth day after the death of Faise and Zineer.

Ayae was not in her room when Aelyn arrived, but on the top of the tower. She had made the walk in the early hours of the morning to gaze at the smouldering ruins of Xeq, a walk she had envisaged since she awoke, a vision that had been conjured in her dreams. When she took the final steps onto the top of the tower, the first thing that struck Ayae was that it looked nothing like her dream. No smoke rose from Xeq, and the black sea lay still around Yeflam, as if it had been stilled by the violence she had created, as if it had been cowed by the cold destruction that rose above it.

'There will be no charges laid against you for Xeq.' Aelyn Meah spoke as she stepped out of the stairwell. She offered no greeting. She wore a gown of blue and white, the latter a thick fabric woven into the waist and hem to give the impression of layers and depth. 'Perhaps you are lucky in the timing of it, but politics is mostly responsible.'

'Politics.' Ayae said the word as if it was an insult. 'What I did was terrible.'

'It was exactly what Bnid Gaerl deserved.'

'I did not mean him.'

'I know.' Aelyn did not meet her gaze, but stared out across Yeflam. 'There was little to discuss in the Enclave, but outside it, I thought there might be a call for justice. Lian Alahn has seen to it that no such call has emerged. He argued the righteousness of your defence to the Traders' Union and the survivors of Xeq.'

Ayae was surprised, but she did not feel relieved by it. Illaan's father would not have done it for her, or for the memory of his son.

'He asked me to convey to you that he wishes to meet,' Aelyn continued. 'He told me that he wants to offer his sympathies. It may be, however, that he desires to thank you for weakening the Empty Sky. Without them, Le'ta's supporters have returned to their old friendships with Lian Alahn, and Le'ta himself has been driven underground. No one has seen the fat man for days, though many have looked. It has given more evidence to the theory that Le'ta has sided with the Leeran god. That he has been publishing *The Eternal Kingdom*. Le'ta's supporters have gone back to Alahn just as quickly for fear of being painted with the same brush.'

'I feel as if I'm being pulled at,' Ayae murmured. 'As if a part of me is trying to break off.'

'All of us feel the same,' the other woman said. 'It is worse when you are near her.'

'You met her?'

'Yes,' Aelyn finally met her gaze. 'She is not the child that

Qian spoke about. She is nearly an adult and quite beautiful. When she walks down a street, crowds flood around her.'

'Maybe she is not the same person?' Ayae suggested.

'She can alter her appearance. That may be why, for the Leerans, and for my brother, she appeared as a child. A child is unable to protect itself and empowers those around it to do so. But beyond the borders of Leera, the image of a child is not what she needs. She will not inspire devotion or adoration as an infant. To be that, she needs to be more. The appearance she has taken leaves behind her need for protection, though not completely. For some, she will still need to be protected; for others, she will be an object of purity, of lust, and of obsession.'

'What is she to you?'

'I am undecided.'

'Why?'

'Because I have said that one day I will be a god.' Aelyn laid her hands on the stone before her, on the house she did not live in. 'It may be that such a path does not exist for me, or for you, or the others who live in Yeflam. It could be that the path is only available to the child who has come to Yeflam — but what I feel around this girl is different to what I feel beside the remains of a god. Yet, whatever she may or may not be, the truth is that the responsibility of how to react to her is mine. I have said to the people of Yeflam that I have a wisdom and knowledge that they do not. I have said that to the Enclave as well. When I say to both that I will go to war or I will know peace, the *I* that I use is *we* and the repercussions are *ours*.'

2.

'How do we hold a god accountable for the crimes it commits?' Zaifyr heard his sister address the crowd before he saw her. 'That is the question at the heart of the trial we begin today. Today, you will stand in judgement of a man who is not mortal. A man who once saw himself as a god. A man who was once viewed as a god. A man who has worshipped and feared. You will stand before him and you will judge him, though not a single one of you is his equal. Not one of you could defeat him in combat, not one of you knows the history that he knows, and not one of you has lived the lives that he has lived. It is only when you stand with each other, when you represent your families, your friends and your loves, that you have authority over him.'

She stood beneath the twisting bone-white branches of twenty-three trees, their pale limbs a crown much too large to wear or assume. On either side of her — a few steps back — were the empty plots of Bau and Fo's trees, the torn earth smoothed over to look like recent graves. Between them was a huge podium made from dark wood so red it verged on black, on which sat a dozen men and women — the judges. Mortal on one side, immortal on the other, they watched Zaifyr intently as he was led through the centre of the crowd. He was unchained, but with a guard on either side of him – one immortal, one mortal. The first was the Soldier, Xrie; the other was a female soldier whose name was Oake. She had close-cut snow-white hair and looked as if she had been carved from ice.

Before the judges was a sealed glass box, small and square, the companion to the dozens of tall glass cylinders that were peppered throughout the crowd.

'The man who is led past you is known by many names,' Aelyn continued. 'Today, he will be referred to by the name he has used the longest. That name is Qian. For some of you, his name will resonate. For a great many others, it will not. Whether you know it or not, what is important to know is that Qian stands before you because he has committed a crime. He has killed Fo and Bau, two Keepers of the Divine. He did this in Mireea, on the back of Ger's Spine, in a city that is now in ruins. In killing Fo and Bau, he broke a law that was made by his peers to ensure that the War of the Gods could not begin again. He was fully aware of this law when he broke it. Indeed, he does not deny that he broke the law when he killed them. What he will insist today is that it does not matter that he killed Fo and Bau. To Qian, their deaths are meaningless because there is a larger threat that stands before us. A threat that must unite us before we are consumed by it.

'He therefore does not argue a mortal defence to you. He argues, instead, an immortal one.'

In the last few days, after the judges had been announced, Zaifyr had learned who they were, had learned so that they were not strangers to him.

He had been unsurprised to find Kaqua at the centre of the Enclave's representation. For all that his presence spoke of bias, either he or Aelyn had to head the Keepers' representation. The crowd would accept no one else. According to Jae'le, Kaqua had resisted, had said that he could not, because of the very public knowledge of his role in the Million Ghosts, but no one would admit that Aelyn's presence as a judge was tenable. When Kaqua had accepted, Jae'le said that he had done so gruffly, angrily, though Jae'le believed a part of it was an act. Still, if he was partial to Zaifyr's guilt – and Zaifyr had to admit that it was likely – his presence paled next to the Keeper beside him. The brittle gaze of Eira, the Cold Witch, had not left him since he had come within sight of the podium.

'She controls what is written about you in the papers,' Jae'le had said to him earlier. 'She has let some bitter things be written about you.'

'I have never met her.'

'She was Fo's lover.'

Next to Eira sat Kalesan, the Beauty, a man whose dark androgynous form held the division between the male and female body with a strange, alien ugliness. Zaifyr had been told that Kalesan claimed to alternate his gender roles, and on the first day of the trial, he was a male, by body and by the black and dark-blue trousers and shirt that he wore. Next to him was a slim, olive-skinned woman named Resao, the Swarm, a woman who was much feared by farmers for what she could – and occasionally did – to land holdings.

After her sat Mequisa, the Bard, who flowed in finery. He had been the first champion and first funder of the fabled presses of Yeflam. Beside him, the last of the Enclave's representatives, sat Fiel, the Feral. He was a squat, red-haired and bearded man who, in taking after Hienka, the god of Zaifyr's childhood, had come to represent anarchy and rebellion against the established order.

On the other side of the Pauper sat the mortal men and women of Yeflam. The head of them was Lian Alahn, present as a high-ranking figure from the Traders' Union. His son Illaan Alahn had been Ayae's partner, a man whose dislike for Zaifyr had been based, Zaifyr assumed, on a bigotry he had learned from his family.

'There was some debate in the Enclave about that very fact,' Jae'le said when Zaifyr pointed it out. His tone was one of dry distaste, for he had found the endless debating of the Enclave to be tedious. He thought, Zaifyr knew, that Aelyn should simply do away with them all. 'He is said to want power to be given to mortal men and women in Yeflam, but he is also a moderate when it comes to war. It is believed that he will be a balance to the Bertan Brothers.'

Fean and Gall Bertan were the largest owners of farmland in the south of Yeflam, a pair of large, hulking white men. They were grey- and silver-haired and had, until recently, been strong allies of Benan Le'ta.

Beside the two brothers sat Saliense Ma'Laar, a small elderly woman whose skin was a dark black. She was an academic who had been born on one of the small islands spread throughout Leviathan's Blood and she had become a strong voice in favour of evolution in the Keepers, suggesting that divinity was the natural end-product of the men and women who ruled the Floating Cities. Next to her, Gaarax Gaarax, a youthful-looking man of pale skin and twisting dark-patterned tattoos, was also an academic, though based in Zoum. According to Jae'le, he argued similarly to Ma'Laar, though he claimed that it was anything but natural and rather a universal necessity.

At the end of the line of judges sat Olivia Raz, a middle-aged woman who had begun to lose shape in her body. She was responsible for a large amount of the cheap pamphlets and newspapers that were printed throughout the cities. Hers was one of the presses that the Enclave had enlisted to help explain the long glass containers that had been secured throughout Nale.

Aelyn continued to address the crowd before her:

'You are a jury of one thousand and one. You have been selected carefully to represent the mortal men and women of Yeflam in this trial.' She held up her hands, revealing a pair of stones, one red and one white. 'You will listen to both the mortal accusation and the immortal defence today. You will hear the arguments that are laid out by the men and women you see before you and the defence. To do so fairly, you should clear your minds. You should listen to your intellect and your heart. You should be modest and you should be proud of your presence here today. You will make history. We will all make history.'

Lastly, as he approached the podium, Zaifyr felt the child. The pain of her sharpened against him, but he did not see her until he was led to stand at the right side of the judges. He had heard that she was not a child in appearance any more, but when he first found her in the crowd, he saw not the woman that she had made herself into, but the broken body she had controlled while he had been no more than a haunt:

he saw what she had done to that body when he recalled Anguish. The image lasted for but a handful of seconds, and when he looked at her again, he saw that she was young and beautiful. Her blonde hair fell in a wave down to her shoulders. Her eyes were green – the green he had seen first in the mind of a haunt – and she met his gaze through the crowd with a casual ease, with no hint of fear.

Beside her stood priests in brown robes and his brother, Eidan. He was behind her, a man who could reach out and snap her neck with a single movement, but he was a man who could not – or would not – do so.

You gave me a name, brother: Lor Jix, Captain of Wayfair. *An ancient dead. What is it that you know that I do not?*

'Each of you holds a stone of red and a stone of white. A stone for guilt and innocence. Only one can be placed in the glass tubes at the end of this trial,' Aelyn said. 'You have given blood for each and the blood you have given will ensure that you can cast only one. The other will crumble into the palm of your hand once your vote is cast. At the end of this trial, your votes will be tallied, and the verdict will be reached – at which point, the men and women behind me, the judges of this trial, will act.

'I have faith in you. I have faith in all of you, but I cannot stand beside you as you pass judgement. Qian is my brother. We have stood together on every continent in this world. We have fought together. We have grieved together. We have ruled together. In the Five Kingdoms, he was the ruler of Asila, the man who was known as the Speaker of the Dead, and later, after all five had fallen, the Madman. He has performed both great and horrific actions. If he is found guilty of a mortal crime, he will be sentenced to imprisonment in the poisoned lands of Eakar. He will be locked in a small tower that has been made by myself and my family. He will have no access to food or water or mortal or immortal company. He will be kept in there until future generations decide he will be released. For, if Qian is found guilty of his mortal crime, if his immortal defence does not convince you to overlook his actions, then it will be you and your kin who will decide when, or if, he is released. Once before, immortals held that key, and if he is found guilty, then it is our judgement that has failed you. If he is found guilty, the key cannot be held by the same people who held it before. Such a change is, we feel, only right.'

3.

Ayae left the house stiffly, heavy still with grief, but not reluctance. She arrived at the Enclave in a small carriage that she shared with Jae'le.

The carriage had struggled through the crowds and was finally forced to stop three blocks from the Enclave. It was halted by Yeflam soldiers who were directing traffic. Ayae had been aware of the swelling crowd as they drew closer to their destination, but she was still unprepared for the sea of people before her when she stepped from the door of the vehicle. The crowd was of such a mass and density that she would have struggled to make her way through to the Enclave had not Faje and half a dozen soldiers been waiting for her and Jae'le. Even with them, the walk was slow. Fortunately, Ayae was not affected by the heat as others around her were. It had come from a mixture of the mass of bodies around her and an unseasonable, eerie calm in the weather that resulted in a dead, clear sky, where not even the flags on the Yeflam Guard's barracks moved. The morning's sun caught the tops of the long glass tubes and food vendors struggled to raise their voices over the crowds. Pamphlets and papers littered the road, torn from the stacks that had been left for people to take. She heard shouts, but mostly the crowd was well behaved, in part due to the increase of blue armour. Yet, as the presence of the Yeflam Guard grew, so did that of the Leeran priests. They appeared in pairs and sometimes more, often standing around the glass cylinders. Had the crowds not been so loud, she would have pointed that out to Jae'le — the first words that either would have spoken since they left Aelyn's home.

Faje led them to a part of the crowd opposite the largest collection of Leeran priests. There the feel of teeth against her skin grew, much stronger than she had ever felt. Yet, it was different, as if the skin that was exposed no longer felt the sharpness of the child's need; the sensation was in the flesh beneath, the muscle and veins and sinew. Composing herself against the feeling, Ayae found the beautiful young woman — the child — that the Faithful followed in the group opposite. For her part, the child's gaze was on the men and women in the podium, and on no one else. Behind her, however, stood the larger figure of Eidan. Unlike the child, the brother of Zaifyr had no interest in the twelve judges, and instead his gaze flicked along the crowd, over the Keepers who watched him intently, over Jae'le, who ignored him, and to Ayae.

His gaze left her a moment later when Aelyn appeared on the podium. In a strong, clear voice, she began to speak, while the crowd parted, and Zaifyr was led through the crowd. Throughout it, Zaifyr stood quietly beside the podium. The charms throughout his auburn hair caught the late morning's sun, and the stillness of his body gave no threat. In truth, he had a closed, almost meditative look that suggested a lack of interest or care in what was being said by his sister. He moved only when Xrie, with a gentle touch on his elbow, drew him to the box that stood behind him. It had been removed from the rest of the podium and held a single seat that he placed himself in, before Xrie and Oake took up positions on either side. Once that was done, Aelyn turned to the judges, and said, 'We are ready to begin.'

The judges looked to each other, paper was passed, a few hushed words were said that Ayae could not hear, and then Kaqua, the Pauper, stood.

'We call Keeper Paelor,' he said.

The Ranger, dressed in expensive leathers that were more ornament than armour, and with his hair slicked back, stepped onto a second, smaller podium that forced him to face the crowd.

'You are one of the few men and women who have travelled to Mireea since its fall. You are therefore one of the few who have seen where Keeper Fo and Keeper Bau died,' Kaqua said. 'Would you explain to us what happened to them?'

'They were murdered in the courtyard of the Spine's Keep.' Beside Ayae, Jae'le gave a sour grunt at the word *murdered* and a murmur from the crowd accompanied the language. 'The bodies of both Keepers were ripped open by what appears to be hand and by tooth, the result of which was a massive trauma to their bodies that they could not overcome. Final death was most likely the result of blood loss. All fluids had been drained from their bodies, leaving behind crushed veins and internal organs in a state of desiccation. This was especially true of the heart of each.'

'How many living creatures can kill a person this way?'

'Spiders and wasps.' The Ranger raised his right hand to

indicate their size, none bigger than a fingernail. 'Not one would be a threat to a person.'

'What else would explain the wounds?'

'Only the dead raised by Qian.'

'Would you expand upon that?' The Cold Witch, Eira, did not rise from where she sat. 'The dead were raised here in Yeflam without any violence.'

'That is true,' the man replied. 'However, the injuries were consistent with the essays that Keeper Fo wrote about the fall of Asila.'

More questions followed, each designed to give more colour to the scene that Paelor had begun to draw. Fiel asked about Fo's connection to Asila; Kalesan added to it by asking for the age of the Keeper, linking it to the date of the fall of Asila. The six Keepers began their narrative with ease, with none of the other men or women challenging them. Gaarax Gaarax asked about the rest of the Spine's Keep, and Paelor spoke of the burnt remains of the tower in Mireea, the broken ground – 'The tower broke apart from its damage' – and, to Ayae's frustration, none of them tried to expand the story beyond what had happened to the Keepers. Ayae felt herself grow heavier with every answer that Paelor gave, a feeling that only increased when, with the judges' questions to the Ranger exhausted, Kaqua turned to Zaifyr and asked him if he had a question for the Keeper.

'No,' Zaifyr said, 'I have no questions.'

The crowd murmured, but fell silent again when, a moment later, Lian Alahn rose. 'We wish to call Faje Metura to the stand.'

The old man emerged from the crowd in the same faded

pale-blue robes that he had worn since Ayae had first met him on the road to Yeflam. He walked with a severe dignity and took Paelor's place on the podium.

'Tell us,' Alahn said, 'on what orders did Keepers Fo and Bau go to Mireea?'

'A request had come from the Lady of the Spine, Muriel Wagan, for aid against the Leerans,' Faje replied immediately. 'The Enclave met in the month of Deuan to respond. It was during that time that the Keepers of the Enclave agreed to send Fo and Bau in an observation roll to Mireea. It was agreed upon by all that the neutrality of Yeflam would not be broken. Both Fo and Bau were instructed to leave before the fighting began.'

'Deuan,' Alahn mused. 'Was that not shortly after the epidemic on Xeq?'

'It was.'

'What was the Enclave's response to the disease?'

'No conclusive evidence has ever been produced to link Keeper Fo and Keeper Bau to the sickness on Xeq. Yet, because of their work in treating the sufferers, it had been reported in the papers of Olivia Raz that they were responsible, resulting in a public outrage.' At Faje's words an angry ripple passed through the crowd and Ayae heard, more than once, a man or a woman claim that it had not been the *papers* that caused the outrage. 'Because there was no evidence that could prove either their guilt or innocence, members of the Enclave, led by Keeper Kaqua and Keeper Aclyn, argued in favour of both going to Mireea so that public anger could subside.'

Lian Alahn waited for the murmur of anger to calm. 'And their response?' he asked, once Nale fell quiet.

'They believed it was a politically weak move.'

The new leader of the Traders' Union smiled as the crowd burst out in complaint.

Once order had been restored, Mequisa, the Bard, attempted to challenge the characterization of Fo and Bau, but his point that both had gone, regardless of what they thought, echoed flatly in the crowd. It was clear that Alahn had dulled some of Paelor's testimony in favour of Zaifyr, and Ayae was pleased when Fean Bertan pressed Faje for other instances of disease outbreak. None could be officially proved, Faje responded, but when Gall Bertan listed two outbreaks in the last thirty years, the steward had to admit that the two Keepers could not be exonerated completely. Yet, with the characters of Fo and Bau sitting on the edge of immoral, needing only to be pushed further to complete such a representation, Zaifyr still did not rise from the box.

As with Paelor, Kaqua turned to Zaifyr once the judges had finished questioning Faje, and asked him if he had a question.

'No,' the charm-laced man said. 'I have no questions.'

'What is he doing?' Ayae whispered to Jae'le. 'He had an opportunity to press — he needs to do that.'

'He is searching for his witness,' he replied. 'He has been searching for the remains of the man all week — he searches still.'

The heaviness of her body felt as if it grew, and she said, 'He should not ignore them.'

'He has no choice.'

4.

After the ruined coastline, Ce Pueral no longer buried the dead.

Lanos led them on a trail that proved, at times, deceptive, and at others, honest. At Enalan, the first village they came to after the coast, the trail told the horror of Aela Ren stalking the edges. Once he had circled it twice, he had sat on the long limb of a branch beneath the afternoon's sun and watched the people end their day and close their gates. He ate nothing, drank nothing, and left no leavings, but his thick-soled boots scored the tree as he climbed it, and he made lines in the flesh of the tree with his fingernail, a count of the people before him. When he dropped from the branch — in the last of the afternoon's light, to judge by the final score on the tree — he moved to the pens of animals and the warehouses. His trail was easy to follow, Lanos's old face in a permanent scowl as the pigs and chickens gathered around his feet, following him into the open barns and silos where food was spilled next to blood. 'He killed them all in here,' the tracker murmured. 'It was not like the beach: they fought him here. They defended themselves. They came into the barns to hold him out. But it did not work. He waited – he released the animals and he waited. You can see by their waste that they stayed behind the doors for a week at the least. Enough time for the smells to get to each of them, for the little fights to begin, for the animals to start calling for them, for the children to hear the animals and want to go to them, for people to start saying that he wasn't outside, that he wasn't who they thought he was.'

Their bodies were spread throughout. They had been killed by hand, by pitchfork and rake and axe, but not once by sword, not even the few that the villagers owned.

'Why didn't he take the swords?' Lanos had asked.

'Because he does not need them.' She dipped her foot under the blade and flipped it over. It was as if new. 'He is sending a message to us.'

Pueral was not flattered and neither were her soldiers. The witch, Tanith, who had become – if possible – even more silent, began to collect blood from the villagers. She scraped the samples into a cracked jar from the blade of an old, dull knife. The jar had to be cracked for the spell to work, but Pueral suspected that Tanith would struggle to use it. The Innocent had left nothing personal in either location, and she doubted that he would in any future ones – and Tanith needed a personal item to give the blood something to grip. Pueral had offered her the letter the Fifth Queen had given her, but the witch had shaken her head. 'He did not write it,' she muttered, before taking her knife to the wounds on the dead, and Pueral said no more. Just as soldiers sharpened blades and patched armour, a witch had her rituals before battle as well, and she did them beside the soldiers. They all knew that the message left was not a personal one: if it had not been them who had discovered the beach and its crucifixes first, and if it had not been them to enter the village, then it would have been someone else, and the message would have remained the same. Regardless of who found it, it was a message of contempt, delivered by a being who believed that the men and women he killed were so far beneath him that he need not even draw a sword.

After Enalan, the trail continued inland, pushing west, deep and far from the main highway that Pueral and her soldiers had used to travel down to the coast. As if he knew that they were behind him, Aela Ren led them into isolated land, where rocks lined the ground and sparse trees stood in lonely contemplation. Volcanic ash and butterflies rose and fell in the morning and the evening. Yet he did not mark a trail to the volcanoes, and Pueral and her soldiers were never forced to wrap their faces for ease of breath. Instead, he led them to another village, and another, with no sense of deceit until they came upon the first village that had not been destroyed. There, Lanos believed that they had lost him, and that Aela Ren had simply disappeared. So convinced of it was he that the old tracker spent half a day going through the trail that he had followed, sure it held a lie, a falseness that he had missed, but Pueral trusted the skill that had led him here, and when she rode into the village, she was unsurprised to be told of a stranger who had stayed a night.

'He was a scarred man,' the village leader, a thick-set woman said, 'but polite. A coop had broken in the evening, and he brought our chickens back.'

'No, he did not speak much,' a young man in a tiny hut said two days later. 'He drank some water from our well and asked the name of the species of butterflies beneath his feet.'

'Did you tell him?'

'What I could.' The man shrugged. 'He did not stay long.'

Despite what she heard, Pueral did not doubt whose trail she followed, and neither did her soldiers. They knew that a game was being played, and they knew, also, that the rules had changed.

In her quiet moments, Pueral would think of the beach, and the barns in Enalan, but rarely of the villages that followed. It was as if, after the first two, she had turned off the part of her mind that recorded memories to spare herself the recurring images of what she saw. It surprised her, for Pueral had been witness to violent acts all her life, and had been responsible for more than a few. But what she had seen on the beach had been singular, not just in the acts of violence, but in the force of will that delivered them — a will that was, she believed, now demonstrating to her just how easy it was for him not to kill, how little life and death meant to him, a statement made somehow worse by the lives he spared after the deaths he had caused.

The hut that Ae Lanos led them to a week after the beach was a mean, malnourished thing, half slumped in the barren land surrounding it. Around it roamed eight goats. A black rooster sat on the rough thatch roof and it remained still and calm even when the door opened and a thin, old man came out. His skin was a dark brown and his eyes were like flint. He had but a few teeth and leant heavily on a long cane of cracked black wood.

'You're for him, aren't you?' he said, stopping before the horses. 'He said that you would be here.'

'Him?' Pueral asked.

'The man with the scars.'

Her soldiers shifted, spreading out like the feathers of an angry bird.

'Yes,' she said. 'We are here for him. What did he say to you?'

'Little.' The old man spat. 'He said that I should tell whoever came looking for him that he had gone up into the mountains, to the castle there.'

'There's no castle there,' Pueral said, looking up into the mountains, to the trails of smoke that mixed with the day's remaining butterflies. 'Just ruins.'

'He said that he had gone up there to pay his respects to the end of an empire.'

5.

On the night of the party, Bueralan placed a large shard from his mother's mirror on a tree outside and shaved, naked. Next to him he had a bucket of cold water into which he dipped the long, straight razor. The white tattoos twisted as he ran the blade along his head first, then his face and neck, careful of the leather strap and pouch. Stubble gone, he dyed his goatee white again, hiding the black roots. He cut his nails after, his left hand first, right second. Then he took a leather sheath from a branch above him and strapped it to the inside of his left forearm. A thin-bladed knife slid into it. Then, and only then, did he reach up to another branch for the expensive black trousers, black shirt and black jacket and begin to dress without pleasure.

Not much had given him pleasure in the week since the Queen's Voice had visited him. He had made a part of his mother's estate liveable – others would argue otherwise – but it was too far from Cynama for the tall grey and him to make the trip there and back each day. He had returned earlier in the week to petition witches: as the afternoon's sun rose and butterflies fell, he had arrived at Samuel Orlan's narrow shop.

He had not wanted to, but the little coin he had was not enough to buy a meal, much less rent a room in the city. After he greeted the old man — who said hello without bothering to rise from the large map he worked upon — Bueralan dropped his pack in the room of Orlan's absent servant and found a small sack of coins on the table.

'Ah, I forgot to tell you, the girl sent me a letter.' He ignored Bueralan's upraised hand that held the leather pouch and moved to the other side of the table that dominated the bottom floor of his store. Nearly complete, the work was a detailed map of Ooila, lined with mountains and volcanoes, each built from the husks of dead butterflies. Bueralan had not noticed that at first: the detailed painting and arrangement hid the materials well, but once the husks caught his eye, he saw only the hollow bodies and empty eyes staring out at him. 'She was married after my last visit a year ago, and her husband and she decided to move out of the city. Such a surprise! She is the same age as me and I am simply much too old and much too sane to get married, much less buy a farm and move to it. Such an awful life. Such an awful choice! Though, given that the farm is located on a plot of land in Gogair, it is entirely possible that she will be vindicated.'

'Just another someone looking for something better,' Bueralan said.

'My store would have provided for her more than a farm.'

'Didn't provide enough to quiet love.'

Orlan dipped a brush into a small green pot of paint that he held. 'You speak like someone who has never worked for me.'

'That's right.' Bueralan dropped the sack of coins on the edge of the map gently. 'I don't work for you.'

The cartographer lowered his brush to the map. 'Take it.'

'I'm not for hire.'

'Which is why you're broke.' He moved to his left, leaving the pouch. 'But you are intent on taking the Mother's Gift and you will not listen to me until you have.'

'I won't listen to you then, either.'

'You will.' For the first time, Orlan's blue-eyed gaze lifted from the map before him and settled on Bueralan. 'You will then see what this new god is. You will see the horror she has placed around your neck. I wish it did not have to be that way, but if that is what it takes, then so be it. Our time here is very limited and I do not wish to increase it.'

'You have been listening to all that talk of the Innocent again.' When he had entered the gate to Cynama, Bueralan had overheard two of the guards discussing a rumour that the Fifth Queen had in her dungeons a man who had seen Aela Ren on Ooila. 'I've told you before, you don't need to stay.'

'*None* of us needs to stay. Take the money. Use it to bribe and to buy whoever you need. But do it quickly.'

He took the pouch.

He had spent much of the week travelling from witch to witch in an attempt to find a woman selling the Mother's Gift. It wasn't easy. Despite the proliferation of soul-catchers, the amount of men and women who were reborn was slim. The cost was prohibitive and it had only become worse in Bueralan's lifetime for, despite the stories of disabilities and madness in the reborn, the Mother's Gift was one of the highest status symbols Ooilan society had.

In the first day he visited two witches and both turned him away with a polite, but firm insistence that he did not have the money. On the second day, he learned that the excuse of his personal poverty – even when Samuel Orlan's name was mentioned – was an easy way to turn him towards the door, a polite dismissal for someone who might be in the First Queen's favour.

It was not until the fourth day that he met a witch who would talk to him about the Mother's Gift. Safeen Re, a dark black-skinned middle-aged woman, greeted him at the door of her estate with the first genuine smile he had seen in a week.

She lived in a large, beautiful building dominating a large tract of flat land to the west of Cynama. The long, tiled hallways of her home had alcoves holding expensive, dark glass jars, at times beside bones, and at others beside charms of gold and silver. In each jar, however, there was a swirl, a hint of a chill that reached out to him, and Bueralan was pleased to see that the office of Safeen Re was large and spacious and occupied only with books and bones.

After she had seated herself, the witch said, 'My brethren have been telling you that you have no fortune, Bueralan Le. What makes you think I will be any different?'

'I have Samuel Orlan's fortune.' It grated on him to say it, and it had become harder since he had first said it. 'Is that not enough?'

'For you, no.'

'The Queen's pardon means so little?'

Safeen Re let out a loud, healthy laugh. 'Have you truly been gone so long, or are you just desperate?' she asked. 'Bueralan, you may take the Queen's name so easily in this conversation, but we both know she does not support you that much. If she did, you would have her money, and she would have brought you here first, and you know it. I have watched the Queen drink from jars that I made, and I am above reproach. We both know that. It is both our business to know that — and it is the business of the women who come to me to know that as well. After all, what they want is a very rare and difficult thing.'

'I know that.'

'You cannot offer them enough to risk that.' Bueralan began to speak, but Safeen Re cut him off. 'You know that as well,' she continued. 'You are a man with no title, no family, and the soul around your neck is of a blood brother.'

Bueralan began to rise. He had not come to be insulted. A simple no would be enough. There were other ways, less desirable ways, he knew—

'But you do have something quite unique,' Safeen said. 'If you but have the patience.'

He remained standing. 'I have no favours to offer.'

'It is not the patience of the Queen's court I speak of, I assure you. Rather, it is the concern that more and more families have with a life outside Ooila.' To her left, a door opened, and a young man in robes of mixed streams of yellow and orange and blue entered, a silver tea tray in his hands. 'I am not a fool. I hear the whispers. So do my clients. As they grow into a shout, we will all be forced to listen to them, even the Queen. In this situation, what you bring is something unique, for Samuel Orlan's fortune is not tied to this country, just as you are not, either. Should you take a step back from the visits you have been making, should you opt for a little patience, people around you will realize that the ability to provide a life of substance outside the borders of our home is one of rare value.

I would imagine that, in a short time, such an awareness will give you your choice of mothers and their gift.'

In old black leather boots, but his other clothes new, Bueralan walked down the overgrown path of his mother's estate. An extravagant carriage waited at the ruined gate. After he had left Safeen Re, the child's words had followed him — *call only when what is at stake is innocence* — and he had come to realize that, despite what he said to Orlan, he too had begun to believe that there was not much peace left in the country. Soon, Bueralan knew, a man would step upon its shore, and begin a war that he had no desire to be part of, and feared that he would be unable to escape.

A black-and-red-armoured guard opened the door to the carriage. Inside, two women waited in an incomplete darkness.

6.

The Spine of Ger was in ruins.

For the man who had been the Captain of the Spine, the extent of the destruction unfolded over days and nights, a jigsaw puzzle he assembled slowly in his mind to replace the image he had previously had. Heast's arrival at Mireea was late in the week, for neither he nor Kye Taaira had wanted to use the main road, believing that the risk of encountering Leeran soldiers and priests was high. As they approached the Spine, Heast would often lose track of it behind trees that lined the obscure back trails he rode, and when the long stone wall reappeared, his vision of its injuries was always more detailed than the one he had seen before. Cracks appeared in the parts of the wall that were not yet broken. The crude wooden walls he had ordered built stood in splintered isolation. Buildings sank while birds stood on the roofs that were at times nothing more than wooden spines. But for Heast, the devastation was only complete when, beneath the morning's sun, he arrived at the fallen gate of Mireea and stepped onto the empty, fractured cobbled roads that led deep into it.

Heast had left Wila in the middle of the night, just over a

week ago. Wading out until he was waist deep in the cold black ocean, he had been pulled into the dinghy by Kal Essa, the mercenary's thick arms lifting both him and the tribesman into the boat. Once they were seated, Essa gently dipped the oars into the water and began to row. They had left as close to the low tide as they could, but the first half hour had been a struggle against the last of the high tide, not because it was powerful, but because the sound of the oars in the water threatened to grab the attention of the remaining guards on the bridge. Yet they made it to the shore before the morning's sun threatened to rise, and were helped onto land by half a dozen mercenaries from the Brotherhood. Once the three of them were on land, a pair of large men loaded the dinghy into the back of a wagon and threw a tarpaulin over it before the ox began to pull it up the hills.

'You sure you don't want a few of my boys?' Kal Essa asked. He was sitting beside Heast in the wagon. 'Lot of bad land between here and Faaisha.'

'Just some supplies, horses.' The captain's steel leg was wedged painfully against the wet boat, but even so, he did not relish the idea of trading the wagon for a mount. 'You and your men have your orders.'

'You're making farmers out of them.'

'The land cannot look abandoned.'

In the months since Heast had begun purchasing the land, Essa and his soldiers had proved to be more than dependable on the land. Other soldiers — soldiers Heast had both commanded and served beside — would have chafed at the idea of picking up ploughs, of setting aside swords for scythes, and of long, hard days harvesting food they had not planted. But the Brotherhood had done it with no sign of disgust, no hint that they had been given a job that was beneath them, and Heast had been more than satisfied.

The ox came to a halt outside the large farmstead that the mercenary unit had made their home. The scarred mercenary captain dropped from the back of the cart before Heast or Taaira and began giving out orders for supplies to be prepared and for two mounts to be found. Once he had done that, he disappeared into the house and reappeared with two travel-stained leather packs and two swords, one of them a heavy two-handed blade with worn leather around the hilt.

He gave the latter to Kye Taaira.

'I did not think that even Hollow used swords,' Heast said.

A worn, thick leather strap held the sword over his back. 'It is not forbidden,' the tribesman said. 'In this case, the weapon belonged to one of my ancestors.'

'One who left the Plateau?'

'No, one who ensured they stayed.'

'Our warlock wanted to bury the sword,' Essa said. He passed the second, a plain longsword in a leather sheath, to Heast. 'I'm told he forbade anyone to go near it while we were gone.'

'A wise choice,' Taaira admitted.

No more was said of the sword as the two packs were filled and horses led out and saddled and supplied.

The tribesman would have made quicker time without him, Heast knew. In his youth, he had been a capable rider, though he had never owned a horse. In those lean years, the beasts had always been the property of the men and women he worked for, and their deaths had been paid for out of his own pocket. It was a way, he learned early, that some employers used debt to bind you to their service. He had owned horses eventually, but after the loss of his leg, riding had become a chore, and though he had kept the skill, he had not kept the animals. Kye Taaira, in contrast, was a fine rider who enjoyed being in the saddle, and who could have taken a day from the journey if he had ridden at his natural pace — and perhaps another day if he had not suggested that they should wait until the morning to ride through Mireea.

Turning his gaze away from the sun's cold light, Heast shifted himself stiffly in the saddle and dismounted.

'I rode through the city on my way here,' the tribesman said. He stood before his horse, the reins held in his left hand, the morning's light leaving his hair and beard a burnished red and gold. 'I had heard that ghosts held rule here, but I had not given it much thought until I saw that the priests who preceded me did not enter the city during the night. Their concern, I thought, was one that had been earned and so I did the same.'

Heast did not argue with him, though he did insist that they ride through the main streets of Mireea, and not skirt the edges as the priests had done. With that agreed upon, the pair made their way along the uneven broken road. Tremors threatened to turn into earthquakes, but neither man responded to the sound, or the occasional shift from a building on either side of them. The tremors had been a constant companion for the last few days, with more than one path ended by a sudden split in the land after the mountain had collapsed on itself. He had heard from both Ayae and Zaifyr that Ger had died during the battle with the Leerans — time, Zaifyr explained, had caught up with the god's injuries — and that the god would no longer function as the foundation for the mountain.

Heast was not given to philosophical thoughts about the nature of gods – they were dead, simply that – but as he walked along broken roads, passed toppled houses and stood before dark and endless cavernous openings in the streets, for the first time in his life he had a true appreciation of what people would have felt during the War of the Gods.

It was not just an assault against the physical dimensions of the world, but the intellectual ones as well. He passed The Pale House, one of the tallest buildings in the city. Only months had passed since he stood on the roof and directed the battle against the Leerans, but he could have stepped onto the roof from the street, so far sunken into the ground was it. It would never be rebuilt, never be reclaimed. It was lost, and so, really, were all the practices that went on inside it, the support of the men and women for the Mireean Guard, for him. The fund-raisers they had held without him ever having to attend. After The Pale House, he passed the markets. In a corner where there had been a small stand and a Faaishan woman had sold sand-wiches, there was now stone, punching deep into the ground. Never would he stand there on the final day of a week and eat the roll she gave him, filled with pulled beef and a spicy gravy, and the small bag of chips she cut from potatoes. She was gone. The ritual was gone. Ahead, the Spine's Keep remained upright, but a part of the mountain it had been built into had fractured, and stone had fallen off it and into the Keep, destroying the corridors he had walked through and rooms he had sat in.

It continued, sight after sight, as the Captain of the Ghosts walked through the city and out into the ravaged mountains.

7.

Inside the carriage, the Queen's Voice spoke first.

'When you're dressed like that, Bueralan Le, no one could mistake you for a servant.'

'Was I was required to look like one?' The roof of the carriage was low and he was forced to hunch before he sat himself across from the Voice of the Queen. A moment later, he heard a whip crack. 'Is it too late for me to go back and get a collar?'

'What makes you think I don't have one here for you?'

'I wouldn't think of denying you the gold around your neck.'

'*Children.*' The First Queen, Zeala Fe, spoke in a voice disintegrating in illness; but even in her weakness, her voice commanded. She sat in front of Bueralan, wearing a long gown of black, the folds of it hiding her thinness, but hinting at red, as if wounds had opened on her. The macabre nature of it was only further emphasized by the arrangement of her thin hair, which had left it in a translucent shroud about her face. 'I am headed to the home of my third daughter. She would have both of you murdered for festivities, if she could. I would prefer politeness until we get there.'

'Forgive me.' The Queen's Voice inclined her graceful neck,

her face still and composed; but her dark eyes did not leave Bueralan. She wore a gown made from a dark burnt orange, and it had been touched with red at the cut of her neckline and hem, where she wore dark-red flat heels. A single slender red-and-gold chain with a smoked-glass centre – the piece cut from a jar similar to the whole ones in Safeen Re's house, a piece of rare expense – rested at the top of the smooth curves of her breasts. Around her hands and wrists were red-and-gold bracelets and rings, with chains that made intricate connections with each piece to link her body and gown together. 'I appear to simply have been carried away in the moment.'

'My charm.' He gave a shallow nod of his own. 'I apologize, my Queen.'

'You are like your mother,' she replied drily. 'She could never call me her Queen without it sounding like an insult, either.'

He could not remember his mother saying such. 'My apologies,' he said, again.

'Just like her.'

The carriage rocked slightly after the Queen's faint words and the whip cracked again. Bueralan wondered why the driver did not spare it – because of the Queen's fragility, the carriage was never allowed a great speed, and it slowed for any rough patch of ground. There was no point in using a whip on the horses that pulled the carriage.

'I have a personal question, before we reach my daughter's party,' the old woman whispered. 'That crystal around your neck, the one in your pouch – do you truly believe that it is your blood brother?'

'Yes.'

'Not even a hesitation?'

'Do you hesitate to believe?' he asked.

The First Queen wore the thinnest necklace of gold, the end of which was lost deep beneath her gown. 'I do not hesitate to voice my opinion.' Her hands did not reach for the charm. 'But your mother never supported it. She said it did more damage to us as a culture than good. I was always told that you shared your mother's belief.'

'Once.' He thought again about the child and saw the way her eyes had held his, eyes that were unlike any he had seen before. 'After it was given to me in Leera, I thought that I had a chance to right a wrong.'

'You and Samuel Orlan have that bond.'

She was not asking a question and when Bueralan responded, it was not to her. 'Yes.'

'But what of Leera?' the First Queen asked. 'Until a month ago, I do not think I ever thought to say the word, but now I hear it frequently in reports.'

'You will hear it more,' he said. 'I do not think that they will stop with their neighbours.'

'Yes, I have thought as much.' Beside her, the Queen's Voice raised a single, fine eyebrow, but remained silent. 'Tonight, however, there is my daughter's party,' the older woman whispered. 'It will be attended by a foreign diplomat, Mister Le. His name is Usa Dvir.'

Bueralan almost laughed at his fortune. 'I know him.'

'I suspected as much,' she said. 'Have you worked for him?'

'The Saan do not hire mercenaries.' And Usa Dvir was not just a part of the Saan: he was the war scout for the largest tribe, the Dvir. Very little of what happened in the Saan travelled down the wormed tunnels that kept them isolated from the rest of the world, but what had come through was news that the Dvir had conquered the Saan over ten years ago. It held the country together through the strength of its soldiers, but its gaze, unlike other tribes on the Saan, was not internal. 'I can't imagine Yoala has much to offer Dvir in marriage.'

'No, you are wrong.' She paused as the carriage tilted to the left, gently, then righted itself. 'My daughter offers Dvir the slave trade of Ooila so that Miat Dvir may tap the wealth of Gogair.'

'You could end that trade.' As Bueralan spoke, he was aware of the Queen's Voice watching him intently. The gold around the tips of her fingers had become a solid twist in her hands. 'Before the day begins, you could outlaw it and she would have nothing to give to him.'

'It would be foolish to do so,' the First Queen said simply. 'It was such thoughts that led to Illate's failed revolution. We have all suffered for that and I will not make the same mistake. In the time that I have left, I will push Ooila into stopping the trade, but to outlaw it tonight would merely be to entrench it. The minds of Ooila must be with me as I turn this corner, and they are nearly there. They will be with me even more once I know the names of all the important people here tonight, all the people who support my daughter.'

The saboteur — for that, he knew now, was why he was the First Queen's companion tonight — understood. He was to collect names, to watch those who kept away from the Queen, to remember who stood beside her daughter. 'But I can leave you off the list, because you were not invited.'

The First Queen's laugh was dry. 'None of us were invited, Mister Le.'

'We may not leave,' the Queen's Voice said. 'It is a very real possibility.'

Bueralan admitted that it was, but he did not try to argue against the move, or attempt to leave the carriage, for which, he saw, the First Queen patted his knee. She offered him nothing for what he would do tonight – and what he would do, he knew, would depend on her daughter's response – and when the morning's sun rose, and the butterflies filled the air, he would have earned no coin and no favours with her. But he would not expect otherwise. If the slave trade was returned to the strength that it had enjoyed before he was born, then Zean would have no station from which to make a life after he was reborn. Much in the way a Queen was always a Queen – even a third daughter who would have to kill her sisters to ascend the throne – a slave was always a slave.

Yoala's estate appeared on the horizon, lit brightly by a smear of lanterns, an image, at first glance, that appeared as if a million butterflies had caught fire and were frantically trying to flee.

He wished he had brought more than one knife.

8.

Before Pueral reached the ruins, but after she had tethered her horse to a stake in the rocky ground, she wrapped a black cloth over her nose and mouth. The Eyes of the Queen did not do this out of secrecy, though she knew others would have, for the moon sat high and full in the sky, revealing the ground in clear detail by its pale light. Instead, she wrapped the old cloth around her face because she had started to smell sulphur. It came from the shadows of Maalikanos and Beeintor, the large volcanoes that sat on the horizon like ancient monsters. She had been content to ignore the smell at first, but it was growing stronger. She had taken the cloth from the bottom of her horse's pack before she left the beast, fearing that she would have to use it — fearing because she had not used it for over twenty years and it smelt of leather and food and whatever else had worked its way to the pit of her worn saddlebags. Once she had tied the cloth, she and her soldiers stepped into the ruins that lay before them like broken teeth, rotted and cracked through centuries of neglect.

Pueral did not know the name of the ruins, but she knew that they were old, knew that they reached back to the Five

Kingdoms, when Ooila had been Mahga. Children were taught about it in school, but it was not until she had become the Eyes of the Queen that Pueral had learned just how much the old history had been responsible for the creation of Ooila. After she had been given her position, the First Queen had taken her into the basement vaults of her castle, to where a series of paintings were kept. They were ancient, huge pieces that depicted castles of black rock rising from the ground, with silver lining the edges of doors, and their peaks like thickly chimneyed roofs. At the foot of each castle – there were twelve – spilled pools of molten gold, each filled with precious-metalled fish. The First Queen had told Pueral that the painting held the reason why the Five Queens had risen up and taken control of Ooila in their violent revolution.

Pueral had nodded dutifully, but the massive paintings, despite their flaking, the runs of colours in corners, and damage done to the frames, had conveyed only greed to her.

'What you see is the wealth we lost,' Zeala Fe had said quietly, mirroring her thoughts with a voice not yet wasted by illness. 'The Queens wanted it returned, even though the mines were long emptied.'

'That is why they began the slave trade?'

'Yes.'

After that day, Pueral had been awakened to the conversations that nobles had about Mahga. She had heard them before, but whereas before she had passed it off as history, now she heard in their voices an emotion similar to the painting in the vaults. They knew not the shape of the kingdom, or what its social structures had been like, but they knew intimately what it entitled them to, and they ignored the consequences of it, just as they ignored their own creations of horror in its name.

Beneath her feet, the paths of the ruins were broken, but the tracks Aela Ren left were clear. Her soldiers had spread out like a fan around her, their hands on their sheathed swords and on the triggers of their crossbows. But Pueral's mind would not settle on the job. She wondered if the Innocent had chosen these ruins because of the message they imparted. Surely he could not know the meaning they had for her. Nor could Pueral believe that he felt the need to justify his actions.

She forced her mind clear. Ahead of her, the pale light picked out the edge of a roofed building. The trail led towards it and her stomach began to feel hollow with the anticipation of battle. Aela Ren would not be inside the building, she was sure of that: what little cover it provided would pale against the fact that he would have no way to retreat, no way to fight except by charging, and she did not believe, even after the horrific visions on the beach and in the villages, that the Innocent would charge twenty-three seasoned soldiers head on.

He would draw them to the building. He would use it as a lure. He would underestimate her and her soldiers.

He would seek to strike quietly and swiftly as they closed into it.

Yet.

Yet not a single soldier saw a new trail.

Not a single soldier saw the sign of an ambush.

And not a single soldier was attacked.

The building beckoned, the stump of a good tooth in a destroyed mouth. It had been made from black stone, but its shape was long gone, the walls having fallen, the beams rotting. The stone roof remained standing because someone – perhaps Aela Ren, perhaps a bandit – had pushed and pulled the roof back into place on top of the building's remains.

There was a camp inside, but it was cold. Loosening her sword, Pueral entered.

'There are no tracks out of here.' Ae Lanos stepped behind her lightly, his voice soft, but his movements and words echoed to her. 'If he came here, I do not know how he left.'

'He was here,' she said.

Before her were the marks of boots, the same as those in the tree outside Enalan. The two boots circled the cold pit of fire, the ashes not yet solidified. A single stone lay in the centre.

A stone that held a note.

An old friend of mine has arrived, it said, *with a friend of new. I regret that our meeting will have to wait.*

'I do not know what this means,' the tracker said, handing the note back to her. 'A friend of old, a friend of new? The Innocent does not have friends.'

'He has gone to Cynama,' she said, a rawness in her throat. 'To find Samuel Orlan.'

'The cartographer?'

She left the camp, the words dying on Lanos's lips as he, too, realized that there was but one man in Ooila who was as famous as Aela Ren was infamous. Only one man's name could have travelled down the roads, to the villages on the coast, quicker than they had ridden.

'Tanith.' Pueral held out the letter to the witch, who stood staring over the broken landscape of the moonlit ruins. 'Is this letter enough?'

Gently, the other woman took it, the old, yellowed paper curling around her fingers. 'He has written it in his own blood.' Her voice trembled with excitement. 'It will be more than enough.'

9.

Beneath Ayae's feet, the stone cracked. She did not hear it, but when the fourth speaker – Pyo Sen – left the podium and Zaifyr repeated for the fourth time that he had no questions, Ayae lowered her head in frustration. There, she saw the cracks, the thin lines spreading out from her feet, from the edges of her boots in an embarrassing web of lines.

'They have called their first break,' Jae'le said.

When she lifted her foot, stone flaked off the sole of the boot.

'Ayae, did you hear me?'

'Yes.' Despair had begun to sink into her the more she heard. Pyo Sen, who was a dark-skinned historian, had been called by Keeper Eira to build on the testimony of Keeper Ialee, who had spoken in more detail about Asila. A small, olive-skinned woman, she had detailed Fo's birth in a soft, reluctant voice. She, after Aelyn and Kaqua, was the oldest of the Keepers, and she had been to Asila both before and after its destruction. Ialee had spent decades, according to her testimony, helping the survivors of Asila's fall, and the horrors that she described – suicide, self-mutilation, a list of damages to men and women of all ages that felt endless – had painted a vivid picture in the minds of the men and women around Ayae. Pyo Sen, who had run dig sites in Kakar – the name Asila was not spoken by anyone but the Keepers – detailed the bones he had found, the sacrificial instruments, and more before he left the podium. 'Jae'le?'

'I hope my brother knows what he is doing, but I have begun to fear otherwise,' he continued quietly. 'This is not what he should do. He should let you and I speak—' Ayae's hand fell on his arm and he stopped, and turned to her. 'Why did you hit me?'

It had been the lightest movement she could make. 'Jae'le.' She directed his gaze down to her feet. 'Something has happened.'

The quiet of his voice turned into a whisper. 'The earth.'

His long, hard fingers wrapped around her arm before Ayae could reply and she found herself pulled through the crowd.

It was difficult for even Jae'le to move quickly. The thin lanes that had existed through the crowd before the break was called had disappeared as people began to make their way to the street vendors and the curtained bathrooms at the sides of roads. A dim roar had begun to emerge as the cries from men and women selling food and drink was drowned out beneath the conversation of a thousand-plus people. It was as if, finally, the men and women who held stones had been released from an iron grasp – for during the trial, silence had reigned as they strained to hear what was spoken. Ayae tried to call out to Jae'le as he pulled her, but it was not until he shouldered through the doors of the Enclave that she could finally be heard.

'What did you mean, the earth?' She lowered her voice suddenly, aware of the small clumps of people at the ends of the hall. 'What is happening to me, Jae'le?'

'Ger was the Warden of the Elements,' he replied softly. 'Of fire, Ayae, of water, of air, and of earth. He could control them *all*.'

'What do you mean?'

'Touch your skin.' He held up his hand, palm first. There, in the deep lines, she saw grains of dirt and scrapes that threatened to bleed. 'You are turning yourself to stone.'

'I can only do—' She knew that it was not true and her voice faltered. 'I just have fire,' she said.

'Grief is a powerful thing,' Jae'le said. 'It can consume you if you are not careful.'

Numbly, she touched her arms, but could feel nothing, not even her skin. She pressed down harder, feeling for bone, but found that her skin did not yield. 'Do you remember Tsi?' she asked. 'Zaifyr mentioned him briefly. He was someone like me – but I can find no mention of him in the library here.'

'You will find none.'

'But you remember him?'

'It was a long time ago,' he said, a note of weariness in his voice. 'I do not remember exactly when Tsi was born, but I met him during the first years of the first war Zaifyr and I made. We had not yet met Tinh Tu, or Aelyn, or Eidan. They would come many years later. As for Tsi, he came to us as a soldier, but the power was upon him at the start – you could sense him when he walked into our camp, for beneath his skin he burned.'

'He was consumed by the fire.' Zaifyr had remembered little

more: he had sat outside in the garden of the hotel he was living in and told her his name, and admitted he had only known Tsi for a short time. 'He said that Tsi had no discipline.'

'He was not like you. Fire was all he had.'

Ayae wanted to close her eyes, wanted to put her hands over her ears, wanted to walk away from Jae'le, but she could not. Further up the hall, the clumps of people she had first noticed had now become focused and she saw Lady Muriel Wagan and Aelyn Meah in conversation. A few steps away from them stood Caeli.

'Tsi had no balance in him, nothing to stop the fire from consuming him. There was no sense of earth, water or air within him. To say he had no discipline is not fair, for he was incomplete from the start.'

She heard Caeli call out her name.

'You need to temper your grief,' Jae'le continued, his voice dropping to an even softer tone as the guard came closer. 'If you do not, it may be that you will be nothing but stone.'

The guard appeared next to the tall, thin man and his cloak of green feathers and she took in the situation in a quick glance. 'Is everything fine, Ayae?'

'Yes,' she replied. 'This is Jae'le—'

'Qian's brother, I know.'

'My reputation.' His smile revealed filed teeth. 'If you will excuse me, I can see that my sister wishes to speak to me, as well.'

After he had left, Caeli said drily, 'You have horrible taste in older men.'

Caught off-guard, the younger woman did not know what to say, and struggled with a quick quip. With a smile, Caeli turned to her – but the smile faded when she saw Ayae's face and her hand reached out for her shoulder. 'What happened?' Caeli asked.

'Faise and Zineer.' Saying her name, not just thinking it, caused her throat to close. 'I'm – I am sorry.'

Caeli's hand tightened on Ayae's shoulder.

'I hear a name and it is not spoken in happiness.' Muriel Wagan did not smile; nor did she reach out for Ayae. Instead, she nodded, once. 'I knew. When the fire burst into the sky and I heard your voice, I knew. The loss is all of ours, Ayae.'

She had no response.

'Walk with me a little.' Lady Wagan pushed open the door of the Enclave. The midday's sun was high in the sky and its heat seeped off the ground strongly, but Ayae could not feel it. 'Aelyn Meah confirmed for me that I will be called as a witness after this break,' Muriel Wagan said. 'I do believe I have made a mistake by agreeing to be part of this mortal and immortal trial.'

She was taken aback by the other woman's tone. 'What did she say?' Ayae asked.

'It was what she did not say.' After a dozen steps, Lady Wagan stopped. Ahead of her, the men and women who held stones in their hands moved like a large, slow animal. Above them, the ends of the glass tubes rose like spears that had pierced through the crowd's body. 'You will need to be careful, Ayae. We all will, for that matter, but you more than others will need to watch yourself.'

10.

Zaifyr knew that the trial was unfolding poorly for him, but that only strengthened his search for Lor Jix.

Kaqua had surprised him. The rest — from the Keepers to the mortals — had said and done much of what he thought they would do, but the Pauper had caught him off-guard. He had not expected Fo and Bau to be presented as victims. Despite his surprise, he could afford to give only a small amount of attention to the trial as it unfolded around him. It was becoming more and more difficult to speak, and he thought that the next time he was addressed, he might not answer. By that time, he knew, he had to have found Lor Jix.

His awareness pushed through Nale's stone ground and to the haunt of a drowned child near the surface of Leviathan's Blood. She was startled by his touch, and he felt her panic wash against him like the waves against the stone pillar of Nale. She was young, so young that she had not the ability to form words or desire and he felt a deep sympathy for her wordless fear. Yet he did not stay. He could have offered her a little comfort, but it would not have lasted, and from her, Zaifyr moved to the haunt of a young woman further beneath the waves. A middle-aged man followed. An old woman after. Each of their pale, flickering bodies formed a thread that allowed his awareness to stretch further and further from him, until he reached the floor of the ocean where he believed Lor Jix waited.

He had found little reference to the man since Anguish had spoken to him. He had searched in books, searched because he wanted to know as much about the ancient dead as he could, but he had found little. That had given him some pause and, he admitted, some trepidation, but it had been mitigated somewhat by the fact that he had found a great deal in relation to the ship, *Wayfair*. It was listed in a number of books as one of the great shipwrecks of the War of the Gods. It had been lost in one of the worst storms to rampage through Leviathan's Throat, its hull low with the weight of gold and silver from sixteen nations. According to the majority of the writers, *Wayfair* had been contracted to make an offer to the gods to stop their war, and while the exact amount of what it held differed wildly, the lost contents had become one of the great wrecks. It was made even more tantalizing by the fact that it was captained by one of Leviathan's holy order.

Periodically through his research, Zaifyr had thought of Meihir, the witch who had greeted him on the morning his parents had died. She had been the first ancient dead he had met — and, in the years that followed her punishment by the god Hienka, he had watched a madness creep over her, but it was not until centuries had passed that Zaifyr truly understood the horror of what the god had done to her.

In the black ocean, he drifted to the haunt of a young cabin boy, his haunt so old that he had become numb to the cold and hunger that drove him.

When Zaifyr had finally returned to Kakar after he and his siblings had finished their war, when he returned to begin the construction of his kingdom, Asila, he had seen so much more of the dead that he was, at times, overwhelmed by a deep sorrow. He had seen friends and enemies die, both by his own hand, and no matter who they had been in life, they had decayed before his eyes in death: they lost their sense of self and become a shell of what they had once been, forever trapped. Even in the depths of his depression, he knew that Meihir had not suffered exactly like that.

He could still recall the old trail that led to his village, the narrowness of it that had once seemed so wide, and the melted snow that left some steps more dangerous than others. Each step he had taken on that return to Kakar had been heavy with the memories of his early life. The charms being wrapped around him by family members. The sword his father gave him, the straight, new blade, and the hilt wound tightly in leather. The stone bears that moved in the forest. He had become so lost in his memories that when he finally came to the clearing of his village, defined now by a handful of broken stone kilns, he did not see the ruins, but the living, breathing site of his childhood with the old witch standing in its centre.

Then she had turned to him and the light had broken through her frail body. *Zaifyr. Hello*, he had replied. *You are my shame, Zaifyr, you are the other half of my curse, my failure.* Her voice gained a fury with each word, and then suddenly, it stopped. *Zaifyr*, she whispered, again, and began to walk away.

Hours later, she returned to him, to speak to him, though

her conversation was not easy. Her difference from the other haunts became clearer with each day he spent around her, and with each day he saw a clearer picture of her fragmented mind, broken not just by her god's betrayal of her, but by her own betrayal through her loss of faith. At times, she was lucid, and aware of how she suffered; at others, violent, and in the worst of her anger, she would be able to touch him, but only very rarely. Most of the time, she was as he knew her, a broken woman. He longed to provide her a final rest, and it was there, he realized as he drifted through the black ocean to another haunt, there in the ruins of his childhood home that the desire to provide rest to all the dead came to him — a desire that would ultimately manifest in his building of the city Asila, and the nation by that name, where, even in the final days of it, he had thought only to release the dead from their pain.

Zaifyr plunged deeper into the water as he stretched out to another woman's haunt.

Just as Hienka had punished Meihir, Leviathan had left her heretics in purgatory, with no chance of relief from their watery prisons. He remembered dimly stories of her dragging ships down herself, of others sunk by her captains. The books he had read had suggested that *Wayfair* had sunk because the offer of gold and silver and whatever other riches was within its hull had insulted the gods. A few, believing the captain to be a holy figure, wrote that the insult had been much, much worse because of that, and that accounted for the storm that ravaged the area as well.

Zaifyr drifted to the haunt of an old sailor. He felt his awareness stretched tight, as if it was reaching an end, and he could go no further, even as the ocean filled with the faint outlines of the dead around him.

A voice spoke, then:

You risk a lot being so deep, godling.

It was a man's voice, deep, and with a wet echo in it. It was neither friendly, nor marked by hostility.

I am not a god, Zaifyr replied.

I did not call you one.

The shadowed outline of a ruined ship began to form on the edges of his awareness, the hull broken, the mast snapped. Long, ugly fish moved between the broken wood, their white forms like distorted slugs that would dart between the broken halves. It was from that space that the ancient dead emerged, his hands first, as if he could grip the wood around him. A broad and bearded face, a smooth, bald head; one eye a solid pale colour, the other not. He wore long, tattered robes, and around his waist were the remains of a once-elaborate belt.

I have watched you flit and flutter down to me, godling, the ancient dead said. *At this depth, you are little more than a bad thought to me.*

But you are Lor Jix, are you not?

That is a real name.

If it is yours, I will pull you to the surface with it.

His laugh was rough and violent. *I am not one to make deals.*

Not even against the last god?

11.

Alone, Ayae slowly walked back to where she had stood earlier.

She felt numb. Before her, scenes of Nale passed rapidly and silently, a cartoon booklet of meaningless pages, until a table was sketched, until a podium emerged from that, and the long body of Lian Alahn sitting on it.

Yet, in her mind, she did not see the podium where he sat. Rather, she saw the table on the top floor of Ciree, one of the finest restaurants in Mireea, the wood polished until it shone. There, Lian Alahn's dark eyes watched her as she sat in the chair Illaan pulled out for her. He was an older man, but not old enough for his hair to be the natural two-toned grey and white it was dyed. She would think, later, that it revealed a secret about him, that it explained his coldness to her and to his third son. He barely said a word to her throughout the dinner, his lips a straight line for much of the flip book of her memory. Of the few words he did say, it was those that he spoke in the middle of the meal that she remembered most. He had asked her name, again. He had already asked before she sat, and even after she answered a second time, he had asked a third. When he asked again in the middle of the meal, she had placed her fork and knife down and said, 'There is no more to add to it than what I have told you.'

She knew that he was asking to remind his son that she had only one name, as if somehow, the girl who was an apprentice for Samuel Orlan had need for the gold and for prestige of a Traders' Union official in Yeflam. But facts, she knew, had little to do with bigotry. If Lian Alahn had come to Mireea but six months later, Ayae knew that he would have found a more receptive audience in his son. The cracks in her relationship with Illaan had begun, though she would not have been able to acknowledge it then, and perhaps neither would he. Yet if Lian Alahn had torn himself from the Traders' Union to present his race-driven fears to his son again, his last memory of Illaan would not be the stiff formality in which his son had told him that he had overstepped his boundaries.

In Yeflam, the father of Illaan Alahn now rose to his feet.

He lifted his hands to quieten the crowd. A moment later, members of the Yeflam Guard cried out for silence.

'Thank you,' Lian Alahn said. 'We are to resume with the trial of Qian, as held by the people of Yeflam. With the afternoon's sun soon to be above us we begin the second session of the day, and the judges respectfully request the presence of Lady Muriel Wagan of Mireea at the stand.'

The crowd murmured. Ayae could hear clearly only those around her — 'She was allowed off the island?' said one, 'So early!' said another — before she turned with the rest of the crowd towards the far edge of Nale. 'Can you see her?' a woman asked of no one in particular, but Ayae had to admit that she could not. She was too short to see clearly, but while she could not identify Lady Wagan, she could see Caeli's blonde head, turned almost white beneath the sun. With a slight push against the woman who had spoken, Ayae began to make her way through the crowd, aiming for the very front, and reached it just in time to see the Lady of the Ghosts emerge from the crowd.

After months of newspaper articles, pamphlets and rumours paid for and naturally occurring in Yeflam, it would not have been difficult for the crowd to underestimate Muriel Wagan. Certainly, they had no respect for her, for her solitary walk to the podium was littered in jeers.

For her part, Lady Wagan did not appear bothered. She was not a tall woman, so she could not hold herself in the fashion that conveyed a sense of superiority and power. She was not young enough, either, that she could cultivate a sense of innocence and a need for protection that would appeal to the crowd around her. No, Muriel Wagan, on the wrong side of being middle-aged, her body giving over to a loose fat after months on Wila, could not stand before the Yeflam people in any such form of grace or innocence. So she stood before them in disregard, the hem of her green and white gown trailing along the stone ground, the ends of it pulling and threading until she stood on the podium where others had and regarded those before her with an air of dismissal, as if she had heard what they would say already.

'Lady Wagan.' Lian Alahn raised his hands for quiet again and waited for the crowds to fall silent. 'Muriel,' he said, once they had. 'Would you please tell us what happened between you and the Keepers Fo and Bau?'

'Keepers Fo and Bau were sent to Mireea after I requested aid,' she replied evenly. 'We had a long-standing treaty with

Yeflam regarding attacks, one signed before the first city was complete. Without going into all the details of it, our agreement was that if one of us were attacked, the other would help in defence of the land and people. I had a similar treaty with the Kingdoms of Faaisha and Leera. No such treaties exist between any nation and the Tribes of the Plateau, but others in regard to trade and border recognition do. We had never been forced to act on our treaties, but we were no longer confident that the number of attacks from Leera would remain small. Over the previous six months we had seen them increase and it was the belief of myself and Captain Aned Heast that the attacks were indicative of a larger force. Keepers Fo and Bau were sent in direct regards to that.'

'If I may interrupt?' Gall Bertan rose from his seat, not waiting for an answer. 'I do not see the Captain here – will he be making himself available for us?'

'I cannot answer that,' she said.

'Why not?'

'Because he no longer works for me.'

'You have fired Aned Heast?' Olivia Raz spoke in a dry, cynical voice. 'Lady Wagan, you must think we are foolish to believe that.'

'Serious allegations were made against him,' Muriel Wagan replied without pause. 'I believed that they were a serious threat to the political harmony between Yeflam and Mireea. Because of this, I was forced to dismiss him from my service.'

'He is surely still on Wila?'

'No.'

'No?' Gall Bertan picked up the thread, outrage in his voice.

'I am afraid,' Lady Wagan said evenly, 'that Aned Heast is his own man. He left Wila as a free man should.'

'Thank you.' Lian Alahn's hand fell on Bertan's shoulder, silencing him. 'Muriel, you are not here to answer questions about your Captain.'

'As I said, he is no longer in my employment.'

'We are here to talk about Keepers Fo and Bau,' he prompted.

'Of course.' A laugh ran through the crowd, but the Lady of the Ghosts did not react to it. 'They arrived in Mireea under orders that they were observers. I had initially hoped that they would be part of my defence against the Leerans. Both would have made the war easier, but they had been given strict orders not to take part. Eventually, I was forced to accept this. As befitting their station, I gave them a lodging in one of my Keeps and allowed them access to what was happening on the Spine of Ger. Apart from state matters, very little was kept from them, and even some state matters were shared. Both attended a handful of public meetings, but largely, they stayed in the tower. I was horrified to hear later that they had been requesting staff to buy them small animals. Their superiors reported a high rate of mental trauma in the staff who had to pick up the remains of the creatures in the following days.'

'I do not see what the studies of Keepers Fo and Bau have to do with this.' Eira's voice was cold. 'Their dedication to their studies is well known.'

'That dedication is well known,' the Lady of the Ghosts said. 'Even in Mireea, we heard about the plague on Xeq that had led to their arrival. In this particular situation, Keeper Fo's work allowed us to make the connection between the animals he killed and the plague that he was responsible for unleashing on Mireea.'

A different muttering emerged in the crowd around Ayae. To her left, she overheard a woman's voice say, 'Xeq', and she heard the name of the city again and again. She could see the flames again falling from the sky and closed her eyes to block out the image. Behind her, Ayae heard a man mutter, '. . . compensation to the families!' while another said sourly, 'We were all his rats.'

The Pauper rose from his seat. 'You are making quite an accusation, Lady Wagan,' he said over the crowd. 'Do you have proof?'

'Keeper Fo walked out of the hospital where it began,' she replied evenly. 'A report prepared by the Healer Reila Juloya is readily available to all here. She makes the connection between various events in the bodies of victims to a number of diseases that have been claimed by Keeper Fo as his own. Most notably, she suggests that it was a variation on the disease known as Divinities Facade. I am sure the name is well known in Yeflam. We found it in the remains of birds that Sergeant Illaan Alahn kept, and later in his body. Because of that, Reila Juloya was able to make the connection quite easily.'

'We will examine the sergeant's body—'

'My son's remains,' Lian Alahn interrupted, 'did not return from Mireea, Keeper.'

'The bird did,' Lady Wagan said. 'Benan Le'ta has it.'

The Yeflam Guard were forced to cry out for silence as the crowd erupted.

'Why did you not bring the bird to us?' the Pauper asked, once silence had been restored.

'I was forced to use it as political leverage for the safety of my people,' she replied, a hint of steel in her voice. 'The Keepers had abandoned me on the Spine of Ger, and it was made very clear that I could not retreat to their gates. The Traders' Union, however, disagreed. With the bird in his hand, Benan Le'ta planned to use it in a campaign against the Enclave. Yet there was resistance to his methods in the Traders' Union – I would be correct in thinking that, would I not, Mister Alahn?'

'I am not here to speak for the Traders' Union,' the man said in a sombre tone. 'Sufficient to say, I did not agree with the use of my son in this matter.'

'You had—' Kaqua was forced to raise his voice over the crowd. Their discontent only grew and shouts could be heard at the back of the crowd, a verbal anger gaining momentum as it rolled towards the podium. 'You had Qian,' he repeated, after the guards cried out again and stopped the noise. 'And you had suffered at the hands of the Keepers Fo and Bau. No one here denies that. That is why we are holding this trial. You need not speak ill of them unless your goal is to create a defence of Qian by doing so.'

'Qian brought himself to Yeflam,' Lady Wagan said. 'He may have arrived in chains, but I had no more power over that than I had in putting Fo and Bau in chains.'

'Remove her from the stand!' Eira's voice cut out sharply. 'She is not a credible witness. She portrays Keepers Fo and Bau as if they were common criminals!'

'No,' Muriel Wagan replied easily. 'I portray them as rabid dogs who deserved to die. Dogs I tried to kill myself.'

The crowd erupted into shouts.

Ayae felt a note of alarm run through her as the voices rose over Nale. The Yeflam Guard shouted out again, attempting to return order to the crowd, but they were drowned out. At the podium, both Xrie and Oake left their position beside Zaifyr to call out orders to the guards, who were looking increasingly frustrated. Ayae saw Kaqua raise his hands in the air and shout, but his voice could not be heard, either. She took a step forward awkwardly, the stiffness in her legs surprising her – but she forced herself to take another step, to push out of the crowd, to prepare herself to help Lady Wagan or, should the crowd turn on him, Zaifyr. By her third step, all the judges on the podium had risen, but none of their voices could be heard over the crowd.

'*ENOUGH!*' The Pauper's voice thundered across Nale, the sheer force of it silencing the crowd. 'Lady Wagan, you will explain yourself!'

'I will?' At the podium, the Lady of the Ghosts stood calmly. 'Two men released a plague in Mireea and I responded in a way that accorded with my position. Soldiers of mine, along with members of the mercenary group Steel, and a woman you know, Ayae, were sent to kill both Keepers.' At the mention of her name, Ayae felt suddenly exposed. 'The casualties were very high, but I knew they would be. In truth, I did not know that any would survive. I had little choice, though: I had an army at my gates and no time for mercy. At the time I sent soldiers to kill Keepers Fo and Bau, Qian was near death. He had been a victim of Fo's attack in the hospital – we believe he had followed the woman who had been the initial carrier into the building. My healers were not convinced that he would recover from it.'

'Yet he did,' Kaqua said. 'Shortly before he raised the dead as ghosts in your very own city, very similarly to what he did in Asila.'

'But unlike what happened in Asila, his actions saved the people of Mireea,' Lady Wagan replied. 'At no point should anyone forget that. Afterwards, he offered to come to Yeflam in chains, to ensure that a place of safety was provided for the Mireean people. I was surprised by that, but I agreed. The Leeran Army was still in place. The mountain itself had begun to crumble. My people were afraid and confused. I had little option, and I still believed that Yeflam would be the best place for myself and my people. Had I known that we would be treated as prisoners, I might have turned down Qian's offer.'

'You are safe here, Lady Wagan,' the Keeper said. 'All the Mireean people are safe here. It pains me to hear that you doubt that.'

'I doubt it because my enemy walks the streets and I do not.'

The silence that greeted Lady Wagan's words was, Ayae thought, worse than the shouts that had arisen before. She turned to the judges, but could not find the discomfort of the crowd reflected upon their faces. Rather, her gaze found the Keeper known as the Cold Witch, and discovered that the woman whose anger had been so focused on Zaifyr, now regarded her with the same intensity.

'Thank you, Lady Wagan,' Lian Alahn said. 'You may step down, unless Qian has questions for you.'

'No,' Zaifyr replied, his voice sounding strangely hollow, as if it spoke from a great distance. 'I have no questions. However,' he continued, and as he did, his voice seemed to return to him, as if it had travelled a line to speak to the crowd, 'I do believe I will speak now.'

What the Leviathan Saw

'You are given three chances to embrace the Leeran God,' Jiqana said to me. When I found her, she was owned by a rich Gogair family in Xanourne who had put her to work as a cleaner and cook for a private residency for diplomatic visitors. Before she had been blinded, Jiqana had been a chef, and it was because of these skills, in combination with her injury, that she was purchased for a good price. The owner promised his visitors that no face would be remembered in the new home he did not live in. It had turned out to be a popular promise, but on the evening that I met Jiqana, no one was in residence, and we talked long into the night while I made her tea in the kitchen. 'The first time you are asked to embrace their god,' she continued, 'is when you are first brought into the camp, but no one agrees. Everyone knows that if you agree the first time you are seen as a liar. The Faithful kill those who do agree and then feed their flesh to their animals.'

Jiqana saw other horrors before she was blinded. She saw men and women who were horribly distorted, and whose bodies were being modified by other Leeran soldiers upon their request. 'Spikes, bones, furs, they asked for it all to be fixed to them permanently,' she said. 'There were not many of these men and women though: I saw only two, for example, but I heard others talked about. They all had two names, one for the past, and one for the future. The past names they spoke in a tone of reverence, while the present names were spoken in fear.'

—Tinh Tu, *Private Diary*

1.

'They talk, Mister Le,' the First Queen said in her whisper-thin voice. 'Behind our backs, in the corners, and with the dark to help hide their raised hands. They talk about me. They talk about you. Occasionally, they talk about us together. They talk about how you did not show enough remorse when you asked for forgiveness, and they talk about how I forgave you too easily.'

Bueralan pushed her chair to the edge of the balcony, the sound of Yoala Fe's party muted behind glass doors. The First Queen rested in her heavy intricate wheelchair, a dark red blanket across her frail legs, the image of a woman in her final years, in her decline of power, an image that she had maintained before the men and women inside her daughter's mansion. She had spent her first hours silent, offering smiles and nods to those who greeted her, before, seemingly reluctant, drawn into conversation. The people who spoke to her were Ooilan for the larger part, but a few brown-skinned Saan offered greetings, including Usa Dvir. The tall, thin man had bowed slightly, and his gaze had lingered on Bueralan uncomfortably, but he had not greeted the saboteur. Dvir, like most in the room, turned his attention to the Queen's Voice, who stood beside the older woman. As they walked up the stairway to the mezzanine that overlooked the main floor, the Queen's Voice replied to all the questions given to her with gentle humour, a simple warmth and, occasionally, coldness. She was still in the party, holding court just before the glass door Bueralan had closed.

'You hear more than me,' he told the First Queen.

'Most of it I don't hear at all, but they move their lips so clearly.' A raspy laugh escaped her. 'How quickly do you think they would hang you after my daughter kills me?'

Earlier, when the carriage had drawn up to the entrance of Yoala Fe's massive estate, they had been greeted by the First Queen's youngest daughter. The Third Princess, Yoala Fe, had opened the carriage door with her own hands – hands that were bare of all jewellery, as were her wrists and arms. Only her hair held any adornment: the long darkness of it had been wound around the crown of her head and threaded with gold and copper. Following such simple fashion, Yoala wore a plain but elegant gown of yellow and orange that, despite its flattering cut, did not hide the age that had crept onto her since Bueralan had last seen her. The years had stripped away much of her youthful beauty, leaving a hardness about her as she approached middle age – a hardness that greeted him not just when her dark eyes met his as he emerged from the darkness of the carriage, but when two brown-skinned men who stood behind her crossed their arms, their thick copper bracelets sounding like swords clashing.

'They might let me live,' Bueralan said, 'once I said I had some remorse.'

'Saan warriors with that many bracelets do not recognize remorse.'

'With that many bracelets, they are not usually guards. They're soldiers, veterans of the wars of the Saan. You only get a piece of copper after you've proved yourself against another Saan. For most, it comes after you kill another in single combat. With their small populations, the Saan do not go to war like us. They choose representatives and those representatives are here.' Over the wooden railing of the balcony, he could see the long poles that punctuated the estate, and the flames that pushed back the dark. 'I enjoyed our carriage ride. It is a better memory than any I have of the Hundredth Prince.'

'Such flattery.'

He smiled.

'I remember him only vaguely, but I like to think that I am very much different to Jehinar Meih.' The First Queen's light hands lay in her lap apart, as if between her fingers was the memory of a shape she had once loved. 'I did not, for one, change my last name to mirror Aelyn Meah's. He was such a fool, he believed that it gave him some claim to power. I told him once that a name did not give one the right to rule, but the womb did. The right womb.'

'He often quoted that.'

'I said it in jest, but it has proven true.'

'I have found it so.' Further out, Bueralan saw one of the flames go out. 'It has made poorer rulers than better ones in my experience, but Jehinar would not have been better than you. Perhaps in my youth, I would have been better if I had seen the world before I met him, and not after.'

'You were like so many of the young,' the First Queen said quietly. 'You wanted your change then, not later. You could not wait for the glacial slowness of our people to reach the corner you had already turned. Had you been older, you probably would have died in Illate. But you were not, and so you had the Prince.'

'I do not think now that Jehinar would have ended the trade.' Zean had always said that, but it was not until after he had saved Bueralan and the Hundredth Prince that Bueralan had seen the truth in his words. 'At least you are turning.'

'Your mother would enjoy your cynicism.' A man's shadow emerged on the road, making his way towards the dead light. 'I would like to tell you that I forgave you because of her, but that is not entirely true. If Samuel Orlan had not stepped out to speak for you, I would have used her memory to justify your return, but the truth is, Bueralan, what you have returned to do is of great help to me in turning that corner. It was not what I expected, and I hope for your sake it is not a lie that has been chained around your neck, but even should it be, your blood brother would be proud of what it will accomplish.'

Zean would think it foolishness. He said, 'Do you not believe that a soul can be reborn?'

The First Queen, the reborn Queen of the original five who had refashioned Ooila with steel and blood three centuries ago, chuckled drily. 'Oh, it is true enough. If you have read the books I have read, you would not doubt it,' she said. 'But I do not feel as if I am hundreds of years old, and I do not remember the intricate details of those lives. I remember merely flashes, and those are of revolutions and changes, of sweeping away old, stagnant power that had been so much like a cage. Occasionally, it causes me to think that the cage still exists, and it holds me and my daughters so very tightly.'

Far out on the estate, a flame flickered and rose. 'The Saan that stood behind Yoala,' he said, 'are bridal gifts.'

'To ensure that a Dvir son sits on a throne beside my daughter,' she said. 'It will be announced tonight.'

'She is too old to have a child, by Saan standards.'

'She is too old to be a princess.'

Bueralan did not reply.

'You should have married her,' the First Queen said sadly. 'Like your mother and I wanted, so long ago.'

2.

As the afternoon's sun began to rise, Kye Taaira said, 'We are being followed, Captain.'

'We are also being watched,' Heast replied. As he spoke, he pulled on the reins of his horse: ahead of him, the road that he and the tribesman followed, the road that led out of the Mountains of Ger, broke down into jagged rips of soil and rock. It was different to the damage that had been caused by the earthquakes, much straighter and consistent. Ropes and ox had done most of it, but amid the rope-burnt tree trunks that had been pulled to the ground and the rough edges of ploughed ground were the marks of axes and the remains of fires. It was destruction that had been caused by the Leeran Army as they retreated down the mountain. Retreat was probably too strong a word for the path they took, Heast knew. General Waalstan and the Leerans had been bloodied in Mireea but they had not suffered defeat – a fact as clear as the exposed roots of the large, broken limbs that had been torn from the ground. 'It started in Mireea.'

'It is an interesting distinction that you make. I would have thought to be followed was to be watched,' the tribesman said.

'This damage continues for some distance, by the way. There is a new trail after the trees, but we will have to climb over the remains here.'

Awkwardly, Heast lifted his right leg over the back of his horse, trying his best to ignore the pain that ran in a line down his left leg as he did. He knew that the scar tissue where the steel and flesh met had broken open – the sharp pain was what he felt when it was particularly bad. On the ground, his left hand fell to where the two met, while he held the horse's reins in his right. 'Is the person following us one of your ancestors?'

'I believe so,' Kye Taaira replied. 'He is at a great distance and he is careful, but I sense him well enough.'

'Will he attack alone?'

'Perhaps.' High over the tribesman's shoulder, the heavy hilt of his two-handed sword caught the sun's light; but it did not reflect the brightness, or glint beneath it. Rather, it looked like a darkly tarnished, brittle piece of metal. 'I do not know which one it is, and how he or she acts will depend greatly on who it is. Who do you believe watches us, Captain?'

'I am not sure.' Heast turned away from the other man, away from his sword. A long, broken limb led up to the fallen trees, where he could see the vague suggestion of a path made by sword or axe. His good leg guided him up it, and the horse followed without reluctance. 'Does it surprise you that the Leerans destroyed the road like this?'

'I thought it strange when I first came through here,' Taaira admitted. 'It seemed to me that the road to an enemy had been cut off. But I told myself that it was cutting off an enemy's road as well.'

'It is not what I would have expected from General Waalstan.'

'I was not under the impression that the two of you had met.'

'We haven't.'

Heast slowly made his way along the thick trunk. The cutting of smaller branches and leaves had not been done to ease the path of horses, and twice, before he reached the huge rounded knot that joined it to an even larger log, he was forced to stop and snap off sharp broken ends that would have dug into the horses' flesh. Yet, as he continued, walking carefully over the uneven lane of tree trunks, Heast's memory returned to the night that he had led the retreat out of Mireea. He had expected the Leerans to follow them, to use the lightly armoured raiders to trail them down the mountain, attacking their flanks. Each morning for the first week, he expected to awake to the report of men and women with filed teeth attacking, but no such report came. He had eventually explained it by the presence of the ghosts in the city: any general would have a hard time pushing his or her soldiers through the broken streets, even more so with the earthquakes. Waalstan had made a few mistakes assaulting the Spine of Ger, and while Waalstan had revealed himself to be a well-planned and thorough general, Heast had thought that he reacted slowly and poorly to changes on the battlefield. Eventually, that characteristic had bled into his assessment of Waalstan and he had reasoned that the lack of pursuit had been unsurprising, but this . . .

'It is the kind of destruction that would force the Yeflam military to travel by sea,' Heast said. 'If they were to go to war, that is.'

'Yet the Leeran god arrives in Yeflam,' the tribesman said. 'Surely she would not be there if she was at risk.'

'The trial may have been worth such a risk, but perhaps we are overlooking the obvious.'

'Such as?'

'Where are the ghosts of Mireea?' A thick branch appeared before Heast, the first in a series of limbs that led down the trees. 'Our caution was unnecessary. We could have gone through the city in the night and seen what we saw during the day. We took a safer journey, but it turned out that it was only safer for us because we could see the ruined road we walked. The priests you followed obviously thought that there was a threat — they believed that enough that they skirted the edges. You do not do that unless you have seen what your threat is.'

Behind him, the tribesman was silent. A gap appeared before Heast. 'You believe that the Leeran god drove them away,' Taaira said, finally.

He stepped awkwardly across the gap. 'Is that so hard to imagine after what you saw in your own home?'

'It is not,' he said. 'Nor is it hard to imagine that she did not drive them off, but claimed them as her own.'

'If that is true, we are both in trouble.' Heast stepped onto the hard ground and began to lead his horse to a narrow path that had been made, again, by axe and sword. 'The ghosts of Mireea are watching us, Taaira. They have been watching us for some time now.'

3.

When Zaifyr first spoke, his words felt as if they had come from a distance, and that they tasted of the salt of blood and seawater. He said, 'No, I have no questions,' and the words echoed in his head, mingling with the final exchange between Muriel Wagan and the Pauper, the combination of which left the latter's words, his admonishment of the Lady of the Ghosts that she was protected in Yeflam, even more hollow than they were in truth. The echo faded as he rose, much as if he was surfacing from beneath the black waves of Leviathan's Blood, and he said, 'However, I do believe I will speak now.'

'You must wait until you are called.' It was Lian Alahn who spoke then, his voice a series of snaps. 'We have established a process, Qian—'

'That is not my name.' He could still taste salt in his mouth, and spat. 'Not any more.'

The silence that followed was sharply pronounced. The emotional intensity of the crowd was still strong from Muriel Wagan's testimony, her denunciation of Fo and Bau connecting with the crowd's animosity. His spittle — a mistake, he knew

– allowed for that emotion to flow into him, for the arrogant actions of the two Keepers to appear like an echo of his own.

'Your complete lack of respect for us,' Alahn said coldly, 'and your lack of respect for the people around you has been duly noted. Return to your seat and wait to be called. You must abide by our process here today.'

'Or?'

'This trial can be ended,' he said. 'This day can end. You are not in charge here.'

'This trial is nothing but a cardboard set in an expensive play.' Zaifyr could still taste the salt in his mouth, but he knew now that it was not real, and he did not spit again. 'I know this because I helped build it.'

'Qian, you must stop this.' Kaqua raised his hands as he spoke, not to silence the crowd, which remained silent, but to calm those on either side of him. 'We are examining your role in relation to the deaths of Keepers Fo and Bau. We have gone to extraordinary lengths to organize this trial that you wished to take part in. We have all responded to the difficulties inherent in it and we have done so by creating a unique process that is unprecedented in its democracy. A thousand and one men and women from Yeflam have the right to cast votes for or against your innocence. The men and women who sit here on either side of me are but volunteers who will lead the discussion. Some, I admit, are not as neutral as others, but your actions have had repercussions that extend widely. We have endeavoured to ensure that a fair balance exists across the twelve of us. To claim otherwise is merely to insult us and our work. If you believe the evidence that has been presented is against you, then it is possible that what you are seeing is a life of such violence and horror that all who hear of it are properly appalled.'

'With that, I do not disagree,' he said, and turned away from the podium.

Before the white wall of the Enclave, he saw Jae'le and Aelyn. Both watched him intently. Jae'le had told Zaifyr that this moment — the moment where he took control of the trial's narrative, where he subverted it to show the threat of the child — was one that was fraught with dangers. If he lost them . . . well, he would not. Not here. Not so close to what he wanted. 'I was caught by Fo's disease,' he said aloud. 'It was as Lady Wagan said, but what she did not know was that it was an accident that I was. Fo had intended the disease to be spread through the population of Mireea. He had no plans to attack me: I was simply beside the woman he had infected at the wrong time. When he found me, he was surprised. He was not overly concerned, but he did at least acknowledge the fact that he had struck me down. It was more than he bothered to show for the men and women who had been in the hospital with me.'

Before him, the crowd lay like a flat ocean. At the back he could see the lingering undercurrent of Lady Wagan's speech, like a swell rising.

'I am here to answer for a mortal crime — that is, the deaths of two men who were responsible for the deaths of over a dozen others — but you do not ask me about the men and women in that hospital.' Zaifyr saw Ayae, half a dozen steps away from him. She would understand the distinction that he was talking about. 'You do not ask because you have no interest in what Fo and Bau did,' he continued. 'My sister asks you if you will see the immortal excuse for murder, but she does not need to ask. You already do. You believe that immortals are worth more than mortals.'

'You overreach, Madman,' Eira spat. 'They would have been gods had you not killed them.'

The unrest at the back of the crowd rose like a wave, rippling through the people in a deep and profound unease.

'No,' Zaifyr said, 'we will never be gods.'

In the middle of the crowd stood Eidan, and beside him, the child. His gaze fell on the latter as he continued forward.

'We must all admit that, if we wish to repair the world that the gods have destroyed,' he said, his voice raised for all the men and women around him. 'We can no longer alter history, rewrite deeds and reclaim morals. We can no longer carry the deceit of the gods as if they were ours. We can no longer carry their prejudices and their hates. We can no longer hold tight to their belief that all other creations were imperfect in comparison to them. It is a cage to us.'

'Qian.' The child offered him a smile. It was beautiful because she was beautiful, but he saw only the empty conscience behind it. 'I am not on trial here.'

'No, there is no trial for you,' he said.

Behind him, the ghost of Lor Jix emerged on the stone platform. He did not need to turn to confirm it: the charm-laced man could feel the chill of the ghost as he drew closer, a chill that was different to the coldness of the haunts and their broken forms around him. It was a chill that passed through the clothes of those nearby, a chill that sank into the flesh, and into the bones.

'So this,' Captain Lor Jix of the lost *Wayfair* said in his water-logged, awful voice, 'this is your god.'

4.

The ancient dead circled the child.

His colourless boots marked his path in an ominous and deliberate step, each fall of his foot forcing the crowd back, each new tread cutting her and her followers from Yeflam. After a complete circle, he stopped beside Zaifyr. 'You do not speak like a god,' Lor Jix said, his voice cold and hard. 'You speak with the air. You speak with your mortality. A god does not speak like that. A god speaks in your head. It is a terrible thing to hear. It is made from words without breath. It is endless. A word could drag itself out for years. A paragraph in a second. There was no respite once a god knew your name.'

'Are you,' the child said, 'suggesting I am not a god?'

Lor Jix laughed.

It was a terrible sound: without humour, it echoed, as if a hundred souls had been forced to laugh by his command.

The crowd withdrew further from him and in doing so, revealed the Yeflam Guard who, like teeth unveiled in a smile, had moved from their positions. At the head of them stood the Soldier and his second, Oake. Their swords were still sheathed at their waists, but the soldiers who had emerged from the crowd around did so with swords in hand and shields over arms, both of which they put before the civilians of Yef-lam. Only the twelve judges from the podium were not so protected, for they had pushed their way past the steel and flesh to stand behind Zaifyr.

'At the bottom of the ocean, you do not hear much of the world,' Lor Jix said. 'But I was not always caged, child. I remember you from my time on the waves.'

'*Qian*.' Aelyn descended from the sky and landed across from him. 'What are you doing?'

'Captain Jix is going to reveal to us a truth about this child,' Zaifyr said. Before him, the smooth black figure of Anguish climbed out from beneath Eidan's shirt and sat on his shoulder. His eyes were still closed, but his small body moved quickly and surely. 'I came here to talk about the gods, but we have made that difficult. We destroyed so much during the Five Kingdoms that all that remains is fragments and lies and mis-direction. That is our legacy, Aelyn. We believed we were gods, but we knew that we were unlike those who had been before. We did not stand in the clouds. We did not sleep beneath the ocean. We could not change our bodies. Our blood did not give life. And we had no paradise to offer the dead. We were the children of the gods, but we could not live beside the words of our parents: the stories of their power diminished ours. To hide that, we destroyed their words and destroyed their history. There are few left who can tell us about a god.'

'I have pleaded with you, brother,' Aelyn said. 'Pleaded with you not to go down this road.'

'He must.' Eidan's voice announced itself for the first time, a voice so deep it sounded as if it had been drawn from huge, dark caverns. 'Our brother has lived with the horror that the gods left in our world. He, more than anyone else, knows the pain.'

Around the child, the ring of brown-robed men and women turned to him, but it was she who spoke next. 'You would do this?' she asked coldly. 'You would make your choice here?'

'I have,' Eidan replied.

'And Anguish?' At the sound of his name, the black-skinned creature pressed against Eidan's neck, as if he could be hidden there.

'The first true betrayal.' An anger simmered in her voice. 'Upon both of you I will craft a lesson.'

'You have done enough to him,' Eidan replied.

'No, I have barely begun.' The crowd watched his brother and the child, but Zaifyr watched the ancient dead intently. The dead man's gaze had not left Anguish since the child had spoken to him, as if, in the first pass he had made around her, he had not seen or felt the tragic being. Now, though, his haunted gaze did not leave Anguish, and Zaifyr recalled their conversation in the ruins of *Wayfair*. Lor Jix had not argued with him after he had mentioned the child. Instead, he had raised his head, as if he could see through the dark depths, as if the huge constructed country of Yeflam was a shadow he knew to be above him. *I have waited for a time longer than I could ever have imagined, godling,* he had said, *but you have finally arrived. Tell me, is she yet named?*

She is not, Zaifyr said.

On Yeflam, Lor Jix lifted his hand to Anguish. 'A god must create. It is an urge within, a mark of their divinity – what does your blind creature of pain say about you, child?'

'You think to question me?' She almost snarled the question to him. 'I will not be spoken to in such a way by an old ghost, angry at the curse laid upon him.'

'There is bitterness in me. I will not deny that,' the Captain of *Wayfair* said. 'But it is not for the reason you believe, child. I have sat in the remains of my god for ten thousand years, and for all that time, I have been reminded of her anger. The Leviathan was not an angry god until the day that you began to exist. I will not claim that all her words to me were a delight. Her words would burn in me when I disobeyed, but her pleasure . . . ah, but that was a pleasure without comparison. On the day you came into the world, however, her pleasure ceased. An anomalous future had created a new truth, one that betrayed how the world worked.

'Linae, the Goddess of Fertility, wept when she realized such a thing had been born of her. She came to the edge of the ocean to ask the Leviathan what she should do. It had not been her will that had made the child inside her. She had the appearance of a woman in the state of pregnancy, but her body was an illusion. A symbol. But her body had manifested a real pregnancy, had allowed for a birth so rare all had thought it impossible. I remember well the day the Leviathan met her. The ocean was rough, the waves high, and the paths we knew arduous to sail. I do not know what the two spoke about, or who called the other gods, but soon all were at Eakar. They talked for days and nights until five years had passed.

'It was on the last day of those five years that the war began.

'My crew and I arrived at the long docks of Eakar that day. Our hold was heavy with food for the people who lived there. In the distance, you could see the outlines of the tallest gods, and of the tallest, Ger. None of us paid it any special mind, except that after Sei, the God of Light, struck Linae, they were all gone. It was a week before we noticed, however, for the light that struck down Linae was so powerful that those who had stood on the deck of *Wayfair* were temporarily blinded. On the day our sight returned, we saw that the high mountain peaks had been broken and sat like a dented crown.

'In the wake of that destruction, my crew and I joined the Eakarian people who lived in the coastal cities and rode to the centre of the mountains. Many died on this journey. The ground had become so septic that the hooves of our mounts were eaten away. Streams ate at our skin. A poor man dipped his hands in before we realized, and I can still remember his screams. Within hours, the food and water we had brought turned foul. Many times did we consider turning around, but each day brought new horrors, new deaths, and we could not go back. Eventually, we found the ruined paths to the floor of the basin where the gods had stood. Nothing lived. The bones of human and animal were stripped of flesh. Trees were splintered. But of all the horrors we had seen, the worst was Linae, who in her pain had dug beneath the soil. She had been burned terribly, and her swollen belly was cracked and weeping.'

Zaifyr watched the child intently as Jix spoke. The anger that had erupted in her so suddenly had turned into something more while the ancient dead spoke; it had left the betrayal that she had felt and had become, now, an offence. She had told Zaifyr that Linae had not given birth to her from a womb, but that she had been born in the soil, in the earth, and that her birth had been the work of fate. She was its last strand. She was destiny. She had accepted that because of her birth from the soil, some of the gods had been afraid of her – she was to replace them, after all – but she had been certain that the War of the Gods was one of love. To hear that it was one that took place because each and every one saw her as an abomination struck deeply at her.

'I asked the Leviathan what had happened.' Lor Jix's voice was unrelenting in its retelling of history. 'We mortals thought to stop the war. Only the most foolish had believed that it would serve us well. But for days I lay upon bed, my senses destroyed by the pain of the Leviathan's reply. I could not speak except while I dreamed, and it fell to my crew to record the words. I lay like this for a decade while my crew fed me and washed me like a babe until her words were complete.

'At the end, I understood that the fate that everyone was following was recreating our understanding of the world and that the gods had not gone to war for dominion of it, but had gone to war to destroy it. What we mortals saw was suicide, an attempt by the gods to remove themselves from this point of fate, to deny its creation. By their acts they did this.' The ghost took a step towards the child. 'Once I had heard it all,' he said, 'the Leviathan gave me a task. She would drown me for it. She would load my ship with riches beyond count, and then she would sink it and drown all my crew on board. She told me that. She told me my task would deny me paradise and she would curse me to complete silence until the day I could stand on the artificial continent. On that day, she told me, I would be able to speak against the abomination, the remains of this piece of fate, and strike out against the last of its form.'

5.

'I have underestimated you,' Ayae heard the child say.

She pushed through the crowd with her heavy hands, her murmured apologies following as people parted before her. They were reluctant, but she persisted, and soon she could see Zaifyr. At his side was a ghost, unlike any she had seen before: he was not like the ghosts Zaifyr had made in Mireea, or the haunts that she had seen. No, this ghost – this being known as Lor Jix – wore his age. It was in the tatters of his robes, in the creases in his boots. The years that had passed, the years that he had been forced to watch, to know that he was watching, were as much a part of the cold, pale, insubstantial flesh that made up his being as the earth was now in hers.

Yet, for all that Lor Jix was a terrifying figure, the child was anything but afraid of him. It was clear that she was furious, that a rage was threatening to consume her. 'What you say changes nothing,' she said as Ayae stepped through the last line of men and women. 'I will have what is mine.'

A woman behind Ayae gasped and she looked up. The sky

had begun to bulge, as if it were a mother's stomach and an infant's hand or foot had pressed against it.

Yet, rather than rising and falling, the force behind the sky continued to press outward. It revealed itself first as a large, shapeless black mass that was more a shadow than anything defined. But with each push it began to split the sky, began to tear it open. Around Ayae, people raised their hands skywards, and their voices turned into shouts – 'What is—' 'Don't look, don't look—' '—my hand, take my—' 'The Keepers! The Keepers must—' – and then their voices turned into screams as the black mass began to take on form, as if exposure to the sky cooled its seething black mass and rendered it into a nightmare for all to see. Thick claws defined themselves first. They wrapped around the edges of the torn sky, grasping onto what surely could not be grasped and used it as a leverage by which a misshapen head could push itself out. It thrust itself into the sky in a horrific parody of birth, looking both wet and newborn, with steam rising from it. Once it was in the sky, its blunt, brutal head began to take shape. So did the huge black teeth. The teeth that were revealed when the creature took a breath. A breath that showed a long, split tongue – a tongue that trailed rising wisps of black smoke, as if it could not be rendered solid.

'Guard!' Xrie's cry reached over the noise. 'Shields raised!'

The Yeflam Guard lifted their shields, making an upraised, interlocking defence. But as the shields rose, the people beneath panicked even more. Their shouts turned to cries and they began to flee, began to push over others, elbowing over guards. They did so until they found that the men and women they pushed through were not substantial, but rather cold, and were multiplying around them at an ever-increasing rate. The ground started to groan and Ayae found her gaze on Eidan as the stone beneath him began to vibrate the most. It did so in a way that was similar to the way the sky had just bulged, and she wondered if another creature was being birthed into the world—

'*No!*'

A huge burst of wind rushed over the crowd, flattening all but a handful.

'You will not do this here.' Ayae, still standing, standing behind Zaifyr, Lor Jix, the child and Eidan, watched Aelyn step between them. 'You will not bring this war to Yeflam.'

'War is already here,' the child said.

'But it will *not* happen here.'

'Look at your brother. He knows that there is no peace. I thought he might be like you when I first spoke with him. I thought he might see reason. That he might see truth. But no.' In the sky, the creature had pulled itself further and further out into the emptiness. It was truly massive, its body of such size and length that it obscured the midday's sun across Nale. 'But I think that I made a mistake before that. A mistake that Eidan allowed me to make. He led me to think that you and he were reasonable. But I think it is Qian who knows reason. He knows what stolen divinity is in him. He knows what I will do to take it back. So does the bitter ghost he has conjured up. That is why his ghost tells lies. He wants them repeated all across this false country – repeated until it is dragged to the ocean's floor.'

'You forget,' Zaifyr said, his voice calm. 'I do not stand here alone.'

'In terms of power, you are very much alone.'

'No,' he said. 'I have my family. My brother—'

'Jae'le.' The child laughed suddenly, as if it were a primal exaltation. 'You do not know, do you? After all this time, you do not know what he gave up.'

'That is enough,' Jae'le said. He did not shout, did not cry out, but his voice carried in the silence as if he had. A moment later, he stepped from behind Ayae, his cloak of green feathers folded over his left arm, over the hilt of his sword. 'You have said your piece, child.'

'You have kept secrets,' she said. 'You have not told them what you were forced to give up when you made that tower.'

'I gave it willingly.'

'Did you?'

'I did,' he said. 'Now look around you.'

On either side of the child emerged the Keepers of the Enclave. 'They are not your allies,' she said, but as she spoke, Ayae could see the restraint that the child had been forced to adopt, the sudden halt on her anger. 'They may stand by you here, but they will not follow you. When they no longer fear you, they will only fear me.'

'You're so young,' Jae'le said.

Then darkness fell over Nale.

In blind panic, Ayae thought that he had done it, that he had somehow plunged the world into night.

But the darkness was not simply an assault on her sight, Ayae realized. She could feel it run over her. Within moments, it pushed into and through her as if it was a hard blade, the edges of it notched and broken. She felt herself catch on it, felt it rip into her hard skin; but more, she felt it tear into her being, into the very concept of who she was. She felt herself begin to split and her identity fracture. She began to think that Ayae was not truly a person but a construct, one made in the world where she lived, one built from her experiences. Underneath that she was nothing but a spirit, an unquantified, undefined spirit that held no central beliefs or ideals. She felt the blade separating the two and she tried to recall her name. As she did, the darkness left abruptly and the midday's sun suddenly burst out around her. She saw her body, whole and unharmed, and she saw that where the child had been standing, the long, tapered end of the black creature's body was disappearing – not into Nale, not down into Leviathan's Blood. No, it plunged into the nothingness out of which it had pulled itself and as it did, it took the child and her priests with her.

'Find her, godling,' Lor Jix said. His awful voice offered no comfort in the silence. 'Pray she has not left this stone nation. Pray she is found and destroyed. Once she is named, I will be bound differently to this world.'

And then he too was gone.

6.

Zaifyr ran his hand through his hair, his fingers tangling with the charms, his breath ragged. He had felt — he had felt himself being split as the dark shadow passed through him, as the child escaped. He had seen her, cradled in its claws, her priests around her. He had felt its teeth and claws. But he had thought, as it passed through him, that for all it had torn the sky open, for all that he felt himself being prised open, the creature had not been here completely. It had been somewhere else. It had been a step outside the world, just a fraction elsewhere. *Find her, godling.* Lor Jix's words repeated themselves in his mind, an urgent chant, the start of a sequence of events that would not end until the child's body had been destroyed. That would take all of them. All his family. All the Keepers of the Divine. It would not be done alone, or even with half of them, he knew. He would need all of them. He would need them to hunt and find her. It had been the threat of fighting all of them that had driven her away — not the threat of him, or Lor Jix, or his family. Even as he realized that, the child's words about Jae'le returned. *You have not told them what you were forced to give up when you made that tower*. Her words, then the ancient dead's. *Find her.* Repeating in his head until he heard his sister.

'Xrie,' Aelyn said. 'Clear Nale.'

'Guard!' A ripple of protest sounded throughout the crowd. Xrie shouted over them. 'Form them into an orderly line! Show them care, but be firm!'

Another voice tried to carry over Xrie's, but the Yeflam Guard followed his orders, and soon the shields that had so recently been used to protect were being used gently to help disperse the crowd.

'I think the citizens of Yeflam have questions that need answering, Lady Meah,' Lian Alahn shouted a second time, trying again to stop the crowd. 'We all heard the words that this *child* spoke to you. She spoke to you as if she was an old friend. I think – and I do not think that I will be alone in this – that an explanation is in order.' His voice reached a small group of men and women around him and they turned to him, stopping the guard. 'What agreement did you make with Leera, Lady Meah?' he said, trying to project his voice to those who were still leaving. 'We have wanted only peace, but what have we traded for it?'

'You would do best, Mister Alahn, to remember where your loyalties lie,' Aelyn replied in a cold voice. 'Xrie, please continue.'

The leader of the Traders' Union yelled in protest twice more but, Zaifyr noted, the conviction of each shout lessened, and by the third, Lian Alahn had joined the crowds directed out of the square. At the tail of the crowd, he saw the ground revealed behind the politician, the litter a series of small indiscretions that grew in size until a lone glass cylinder could be seen lying on the ground, broken at the base and surrounded by red-and-white stones.

'Jae'le,' he said, finally. 'Was she—'

'—right?' His brother had stood next to him patiently, waiting for him to speak. 'No ordinary tower would have held you.'

The sun had been in Zaifyr's eyes when he stepped out of the tower. He had reached up with his free hand to wipe away the tears, using his other hand to balance himself against the frame. Jae'le had spoken to him, but it was only when the glare had truly faded from his eyes that Zaifyr had seen the thinness in his brother. *I have given up food*, he had said, and Zaifyr had believed him. It had been presented to him as an act of kinship, an action of love and solidarity, a mirror to his incarceration in the tower. Yet, when the two had returned to Jae'le's twisting home among the trees, his brother had still not eaten. He had fruit and vegetables for Zaifyr and the newly charm-laced man was thankful. His brother ate meat and, for a while, Zaifyr assumed that Jae'le was eating it privately, to spare Zaifyr the sight of it. But it was not until months had passed, and Jae'le had still eaten and drunk nothing, that it had occurred to Zaifyr that a deep, fundamental change to his brother had taken place.

'We made the tower with our hands,' Jae'le said now. 'We made the bricks from poisoned water and tainted dirt in the Broken Mountains. We shaped them as best we could, but it was Aelyn and Tinh Tu and I who laid them, not Eidan. He held you while we built. But even had his hands been free, he could not have built a door strong enough to hold you. He would not have built a wall that you could not pull apart. No, brother, we could never leave you in an ordinary tower. It had to live and breathe, it had to be able to combat both you and the dead.'

'You went back to give it life, didn't you?' Eidan said. He crossed the stones that separated the three of them, Anguish perched on his shoulder. 'That is why I did not feel it at the time.'

Jae'le nodded once.

'You took a great risk.' Aelyn left her Keepers a handful of paces behind as she drew next to them. 'He could have awoken.'

'He could have,' Jae'le agreed.

'How do you give a tower life?' Ayae said from beside Zaifyr. 'I was told that only a god can create life.'

'There is life in the soil and in the water,' Jae'le said. 'It had only to be woven together and bound again, piece by piece.'

'How long did that take?'

'A decade.' He shrugged. 'Maybe a year more.'

'How is it that no one noticed?'

Zaifyr felt a sudden deep and profound sense of shame before his brother spoke. 'We did not look,' he said.

'Yes, though I hid myself as well,' Jae'le said. 'I am not the beacon our sister is in the land she made. Nor am I like others.' His free arm waved across the Keepers and the Enclave. 'I do not reek of the cold, I do not feel like steel, I do not have the earth in my voice. When my power awoke in me, the gods walked the earth still, and their servants were everywhere. I learned to hide who I was long before I celebrated it. When I gave up a portion of my power, I gave up little anyone would notice.'

'But someone did,' Aelyn said, the bitterness unhidden in her voice.

'Aelyn,' Zaifyr began.

'*No*,' she said, and in the word he heard a finality, an end that she had been driven to. 'Look what you have done, Qian. Look what both of you have done. If you had both listened to me and not pushed this trial, we would have more time to deal with this child god.'

'Where is my sister?' Jae'le said. 'She would not be this weak figure before me. She would be cruel and hard. She would advocate that we must strike before the child is named.'

'Her name does not matter. We have known about the child for a long time, brother. We have had our plans for many years.' A frustrated sigh escaped her. 'Do you think I do not feel those teeth on me? She wishes to devour us to rebuild herself. It could not be tolerated – but it could not be fought as you and Qian once fought, brother. You could not grab this creature by the neck and wring it like a poor animal. She is much more than that. That is why we sent Fo and Bau to Mireea. They were to watch. They were to learn.'

'Mireea was a test.' Kaqua's usually calm and measured voice mirrored the bitterness in Aelyn's. 'Lady Wagan is a capable ruler of the Spine, and Aned Heast's reputation precedes him. We had an agreement that no force from Leera would come to Yeflam, an agreement that meant Yeflam would not contest the body of Ger once Mireea fell. But it was more than that. It was a chance for us to study. For us to learn of the child's general, to learn of her soldiers, her priests, and her. Let us not be hypocritical here, Qian. You and your brothers and sisters conquered most of the world. I am one of the few people here who remember enough of it to know the blood that was spilt. Mireea was a small price to pay to learn what we needed.'

'But you couldn't pay it,' Ayae said.

'No, we could not,' Aelyn said. 'None of us knew that Qian would be there. If we had, we would not have sent Fo.'

'You'll pay a different price now,' she said, her voice hard. 'How does it feel?'

Aelyn ignored her, deciding, instead, to turn, to join Kaqua and the Keepers. With them, she began to walk towards the Enclave as a united force.

Zaifyr wanted to tell her that she was not being asked to sacrifice Yeflam. He wanted to tell her that she was being given a chance to defend her home, to defend the people in it, but he did not raise his voice. Instead, he watched them leave. *If you could only see the dead,* he thought. *If only you could see their suffering and live with it for a thousand years. You would know that to stop the child would be the greatest thing you could do, and you would pay any price for it.* But none of them could see the dead as he did. None of them could see the world that Zaifyr did.

7.

Ayae's office in the Enclave was small and bare. When she pushed open the door to allow Zaifyr, Jae'le and Eidan to enter, the contents were revealed in three shadows. A table and chair sat on the right, the two pieces barely distinguishable from each other, while a quarter-filled bookshelf stood to the left. Between the two was a small window. What little pale light that was in the room came from it and the darkening night sky outside. She had a light beside the door, a copper lantern, but after she had bent to pick it up, she realized that she could not light it.

'Sorry,' she said, putting it back down. 'I never kept matches.'

'It's okay,' Zaifyr said. 'We won't be here long.'

They left the door open and the light from the hall slanted in. Ayae moved to the window, afraid to take the chair or table, sure that they would crack beneath her weight, much as the stone in Yeflam had. She stood at the window because it put all three brothers in her field of vision and allowed her to retain a sense of distance. Zaifyr was the closest to her, sitting on the edge of the table. He would turn occasionally in the conversation that followed and attempt to draw her into what was being said. Jae'le had taken the chair and placed it near the door. He had thrown his cloak of green feathers over the back and its colour was a stark splash in the room. He kept glancing at her as they spoke, but half his face was shadowed and unreadable. Only Eidan, who stood beside the open door, paid her no attention – his focus was on his two brothers and the dark figure on his shoulder, much like a bird.

It was Eidan who spoke the most of the three. His voice was deep, and each word felt as if he had chosen it carefully. 'I am glad you heeded my advice,' he said to Zaifyr. 'I found *Wayfair* many years ago when I built Yeflam. I almost dragged its wreckage from the depths on more than one occasion, but a part of me held back. I have wondered about that, of late – wondered since a man searched for me in Ranan and told me Lor Jix's name. He told me that he was god-touched, but I felt nothing of him.'

'You do not,' Jae'le said. 'The god-touched are not like us.'

'You have met them before?'

'When I was young,' he said, 'when the War of the Gods raged around me. One came to me in the final years of the war because he had heard stories of my power and he thought I might be a return of his master. I was not, but what I learned about the gods, I learned from him. He and his kin were who defined the gods to mortals. It was he who told me that they were but strands of fate given form. He believed that the gods' war was an act of rebellion against other strands. He said that in fighting it, they had destroyed any notion of truth. I gave him little thought after he left me, for he was mad, truly mad. That was what the War of the Gods had done to him. But the words he spoke to me were the same as the words of Lor Jix.'

'The man I spoke with was mad as well,' Eidan said. 'Perhaps they were the same man? The one I met was old and scrawny and white.'

'No, the one I knew was different,' Jae'le said. 'But it could be that they are all simply mad. I would not struggle to believe that.'

Against the wall, Ayae's hand curled into a fist, but it was Eidan who spoke again. 'It would be easy to become mad in the shadow of a god. In the shadow of this child, many things that I had prided myself on have been betrayed.' The dark shadow slid down his arm, and onto the back of Jae'le's chair. 'I had my reasons, but I have questioned them. Often.'

'Perhaps,' Zaifyr said quietly, 'fate and the gods are in collusion.'

'Or conflict,' Jae'le said.

'If we believe Lor Jix, that is,' Ayae finished. 'No offence, Eidan.'

'I have thought it myself,' he admitted. 'On the Mountains of Ger she ordered the land to be ripped apart and torn up, to limit travel across it. It gave me pause to think about what might befall here, for the child can see a fate. It is a single strand, but it appears to be her own, though she has no control over it yet, and cannot see the others that surround it. I have heard her talk about the fate she sees often, and I believe that it is very incomplete. She can see an event two years into the future, then another in ten. But she cannot see consistently a whole year, or a month. She is frustrated by it, but she has used it well. That sight allowed her to find me five years ago. I had been working on the southern edge of Leera, rebuilding a series of smuggler hideouts that had sunk into a bog.

Beautiful buildings: they had been made with fired stones that were lined with holes for their riches. The traps still functioned, and one almost took my hand off, a fact that she related to me in our first meeting.'

'Has she seen what will happen here?' Jae'le asked.

'I do not think so,' he said. 'She is not complete. Her lack of a name is but an easy part for us to identify, but there are others. She has relied upon mortals to do her work for her, men and women she called her beloved. Mother Estalia was one. General Waalstan is another. Both are her voices to the Faithful, and she has long told the General about his death; but the old woman's was not one she foresaw. The child cried out when she died – it was a scream that tore through all of Ranan. When I found her in the cathedral she was a statue in the middle of the floor. She had projected herself to Mireea, in search for the soul of the woman she had named Mother. That was when you encountered her, Qian. She had not expected that – not in the realm of the dead. It frightened her and in her fear, she made Anguish.'

'Her fear?' Zaifyr turned to the creature who stood on the green feathers, rubbing his feet. 'I did not hear that.'

The creature's blind face turned up to him. 'I was a deceit from the start.'

Ayae frowned. She began to speak, but Eidan interrupted her. 'He does not mean it how it sounds, I assure you,' he said. 'He does not want to harm us.'

'Unless he opens his eyes,' Zaifyr said.

'But they're closed.'

'Is she still here in Yeflam?'

'In a way, I suspect.' Anguish dropped from the cloak,

slipping into the shadow of the room. 'But you should be more concerned if she sees herself here.'

'He is right,' Eidan said bluntly. 'On the edge of the bog where I met her, she told me that I would betray her before a century had passed. I could feel her power – the way we all feel it, I believe – and I remember that I held a long steel pipe that I had pulled from the water.' He held out his large hands to show the girth, but in the dark, Ayae could only see the edges of his knuckles, huge and blunt. 'I have often thought back to that moment, for she was unsure how I would react. I could have thrust the pipe through that small form she wore. She was afraid of me, then, but that fear of me never returned after I followed her into Ranan.'

'We will have to find her,' Zaifyr said.

'That is why the Enclave is meeting,' Eidan answered.

'They are not a unified whole,' Jae'le said. 'They tear at each other, now. They may not stand united against her.'

'They cannot allow the child to live,' Zaifyr said.

Though she remained silent, Ayae agreed. Aelyn did not have much choice, as far as she could tell. She had made the agreement to sacrifice Mireea – the knowledge of which sat hard and heavy in Ayae's stomach and had done so as she walked through the Enclave halls – but to maintain the agreement would be to seed a deep ideological threat in Yeflam that she would never fully remove. To accept the Leeran god meant that the Keepers acknowledged that they were not, and would not be, gods themselves.

Jae'le rose from the chair, his cloak a green ribbon that he slung over his arm. 'We should head up there,' he said. 'She may agree with us, but we should take care to support her.'

'Yeah,' Zaifyr said. 'I'll be along in a moment.'

The other man nodded and at the door was joined by Eidan. A moment later, the small, dark figure of Anguish appeared, and in quick, strange movements, climbed up the latter's leg and to his shoulder.

Once the footsteps of the two had faded, Zaifyr turned to Ayae and met her gaze. 'You're quiet,' he said.

'I am,' she said.

'You all right?'

'Not really.'

Ayae laid her heavy hand on his, but could not feel his skin. 'I can't feel anything,' she said. 'What if it doesn't stop?'

Gently, Zaifyr tapped the back of her hand. 'You just have to take control of it,' he said, and turned his hand around to hold hers. 'It's discipline, remember?'

'I don't – I lost that a while back, I think.'

She wished that she could feel his hand tighten around her own, but she could only see the pull of the muscles. 'It happens to us all,' he said. 'You'll get it back.'

'I don't know that I can do this war,' Ayae said, after a moment. 'Not today. Not this week. I can't fight a god this week, Zaifyr.'

'Maybe in a month?'

'A month is fine.'

In the faint light, she saw him smile. 'A month and it'll be over.'

Ayae did not believe that. It could not be true, though she saw in Zaifyr's gaze a confidence that it would be, and she wanted to reach out, to warn him not to take that belief to the Enclave, but she did not know how. She still did not know after his hand left her own, after he had left the room, and any chance she had to know was ruined when a shadow fell across the open door.

'Well, it is just as I thought: you are not coming to the meeting.' Eira spoke quietly from the doorway, her voice almost a purr of pleasure. 'A wise choice, now that everyone knows that you went to kill Fo and Bau. You should know that no dark hole will save you.'

'I don't need a dark hole.' Her voice was rough. 'I have nothing to be ashamed of.'

'Listen to yourself,' the Cold Witch said, contempt clear in her voice. 'You sound as if your tears are all caught in your chest. As if they're frozen down there, trying to get out. I know that they are not tears for me, but I will believe that they are. I will believe that you know what I have lost. For over two hundred years I loved Fo. He had the most beautiful mind I had ever met. To talk to him was to see connections that no one else could, or would. It will never return and I will have to live with that absence.'

'I am not looking for a fight, Eira.'

'I do not even remotely care what it is that you want.'

And then she was gone and the doorway was empty, but for its faint light, and its promise of fire.

8.

The afternoon's sun had begun to set, its light catching on the broken edges of trees, a burnt orange offering to the violence that Heast and Taaira were following.

The trail that the two rode along alternated between sunlight and the heavy, broken shadows of the trees as it climbed a ridge. Heast had not expected the path, and the two had come upon it in a sudden turn to the east, away from the Kingdoms of Faaisha and towards the plains.

'Once we reach the ridge at the top,' Kye Taaira said at the start of the narrow trail, 'you will see that a part of the mountain has broken and fallen through the ground. It has left a huge expanse where rivers run like veins in your arm. But by the morning, the trail will have turned again and we will be back in the direction we want.'

In a year, Heast believed, the Mountains of Ger would be too dangerous to journey over. The rot in the mountain would reveal the hidden tunnels and rivers that flowed throughout the range and it would bring the Cities of Ger and the corpses of men and women to the surface with it, just as it had claimed Mireea and the towns that had been above it. It would claim people, those who came to live on the shuddering land – Heast had no doubt that there would be men and women, desperate and opportunistic, who would come onto it. Animals would do the same, and they would die beside the humans.

On the trail, Heast's horse baulked twice before they reached the end of the steep climb. The second time, Heast stroked the beast's neck and listened to the eerie silence that filled the broken trees around him, but it was not until the third time that he said, 'Your ancestor is no longer far away.'

'I fear he plans to attack us after nightfall,' Taaira said. 'He must not consider us much of a threat.'

'Is there another path we can take?'

'Not that I know of.'

Heast's heels nudged his horse up the trail.

The ancestor would not consider him much of a threat, he knew. His sword was steel and he could use it passably well, but given what Heast had been told about the creature, he did not expect to be its equal. Yet, a certain part of him anticipated the conflict, for he had never seen one of the Hollow fight before. He had heard stories, of course. Had heard about them fighting with fists and with staffs, and had heard how they fought as no other warrior did. But he had heard enough in relation to his own life over the years to know that the stories of one's achievements were much like a bloated and distorted corpse, no matter how flattering they might appear on the surface.

'Soon we will be at the Faaishan border, Captain,' Kye Taaira had said earlier, when they had broken for lunch. 'When we are there, we should make good time to Vaeasa.'

'We won't be heading there,' Heast had replied. 'At least not first.'

'Where *will* we go?'

'Maosa first.' Heast cut two slices off the thick black bread that Essa had given him. Cheese and pork followed. 'It was where Baeh Lok was taking you, before you were caught.'

'It may not be standing,' Taaira said. 'Have you considered that?'

'I have.'

'But still we will go?' He regarded Heast intently. 'What is there that is so important? I have been there before. It has little to recommend it.'

'It is where Anemone lives.'

The tribesman chuckled.

Heast smiled. 'You've met her, I take it.'

'She is a cranky old woman,' he replied. 'Our shamans always visit when they are there. It is a sign of utmost respect, but you would not know it to hear how she speaks to them. Why would she treat you any differently?'

'Because she is the witch of Refuge,' he said.

After lunch, they had continued up the trail, and now, as Heast entered a clearing, he saw a single body lying in the centre.

The horses, which had baulked earlier, did not do so now. With gentle nudges, Heast and Taaira split to the left and right as they rode into the clearing, but the precaution was unnecessary.

The man — for it had once been a man — lay on his back, quite obviously dead, his body a mix of injuries and deformities. Heast lifted himself from his saddle and walked closer to examine the body. It appeared as if a second skeletal structure had been fused against the first, enlarging the cheek and chin on the left hand side of his face, the skin breaking beneath the growth to reveal hard bone. The man's forehead had suffered similarly, with the bone above the right eye protruding, and a lidded and blind third eye in place. The distortion continued down the limbs. On the right arm, the elbow joint fused oddly, and the right hand had four fingers growing from the back, leaving nine – including the thumb – in place.

But it was not that which had killed the man.

He had been killed by blunt incisions, each wound tearing open his skin. No sword had made them, nor a knife. Heast suspected, as he lifted a flap of skin aside to reveal damaged organs, that it had been done by hand.

'This is what the child did,' Taaira said quietly. 'This is one of my ancestors. But where is his blood?'

'There are no tracks.' Heast left the body, walked to the side of the clearing that broke into thick trees that still grew on the mountain. 'Except the ones he left.'

'He did not do this himself.'

'No,' he replied. 'Look at his legs, arms, at where the wounds are. They were to immobilize him first.'

The tribesman rose from beside the body of his ancestor. 'I know of nothing that could do this, Captain.'

'I know,' Heast said, turning away from the trees, away from the ruins that were defined by the broken Spine of Ger, clearly visible from where he stood. 'It is as I said: the Ghosts of Mireea are watching us.'

9.

Just after midnight, the marriage was announced.

The groom was the youngest son of Miat Dvir, a skinny boy no older than thirteen who had found the joys of masturbation, but not yet shaving. He was presented to Yoala Fe by Usa Dvir, who stood head and shoulders taller than the boy and spoke in a strong voice about the deeds of the boy's father, who had bonded the Saan together by blood, long before his son, Hau, was born. He was true blood from the warlord, though Bueralan doubted that Miat had any real care for the boy: the old man had had close to a dozen children, but all the stories and rumours the saboteur heard claimed that he had little love for any but his eldest two sons. Regardless of how much Hau's father had loved him, the boy was a legitimate Saan prince, and his presence here beside Usa Dvir, coupled with two dozen guards in copper bracelets, was a clear message to the First Queen of Ooila: succession and change was the bride's price.

Yoala had spoken to her mother shortly before the announcement. Bueralan had been with the First Queen when her daughter had opened the glass door, dismissing the Queen's

Voice with a wave of her hand, before walking determinedly across the balcony. As she drew closer, Bueralan thought that the hardness in her matched her older self well. In their youth, he had always thought that it ill suited her and Zean had laughed at his attempts to soften her. His marriage to Yoala had been decided at a very early age, and he had adhered to it until he was old enough that his interests, along with her own, had diverged to such an extent that the prospect of marriage was simply one of unhappiness on both parts. By the time he had become involved with the Hundredth Prince, his engagement to the Third Princess had been over for three years, and the two of them had not spoken since.

'If you don't mind,' Yoala said to him coldly, 'I'd like to speak to my mother alone.'

Bueralan glanced at the First Queen, who replied that she would be fine. He nodded and left. After he closed the door, he stood beside the Queen's Voice and watched the party before them.

'Are you having fun?' she asked him.

'I was promised that,' he said drily. 'I keep waiting for someone to ask me to dance.'

'Don't look at me.'

'Perish the thought.' A moment of silence passed between them. On the floor, people stood close to each other, clumped in sections while young men in robes of pale yellow walked among them, holding trays of food and drink. 'You want a drink?'

'Very much so.' The Queen's Voice shook her head. 'But just water, and if you don't mind, could you pour it yourself?'

'The Saan rarely poison,' he said.

'Who said I feared the Saan?'

He left her on the first floor, taking slow, lazy steps down the large staircase that ended on the smooth stone floor. At the far edge of the room were a series of long tables dominated by a set of ice sculptures. They depicted half a dozen warriors fighting a single Saan warrior, who held two broken blades in his grasp. The Saan warrior loomed over the others, and though his swords were in a defensive position, there was no doubting that he would fend off these attackers, who had begun to melt into large pools of water from their torsos, giving the impression that they were about to drown in their own blood.

'Impressive, is it not, Captain?'

Bueralan dipped a glass into the cold water. 'Hello, Usa,' he said.

'It is meant to be a depiction of the Blade Prince in his famous battle at the Jajjar. He had been cut off from the rest of the Dvir army and found himself isolated in the small town. Over one hundred warriors swept into it to kill him, and in a battle that took over a week, he killed each and every one of his opponents. It was said that on the third day his blades broke, and he fought for four more days with the shattered remains. Personally, I suspected he picked a fresh blade, but legend is a strange thing, beholden to no fact.' The Dvir war scout moved to stand beside Bueralan, his back to the sculptures, to the fragile glasses and beautifully arranged plates of food, his gaze on the floor above. 'Do you know, I did not think the old woman would ever let you out of her clutches. She must like the fame you come with.'

'There will be a new topic tomorrow.' He dipped a second glass for himself into the water. 'You know that as well as I do.'

'Yes, but the shock of the marriage will be greater, thanks to you. I ought to pay you for that.'

'The Saan do not hire mercenaries.'

'I have heard such a thing said myself.' He smiled faintly. 'She is a beautiful woman, is she not?'

Bueralan followed the other man's gaze and found it centred on the Queen's Voice. 'I don't think she is your kind.' He recognized the insult as he spoke, knew that he should stop himself, but found that he continued drily, regardless. 'She has too many opinions and is much too old for you.'

The war scout's smile faded. 'We're all just flesh, Captain.'

'A fascinating insight, Usa.' Bueralan picked up the two glasses, the moisture running over his hands. 'Do you have more written down?'

'It was always said you had a soft spot for slaves.'

Bueralan left him, then.

He walked up the stairs slowly, returning to the Queen's Voice without rush, aware that he had most likely made an enemy of Usa because of her. He was surprised, despite himself. He had gained a greater respect for the Queen's Voice over the night, at times watching her converse with men and women while the First Queen was silent beside him, watching the sureness and confidence by which she maintained the standards of royalty without compromising her own grace. She had made his job much easier, allowed him to learn faces, names, to note those who approached and those who did not. But he did not think that he had been so impressed that he would insult the war scout of the Dvir family. But he supposed that it did not truly matter: any retaliation that Usa could undertake would have to be done outside the Dvir interests, and once the night was over, the war scout would be busy enough that he would be forced to put aside Bueralan's words.

Yet, as the announcement of marriage was made, and Yoala Fe took her young fiancé's arm in her own and stepped into the middle of the downstairs room, which filled with applause as orange-and-yellow confetti dropped from the ceiling, Usa Dvir turned to stare at Bueralan.

'You've made a friend,' the Queen's Voice said.

'I'm very charming.'

She might have said more if the applause in the room had not faded to one strong, steady clap, much like a war drum's beat.

'I did not know that I had arrived for a wedding,' a man's voice said. 'Samuel, did you know anything of this?'

A brown-skinned man stepped into the room without waiting for a reply. From his position upstairs, Bueralan could not see his face, but he could see the old dust-stained leather armour that he wore, and the hilts of two worn weapons, one a dagger, the other a sword. But it was the chain in his hand that drew Bueralan's attention, the chain that fell in a slack loop behind him, and was connected to the neck of Samuel Orlan.

'Guards!' Yoala demanded. '*Guards!* Who has let this man in?'

'I am afraid they all stepped aside for me.' The hand that held the chain was heavily scarred. 'They knew my name, both my names, and they laid down their weapons for me. One even called me Mister Ren, but I told him that that was my father's name, and that I was simply Aela.

'Aela Ren.'

Three Stories of
an Innocent Man

'The second offer,' Jiqana told me, 'was given a week after we had been in the camp. In the days before, the soldiers would come up and talk to you. Some were frightening: they had filed their teeth down, or dug trinkets beneath their skin, but some were not. Some were normal. Friendly. But both would ask you about your life, about the things that you had done, and the things you wanted to do. It did not seem to me that anything anyone said was right, but nothing appeared to be wrong, either. In some of us, it bred a kind of confidence. After two or three days, they would begin to whisper about what they saw in the camp. They would point out that the Faithful did not have much food. That they did not have a single uniform. That their siege weapons were made from town walls and buildings. By the sixth day, some were even talking openly about how many of the Faithful weren't even soldiers.

'When the second offer was made, it was those people who said yes. They did not believe it, so I do not know why they did agree, but I believe there was some sort of compelling notion within them, something that forced them to raise their voice.

'The Faithful cooked them alive. They sat the rest of us around the fires they lit and made us watch as they pulled the flesh off the men and women we had known and devoured them.'

—Tinh Tu, *Private Diary*

1.

Aela Ren was not a tall man. He was five and a half foot and was neither thick-necked or muscular in frame, and at first glance, that lent him an air of innocence. A second glance revealed a leanness that spoke of a soldier who had spent years on campaign. But it was the third glance, the glance that turned into a stare, that allowed the terrible nature of the man to unfold. From beneath the shorn black stubble of his hair to the ends of his fingers, Bueralan saw a man whose body was mapped by scars, tattooed by extreme acts of violence. They were old wounds, dried and puckered and faded into his skin until they would fade no more. There was no uniformity to them: the injuries had not been caused by a single blade, mace or arrow; they corrugated across his arms and neck like bites and ran in cuts both thick and thin between. Both the number and the age of them left no doubt that the Innocent had come as close to a violent death as any man or woman could, and that only by sheer force of will had he overcome it. Yet, when Aela Ren turned, his gaze running over the people before him in a curiosity before it settled on Bueralan, he revealed a face that was neither defined by pain or stubbornness, nor a face that by the story of his body had a right to be taciturn and abrupt. No, he revealed a face that was alert, intelligent and – despite its scars – approachable.

'Mister Le,' he said. 'Just who I came to see.'

Call only – Bueralan's hands tightened on the railing at the top of the stairs as he remembered the child's words – *when what is at stake is innocence.*

'Samuel did not want to bring me here.' Aela Ren released the chain he had wrapped around Orlan's neck and let it clatter to the floor. 'I arrived at his shop this afternoon and he began to argue once the door opened. My first time seeing him in over two hundred years and his first word to me is no. He tells me he has done enough to you, Bueralan, and enough has been done to you. If I were to be truthful with you, I expected as much. Samuel Orlan has always argued with me. It is the name, naturally. The first Samuel Orlan sounded like the fifty-eighth, and the eighty-second is no different. They are all the same.'

In the silence that followed Ren's words, Bueralan heard the old cartographer unwinding the heavy chain around his neck in painful grunts and gasps. The rest of the mansion was caught in the words of the Innocent and, a handful of steps away from him, Yoala's young groom, Hua Dvir, best exemplified the fear of those around them. He appeared as if he had been caught in amber. He was unable to move from where he had been when the celebration of his marriage announcement began. The same, however, could not be said of Yoala, whose terror was giving way to indignation at Aela Ren's intrusion. She took a step forward without hesitation and said, 'You do not—'

Her body slumped to the floor, her throat torn out.

'I did not invite conversation.' Aela Ren shook his right hand, spraying blood across the tiled floor. 'But that is the problem with people of pride and ambition.'

The Innocent's movements had been swift and sudden, the ends of his fingers tearing through Yoala's neck with a callous disregard that Bueralan had never seen before. *Call only when what is at stake is innocence.* The child's words repeated as Aela Ren began to walk up the stairs. *Call* – the terrified crowd parted before him as his worn boots marked a path to the saboteur – *call only when* – across the smooth stone floor, blood dripping from his hand – *call only when what is at stake* – each step a beat to the child's words – *call only when what is at stake is innocence* – words that Bueralan knew with certainty were intended for the man who approached, words that demanded he speak a name he did not know.

'I am the oldest person here.' The Innocent stopped before the Queen's Voice, his right hand still wet with blood. 'Even so, I can still acknowledge great beauty. Does that flatter you?'

'No,' she whispered.

Aela Ren reached for her dress, gathering it from up high around her thighs, and wiped the blood off his hand.

'I like her.' He said the words to Bueralan, but he remained in front of the Queen's Voice for a moment longer, still holding her burnt-orange gown in his hands. Gently, he released the dress and turned to the saboteur. He approached the railing where he stood. 'She is genuinely terrified,' he continued. 'It took a lot of courage for her to tell me no. Many others would not find it. Most are simply afraid to speak when they meet me. Afraid that if they draw attention to themselves they will die like that woman on the floor. Their fear is a truth deep inside them. It is caused by my name, by my presence and by my actions. I enhance it, naturally. My master gave me that gift long ago – to let the truth inside someone be that which guides them around me. Samuel's mistress gave him the gift of the world's borders. But your master – what did your master give you?' A scarred hand reached for the leather tie around his neck, for the pouch—

Bueralan's hand snapped around the Innocent's wrist. 'That's not for you,' he said.

'Isn't it?' He pulled his arm away. 'Your master did not give that to you, did he?'

'I do not have a master.'

'That is not true.' The First Queen's interruption was a harsh whisper. 'And unlike others in this room, Aela Ren, I am not terrified of you.'

The Innocent turned his attention away from Bueralan, turned to the old woman. 'But you are dying,' he said simply.

'I have been dying for many years.'

'Yet you believe it has made you strong, immune to the fears and indecision of others.' The Innocent's hand waved across the crowd, waved to where Saan warriors emerged, their copper bracelets catching the light sharply. 'But it has made you weak. That is why men of conquest are on your shores, Zeala Fe. Tell me, how long do you think your daughter would have allowed you to live once she was married?'

'That is for mothers and daughters to decide, not men from across the ocean.' The First Queen slowly rose from her wheelchair, her arms shaking with the effort. Upright, she was a thin woman, her shoulders hunched under a weight that no one watching could truly have appreciated. 'Why don't you let these people go home?'

'No.'

'Then kill them now.'

Around the First Queen a gasp escaped the crowd.

Aela Ren's scarred lips smiled faintly. Instead of answering her, he turned to Bueralan, turning his back to both the First Queen and the Saan warriors who drew closer to him. Yet the saboteur did not look at them. Instead, he followed the Innocent's gaze down to the floor where Yoala's body lay alone, her blood forming a tranquil pool around her. At the far edge of the crowd, Usa Dvir had taken the arm of the Saan prince and led him into the crowd, leaving Samuel Orlan alone in the centre of the room.

The cartographer had regained his feet and, free of the chain that had dragged him, walked past Yoala Fe's body to the long table of ice sculptures.

'My master was the god Wehwe,' Ren said to Bueralan, his voice conversational. 'He was the God of Truth, and he died in the middle of the War of the Gods, struck down by Uditos, the God of Necessity. The loss was great to me, but the irony of it did not escape me, even at the time. *For war to continue, truth must die.* Wehwe was the first to say that. He had made me write it. It was one of the few pieces of writing that he did not make me destroy after I had completed it. Over the thousands of years that my master spoke to me, he would have me transcribe whole books and then burn them. He believed that once words became print, they were no longer true, but it was my duty to search for those that were not.'

At the ice sculpture of the broken-bladed warrior, Samuel

Orlan dipped his hands into the bowls of water, bringing the liquid to his face.

'I was a monk when Wehwe first found me,' Ren continued. Bueralan risked a glance behind the Innocent, and saw that the Saan warriors were drawing closer, but with great caution. 'I know that it is not true now, but for the first few decades of my life, I was dedicated to the pursuit of peace and harmony. I had not seen a sword or raised my hands in anger. I lived in a monastery on a mountain that no longer exists and I owned nothing but the robes and boots that I wore, clothing that I made with my own hands. The trail to the monastery was a long and twisting one, made from bridges of rope and wood, and secured into the smooth rock of the mountain by monks like myself. To travel to it was such a danger that few did, and the monks there were forced to grow their own food and sink their own wells for water. The monks would leave twice a year. On both those times, we would travel along our dangerous trails until we reached the base of the mountain, where we would trade for cloth and seeds, and we would help with the ill and take in abandoned children. I was one such child, left by parents too young and too poor to care for me, and I was carried to the monastery on the back of another monk at six months of age. For thirty-four years I lived in the grounds. I did chores, I studied and I lived an unremarkable life until the winter Wehwe noticed me.

'He came to me first as a small rodent, and he followed me around the gardens for a month. He would lead me to hurt birds, hungry rodents, struggling insect colonies, and I would help all of them. I did not know he was a god then, though I knew something was strange about the rodent, and when it died, I wept. Later, he appeared as a woman heavy with child who needed my help. I saw her in a dream, and found her on the mountain, beautiful and alone and vulnerable. He tested me with her in a number of ways, and I resisted them all. After her, he appeared as an old man with no legs. He sent a letter to the monastery by bird, requesting that I make the journey along our paths to reach him and bring him up, in the middle of winter. I carried him on my back for nearly a month as I brought him to the monastery steps.

'And it was there, after I had completed the last of these tasks, that Wehwe informed me that I was his. I had no say in the matter.'

Samuel Orlan straightened. Slowly, he reached for one of the blades on the sculpture, one held by the melting attackers of the Saan Blade Prince, and with a twist, he snapped off a fist-sized length.

Bueralan pointed to the cartographer. 'He said the original Orlan denied his god.'

'It is true, but the same Samuel Orlan could neither deny nor accept the desire of Aeisha.' The Innocent raised his voice. 'Am I not right?'

The old man ignored the shout, sinking instead to the ground, where he pressed the ice up against his neck to soothe the welts caused by the chain.

'Why are you telling me this?' Bueralan asked.

'There has not been a god-touched man or woman for over ten thousand years,' Aela Ren replied. 'I know where each and every one in this world is, Bueralan Le. Even the sad and pathetic one who lives in swamps and mutters pieces of madness as if it were truth. But now there is you. You, a mercenary, a saboteur, a man but a step from being an assassin, a betrayer of Queen and country. A man who was given no trials by a god, no tasks to complete, and no constraints. A man who was simply given a power that does not describe itself and left to the world as the last act of a dying god. If I were a religious man, I would say that it was ordained.'

'I did not ask for it.'

'None of us does.' He settled both his hands onto the railing lightly. 'When I asked if Ger had given you the soul around your neck, I already knew he had not. A different god gave it to you. A new god. Can you imagine what this has meant to me?'

'No.' The word felt as if it were strangled from his throat.

'Tell me the name of this god, Bueralan.'

'I don't—' He hesitated, stopped.

'That,' Aela Ren said. 'That is interesting.'

'I do *not* know it,' Bueralan insisted. 'She never told me it.'

'No, she would not have.'

Then, before the saboteur could react, the small man vaulted over the railing, and dropped lightly to the floor.

'Warriors of the Saan!' He turned to the men who had been closing in on him, the men who had rushed the railing the moment he leapt. 'You want to be able to claim that you were responsible for the death of the Innocent! You want fame! You want fortune! I offer you the opportunity. Draw your swords. Come down the stairs. In this room is a man who has been god-touched and who does not know what it means.

'Let us show him.'

2.

'How long has your name terrorized people, Aela Ren?' Usa Dvir was the first to speak after the Innocent's voice fell silent. He stepped from the crowd on the side of the ice sculptures. Beside him the Blade Prince of the Saan wept, but he was otherwise alone. The young prince was nowhere to be seen, and the hand that had pulled the boy to safety now held the hilt of a long straight-bladed sword. 'I read about you as a child, just as my father had read about you, and his father before him. Your deeds are written on some of the oldest scrolls that we have, scrolls so old that the ink purchased by my father's fathers is but barely visible.'

'Oh, Usa,' the First Queen whispered, 'do not lie to him.'

'Lie?' the Queen's Voice asked.

'The men of the Saan cannot read,' Bueralan answered quietly. Beside him, the Queen leant heavily on his arm as she moved to the edge of the balcony, to gaze down at the Innocent. He was silent in response to Dvir, and Bueralan could feel a tremor in the Queen's hand, as if that silence was worse than any words he could have said.

The first of the Saan warriors emerged from the crowd. He was a tall, muscular man, and the thick bands of copper that curled around both his arms and reached up to his chest. He did not pause to wait for others, but instead drew his scimitar and continued towards the Innocent.

His first slash was fast, the slice not just of a seasoned warrior, but of a skilled one. Yet it met with little more than air. Aela Ren's left foot took a single movement to pivot him before the blow, while his right continued the circle as the blade came slicing back up, passing through air again. The steel was close, achingly close to the small man, and for a heartbeat the crowd around Bueralan believed Ren had been cut. The saboteur felt the First Queen's fingers dig into his arm in hope, as if the tremor had been nothing, but it returned when it became clear Ren had not been injured.

On the floor, the Saan warrior's scimitar repeatedly slashed through the empty air as Aela Ren stepped around his attacks. It looked very much as if it were a dance that the two had prepared, an entertainment that they had spent years perfecting so that neither was hurt. A slash diagonally across his chest, a thrust that the scimitar was poorly designed for, a hack at the neck: all of it came within a breath of the Innocent as he weaved and twisted out of harm, his hands not yet reaching for the sword and dagger at his side.

The warriors of the Saan had formed a circle around the two fighters. Bueralan counted twenty, and he could add another two if he included Dvir and the missing prince. But neither of those two was the threat that the warriors were. The thick copper bracelets proclaimed their skill and valour. If that was not enough, the scimitars and long swords that they held, the leather whips and chain maces that they allowed to unravel, were all held with the ease of familiarity.

Not one of them moved to help the warrior who fought against Aela Ren. Instead, each man watched, their eyes following the darts of their companion's blade, the weave and shift of the man he attacked, each of them learning from their companion until, with a scream, the warrior drove his scimitar at his opponent's midsection.

Aela Ren stepped around the warrior smoothly, grabbed the man's head in his scarred hands and twisted.

The scream that came as the warrior slumped to the ground came from somewhere within the crowd. It was followed by another so quickly that Bueralan could not see if it was a man or a woman who had first let out the noise. He felt himself respond to it, as if the scream spoke to a fear that was being activated in him, but he remained silent. The cry, however, repeated itself again and again, as if that terror had been awoken across the crowd, but it was only when all the voices rose in a uniform pitch that the sound finally broke the stillness that had gripped the mansion. Like a ripple on a pond, movement raced through the crowd and soon men and women were running. They ran towards the Innocent, towards the Saan, and they ran away from both. They dashed for doors at the front of the mansion, the doors at the back, and for a moment, the Saan warriors and Aela Ren disappeared beneath the flesh of others seeking escape.

But only for a moment.

'I trust,' Aela Ren said to the remaining warriors, once the main floor was empty of guests, 'that you will do better than your friend.'

The Saan charged.

A long whip lashed out first, forcing the Innocent to move

to his right. He ducked beneath a scimitar's slash, only to run into another blade that sped downwards – only to be blocked by Aela Ren's sword.

It was an old blade. The steel had long ago lost its shine, stripped away by time and use, but it was simple and elegant in its make and it was partnered by a dagger that appeared in the left hand of the Innocent. The two were complementary, for where the sword's blade had been made with a single edge that came to a thick point, designed for slashing and thrusting, the dagger was lighter, made with a double edge that came to a wicked point to not just thrust and pierce, but to tear open and spill what was inside another human being.

'Why do we not leave?' the Queen's Voice asked in a whisper. 'It is our chance.'

'We must see this to the end,' the First Queen replied.

The plan of the Saan warriors, Bueralan saw, was to keep a tight circle around Ren, to limit his movements and use their sheer number to force him into the blades of their companions. They had witnessed a fearless display against their first comrade and knew that to permit him space, to allow him but simple room to engage them singly or in pairs would give his sword and dagger the chance to pierce them and begin, one by one, to take away their advantage of numbers. To stop that, they had to starve him of space, to deny him freedom.

Yet the Innocent denied them.

As if he were but a flicker of an eye, a trick of shadow at the edges of vision, he blocked and parried, and within moments, began to dictate the movements of the Saan warriors. When Ren moved to the right, the group followed, as if a chain had been wrapped around them. Bueralan felt the weight of it around him. He watched without hope as the blades and maces and whips lashed out around Ren, but each fell in emptiness, passed through air he had just left by turn, twist, or, twice already, a cartwheel flip he made with the strength in his legs. It would be only a matter of time before one of the Saan warriors fell, before a hole was revealed in those around him.

But when that happened – when a man's face parted in a straight cut across cheek and nose – the Innocent did not press towards the gap to exploit it.

Quickly, a length of whip rose high above the Saan, the long black leather end like a snake that prepared to strike . . . which it did through the closing hole, snapping with a loud crack around the Innocent's sword arm.

The Saan warrior pulled Ren, hoping to disturb his balance, to pull him from his feet, but the scarred man turned into the length of leather instead. His free dagger sliced up on the turn, cutting through the whip to free his sword, allowing it to catch the blade of a slashing scimitar and spin it out of the wielder's hand. Yet, the whip had broken the Innocent's control over the Saan movements and warriors surged forward, sensing weakness – a weakness Aela Ren raised his sword to, before he plunged into their midst.

'I met Usa Dvir, once before.' Bueralan's voice sounded distant, as if it belonged to a stranger. 'It was three years ago. Dark was hired by a town called Oeissi. It's on the edge of Gogair, near the Saan.'

'I have heard of it,' the First Queen replied quietly. 'Oeissi was a day's ride from the tunnels.'

'The town and the Saan had an agreement.' On the floor, the Innocent's charge scattered the warriors, but not before his sword had swept past the defence of one man and tore through his neck. 'It had been made five centuries before and it ensured that the Saan paid low prices for the food and metals that they bought from the merchants. In return, the Saan would defend the town. When the agreement had been signed, Gogair had been in civil war, and Oeissi had had the better half of the deal; but three years ago, anyone who could remember an attack on the town had long since died and people had begun to speak out against the Saan prices. The new lord, a young man by the name of Buzeur, was sympathetic to that. He had not been born to the old lord, but had been one of his rivals, and had come to power after the older man died rather abruptly – it was never said openly, but Buzeur was known to make jokes about it, to brag as some men do of bettering another.'

Aela Ren continued to break apart the Saan. His blades thrust forward and, no longer content with a simple defence, he turned each block, each parry, and each sidestep into an attack. The Saan warriors were forced backwards, the weight of their superior numbers lost by the sheer ferocity that was emerging from the small man. One of the largest warriors, bald but for a long braid that ran down his back, thought to challenge Ren, and the heavy end of his chain mace whistled over the Innocent's head . . . but it failed to return as his fingers lost their grip on the long hilt and Ren's dagger plunged into his thigh moments before ripping upwards and tearing across the warrior's genitals.

'When he came into power, Buzeur told the Saan that they would have to pay market prices, as well as compensation to merchants who had lost income during the last lord's reign.'

Bueralan wanted to close his eyes, to look away from the slaughter that he was witnessing, but instead, he kept talking. 'According to Lady Farlay, who hired Dark to ensure her power base against the new lord, the Saan were amenable to the idea of paying market prices. She believed that they had already acknowledged among themselves that after the death of the old lord, such a demand was likely. The reasons for the treaty had long passed and Gogair was a united country, now. But the compensation that Buzeur insisted upon was nothing but an insult. More, Dvir had been given the ultimatum in a letter when he went to greet the new lord, but no mention was made of its contents to him at the time. Instead, Buzeur enjoyed the gifts the Saan brought to him and ate at the feast that they prepared in his honour. Buzeur's insults were many, Lady Farlay told me, but he made them with the clear understanding that, should the Saan march on Oeissi, then the rest of Gogair would respond – she believed he had been ordered by the capital to incite this.'

On the floor, the Innocent had begun to stalk the Saan. He was silent, swift, his movements nothing short of predatory, but he was not like any animal Bueralan had seen. He did not pause after his kill to savour it, to dig deep into the meat he had carved open, to taste the blood and sinew. For Aela Ren, the remains of a man was nothing but waste, fit for the scavengers that followed him, the birds that would pull the eyes and tongues out, the animals that would rip at the rotted meat. He was primal but he possessed no appetite and the men before him fell beneath his strength and speed, falling into defensive patterns that he broke apart easily. One man's scimitar clattered to the ground, his hand still on the hilt; his head followed, hitting the ground hard and rolling along the floor, its uneven path leading beneath the table that held the melting sculpture of the Blade Prince and finishing before Samuel Orlan.

There was no horror in Orlan's gaze. The head that came to rest at the ends of his boots was met with a tired acceptance, a fatalism born from the inevitability that Bueralan himself felt: that no other outcome could take place, no other grisly reminder of mortality could be presented to him, or to any of the others that remained in the mansion. When the cartographer did, finally, use the toe of his boot to push the head away from him, it was done without revulsion, without a sense of rejection, but rather with a morbid sense that it should roll back into the battle and that it should return to the shouts and screams. It should finish next to another fallen Saan warrior, this man gasping for air from a cut that ran clear through the centre of his throat and up his chin – a cut that threatened to part the skin of his face, as if the blood and bone beneath were a secret that needed to be told.

'Bueralan?' The First Queen's voice held the tremor that had been in her hand. 'Please – please continue your story.'

'Dvir agreed with Lady Farlay, but he would not allow the insult to stand unanswered.' He spoke quietly, unable to raise his voice. 'He made that very clear to me when I met him, half a day's ride into the tunnels. Lady Farlay did not want war, and worried that the Saan would ride out in force, so she sent me to meet with him. Dvir was too smart for the trap that had been laid to draw them into war with Gogair. He is the war scout for the Saan and he understands that war does not begin on the field, but in the quiet halls, in backroom talk. He understood that the talk of war was much like the dark, twisting tunnels where he met me. He knew it was an echo that twisted around you, robbing you of all sense of its origin. He accepted the apologies of Lady Farlay for Buzeur's insults because he knew that the promise of war came from distant parts of Gogair, but he would not accept her justice. That he wanted for himself, and the Lady agreed, quickly enough. It left Dark with the job of weakening Buzeur's supporters, to undermining his power while building up Farlay's, but that is not so important, not now.'

On the floor five Saan warriors remained, not including the war scout. Usa Dvir had not yet moved from his position beside the weeping sculpture and the sword that he held had come to rest, point-first on the tiles.

'On the night Buzeur was removed from power,' Bueralan continued, 'Dark opened the gate for the Saan. We were advised to return to our rooms and to stay there. We did not, obviously. In curiosity, we made our way along the streets and found a perch outside the vast grounds of the estate, where we watched the first fires lit.'

Aela Ren moved swiftly against the five warriors, but the Saan did not fall from him. The tallest of them met his charge with a wide sweep that was aimed at the Innocent's midsection. It was a wide but controlled cut that forced Ren to use his sword to block, while a second and third man charged him from the left and right. Yet Ren, with the slightest sway to his body, avoided the second man's slash, while his dagger plunged into the man's chest, and the two steps he took to follow the thrust allowed his sword to slip away from the other man's block and to arc, high over the heads of all the warriors, before it rushed downwards.

'I have seen all kinds of soldiers and all kinds of killing,' Bueralan said, his stomach heavy. 'But there are few who enact their justice so exactly and violently as the Saan. No member of the staff who worked for Buzeur escaped. No one who cooked, who made beds, who kept the garden. Not a single one of them left the grounds. They were cut down, slaughtered for the most part, for few were armed. Guards offered a little more resistance, but Dvir's Saan were not bloodthirsty or wild. They were disciplined. Controlled. Exact. Even when they set out on the long night of torture for Buzeur and his family, they were that.

'Nowhere in Ooila,' he said, and for the first time, bitterness entered his voice, 'is there a force like the Saan.'

On the floor, the final three warriors closed ranks, attempting to pull Aela Ren into a pattern of feints and blocks, the frantic speed of their weapons seeking to seed doubt in their opponent, to mirror the fear that showed itself deep in the lines of the warriors' faces. Yet Ren, unconcerned with the three, strode forward, beating aside the scimitar of the man on the left, thrusting his elbow into the face of the man on the right, before gliding past the defences of the third warrior, his gory dagger ripping through the man's leg, before reversing to plunge deep into his thigh. With sheer strength, Ren lifted the warrior from his feet, and as he fell, the straight edge of the Innocent's sword sheered down much like the blade of an executioner's axe.

The second warrior fell moments later, an ugly parry turning into a thrust that slammed deep into his chest. The third followed in a graceless tumble as he turned, as he finally broke in fear and began to run to the tables, but instead sprawled across the ground, Ren's dagger buried in his throat.

Slowly, the scarred man gathered the weapon. He did not wipe it, did not clean it, and with it still wet, he turned to Usa Dvir.

The other man's sword rose.

'No.' The Innocent dropped both his blades on the floor, where they landed in a hard pair of noises. He began to walk forward. 'You do not get that.'

'I will kill you,' Dvir spat. 'I will run you through like a pig.'

Aela Ren did not reply.

Usa Dvir, the war scout of the Saan, the man who had watched the deaths of his men in such a short, brutal time, the man who had stood beside the melting ice sculpture of the most famous of swordsmen of the Saan, the man who had stood there and done nothing to help those who had come to Ooila under him to take power from a sick Queen . . . that man let out a scream of raw frustration and anger and charged. He levelled the sword as he would a spear and the hard blade did not pause as it plunged into the chest of Aela Ren.

And neither did he.

Silently, the Innocent pushed himself along the blade, each hard step succeeding in plunging the steel deeper and deeper into his chest, until it pressed against the skin of his back and burst through, continuing for a forearm's length before his hands closed around Dvir's head.

The sickening crunch of bone giving way, of a head losing shape and collapsing, sounded a moment later.

3.

Aela Ren's scarred fingers curled around the leather-bound grip of the war scout's sword. Slowly, he began to withdraw it from his chest. Bueralan watched in horror as the small man pulled the blade out of himself inch by inch, the steel slippery with his blood, but not enough that, when his hands could no longer reach the pommel, Ren hesitated to grip the slick blade. When he had drawn the last of it from himself, he let it fall to the floor, where the sound of the sword hitting the ground was shallow, as if it were nothing but a toy, its very composition material that would not harm a child.

'Once—' Aela Ren's voice was rough, bestial, and he stopped, as if the nature of his voice was a truth he did not wish to hear. 'Once,' he began again, his voice returned to its normality, 'I thought the gods had returned. It was towards the end of the war. The sea level had not yet risen. Churches still existed. I had not yet grieved for all that I had lost, and neither had those I knew. The war was terrible to men and women like myself and we suffered more than any other. For each god-touched man or woman, the death of a god, the death of their god in particular, was a pain that transcended flesh and

484

consciousness. It was of such pain that words are inadequate to describe it. Death was denied us. We had to live through it all. Many would eventually live in *Glafanr*, but not all. For some, anger and resentment drove them out into the world.'

The Innocent's right hand came up to his chest, to where the sword had pierced his skin, to where blood now seeped.

'I believed that only the return of the gods could alleviate our pain. To discover that one did exist, one that was born while they still killed themselves, was a cause of celebration.' His hand curled into a fist. 'It was not to be, of course. In their demise the divine nature of the gods had spilled out into our world. It changed ordinary men and women, made them something new. It would take years for me to understand that, but one thing was true: when I found the first of these men and women, I knew immediately that he was not a god.'

Aela Ren turned to Bueralan and the saboteur saw in his gaze a dark fury.

'He had called himself the Animal Lord,' the scarred man continued. 'He would have many titles throughout the years, but to me, Jae'le would always be the Animal Lord. The title had been given to him because he kept beasts by his side, but it revealed a more intimate awareness of the man, for he would hunt other men and women. He believed in strength and cunning. He believed that only the strongest deserved life. When I found him first, he was a crude deity to the small tribe on the island of Tuia. He had been born there, but had not thrived until a god's power had worked itself into his being. Now, he had all that he wished, and like a beast, he was sated with domination over his small part of the world.

'He kept his home on the side of a mountain. It sat on the

horizon with a dark finality, and I walked through silent camps of men and women before it to reach him. In each, I was forced to fight a warrior. In the seven camps, four were women and three men, and in each camp no one else sought to attack me once I had defeated their first warrior. Their skill increased as I drew closer to the cave where he lived and it became clear to me that there was a ranking in the men and women I passed. I was able simply to disarm the first two warriors who opposed me, but I was forced to kill the remaining five. Once the last of them had fallen, I followed a narrow path that wound up around the mountain, and at the end, I found the Animal Lord living in a shallow cave.

'He was a frightening figure to behold with a calm eye. Lean and dark-skinned, he rested on his haunches in tattered furs on the lip of his cave. He gave every impression that he would soon leap down upon me, even though he held no weapons. But his teeth had been filed down to points and, later, I would learn, he used them to rip the flesh off the men and women he had killed. He would only eat that flesh, he told me from his perch, though he did not offer a reason for it. I almost wept in despair to hear him speak, but instead, I allowed something much worse to take place. I allowed myself to believe in a lie.'

Bueralan felt a shiver pass through him, the scene clear in his mind's eye. He could see the Animal Lord looming above him, the darkness blending into his skin, obscuring his face, leaving only his burning, dark eyes, the hint of his teeth, and the hints of fur that he wore. When he rose, he was tall. His body was twisted, lean muscle and ended in fingers long and hard. He left his perch suddenly and without a word, landing on the ground at the opening of his cave in such a swift fluidity that it was startling to behold.

'Jae'le believed himself to be a god and I allowed myself to believe that he might one day become one.' Aela Ren's fist fell away from his chest and revealed the wound, which had begun to heal. 'For two decades, I was his companion. I taught him languages he had never heard. I introduced him to the world beyond Tuia. I educated him about the gods. In my need to have divinity returned to me, I believed that I saw strands of fate gather around him, and thought that it would only be a matter of time until he could reach for them. But it was an illusion on my part. The paths of fate that the gods navigated were created by their own desires and fears and were divine in their nature. Their very existence was a reaction to the gods. A touch spawned another, and another, and the result was that an equilibrium was reached among all the gods. But with no gods, no new strands of fate could be made. Without them, we were truly without truth. As my years with Jae'le drew to an end, I began to realize that our world was one of emptiness. We lived now in a world where the only meanings that could be given were our own, and where, without any real truth, those words and actions could be used to make legitimate our most base desires. It soon became true that we were now living in an existence of deceit and that Jae'le was the centre of it.'

'But you could not kill him.' The image that Ren had built crumbled beneath Samuel Orlan's voice. The old cartographer had pushed himself to his feet and stood before the weeping statue of the Saan Blade Prince, the melted figures around it indistinguishable from each other. 'For all that you have said about him, Aela, you were unable to kill him. Jae'le and his brothers and sisters would make the Five Kingdoms – and you did not challenge one of them.'

'You and your kin were too quick to be their friend, Samuel.' The Innocent did not turn from Bueralan. 'But he is correct. I could not kill the Animal Lord.'

'You were not stronger than him?' the saboteur asked, his voice cracking as he spoke.

'No, I was not.' He extended his arms. 'These scars you see were made by him. He had not displayed such power in the years we stood together – he had hidden it for all that time, waiting for when I would betray him. Can you imagine the mind that it takes to do that? To purposely hold yourself back for two decades and more? I will not pretend that I had the better of him, then. I had underestimated him greatly, and on the day I drew my sword against him, I was defeated within no more time than it takes for a heart to beat. In the depths of Faer, Jae'le strung me across a great tree and impaled me on its branches. It moved, like you or I would, and it drew me against its trunk, where it held me as branches burst through my skin. In places, it was like a series of pins driven into me, in others, thick blades. If that was not enough, Jae'le then drove nails and spikes into me. It would be thousands of years before I could remove myself from that tree, but the wounds would never heal completely. In my darkest days, I despaired that I was being punished by my master, that he had seen this fate for me and bound me to the strand of it – but I had no reason to be punished, and the meaning was one I gave myself. I have lived with that realization for many, many years. It was not until I heard of you, Bueralan Le, that I began to think differently.'

'You believe there is another god,' the First Queen said, her frail voice gaining strength, a hope it had not previously had. 'That is why you are here?'

'It would change everything,' he said simply.

'She is not a god yet,' Orlan said, a certainty in his voice that Bueralan did not share. 'And if she has thought to take on Jae'le, she might never be.'

'He is not what he once was,' the Innocent said. 'You know that as well as I do, Samuel. Yet, nonetheless, I will show caution where I once did not. I will wait to hear her name spoken and I will remain here in the house of your daughter, Zeala Fe, until it is spoken. Both these men will keep me company, and so will your Voice, until it is that you and I need to speak again.'

A Gravedigger's Name

'During the meal, the Faithful stopped speaking to us,' Jiqana said. Around her face she wore a black bandage, and as she talked, she would scratch beneath the cloth. 'A terrible silence fell over the camp. In the last week, nothing made a sound, not even the animals. They would answer the silent call of the soldiers, just as the soldiers responded to each other without words. On the second day of that silence, the soldiers began to read from a book entitled *The Eternal Kingdom*. It was the only noise you heard for the entire week.

'At the end of the second week, you were asked a third and final time if you embraced their god. I was asked by General Waalstan himself. He entered the camp that I was in on the last day and took each of us to his tent, one by one. We never saw anyone emerge. By the time I entered his tent, I was terrified that I would find the others dead on the floor, but instead, I found it filled with diaries, with maps, and with a small golden dish from which smoke rose. He sat on a chair in the middle and beckoned me to the one opposite him. I remember that he spoke in such a gentle voice that when he asked me if I would embrace his god, I could not lie to him. I wanted to tell him yes, but I could not. I told him that the book had made no sense to me. That it sounded silly. I remember that I began to weep as I spoke, but he reached for me, and hugged me. For a moment, I felt safe, and then another hand touched me, and I felt my head pulled back. The last thing I saw was the smoke in the ceiling of the tent, twisted into the form of a strange creature, as if it followed the definition of something real in the shadows.'

—Tinh Tu, *Private Diary*

1.

Beneath the morning's sun, Bueralan dug the fifth of twenty-four single, unmarked graves.

He had begun in the last of the night's darkness, the emptiness of it stretching around him, its fading depth a voiceless articulation of the situation he was in and the mortality he felt so keenly. Earlier, he had ridden beneath the sky at its darkest as he drove the carriage to Cynama, the long road revealed in scraps of light, the path poorly illuminated for both him and horse. The two beasts had made their exit from Yoala Fe's grounds as if the very wood of the carriage held the heavy weight of the night's violence. On the road, he had passed men and women from the party, each of them still in their fine clothes, each of them the debris of a much larger wreckage, but Bueralan did not stop for any. He entered the quiet roads of Cynama alone, the canals giant shadowed wounds in the distance, and it was not until the firm and unpleasant grip of Captain Lehana took his arm that the reality of the night returned to his stomach in a sick rush.

'Where is the—'

'Unhand him, Lehana.' The First Queen interrupted the

soldier's question from the door of the carriage. Her voice was still frail, and she emerged from the dark with the shadows entwined around her, but she did so under the strength she had shown in her daughter's home. 'He must return before the night is over, though he would be wise not to do so.' Slowly, she stepped onto the ground. 'He should unhitch a horse and ride from this city, ride from this country. But you will not do that, will you, Bueralan Le?'

'No,' he said. 'I will not.'

The First Queen waved away Captain Lehana's offer of her arm. 'You will bury my daughter with her soul around her neck, won't you?'

He nodded, but did not trust himself to reply.

'She would have killed me, or I would have killed her.' She released her hold upon the door and began to walk to the palace gate. At his side, she paused. 'But she was still my daughter and my fury is a mother's. You will not forget that, will you?'

'No.'

When he returned to Yoala Fe's estate, the lamps to the mansion lit a half-extinguished trail for him to follow.

The Innocent's silhouette stood on the balcony, but Aela Ren made no move to acknowledge him. Beneath his gaze, Bueralan unhooked the horses and led them into the stables. Once inside, he rubbed them down, fed and watered them, and then did the same for all fifteen horses in the stables. When he finally emerged, an empty, dark space greeted him on the balcony and Bueralan, his body unable to stop, unable to rest, walked into the mansion and began to move the corpses outside.

The butterflies rose with the morning's sun, pulling themselves from the broken dirt beneath Bueralan's feet. They rose with the warm humidity and drifted around him, landing on the bare skin of his back and the tattoos on his arms; they touched the cold pouch around his neck; they settled on the knife he had thrown on the ground and on the shirt next to it; they flocked to the handle of the shovel when he paused in his actions; but mostly, they drifted around the bodies that lay in front of him, where many would settle between moments of flight to obscure the dry wounds.

Samuel Orlan joined him before the first of the butterflies began to die. He had with him a pair of shovels, both of which he laid on the ground before he took off the jacket he wore, rolled up the paint-splotched sleeves beneath, and began to dig wordlessly.

It was not until the Queen's Voice said, 'Is this to be our morning ritual, then?' that someone finally spoke.

She stepped out of the mansion without her gold chains, or her beautiful, bloodstained dress. Stripped of her finery, she had changed into brown leather trousers and a dark-orange shirt, though the latter, Bueralan saw, was a size too big, and cut for a man with square shoulders. On her feet, she wore a pair of old boots, the type that folded over at the top, the type that, he knew, held a sheath that you could slide a dagger into without it slicing against the side of your foot.

'There's a third shovel,' he said.

She did not move to pick it up. 'So it is, then?'

He turned from her and thrust his shovel into the ground. 'What's your name?'

'I told you—'

'The Queen is not here.' Bueralan bit the words off harshly. 'It's just the three of us, waiting to see if I know a name.'

She was silent as he dug and he half expected to hear her turn, for her to return inside, where the Innocent sat in one of the many rooms.

'Zi Taela,' she said, finally.

It was not *the* name, but then, how could it be? A god's name would not announce itself with its family name first, would not follow with its first name, would not allow such a simple act to ensure that it was distinguished from the wealthy noble families in Ooila. A god would know better than to begin fighting for two letters that it could claim as its own.

'It is a lovely name,' Samuel Orlan said when the saboteur's shovel bit back into the ground. 'Any one of the women who wanted to marry me would have been lucky to have such a name.'

'Is that a proposal?' she asked archly.

'I fear the grave I stand in is much too morbid a place.'

'If the two of you are done,' Bueralan said, his voice kinder than it had been before, 'there is still a third shovel.'

She picked it up, but did not approach either of the two graves that were being dug. Instead, she said, 'Samuel, why did he not die?'

The Innocent. She did not have to say his name and the cartographer did not need to ask it. 'He is god-touched,' he said.

'He said that both of you were.'

'He was wrong.' Bueralan turned to Orlan as he spoke, surprised by his answer. The old man stood in his shallow grave, stained in sweat and dirt, neither of which hid the red marks of the chain that the Innocent had wrapped around his neck.

'I am just a fat old fool who has forgotten that the task of cartographers is not to define history, merely bear witness to it. My name is worth more than I am, worth more to all the lords and ladies and gods than myself. But you cannot test a name, you cannot measure its moral quality. But you can tie it to a strand of fate, just as the God of Truth did to Aela Ren. You can make it mean something. You can make the people who take it mean something. That is how immortality is given. A god locks your death in a moment of time that may have already taken place, or will never take place. It locks you there with all you may have once been, or once become. It takes away all the freedom you were born with.'

'That's what happened to Bueralan?'

'Nothing happened to me.' He thrust the shovel into the dirt, left it upright. 'Let's be clear on that. A dead god used me for one moment. I don't know how, but there were no trials, no ties to fate. His mountain fell on him afterwards and it nearly fell on me. I would have died if it had.'

'You,' she said, her dark eyes holding his, 'you don't react well to change, do you?'

'I am not your saviour.'

'I do not need a saviour. I am the Queen's Voice.' She turned from him and walked over to an empty piece of grass. With a solid thrust of her shovel, Taela pierced the ground. 'She will not abandon me.'

2.

Ce Pueral killed two horses returning to Cynama, yet still arrived a week too late.

The city was quiet when she rode through the gate, her soldiers an exhausted line behind her. The streets were empty but for soldiers and butterflies: the latter had settled onto the walls and roofs of the buildings she rode past. Pueral saw boarded doors and windows painted with symbols of dried animal blood on them. It was an old protection ritual, useless in Pueral's opinion, but when one of their horses stepped hard on the paved road, or a sword in her pack jangled oddly, the hard, sharp sound tore through the city, and she understood the need another might have for the symbols' comfort.

In the middle of Cynama, the presence of the First Queen's soldiers began to increase and with it a sense of normality returned to the city. Guards started to appear regularly on the streets in pairs, their black-and-red-metalled hands on the hilts of their swords. Pueral saw citizens as well, and many worked at constructing barriers and roadblocks, further strengthening the defensible line that had been created. Yet, by the time she rode through the final two blocks to the palace itself, Pueral had become aware that it was not just her soldiers she led to the gate, but a wave of anticipation, and when she finally came to the palace, rows and rows of soldiers had turned out to await her.

She dismounted before their gaze. Her first quiet words were to her soldiers, whom she ordered to retire and see to the care of their new horses. Once that had been done, she began to walk through the lines of soldiers, and stopped only once Captain Lehana emerged from the back of the square, the palace gate a webbed mouth closing behind her.

'My Lady.' The lean, middle-aged woman saluted. 'It is a pleasure to see you.'

The salute surprised Pueral, but she returned it. 'The First Queen?'

'She is in the palace,' the other woman replied. 'She has left orders for you to be brought to her as soon as you arrive.'

As she walked through the gate to the palace, Pueral was aware of every soldier's gaze on her.

She was uncomfortable. The First Queen had three generals who oversaw the military and in Pueral's opinion, each of them was as capable as the other. Each was as loyal to the Queen as they should be, the Eyes of the Queen knew, but Pueral was also aware of the fact that, in the last half-dozen years, she had gained a reputation among the soldiers as the spine that kept the army upright. She had overseen a pay increase. She had weeded out a small corrupt element in the higher ranks. She had changed their armour – though she felt its weight keenly as she walked along the tiled floors – and she had expanded their training to include practices both on and off the black ocean. Many of the decisions had been made with the Queen's generals, and she had been sure to acknowledge each of their contributions over her own, but it was clear, as she mounted the stairs, just who the average soldier relied on.

Inside the Queen's private chamber, Pueral found Zeala Fe alone. The First Queen sat in one of her heavy chairs in front of a large window, the table beside her littered with papers and letters, an ocean of activity around a single, delicate teacup that trailed steam. Yet, what concerned Pueral most was the Queen's health: her frail skin had sunk further into her bones and, as the last of the midday's light came into the room, it appeared to pierce the skin of her hands.

'You have heard, no doubt,' Zeala Fe said in a voice stronger than Pueral had heard in years. 'He is here.'

'I thought that I had found him in the Fifth Province.' She picked up a chair and placed it beside the Queen. 'Instead, he left a letter telling me he would be here.'

'He does like to talk.'

Pueral grimaced as she sat. 'You met him, then?'

'He killed twenty-three men and my daughter.' The gaze that turned to her was haunted. 'He did not take a backward step once.'

She had heard about Yoala. A nobleman's guard had stopped her on the highway to impart the news. He had seen her and her soldiers riding hard, and had left his charge to stand at the edge of the road to flag them down. If Pueral had not known him from his decade of service − if she had not fought beside him in those years − she might have ridden past him. 'I have also heard that he took your Voice.'

'Yes.' The strength in the Queen's voice faded with the

admission. 'My generals tell me that I should flee, that I should seek safety in another province or another country.'

Pueral did not reply.

'But I am the First Queen. I will not run. I will not desert my land, I will not abandon my people, and I will not allow him to silence me.' She indicated the papers at her side. 'My Voice is kept on Yoala's estate with Bueralan Le and Samuel Orlan. He has not touched her. He talks a little with her and Samuel Orlan, but mostly, he converses with Bueralan. He tells stories. He talks of the gods and of the future and the past. Sometimes, what he speaks of is nothing but horrors. At others, it is nought but triviality. I will have her returned when we kill him.'

Pueral did not reach for the papers. 'What you ask for may well be impossible.'

'It may well be,' she replied. 'But would my Eyes be as foolish as my generals to ask me to turn away?'

The Eyes of the Queen would not.

Pueral remained with the First Queen until the afternoon's sun began to set. It was then that the weight of her armour began to fall painfully onto her bones. She found herself constantly trying to rearrange the weight of the leather straps and was eventually dismissed by the Queen, who told her to return in the morning after she had bathed and eaten and slept. In her own chamber, Pueral sank into a hot bath with the words of the report in her mind, with the images of the generals – two women and one man – once again lobbying for the Queen to leave. They had appeared within the hour of Pueral's arrival, but while she could understand their point, she knew also that the First Queen simply could not flee. It was not about the Queen's

Voice: the three generals had seen that as a point of weakness to exploit, but in doing so, they had failed to acknowledge the demands of a Queen's power. It was her duty, her responsibility, and the cruel acknowledgement that all the First Queen had done — all the changes she had brought to Ooilan society — would be no more if she ran from the Innocent.

After her bath, Ce Pueral did not pull on the soft bedclothes that had been laid out for her, nor did she slip into the bed that had been turned down by servants she had not seen.

Instead, she dressed in her leathers and tightened the belt holding her sword on her waist. As darkness began to set around the palace, she walked across the courtyard. She returned the salutes she received and entered the barracks of the Queen's soldiers. Inside, she walked down the long hallways until she found the witch, Tanith.

'Tell me.' Pueral picked up the jar that held the letter written in the Innocent's blood. 'How will this work?'

3.

Before the morning's sun rose, Heast sat wrapped in his cloak beside a dead fire and stared at the Mountains of Ger. He would leave the last of the mountains today: the narrow path that he and Kye Taaira followed would lead them into the Kingdoms of Faaisha before the midday's sun had set. From there the land ran into a vast scrubland.

The journey over the mountain had been without incident after they had discovered the body of Taaira's ancestor. That had been the cause of greatest concern for the pair of them and, on the night after finding the body, the tribesman had explained it to the Captain of the Ghosts. 'I could find no trace of him,' the tribesman said. 'No sign of his blood or his soul.'

'It could be that the ghosts took him.' Heast had laid his saddle on the ground and sat against it, his steel leg stretched out before him. 'If a ghost can do such a thing, that is.'

'In truth, such knowledge is beyond me.' His gloved hand dropped to the large sword beside him. 'But I have a duty.'

'There are still others.'

'I must return with them *all*, Captain.'

Heast sipped his water. He had not liked the tone in the other man's voice, but he made no comment about it.

'But we have a more immediate problem.' Taaira began to pull off his gloves to eat. 'The name of the ancestor we found was Myone, I believe. Certain older wounds on his body were reminiscent of scarification and he had been one of four or five who had done this to their body. It was a part of culture on the Plateau during the War of the Gods, but lasted no more than two generations. The others the child raised who would have made similar changes to their own skin were not men and women who would hunt alone. Myone, however . . . shamans would tell a story of how he enjoyed torturing enemy warriors. In it, Myone released those he captured on the Plateau painted with pig's blood. He would use enough to draw the predators of the land to the men he had captured. For two weeks the animals would hunt the soldiers, and once they fell, once the strongest in their packs devoured the enemy warrior, then Myone would hunt and devour the packs.'

'But someone would ride after him, if he was gone for too long,' Heast guessed. 'That is our problem, is it not?'

'His brother is named Nsyan. He is by far the crueller man.'

When the morning's sun rose, there was no sign of Nsyan, and neither Taaira nor Heast saw any over the following week. In truth, they had seen little beside birds and animals and each other. Even the ghosts of Mireea could no longer be felt.

The trail the two men followed had twisted along the Mountains of Ger on paths Heast had not expected to take. It rose where he thought it should have dropped and turned south when it should turn north. He had not been worried, for the breaks in land had been the clear reason for the change in direction and, ultimately, the paths had taken them towards the border of Mireea without incident until the last day.

As they had broken camp that morning, both Heast and Taaira had heard a loud, shuddering sound a moment before a serious earthquake shook the ground beneath them. The sound of stone being torn open roared in the sky around them, joining the birds that had lifted up like a flood, but it had not lasted long. Despite the sounds, very little had changed around the two men and their horses and it was not until the afternoon's sun had risen that they saw anything that had altered. There, the trail they had followed dropped away suddenly and Heast found himself standing before a sight unlike any he had seen before.

The earth had been torn apart, as if a pair of hands had thrust into a wound, and then pulled it back to reveal the ruins of a City of Ger.

It was not a large city. It consisted of nearly two dozen large stone buildings, the edges of each long worn away, leaving them with a rounded appearance. Lichen and moss covered the great majority of the buildings, and a myriad of green and blue and white and grey blended together to give the city a luminescent quality, an unearthly sheen that suggested the buildings had never been designed for human habitation. Yet, Heast knew as he rode his horse around the edge of the broken earth, they had. The windows still held rotting frames and curtains, while the remains of doors were blackened so very similarly to the houses that Heast had seen throughout the world. A mother or a father would push it open. A child could emerge.

It was the first time he had seen a City of Ger. When his

men had dived into a flooded mineshaft in search of Leeran bandits, he had left the work to others. His leg would have made it difficult, but it was not the work of a captain anyway. Instead, he had read the reports that had been written, but none of them had captured the strangeness before him, none of them gave voice to the unsettling realization that here were the remains of a society that had, for generations, lived beneath a stone sky.

Silently, he nudged his horse off the trail and, with the tribesman behind him, rode along the broken expanse of the land, his gaze on the ruined trail of the city.

Then—

Then the ground had opened.

The wounded fissure that ran through the ground became a huge empty space. It was of such size, such magnitude that, as he first gazed into it, a sense of vertigo assailed Heast. The City of Ger ended suddenly at it, half a stone house still present on the edge of the hole, while another leant at an odd angle into it, as if it were falling, piece by slow piece, into the emptiness below it. If Heast had been riding in an earlier part of the day, the sight of the two buildings over the vast blackness of the mountain's wound would have been all he saw; but he came to it when the afternoon's sun was at its peak and its light reached down into the dark and left it dappled.

In the depths of it, the very, very depths, Heast could make out an outline. It was but a curve at first, a dark shadow, a sight that could easily be mistaken for a part of the mountain until the eye made out another outline. It traced from the edge of the first, further into the splotched shadows, to the centre of the great expanse. There a monstrous shape could be made out and he saw not the broken stone of a fallen building, but rather a splintered bone, a forearm, he thought by its shape, but a forearm of no creature he had known, a forearm so thick and heavy that it could only have belonged to a being that had been so large that, once standing, its head would have risen beyond the clouds.

'Only in devastation is truth shown clearly to us,' Kye Taaira said in a hushed voice. 'Only here is the artifice of belief and intent stripped bare. Only here is what binds us together revealed.'

In the darkness of the camp, Heast continued to gaze at the dark shape of the mountains. If it revealed a truth to him, he did not speak it.

4.

The storm that struck the Floating Cities of Yeflam the morning after the trial lasted three days. In the morning, the darkness of the night failed to lift completely and, from within the bruised sky, an ugly, late-season storm came. The streets emptied, the bridges closed, and the ocean rose in black waves to crash against the pillars as if the angry hands of the dead had begun to beat against the stone. Zaifyr was restless at that thought – he imagined Lor Jix standing on the shattered deck of *Wayfair*, leading the procession – but on the fourth day, the sky was empty and the ocean flat and still.

At the end of that week, the calm had given way to restless, erratic air as Yeflam waited for the Enclave to begin the march of war.

The papers, be they run by the Enclave, the Traders' Union or independents, made no secret of the fact that the Enclave would issue a statement declaring war soon. The presses reported that the Keepers were embarrassed and outraged, and the Traders' Union littered its papers with images of a giant, misshapen leviathan in a variety of poses. In some, it crushed the Keepers. In others, the Floating Cities were covered in its corpse. Yet, no matter what Zaifyr saw or read, he did not disagree that Yeflam was preparing for war. He watched the slow militarization of Yeflam from the tower ledge. From there, he saw the increased presence of armoured soldiers on the streets. He saw them begin during the storm at the bridges, and he saw patrols and small corner outposts spring up beneath the rain. After the storm stopped, he saw for the first time the Yeflam navy patrolling Leviathan's Blood. The beating of the drums in the long vessels took the place of the noise the waves had made against the stone, as if nature had given way to the demands of humanity.

On the day of the trial, he, Jae'le and Eidan had entered the meeting room in the centre of the Enclave and found the room united.

'We will find this child of the gods,' said Kaqua, the Pauper. 'We will find her and bring her to justice.' He had folded his arms in the faded sleeves of his robe and spoke with a serenity that Aelyn, who stood beside him, did not have. Her fury spread over the Keepers behind her. 'However, all three of you must understand that the Enclave has responsibilities to Yeflam,' Kaqua continued. 'It cannot abandon these responsibilities in search of revenge. If you cannot agree to that, then you will be at an impasse with us. Worse, you will be in conflict.'

'Anguish believes that she is still here.' Zaifyr directed his reply to his sister. 'Millions will die if you allow her to leave Yeflam. To kill her here is to end the war in a day.'

'Do you truly believe that?' she asked in a hard voice.

'Yes.'

'Then you are a fool, brother,' Aelyn said bluntly. 'The Faithful will not awake the moment she is dead. They are not under a spell. They believe. They will not stop because she is dead. We do not even know how long it will take her to die. It could be another ten thousand years, in which case her Faithful will claim she is alive. They will even make up a name for her if she falls without one. They will keep marching. You cannot stop what is happening here, and over the mountain, by destroying her.'

Zaifyr sensed that his sister was afraid. Everything she had done – from a treaty with Leera, to sending Fo and Bau to Mireea, and her reluctance to begin a trial – had been a manifestation of that. She had been more damaged by Asila and by the fallout in her home than he had realized. For a moment, Zaifyr thought that he could see her memories, that he could see the crumbling spirals of Maewe, the riots in the streets and her deep despair at it. But he also believed that a moment had been presented to them *now*. Lor Jix might not have risen on the waves during the storm, but Zaifyr could still sense him beneath the stone of Nale, a presence entwined with the sensation of the child, a chill against her sharpness on his skin. In his mind the two had combined with the cold of the dead and the whispers of the haunts, but, as he had begun to speak, to explain that to Aelyn and to the Keepers, Eidan had interrupted.

'She is right,' he said. 'When the child falls, she will remain a figurehead to them. It may be that some will leave upon her death, but not all. They will cross the ruins of Ger's mountains to reclaim her. They will not easily believe that she is dead, and perhaps rightly. Look at our world. Will she become yet another dead god? We do not know the answer to that, just as we are missing so many other answers. We do not know what defences she can call upon, what creatures will answer her. I have seen what does answer in Leera, and if it is but a fraction of what responds to her here, then the stones of Yeflam will be a new colour come the morning if we strike against her.'

Earlier, when Zaifyr had rejoined Jae'le and Eidan, he had found them on the third floor of the Enclave. The former stood alone in the hallway while the latter stood in a dark empty office before an open window.

'The creature with him,' Jae'le answered his unspoken question quietly. 'He says that he has seen her.'

'In the Enclave?' he said.

'Outside.' Eidan emerged from the office alone, the darkness falling behind him while his body was reformed by the light. 'He says that he saw her, falling through the sky. That she was held in that giant creature she summoned. When we looked out of the window, we could not see her.'

'So he left?' Jae'le asked.

'He said that he wished to climb to the top of the Enclave. To look for her again.'

Zaifyr shared the surprise of his other brother who, the hilt of his sword concealed beneath his green-feathered cloak, did not hide his expression. With a sigh, Eidan continued along the hallway. 'It would be better to kill him, yes,' he said. 'It is the more intelligent thing to do, I know, and in the past I would not have hesitated. Anguish would even welcome such a thing, I believe. But all of us know that death is no mercy.'

It was those final words that returned to Zaifyr as he stood before Aelyn. He still believed that *this* was the moment, that all of them should strike – now, before the night was over. He could visualize the violence in his mind with a startling clarity that would linger with him through the storm and in the days after. But he took warning from the vision, and allowed that it was no longer a sign that he should rush towards the idea of destroying the child, no matter the outcome.

Zaifyr's right hand touched the bronze charm beneath his wrist, the simple, worn piece of metal his father had instructed him to tie upon himself first. 'Perhaps,' he said to Aelyn, 'you are right in this.'

5.

The storm had threatened to flood a part of Faise and Zineer's house. When it had reached its worst on the first day, the rain had poured through the broken second-storey window, and Ayae, desperate to stop the floor from being warped, had nailed a sheet of wood over the frame. She had pulled the wood from the back door where someone – Zaifyr or Jae'le, perhaps – had put it over the broken entrance after clearing away the men and women she had killed weeks before. Now the stone floor downstairs was awash from the rain that flooded in from the backyard. When the storm stopped, she organized a replacement of the window and door.

It arrived on the day that Aelyn Meah knocked on the door.

Ayae had left the Enclave shortly after Eira's final words. Outside, the darkness stretched across Nale and had slowly embraced her as the hours wore on.

She could have returned to Aelyn's false home, to the room where she had slept heavily after she killed Faise and Zineer, but Ayae knew that she could not. To go back there meant to be drawn into Zaifyr and Jae'le's war, into their plans to attack the child, and she did not want that. She wanted space to think and to breathe. She knew that she had lost control on Xeq, but it had been harder for her to acknowledge that she had not regained control of herself afterward, and it was why her step left faint webs of cracks along the stone. In the long walk back to Faise and Zineer's — a walk that saw carriages pass her, carriages she was afraid to step into — Ayae admitted that there was a chance that the solidification of her body would continue, that it would start to turn her very organs to stone. There was, as Jae'le said, a very real danger that she could be consumed by grief.

It had not happened by the time Ayae opened the door to Aelyn Meah, but neither had her body returned to itself.

'I thought it would be best for us to talk,' the Keeper said. Ayae's anger at the woman for her betrayal of Mireea was difficult to find, in part because Aelyn had forsaken the blue that she was commonly associated with and looked nothing more than a tired woman in her plain leather trousers and linen shirt. 'An official statement will be given tomorrow. It is the statement of war. We will be issuing it from the Enclave.'

No one had visited the house since she had arrived, not even neighbours, and for a moment Ayae had not thought to respond to Aelyn. Finally, she said, 'What do you plan to say?'

'That we must do this, of course.' The other woman offered a smile that was brief and hollow. 'Is that not what we always say before we march our citizens off to death?'

Ayae held the door open for the Keeper to enter the house. 'People still talk about her being in Yeflam.' A number of papers had, in the wake of the trial, become free. They piled up outside the house. 'People see her — a shadow of her, they say. And they see her priests.'

'Some of it is true, in so far as the people themselves believe. Others are not so true.' Aelyn followed her into the kitchen, still dominated by its long table. 'We have not found her, though. Even Eidan cannot find a trace of her in the stones.'

Ayae pulled back the heavy chair she had brought from downstairs and sat down. 'How do you explain it, then?'

'I do not. I cannot.' The Keeper pulled a lighter chair out to sit upon and spread her hands out. 'However, if we move up the coast with our navy, if we take Leera at its ports and shut down her supply routes, she will appear. In all her fury, she will appear in a country that is not the one I have worked so hard to create.'

She sounded tired and defeated and Ayae did not know how to respond to what she said.

'The rain must have come in during the storm,' Aelyn said, looking at the damp patches that remained on the stone floor. 'I do apologize. Faje warned me that he had been only able to do a minor repair.'

'I did not realize it was you who came here,' Ayae said, caught off-guard. 'Thank you.'

'It was Faje, mostly. My brothers can be kind in their own fashion, but they are terrible men to know in times of grief. They believe you must stare into it. That it makes you stronger when you meet it directly. There is an element of truth to such thoughts but it is what they first said when they were at war. I do not think that they ever truly left that mentality.' Aelyn fell silent for a moment, the stillness that was around her feeling as if it trembled, just slightly. 'No one is sure where Benan Le'ta is at the moment,' she said, leaving the topic. 'In the confusion of Xeq and the trial, he must have slipped out of Yeflam. At the moment, I am quite happy to believe that. It may interest you to know that the Traders' Union is going to compensate those who lost their homes or loved ones, in order to keep the peace as we go to war with Leera.'

Ayae ran a heavy hand through her hair. 'I am happy to help anyone innocent who was hurt,' she said, finally.

'There are no innocents.' She might have said *on Xeq*, but she did not. 'People make their choices — do not forget that.'

'I merely meant that I will not hide from what happened.'

'You speak as if you have a choice in the matter.' Aelyn's second smile was no longer empty, but rather sad and, Ayae thought, lonely. 'Not so long ago, you were probably like so many others in this word. An event befalls them, and they blame someone in authority above them. They say that they could have done this or they could have done that. They say that if they had more money it would be different. If they had more authority, more opportunity, then it would also be different. But for people like you and me, there is no alternative outcome. There is no authority to turn towards. We are it. We are the highest power in the world and we can do nothing but take responsibility for what we do.'

'But the child—'

'—is but us, until she is not.' Her smile faded. 'If we are to take what was said at the trial as a truth — and bear in mind that I think it will be a long time before we can say that — little has changed. We are still striving to make the world whole again. We are still recovering from the War of the Gods. We are not still in it, as my brothers would suggest. Indeed, my great fear is that thoughts like that only begin a cycle for what will happen when others reach this point, when beings like you and me become gods. When we begin to transcend ourselves and become divine, we cannot be at war.'

Ayae had no answer, but she knew that she did not need one. The conversation was not for her alone. They were Aelyn Meah's words to Aelyn Meah, Keeper of the Divine, ruler of Yeflam, and they were in part an attempt to ease her conscience that she and the Enclave were heading in the right direction. While she might have always thought war was inevitable, Ayae could see that the way in which it was unfolding was not the way Aelyn had wished it, and her words sounded much more like a practised speech aimed at regaining the confidence of her Keepers.

For a short time longer, the two talked in this fashion, about subjects otherwise unspoken, about a confession of fears Aelyn could not begin to make, until the Keeper finished.

At the door, the Keeper stopped. 'Are you sure you will not consider coming to the announcement?' she asked. 'It is important for you as well.'

'I am sorry,' Ayae told her. 'But I would not trust myself there.'

6.

In the darkness, the finished graves held a terrible promise that Bueralan could not turn from. For the last week, he had slept poorly, the exhaustion of physical labour providing only snatches of rest and, when he awoke, he would inevitably find himself drawn to the graves. In the early hours of the morning, the mounds of dirt were lit by the moon and the stars, and he would wrap his hand about the leather pouch around his neck until the cold began to burn his skin. Then, he would release it, and the familiar chill would settle against his chest.

On the third night after the graves had been finished, Bueralan realized that a part of him came out expecting to bury Zean's soul.

Aela Ren had appeared before them on the fourth day, after the last grave had been filled. 'It is a strange ritual we keep without the gods,' he said, walking between the mounds of earth. 'Originally, we buried our dead so that the Wanderer would know where our souls were. He was but one of the aspects of mortality, and when he requested that the dead were buried, he also asked for Maika, the God of Ascension, Maiza, the God of Oblivion, and for Maita, the Goddess of Rebirth. It was she who used the soil most of all, for she ensured that a soul's return to human life was one of steps, and it began in the soil, in the worms that ate human flesh. It has often amazed me that only the butterflies in Ooila rise after falling into the ground where the traces of Maita's power give them life again and again.'

'Occasionally people arise,' Samuel Orlan replied. Of the three, the old cartographer was the only one who felt comfortable entering into conversation with the Innocent. 'They are in a terrible state, half-decayed, their mind gone, but they do arise.'

'You have seen such?'

'Yes,' Orlan said sadly. 'I have.'

'Then why do you dig graves?'

'I do not, usually.'

Bueralan remembered the pyres in Mireea and the intricate images that had filled all but two of them, but he made no attempt to intervene. Ren baited Orlan in each exchange the two had, and the latter would reply only in earnest, as if a strange, unspoken debate was taking place.

A light crunch of gravel sounded behind Bueralan and he smelt a mixture of soap and perfume before Taela stood next to him.

'You're supposed to be asleep,' he said.

'So are you.'

After the first day of grave digging, she had returned to speaking to him. Bueralan had tried to keep his distance, but had found himself drawn back to her, to her conversation, to her insight, and to the fact that, in the house that held four people, only Taela shared his experience of being caught in something much larger than themselves.

'Have you decided to bury it yet?' she asked.

He could still feel the cold in his hand from the pouch at his neck. 'No,' he said. 'I see Ren stare at it each time I enter a room. He would dig it up if I buried it.'

'It is a talisman to him.'

Bueralan did not disagree. Each time he spoke with the Innocent, the scarred man would begin to speak of the War of the Gods. He would describe the world that had existed at that time, quite often in language that surprised Bueralan. He would see images in his mind, similar to the image he had seen of Jae'le, the Animal Lord. Each of them had a sweetness, a perfection to them, a sureness that Bueralan found comforting, and he had come to realize that Aela Ren was trying to convince him of his position, as if, by doing so, he might draw a name from him.

'What was she like,' Taela asked, 'this child god?'

'Cruel,' he spoke the word without pause. 'Young and cruel.'

'I used to pull off the wings of butterflies when I was a girl,' she said. 'I would catch them in a net that my father owned and I would cut off their wings, to see if they would be reborn without them.'

'And were they?'

'No, they were reborn with wings. But it was cruel of me – children are often cruel, I have found.'

'I do not think she is truly a child, not in the way you and I understand it,' Bueralan said. 'I had not given her much thought until this week. For the most part, I was interested in making amends for my failure. I had lost my friends, and I had lost my life. To hold Zean's soul in my hand after that . . . it was too much like when we were children. I was not given nets to catch butterflies, but a boy to wear all my punishments, and I did not want that authority. It was a burden that I could not bear.'

'You sound very similar to the Queen,' she said quietly. 'Years ago she showed me the books that she had written. They were difficult to read, filled with violence, and advice, and instructions, all with the aim of building a world power out of Ooila. At the end of my reading, she told me that the words in those books were a burden she felt every day of the year. She placed a cup in front of me as she spoke. It was filled with poison, she said. I would have the option to drink it after she told me a secret. I was not very old: the Queen had purchased me from the opera that my father had sold me to the year before, and the secrets I knew to keep were awful. But it was there that she told me that none of her children were the reincarnations of the women in the books. That her children were her own. That she herself would not be reborn.'

Bueralan wondered if his mother had known. He thought that she had. He thought of Safeen Re, whom he had seen last week, and her advice, and he thought lastly of the Hundredth Prince.

'I could laugh,' he said. 'Almost.'

'Yes,' Taela said after a moment of hesitation. 'I suppose you could.'

Zean would laugh. The cold in Bueralan's hand had almost faded, and he resisted the urge to reach up again for the pouch. It was strange that he barely felt the leather against his chest. He had grown used to it, just as he had grown used to the strip around his neck, and the weight at the end. The burden that he could not at first bear was now a burden, he knew, that he had learned to bear. He had finally begun to understand that, standing before the graves he had dug.

7.

When the second knock came on the door, Ayae considered ignoring it.

Yet, it persisted, a heavy soldier's knock. *A soldier dressed as a priest* – but she pushed the thought from her mind as it started. Memories of Faise and Zineer were never far from Ayae in their house. A cup she held. A door she opened. The rumpled, unmade bed she saw from the hallway. She could see the faint outlines of both, performing the acts that they had done when alive. Walking down stairs. Standing before the kitchen window. Ayae had navigated the memories from the moment she pushed open the door and found the bloodstains, but not the bodies. Still, when the knock sounded again, she resisted the idea of rising because it did remind her of that night, and a part of her wished that she had not answered it then. She would have been in the house when the window broke, would have heard Faise's scream. Would have heard Zineer's shout. She would have been there. She would have, had not the false priest knocked on the door.

After the fourth knock, Ayae opened the door. There, Caeli leant casually with her long back against the frame. Her gaze was on the dark street and she had been knocking with her right hand, a series of heavy raps that did not even require an upraised arm and, when the door fell back, the fist she had held spread into an open palm and gave half a wave.

'You bring a drink?' Ayae asked.

Wordlessly, Caeli's left hand lifted a clear bottle.

'Is that laq?'

'I used not to think much of it.' She pushed herself off the wall. 'But Lady Wagan has a real taste for it. It has rubbed off on me.'

Ayae closed the door behind the guard. She had not seen Caeli or Lady Wagan since the trial, but she had not looked, either. After the storm had broken and she had gone out in search of a new door and frame, she had overheard two men discussing the fact that the Lady of the Ghosts had not returned to Wila. The words had been startling, and she had felt something deep inside her curl in anger, but the men's conversation had no real depth. One of them had spat regularly on the side of the road as he talked and the other smoked a badly rolled cigarette. Both agreed that nothing would come from keeping the Mireean refugees now. Send them away, they said. Push them into the ocean, another said. They'd drown their children first, the other said, and the pair had laughed at a private joke. It had left Ayae feeling combative, though she had said nothing.

Caeli, she knew, would not have reacted in that way. The tall guard wore a thick leather vest, leather trousers and solid leather boots. None of it was new, not even the chain mail that threaded over the sleeves around her wrists and forearms, and which was hinted at around her shoulders and hips. But it was the long sword by her side that would have led her reply to the two men.

'I was here earlier,' she said, approaching the kitchen table, and the same chair that Aelyn had sat at. 'But I waited.'

'Thank you.'

Caeli placed the bottle on the table. 'Glasses?' She began to unbuckle her sword. 'I imagine the head of the Keepers came to tell you about the response to the child?'

The glasses were the ones she had drunk from with Faise, weeks ago. 'Yes,' Ayae said, returning. 'It isn't a surprise, surely?'

'No, the cities are alive with it. You can sense it in the papers, but it's worse when you talk to people. They fear her, they see her, they want her dead. The curfew still exists, the guard and navy are out. But it is near impossible to walk through parts of this city without overhearing someone talk about it,' the guard said. 'It has been hard to hide Lady Wagan, but Sinae Al'tor has been very good at that.'

'Is that why you are here?' She placed the glasses on the table, careful not to put too much weight on it, or to break them with her hard fingers. 'You pour, please.'

Caeli broke the seal with a single twist. 'Yeah.' She began to pour. 'The Traders' Union and Lady Wagan are meeting tomorrow night. Thought I'd see if you wanted to come along?'

She took the glass. 'I'll pass.'

'You going to stay in your dead friend's house?'

'Yes.'

'That's a little morbid.'

'I'm tired, Caeli.'

'Aren't we all.' She lifted the glass in salute, then drank. 'I have spent the last week sleeping on the ground and living in ugly rooms. I rode out of Yeflam the night of the storm because Lady Wagan wanted me to deliver new orders to Kal Essa's

Brotherhood. Without the captain here, the guard is Lieutenant Mills's command, but the other work is mine. I don't mind, but the shoes are hard to fill. And when I returned, I found out that Wila had been cut off from the city. The guard had been increased and no one has been allowed down the ramp. Food and water is delivered by the soldiers, but no one will tell anyone how much or how little is being taken. Lian Alahn has told Lady Wagan that he can do nothing. He claims everything in Yeflam has ground to a halt politically, that everything has been militarized. From one end to the other, it certainly looks that way. A lot of Lady Wagan's people in Yeflam have been leaving while they can. I have walked into over a dozen empty shops, at the least.'

'You don't need me.' Ayae placed her empty glass back on the table. 'You should contact Xrie.'

'But I'm here instead.'

'Why?'

'Maybe I think sitting around in your dead friend's house is morbid and I'm worried about you.' Caeli began to refill the glasses. 'Did you know the captain is in Faaisha? Lady Wagan lied when she said he had been let go. A letter came from Lord Tuael. It had the symbol of Refuge on it.'

'Refuge?'

'Refuge is—' She hesitated. 'Refuge is what desperate people reach for. There isn't much of it left, a few soldiers here and there. It is mostly a myth now.'

'I know what it is.' She took the full glass from the blonde woman. 'The camps on the edge of Sooia were established by Refuge. I don't remember much of the story — I was only little when it was told — but I remember that the camps used to belong to mercenaries. That was a long time ago, though. A hundred years, I'd say.'

'It has been around for a long time, and there've been a lot of captains, and a lot of soldiers in it.' The guard slumped back in the chair, holding her own glass. 'Lady Wagan says that it might not come back. That it might not ever exist again. But she wants the Mireeans off Wila before this war begins. She wants them on the farms and on the land. She wants to be ready to support Heast when he begins to take the fight to Waalstan.'

'But he doesn't have an army. Surely she sees that?'

'I don't know what she sees.' Caeli let out a low breath. 'But I know what I see. I see Wila in my dreams. I can smell shit and salt and blood and I see the tents. They appear tighter, but they are empty, and there is a roar in the background, like the crash of surf. Except, when I turn to it, it looks like a huge mouth, and everything is being drawn into it to be consumed.'

Ayae looked down at the glass in her hands. The last time she had sat and drunk laq it had been with Lady Wagan and she had asked her for help. She had asked her to hold a bird until they reached Yeflam, but Ayae had not done so. Instead, she had walked into the Keep to attack Fo and Bau beside Mireean Guards and Steel soldiers. And Queila Meina. 'You want me to help you,' she began, 'but I lost control on Xeq.'

'I know.' Caeli lifted her glass and the light from the kitchen caught in it, and in the laq it wavered and bent so that nothing was straight. 'Maybe Faise holds it against you. Maybe Zineer. I know you hold it against yourself. But I'd still like my friend to stand beside me while the world of Muriel Wagan and Aned Heast devours me.'

8.

Eidan had taken to prowling the edges of the enclosed land of the estate. Zaifyr did not know why his brother found it so difficult to remain in the building – even the storm had been unable to keep him indoors for longer than an hour – but he knew that outside he searched for Anguish.

The creature had not been seen since the night of the trial. When he and Jae'le had suggested to Eidan that Anguish had been forcibly drawn back to the child, he had rejected their words. 'If she has forced him to open his eyes,' he said in his deep voice, 'he will remain isolated. If she is using him to watch us, then he will stay away, no matter what pain he will suffer.' He stood outside the door of the house, his gaze on the gate at the end of the path. There were no longer any guards made from wind, only a simple gate, but to judge by his brother's stare, a dangerous wilderness existed beyond the steel, one that was without mercy.

What had befallen Eidan in the company of the child would emerge eventually, Zaifyr knew. It need not be demanded, or pushed for; secrets that another held would emerge, given enough time, though they might be too late, or too damaging, when they did. The thought was one that he had as he stepped from the back room of the mansion. He had sensed Aelyn's arrival and, as he walked into the main room that led to the front door, he saw the shadows of her and Eidan pause outside the door.

'You do not need to stay here.' It was Aelyn's voice he heard first. 'There is still a room for you in the Enclave.'

'I am not welcome there,' Eidan said. 'Only you are.'

'This is your home.'

'I wonder,' Eidan said quietly. 'Do I have a choice where I sleep?'

'You always have a choice,' Aelyn replied. '*We* have always had a choice.'

'Unless we have not.' A third voice, an inhuman voice, appeared as a shadow fluttered into view of the window, a storm petrel settling onto the sill. 'As you said yourself, sister, questions will need to be asked.'

'I do not need to ask questions about free will and fate,' she said, a weariness etching itself on her voice. 'I know that it is my own choice.'

'I do not disagree,' Jae'le said. 'But I wonder. When I first entered Yeflam I would listen to the child's priests. They would speak to audiences that did not listen. They would tell them about the future. About how it is not complete. How it changes not with our actions, but with hers.'

The closeness that Zaifyr had not wanted to break between Eidan and Aelyn strained under Jae'le's words. He was the eldest brother, and though his lack of power had been revealed, his authority still remained. In the Enclave, he had led a single, determined argument for attacking the child immediately, and at some points during the night, his sheer force of will almost convinced those in the room to agree. Had not the child's words remained like a wound on Jae'le, Zaifyr believed that he would have succeeded; but the words did linger, and when they returned to the house in the early moments of the storm, he had asked his brother about the tower, and about his power. The other had said he had no desire to reclaim it, but Zaifyr suspected that the truth ran deeper, that perhaps he could not reclaim it. He believed, by the violence in his brother's gaze, that Jae'le would already have done so to kill the child if he could.

'The priests claim that she is making a single truth,' he continued. 'That her actions are creating a world of purity.'

'They speak of it all the time around her,' Eidan said as Zaifyr sat himself on the bottom step. 'She tells them that she will consume the gods like grain to reach that point.'

'Lor Jix's words would suggest the gods themselves feared exactly that,' Jae'le's inhuman voice said. 'If we are to believe the dead, then we are all their creations to be used against her.'

A sigh escaped Eidan. 'I hope you are correct in that, at least,' he said. 'On the Plateau, I was the witness of an awful event. There were those who were victims, and those who went willingly, and both screamed in such ways that I had never before heard as she drew the spirits of killers from the Plateau. I have thought much about that day, for it was a great wrong, and yet I did nothing to stop it. Worse, I took part in it. I have puzzled over why it has troubled me — I have killed men and women in a carnival of ways and seen such sights that to call them horrific is but a starting point. But as I stood on the Plateau, I felt as if I was staring at myself from a distance, and I could see all that I could become, and all that I might do as a divine being, and I was deeply troubled by it. To such an extent that I have wondered if it was not truly my thought, but one given to me, one put aside by a god for this moment.'

'Would that greatly relieve you, if it was true?' Jae'le asked.

'I think it would still trouble me,' he said.

Through the window, Zaifyr watched as Aelyn's shadow mingled with Eidan's. She became lost in it, and it was only with the most careful of inspections that he could see her hands and her hair. But now, as the silence between the three grew, the shadow of her body began to detach itself, and in a quiet voice, she said, 'Tell Qian that the announcement will be in two days. We will march for war then.'

Shortly afterwards, she was gone.

9.

Beneath Bueralan and Taela's feet, the first of the morning's butterflies died in sharp cracks.

They had left the graves together, after a long moment of silence, after Bueralan had rolled his shoulders and, in changing the topic, said that he had stables to clean. He had continued to care for the horses alone during the week and would come to the stables in the early hours of the morning, before the butterflies were thick, and return in the afternoon, after they had died. He refilled the troughs from the well out back, raked out the stalls, fed the horses, and then brushed them. He did it alone, but he felt no intrusion when Taela fell in beside him, and indeed, felt her help would be useful. He had not taken the horses out of the stalls yet. As if they knew the figure that stood in the house up the hill, they showed no desire to leave the safety of the stables, but Bueralan knew that they would have to be taken out to exercise soon, and a second person would make that easier.

'When I was young, my mother had a huge stable built,' he said, lifting a rake from the stand. 'She made the walls from stone and the roof from slate, but the stalls inside were divided by wood. She had a very specific request that it be big enough for them to move around in, and wanted it to open into a huge yard. She would go out each day around midday, when the sky was starting to clear, and let the horses out into that yard.'

'Yoala was not as kind to her animals.' Zi Taela leant against the stable door and watched him intently. 'Do you plan to clean all the stalls?'

'There's another rake.'

She laughed.

'You dig graves, but don't clean stalls?'

Her laughter turned into a swear word, but she reached for the rake. 'This really is the kind of thing you pay others to do, Bueralan.'

'I've been paid to do a lot of things.' He stopped outside the stable of the tall grey. The horse had appeared in the grounds after the night of the party, but it had been Aela Ren who led the beast to the stables. After Bueralan had found him, he had asked the Innocent about it, and he had simply replied that it appeared that it had a bond with him. 'But mostly, a horse is worth more than you. Ask any mercenary who has had to pay for one lost in battle.'

'It's because your horse followed you here that you think this is fine, isn't it?' Taela stood in front of the horse, her hand scratching its neck. 'You should give him a name.'

'Horse is fine,' he said sourly. 'Also, I hope he bites you.'

The horse did not, of course, and neither did any of the other fifteen in the stable.

Bueralan enjoyed Taela's company and for a while he forgot about the man who stood in the house in the distance, and he forgot about the coldness that pressed against his chest . . .

and he might have continued to forget all that troubled him, might have forgotten who he was, if not for the fact that, after raking out the straw in the stalls, he had climbed the wooden ladder to the stable's upper level and begun to push down the replacement, only to hit a body that promptly screamed.

Hau Dvir, a Prince of the Saan, stared up at Bueralan, pleading desperately with him not to kill him.

'Calm down – *hey, kid!*' The saboteur's voice cracked out. 'You're fine.'

'He's still—'

'But he isn't *here*.' The boy was filthy. It was clear that he had not been living in the stable for the entire week; probably, to judge by the mud around his trousers, the split in his boots and the cuts across his face from branches, he had spent no more than the one night beneath the loose hay. 'Not right here, so keep your voice down.'

Taela appeared behind him, her rake held loosely like a staff, ready to strike. 'He can't stay here,' she said quietly. 'Ren will know.'

Bueralan agreed. 'Why are you here?' he asked Hau.

'I-I had nowhere to go,' he whispered quickly, tears welling up in his eyes. 'I've never been to Ooila before! Usa took care of everything! I don't know where to go!'

'You just ride, that's all.'

'Just—'

'The destination doesn't matter.' The saboteur looked at Taela. 'You have any money?'

'Only my jewellery, but that's back in the mansion.'

Bueralan had nothing on him, either. He held out his hand to the Saan Prince, but the boy shook his head and scrambled to his feet on his own. 'Take one of the horses here,' the sabo-teur said. 'Not the grey. The grey is mine.'

'He tried to bite me!'

'That's why he's mine,' he continued, not allowing the boy's hysteria to grow. 'You saddle it and you ride. You ride through everything out there until you hit a port or a town, and you sell the horse, and you buy your way back to the Saan.'

Hau Dvir stared wide eyed at him.

'If you don't do this,' Taela said calmly, 'Aela Ren will find you and he will kill you.'

They had to saddle a horse for him. Bueralan chose a skew-bald one, whose brown and white patches would show on the trails easily for any of the scouts watching the estate. There would be scouts, of course: one of the first things the Queen would have done was ensure that all parts of the land were watched. On the off chance that he made it through whatever net was there, he would be arrested at the first market he went to when Yoala Fe's brand was spotted. The boy would crack and admit everything to the first person who talked to him, and Bueralan was fairly sure he would be turned over to the First Queen in a short amount of time.

Hau Dvir could at least ride, Bueralan acknowledged as he watched the Saan Prince canter across the flat land. Taela had pointed him in that direction; after a few miles, the road met the edges of the property, and he could follow that without having ever to pass the mansion.

Feeling strangely removed from the scene, Bueralan stood at the back of the stables beside Taela until he could no longer see the Saan Prince. It happened gradually, the butterflies lifting and falling like a wave, until they obscured all sight of him.

When he was finally gone, Aela Ren said, 'I wondered if you would find him this morning.'

The Innocent sat to their left on an overturned wooden pail, his legs stretched out in front of him. Butterflies drifted lightly to the scars on his hands and head, and settled on his legs, and on the hilts of his sword and dagger.

'He's lucky,' Bueralan said casually. 'I wasn't even looking.'

'No one was.'

'Do you plan to chase him?' Taela asked. She attempted to match Bueralan's tone, but failed on the final word. 'To hunt him down?'

'No.' Ren rose, scattering the butterflies as he did. 'But she is right, Bueralan: you should name your horse.'

10.

The abandoned siege tower was clearly a trap.

Heast had first seen it late in the afternoon. The afternoon's sun was a solitary orb in descent and a cold wind had begun to move through the air, ushering in the night. The tower was made from wood taken from a Leeran town fence – Dirtwater, or one of the other larger towns – and it had fallen into a ravine where it leant, rather steeply, to the east. He had stopped before the narrow entrance to the ravine, before turning and riding to a thick set of scrub and trees. There, Heast had tied his horse to a branch and pulled out his narrow spyglass.

The tower was spotted with fire damage, but it had not fallen into the ravine from the stone ledge that it leant slightly over. There were tracks leading alongside it, and broken rope, but the truth was, if the siege tower had gone over the side, it would have landed differently. Heast's opinion was that it had been lowered down by horses or oxen, and he said so to Kye Taaira before he handed the spyglass to him.

'Myone's brother, Nsyan,' the tribesman said, staring through the glass at the length of the tower. 'Nsyan would take the captured children of his enemies and let them out in the field of battle. It did not matter when: in the morning, in the afternoon, in the night. He would do it before the battle began. He preferred young girls, no older than five or six, but not so young as they could not use words. He is quoted as saying, once, that the heart's death was the creation of language. He fancied himself, I am afraid to say, something of a philosopher. He would release the children only after he had cut them. Across the abdomen, or chest, anywhere where the blood would flow the best. After that, he would release them onto the field of battle, to wander and cry and to draw out the soldiers he fought.'

'I have seen similar things done,' Heast said. 'The tower is that kind of ploy, would you not agree?'

'But it is not Nsyan's.' He handed the spyglass to him. 'I do not sense him here.'

'Good. That will make it easier.'

'Do you plan to approach the tower? If I may say so, that does not seem a particularly good idea.'

'No, but another will come to the tower. We only have to wait.' Heast began to walk back to where the horses had been tied, the spyglass tapping against his good leg. 'Maosa is half a day's ride from here. The tower is surely a trap for them.'

'Why would they so willingly enter a trap?'

'Because they will be ordered to do so by a fool.'

After the border, the pair had intermittently passed crucified soldiers. They had passed sixteen before they came to the entrance of the ravine and the siege tower. Each of them had died on the wood, the last of them only days ago, Heast believed. The Leerans had stripped each soldier of their armour and their weapons but left, around the waist of each, a crimson sash. Heast had looked at the bodies of the men and women, but all but two were too young for him to have known them. Of the two who were not, Heast had known one, but only briefly.

'You've been to Maosa,' he said now to the tribesman, 'so you must have met Kotan Iata. You must have seen that he is an incredibly vain man who, for years, has wanted to style himself Warden of Faaisha. He has a fantasy of being a man who keeps the peace through his military skill. In truth, it is not a difficult ambition: most of the wars in the Kingdoms of Faaisha are against each other, and Iata's first attempt at being a Warden began by intervening in a series of small domestic battles with his neighbours. He won them because he had more money and more soldiers.'

'Yes, I know of the man. I have not met with him, but I know of him. He was stripped of all but his hereditary land ten years ago,' Taaira said. 'It was said that only the respect his father had been held in allowed him to keep that much.'

'He was a lucky man, but it will have burned him. He will see this as a way to regain what he lost.'

'I am afraid that I do not quite see what it has to do with us.'

Heast reached for the sword on the back of his horse. 'Iata will send soldiers to take the tower.'

'You plan to rescue them?'

'*We* plan to rescue them. Unless you have a desire to step away?'

'No.' A smile flickered on his face. 'No, but I am curious why you would help Kotan Iata? It does not appear that you think well of him.'

'I do not.' He began to buckle the sword around his waist. 'But we will need soldiers, and I am afraid that they will not come without risk.'

'I believe I understand.'

No, Heast thought as he adjusted to the weight of his sword, *I do not think you do*.

Ahead, the tower sat like a dark finger pointing away from Faaisha.

11.

Ce Pueral had never had a family of her own. There had been a man when she had been in her early twenties who had proposed, and another in her mid-thirties, but eventually those two men had been no more than the men before and after. Her parents had died a decade earlier, separated by a pair of years, and her brother, who had been born with a severe intellectual disability, had died before the age of seven. She could still remember the slow tragedy of that unfolding before her young gaze.

Her room in the palace was filled with unused space, and she kept no mementos of her family or the two men. They were indulgences, and she believed such things had to be cut out of a soldier's life, which she had done for all but two pieces of furniture. They were the largest pieces in her room and would not, at first glance, have appeared to be an indulgence. They were two human-sized wooden stands that held her armour. On the right stand sat the lightweight black-and-red suit: half of it had already been removed as she strapped it into place. On the left sat the heavy gold-rimmed armour she had worn nearly two decades ago. She had not put it on since it had been decommissioned and wondered what would be made of it after she failed to return one day. No doubt, whoever opened the door to her room, whoever the First Queen assigned the task to, would believe it to be a memento of her life in the military, similar to the broken swords soldiers kept, the horseshoes, the knives, the boots that had more meaning to them than the medals that they were given. Perhaps whoever stood there would think that the armour had saved her life, had taken on a value to her because of a single act that had nearly seen her die.

It had saved her life, of course, but that was not why she kept it.

The day before last, the Saan Prince, Hau Dvir, had been brought to the palace. One of the scouts around Yoala Fe's mansion had caught him bursting out of the property and had picked him up after it was apparent that no one was following. The scout had brought him back and presented him to Captain Lehana, who locked him in a cell at the bottom of the palace before word was sent to the First Queen and Pueral.

Pueral took an immediate dislike to Hau Dvir. He was weak, and that weakness, she believed, was derived from a mixture of parental indulgence and class arrogance. He stood in the middle of the cell as she and the Queen made their way down to the end of the empty jail. The latter was in her heavy wheelchair, pushed by Captain Lehana, who had taken the duty from a silent young man when the Queen had appeared.

At the cell, however, Zeala Fe rose from the chair and stood before the bars. 'I will be honest,' she said, her voice not yet cold, but cool. 'If I decide to kill you, there will be nothing to distinguish your death from those of the men you arrived with.'

'*Please*, I beg for mercy.' Hau took a step forward, but stopped as both Pueral and Lehana reached for their swords. 'Please,' he said again. 'I was to be married to your daughter.'

The Queen's smile was thin. 'Would I have lived to see the wedding?' she asked.

He faltered and took a step backward. 'I don't — why would — I was never told *anything* like that.'

'So you know nothing?'

'I'm innocent!' The Saan Prince blurted the words out, then took a second step backwards. 'I didn't, I'm sorry!'

'Let us see if you know something,' the First Queen said, the cold in her voice growing. 'Did you know that there were soldiers around the estate?'

'No,' he said quickly, the words falling over themselves. 'No, I ran. I was lost, I didn't see anything until I saw the stables.'

'Who found you?'

'The——' He wanted to say black, Pueral saw, but bit back the word. 'The big man. The one with the tattoos. The girl was with him.'

'The Queen's Voice?'

'He called her something else when they saddled the horse, I don't remember.'

The First Queen fell silent. Across from her, the Saan Prince shifted on his feet, unaware of the importance of what he had said, unaware of the concern he had lodged in the old woman before him, the symbolic value that was contained in the words. 'Did either the woman,' she said, finally, 'or even the man, tell you that you would be found by soldiers?' she asked.

'No,' Hau Dvir replied quickly, 'the man with the tattoos told me to sell the horse.'

Pueral felt a ripple of relief pass through her. She had been waiting to hear that, to hear that their plans were not known to those on the estate. If they had been, Bueralan would have sent the boy out with different words. Oh, she did not doubt that the saboteur knew that people were watching the estate. She assumed all of them — especially Aela Ren — knew that. It was merely the extent that Pueral was concerned with, but the Eyes of the Queen was confident that, had he or the Queen's Voice known, and had Ren also known, then Bueralan would have told Hau a different lie.

The First Queen asked a dozen other questions, each of them probing for information about the force she had around her daughter's estate, and Pueral's initial relief held true. The boy knew nothing. Bueralan had said nothing. The only concern, then, was the fatalism of the Queen's Voice, which, in Pueral's estimation, was a reasonable response to the situation.

Finally, the First Queen returned to her wheelchair and, without a word of goodbye, left the prison. Each cell passed her, dark and empty, and the Saan Prince's voice followed, pleading for them to come back, begging for mercy.

'Put him on a boat to the Saan,' the First Queen said, after they had left. 'Give him a letter and let him explain it all to his father.'

'And then?' Captain Lehana asked.

'We begin,' the Eyes of the Queen said.

Fully dressed now, Ce Pueral gazed at the old armour.

She would not serve another Queen. Pueral had known that from the day she had become a member of the First Queen's private guard. On the day the Queen died, she would be retired. She had accepted the fate when she accepted the position. The only question was how she would be retired: a sword or a quill. It depended on which daughter succeeded and the manner of her succession. But the knowledge had never brought bitterness to her. She could not have asked for more in her life.

Ce Pueral inclined her head gently to the armour, then left the room.

The Eyes of the Queen

She drew the creature for me, but it was nothing that I had seen before. If it is real, if it is not the work of the poor girl's mind trying to hide the horror of a knife descending into her eyes, then the creature is like its god: it is unnamed.

—Tinh Tu, *Private Diary*

1.

The cart held two hundred and six steel boxes, one for each bone in Aela Ren's body.

It followed Pueral along the road to Yoala Fe's mansion, drawn by a single brown horse and driven by Ae Lanos. Beside him sat the witch Tanith, her satchel heavy at her feet. The pair looked as if they were characters from a fable, where an elderly father rode beside his grown daughter on an awful delivery that they fulfilled only because it was required of them. At the front, Pueral believed that she was the guard captain, the loyal servant who knew too much . . . but the indulgence was short-lived. She saw it as a sign that the weight of the situation had begun to overwhelm her, and that in defence, her mind had begun to shy from reality, into a world of fables and myths, where for much of her childhood the Innocent had been such a character.

Before she had left, before Pueral had walked out through the palace gate alone, she had met briefly with the First Queen. Against the morning's light, Zeala Fe appeared to be a frail figure, one whom a stronger light would break apart. Yet, as Pueral closed the door, the Queen rose from the chair under her own strength and spoke in a voice that, a month ago, the Eyes of the Queen would not have recognized as Zeala Fe's own.

'A historian might write that we spoke of ordinary things,' the First Queen said, her hand on Pueral's. 'Strategies and alliances, and the weaknesses and strengths of both.'

'A conversation already had,' she replied.

'I would rather history record that we spoke of our anger.'

It was the fury within the First Queen, not the illness she had battled for so many years, that would consume the last of her body, Pueral knew. 'It will be announced,' she said, placing her hand over the Queen's. 'Soon enough, with swords and fire, and no historian will need doubt our response to Aela Ren.'

'Thank you, my friend.'

In the courtyard, the steel boxes had been stacked onto the back of the cart in order of size. The longest – those that would hold parts of legs and arms – were on the bottom, while boxes that would hold hands, pieces of spine, and fingers, sat on top. Each was uniform in design, made by the chief armourer on specific orders from Pueral, and there was no ornament on any. They were smooth and heavy and, once locked, would be taken into different parts of Ooila, where deep holes would be dug to bury them. Soldiers would stand on the lips of dormant volcanoes before releasing their weight; they would be carried under guard to the ports, where ships would head out into the wide, empty space of Leviathan's Blood; they would travel beyond the edges of Samuel Orlan's maps. All the parts of the Innocent, all but the skull, the crown of his body, would be taken far away from Cynama.

Pueral did not believe it would be simple to kill the Innocent. She had listened to the First Queen's description of the battle with the Saan more than once and, though she did not agree with Bueralan Le's assessment of the Saan and Ooilan soldiers, she nonetheless understood that any one man who cut his way through so many soldiers was not mortal. That Aela Ren had delivered onto himself a mortal wound after he had fought the men, to prove that he could not die, was to Pueral an unnecessary act.

Still, he was one man.

One man, no matter his skill with a blade, no matter his personal strength, and no matter the strange nature of his mortality, could be weighed down by a much larger force.

Around Pueral, Ooilan soldiers began to appear. They did so in fragments, as if being assembled before her, as if they had been made from the sunlight. They were figures from the fable she had imagined earlier, creations given to guard the daughter and her father as they made their journey to the castle of the monster. But of course, it was nothing of the sort: they appeared because the camouflage spells that the witches had laid could not hide them as Pueral rode past so close, as she broke through the shell constructed of sunlight and moonlight.

Pueral rode past black-and-red-armoured soldiers who stood before bedrolls and cold campfires, who pulled off the helms they wore to wipe sweat from their faces, who stood before tents and carts, and before lines of picketed horses. Ahead of her they formed, and kept forming, as over five thousand men and women were revealed around Yoala Fe's mansion. That number was not the whole of the First Queen's military, but it drew from the most seasoned, the most disciplined, from those who had experience fighting on horseback, and fighting with siege machines – machines such as the pair of catapults that she saw now, one already assembled, and one in the final stages of being so. They would be pulled into range of the mansion from here, but the witches would not go any closer to the mansion to work the large spell, and so the last of the distance would be made by flesh.

In Sooia, the Eyes of the Queen told herself, surely such a thing had been tried. Surely such huge forces had met Ren, and surely, they had crumbled. But there, he had been part of an army, a force that was – depending on which books she read – either huge and sprawling and disciplined, or made of such horror that it was clear no human rode at its head. That force had stood beside Aela Ren from the day he had begun his war, but it was not on Ooila. Had she herself not seen the beach on which the Innocent had come ashore, and had she not seen much of his early violence, she might not have believed so easily the reports of her spies that they could find no sign of Ren's army on Ooila. Nor might she have believed the bloodstained assurances of the witches who said that he had walked from the coast to Cynama alone.

Pueral no longer believed that the Innocent had intended to bring his war to Ooila. He had arrived on *Glafanr*, and he had done so with the intention of finding Samuel Orlan and Bueralan Le. He had not brought his army with him. Whoever had helped pilot the giant ship off the shore had stayed upon it and left Ren to his personal quest.

By the morning, Aela Ren would realize that mistake.

2.

The torches marked the arrival of the Maosans long before they came close to the ravine.

Taaira's gloved hand had awoken Heast from a light sleep. 'You will not believe what is to be seen,' he said quietly.

Stiffly, the Captain of the Ghosts pushed himself up, his right hand lifting the sheathed blade that lay beside him as he did so. In the few moments that he had had to process the tribesman's words, Heast reasoned that they had missed their chance. Over the afternoon and evening's observation, he and Taaira had found half a dozen Leeran soldiers hidden in the scrub around the siege tower, and Heast believed that at least two or three were within the tower itself. It was more than enough men and women to close the trap on the Maosans who entered, and when the night had darkened and the clouds had covered the moon and stars, Heast had reasoned that there was an even chance that he and Taaira would not notice the approach of the soldiers into the trap until it was too late. But when he reached the edge of their small camp and saw the torches, he realized that what he was seeing was much worse.

'They're not soldiers,' he said.

'It does not appear so.' Taaira handed him the spyglass. 'They wear armour, but most are armed with farm equipment.'

The lens of the spyglass took a moment to focus, but Heast saw that the tribesman was right. The approaching group numbered a dozen, each with drawn, heavily shadowed faces etched with exhaustion like deep scars. The best of the weapons appeared to be axes, long-shafted and heavy-headed, but he could count no more than three of those: the rest were hoes and staffs and, on the back of one woman, a rusted scythe. Heast's gaze settled on the grey-haired woman for, though she rode at the end, she did not hold a tall burning torch. Instead, she led half a dozen draught horses by a thick rope. For a moment, Heast thought that this was proof that she and the others were not soldiers, but opportunistic farmers in the wrong place, but then she shifted, and he could see the crimson sash around her waist, and quickly, he found one around each of the remaining figures.

'What did we estimate, seven?' Taaira asked.

'Eight.' Heast closed the spyglass. 'But I would expect another three or four.'

'A difficult task for the two of us.'

'We'll take the tower first,' he said. 'But the biggest threat to us will be the ride into the ravine. The odds would favour us better if we slipped in after the trap was sprung.'

'If they charge the ravine while we're fighting, we may not save any, I fear.'

Heast grunted sourly in agreement. He had thought that he could lose up to half of whatever force arrived and had been, if not pleased, at least able to accept that. But the torches that the men and women carried were bright markers, and a seasoned Leeran soldier would make short work of the targets.

Because of that, he and Taaira would have to charge the ravine without any light – and both would have to hope that the ground was not pitted, filled with sudden drops or holes in which their horses could break their legs.

Running his hand down his beast's neck, Heast gripped the saddle's pommel and pulled himself up. 'One last chance,' he said to the tribesman. 'You don't have to fight if you don't want to.'

'Captain.' Taaira wrapped the bridle around his left hand and pulled himself up. 'I am Hollow.'

'Once I start—'

'Is this conversation for me, or for you?' One-handed, he drew his heavy blade from its sheath and, for a moment, it looked as if he held a piece of darkness. 'The shame that is before me is one I have felt before.'

'There's only shame in death, boy.'

Heast was the first out of the camp.

He let the horse have its head in the pace that it set towards the ravine. It was fast and sure, but Heast would have pushed it faster, if he had not trusted the training that Kal Essa's Brotherhood had put the beast through, if he had not trusted the battles it had already fought. Like him, the horse was a veteran, a creature that would find itself on familiar ground once the battle began.

In his hand, Heast's sword was weightless. He held it low and, as the lip of the ravine showed itself in a craggy broken-toothed opening of scrubland, he raised it.

The tower sat five, maybe six hundred metres after the opening, a dark, solid shape. Inside it, he would be able to funnel the soldiers spread around for the trap, he would be able to use the walls as protection against crossbows. He knew he might not get all of them inside, where he and Taaira would be able to control who they fought, but he would get enough in there that the numbers outside it would be in his favour. Behind him, he heard the solid gallop of Taaira's horse, the reassuring fall of the hooves, the presence of a man who, Heast believed, would ensure that little resistance would be offered.

In front of him a Leeran soldier rose from his concealment, hastily aiming his crossbow. The bolt flew wide and Heast's horse did not pause as it rode over him with a sickening crunch.

Movement and sound erupted around him after that. Heast heard shouted orders from his right and heard bolts burst from the positions he had identified earlier. Another two Leeran soldiers were revealed by their voices deeper into the ravine, where it was darkest, but he did not turn to them, or slow his ride to the tower. His sword slashed out, but it hit metal and skidded off, catching the edge of something – but causing what damage, he could not say.

Ahead, the dark bottom of the tower cracked open and a woman stepped out. She was a solid woman, and in her hands she held a heavy crossbow, which she lifted calmly to her shoulder. Only for her shot to go wide as a roar tore through the ravine.

It came a second time and Heast, as startled by the sound as the Leeran soldier, turned to his right to see Kye Taaira drive his horse into the darkness of the ravine.

'*Nsyan!*' the tribesman cried out.

A third roar sounded from the darkness and, to Heast's gaze, it appeared to ripple. With a curse, he drove his heel into the flank of his horse and continued alone to the siege tower.

3.

A certain psychological insight had become evident after they had selected their rooms, Bueralan believed. Taela, the first of the three to take a room, had chosen one at the far end of the building. Located on the first floor, it had a single, narrow bed before an equally narrow window, and it felt, the one time the saboteur thought as he had stepped into it, like a fist closing tightly shut around you. The room he had opted for – a simple guest room that overlooked the dug graves – was larger, but without any of the personal touches of the first. Once he left, no one would know that he had been there. But Samuel Orlan's room was different: the cartographer had chosen the one room equal in size to Yoala Fe's master bedroom. While it did not have the golden handles on the drawers, or darkly polished furniture, or the elegant rugs laced with thin strands of precious silver, the room had clearly been designed for guests of importance and substance.

Bueralan discovered that the old cartographer had stripped the walls of its curtain and tapestries in the early hours of the morning. They lay across the floor, against the wall, and both on and under a small maze of chests and tables that he was forced to navigate to cross the room. Once inside, Bueralan saw that the cartographer had pushed the rest of the furniture into the centre of the room, leaving the bed locked in the centre amid a pile of unmade blankets.

Samuel Orlan stood in the far left corner of the room on a chest of drawers. In one hand, he held an expensive quill, in the other, an ink pot. Before him an elaborate, detailed map of the world sprawled across the first two of the pale-orange-painted walls, beginning at the door frame where Bueralan stood. It gave the impression of a world slowly being consumed by fire.

'It helps me relax.' The cartographer spoke first, his arm outstretched to a high point on the wall. 'Surely you have something that takes your mind off your troubles?'

'I like to drink,' he replied.

'I have not seen you drink once.'

'Maybe I'm not troubled.' Orlan had begun with Ooila, Bueralan saw, as he turned to gaze at the wall behind him. The cartographer had drawn the continent around the frame of the door and, if left open, it looked as if a hole had been dug into the middle of the continent. 'How's that lie?'

'Poor.' The cartographer dipped the quill into the pot, then tapped it on the edge. 'When you first met Ekar Waalstan, I was impressed by how well you held your own in that situation. You were in control, you were dangerous: you clearly should not have been left alive. I have often wondered if that is exactly what happened – that Ger made you god-touched then and that Bueralan Le died then – since I have not seen that man since.'

'Every now and then, Orlan, I start to like you.' He grabbed a chair from one of the tables and turned it upright, before sitting. 'Then I remember that you killed my friends.'

'And for my crimes, I stand here now.'

'Your crimes?' Irritated, he spread his legs out and slouched in the chair. 'For your crimes, you're drawing a map on a wall.'

'And you're sitting in an expensive chair.' The quill tip scratched furiously across the pale-orange paint as he spoke. 'In Jeil, I was given an opportunity to part ways with you. I had expected it for days and I had, for my part, thought to let you go. It would have been very easy for me to do so. I am not a cruel man and I could see how painful my presence was to you, but it was clear to me that you did not understand where you were going. You did not understand what had happened to you. Worse, you did not want to know.' He sighed and lowered the quill. 'I tried to warn you what awaited here, Bueralan. I tried to steer you away from Ooila, from the Mother's Gift, from Aela Ren, and from the child. I may have failed, but I have not walked away, either. Try to acknowledge that I have done that for a reason.'

Bueralan did *not* want to acknowledge that. 'Yeah, I'm in your debt,' he said, but the dry defiance rang false. He cleared his throat. 'Let me ask you, what will happen when Ren hears the child's name? If, that is, he hears her name?'

Orlan turned to him. 'I imagine he'll stop his war, if that is what you wish to call it,' he said. 'He'll pledge allegiance to her and take his army to Leera to be part of a new war.'

'His fabled army,' the saboteur said as he turned the words over in his head. 'How come we haven't seen that, yet?'

'Just be grateful,' he said. 'It is a sad collection of men and women.'

'What about the old man from Dirtwater?' Bueralan asked. 'Was he one of Aela Ren's soldiers?'

'No, not him.'

'How'd he know you then?'

'He had met other Samuel Orlans.' His laugh had a hard edge on it. 'Not one of the men or women who came before me has been beholden to Aela Ren, a point you should never forget. He may view you and I as if we are sacred men, Bueralan, but he is a monster made from the wreckage of the War of the Gods. He has lost everything that gave him purpose, and without it, he has fashioned his own terrible purpose, and of those who have seen it — well, that old fool in Dirtwater is one of the fortunate ones who has avoided it.'

Bueralan began to speak again, began to push further into the mystery of Ren's army, when his voice was suddenly cut off by the front of the mansion crumbling beneath an explosion.

He was out the door ahead of Orlan. At the end of the hallway, where the first floor gave way to the large, open floor where Aela Ren had slaughtered the Saan warriors, sat two huge piles of rocks. Roped together by thick netting, they had torn through the balcony and doors. The rocks had been followed by burning pitch, which was now taking hold of the building.

Bueralan and Orlan ran down the hall towards it, but took the first turn that presented to them, keeping ahead of the smoke that was rolling towards them. But soon its long fingers began to claw ahead, a dark promise as the two turned again and again on their way to the small room that the Queen's Voice had taken. Neither spoke, either to ask about Taela's welfare, or about Ren's, though Bueralan assumed that no matter the damage done to the front of the mansion, the Innocent had not been killed.

The door to Taela's room was shut and the saboteur shouldered it open . . . only to be greeted by an open window.

4.

Ayae walked down to the carriage beside Caeli, a cut of the moon finally beginning to show through the fading cloud cover. She believed that the way it revealed itself mirrored the way in which the world had begun to reveal itself to her. Captain Heast was in Faaisha. Lady Wagan was pushing to move the Mireeans from Wila. Caeli's words — the words that, as that first night had continued, and the laq had disappeared, had become more and more blunt — had not explained everything to her, but it had explained enough that, when she eventually slept, in her dreams the black water around Wila had turned into the battle-scarred walls of her childhood and when she had awoken, Ayae had been able to stand easier than she had since awakening after Faise's death.

Before the two women began to walk down to the carriage on the night of Lady Wagan's meeting with the Traders' Union, Caeli had taken Ayae out into Yeflam. She had been surprised by how many more guards filled the streets since she last left the house, and the sound of the Yeflam Navy's drums had echoed each step she took. Perhaps unsurprisingly, she saw little of the residents: most remained inside; many of the markets and shops had been shut up, with some of the shop-keepers going so far as to board up the windows.

She had thought that Caeli would leave her after they returned to Faise and Zineer's house, but she had not. A day waited before Lady Wagan's meeting with the Traders' Union, a day of quiet if she had wished, but instead, Caeli had looked at the broken remains of the back door, at the material Ayae had to fix it, and the two had begun to repair it as best they could. It was solid labour, work with their hands and, before they left the house to take the carriage to the Traders' Union meeting, they stood before it to admire the finished product.

There, Caeli offered her a dagger.

'I still have a sword,' Ayae said, declining the weapon. 'It's in my room upstairs.'

The other woman spun the weapon over her hand and then slipped it back into the leather sheath at the back of her belt. 'You should bring it,' she said.

The sword lay on the bed, dropped there after Ayae's heavy body had threatened to break the bed frame and she had taken to sleeping on the floor.

The carriage that awaited them now was drawn by two horses, both black. At a casual glance, it appeared as most carriages in the streets of Yeflam did. It was made from darkly lacquered wood, had a single door with a window and a second window at the back, both covered by cloth. Its shell had seen better days, with the salt water leaving stains on the wood, and with an array of chips and scratches around the bottom of the door where people stepped in and out, and where stones had flown up from the ground. The wheels had fared no better. But the driver, a large white man who gave the appearance of huddling deeply in a cloak for warmth, did not quite pull the thick covering around him as he might if he were cold, and the look he directed at Ayae and Caeli as they approached was not that of the casual driver, a man who might appraise either with a gaze she found uncomfortable, but rather he looked at them with a soldier's gaze. His nod to Caeli, faint though it was, was that of a subordinate to a superior. Ayae's observation was further supported when the door to the carriage opened and the Lady of the Ghosts, Muriel Wagan, was revealed to be sitting within.

The carriage sagged with her heavy weight as she climbed in. 'Lady Wagan,' she said.

'Ayae.' The carriage jolted as it began to move, interrupting her. Once it settled into its pace, she said, 'I had thought I would see you here. It is a pleasure, of course.'

If Caeli's appearance at her door the other night had suggested a week of living rough, of a series of cold meals, and a cloak wrapped around a sword as a pillow, Muriel Wagan's appearance suggested an altogether different experience. She wore the green and white gown that she had worn to the trial, though it had been cleaned since, and had neither the rumple nor crease of a gown previously worn. Her hair had been freshly dyed, but while the grey had been removed, so had the red, and her hair had a dark-brown colour that sat oddly against her pale skin. It was her eyes that spoke the most difference, for while Caeli's had taken on a certain flat hardness, Muriel Wagan's were set behind dark bags, and had a sharpness to them that Ayae could not meet for long.

'Were you told,' the Lady of the Ghosts asked, 'that we are going to a brothel?'

Ayae glanced at Caeli who, across from her, shrugged. 'Sin's Hand?' she said.

'That is the place,' the older woman said. 'It is a building I have owned in Yeflam for a long time, just as I own the man it is named after, Sinae Al'tor. Did Aned tell you of him?'

'He was to help Faise and Zineer leave,' she said. 'He helped them get passages.'

She nodded. 'Once we leave this carriage, only he out of the people you meet will be trustworthy.'

'Who will we be meeting?'

'Lian Alahn and Benan Le'ta.'

The carriage bumped as it began to climb one of the stone bridges between cities.

'Alahn has wanted to meet you for a long time,' Lady Wagan said, after it became clear that Ayae would not speak. 'He has wanted to tell you about the Enclave's agreement with Leera. He knew the extent of it before the trial, so his outrage then was opportunistic, of course. I imagine that he still wants to try and convince you to become a tool for him to use to hollow out the Enclave, since tomorrow's announcement will make the task he has been working on for years difficult. Since you've had no desire to meet him, I can only imagine you will say no. Still, he is going to help us move the Mireean people from Wila to the southern land of Yeflam over the next month, so he has his uses, even if the price I had to pay for doors to be opened for him in Zoum was somewhat steeper than I wanted.'

'And Benan Le'ta?' Ayae asked quietly, her voice sounding to her as if it were spoken by another. 'Why is he there?'

'That,' she said, 'is something we all have to wait and see.'

5.

'Do not look for him tonight, brother.'

'He is out there.' The door stood open, a cold wind touching the frame. 'If he is in need, I cannot ignore him.'

'After tomorrow, I will help you. We will both help you, but—'

'Tonight is before tomorrow.'

Eidan closed the door behind him and his heavy steps took him down to the gate.

Zaifyr continued down the stairs to the bottom floor, the shadows of the stairwell falling off him as if he were a spectre. He had been working upstairs when the door had opened and he had arrived only to hear the end of Jae'le and Eidan's conversation, but he did not need to ask where the latter was going. He had watched Eidan go past the gate of Aelyn's estate and disappear into the dark streets of Yeflam after her visit the previous night. Eidan had returned in the final hour of the afternoon only after he had walked throughout Nale, his deep-set eyes and creased face scouring each corner and rooftop with the concern he had for the creature named Anguish. After he had returned, he had done nothing but relentlessly prowl the floors of the house. That was what had driven Zaifyr upstairs.

'You cannot be surprised,' he said, watching Jae'le turn in frustration to retreat to the candle-lit back room he had been in when the door opened. 'He clearly believes he has a responsibility to the creature.'

'He knows better,' Jae'le replied. 'The man he was would never have exposed himself the way he does now.'

Zaifyr left the stairwell and followed his brother into the room. 'He is not the same man he once was,' he said.

'I see that.'

'*None* of us is the same man.'

'I am aware of that, as well.' His brother stood before the chair he had been seated in. Over the arms lay his sword, a whetstone resting on the right. 'Would you like to count the ways, brother?'

'You'll not need the sword tomorrow. It is just an announcement, that's all.' The books he had borrowed were still in the room, the heavy stacks like dark, weighted shadows to hold the world down. 'But you would not have needed it if we were the men we once were, either. Those men would have stood beside the child.'

Jae'le laughed. 'I think you have forgotten who we were.'

'Gods.' Zaifyr took a book from one of the chairs and sat down. 'We would have seen a mirror of ourselves and we would have stood beside her.'

'To varying degrees, Eidan and Aelyn have already done that. You and I have not.'

'We are perhaps the most changed.'

'You are wrong. We would never have stood by her side.'

Jae'le lifted the straight blade up. 'All of us have responded to her power, just as we have always responded to power: if we cannot dominate it, we either kneel before it, or we destroy it.'

'We have never been that simple,' he said.

His brother pointed the sword at him. 'Consider what I hold in my hand as a representation of who we are. We have adhered to the logic of this weapon our entire lives. It has been true from the first of the men and women like us that I met. She was a woman with the gifts of Jeinan, the first Soldier, if we were to use a name we use now. She was called Zelula, but it may not have been the name she was born with, for she was mute and illiterate. When she spoke, she spoke through a man whom she kept by her side. It was he who told me her name. But most of her conversation was done with a sword. With it, she was but the purest distillation of grace and violence I have ever known. When I first met her, she was part of a group that came to the island of my home, and she was part of those who thought to conquer it. But she was there for me, first. She would not allow another to exist who could surpass her. She needed no words to say this to me. I understood intently that I would bow to her or I would die to her.'

'Much has changed since then; even had it not, you and I have never fought.'

Jae'le's sword fell to his side. 'But we did not begin as equals, either.'

Zaifyr had been a prisoner for fifteen years in the marble palace of Emperor Kee when he had first seen Jae'le. The soldiers who had destroyed his village had been sent by the Emperor to enact his law of reprisal for the loss of a relative whom one of the people in Zaifyr's village had killed. A sister, he had once been told. But, after Zaifyr had been taken across Leviathan's Blood, the Emperor had quickly realized that he had gained a much finer prize: an ageless man to sit in a dungeon in the floor of his court, a reminder of the law he held over the people who came to speak to him, a law that remained until Jae'le entered his court.

'Nor should we pretend,' the other man continued, 'that the five of us have always been equals. In our wars, in our kingdoms. Even now, what you have done to Aelyn in Yeflam is nothing but a display of authority and power over her.'

'It is—'

'—true,' Jae'le finished. 'We are dictated by power. It is how we navigate our relationships. It is why Tinh Tu has not come. It is why Aelyn does not stand here with us tonight. And it is why you were able to befriend Ayae so easily.'

'Ayae?' Zaifyr frowned. 'I don't see what she has to do with this.'

'She was in need when you met her, was she not?' He shrugged. 'You will always be at arm's length while she sees you as her mentor.'

'I do not see where you are going with this.'

'No?' Jae'le shrugged again, but this time he smiled, as if he did not believe Zaifyr. He picked up the whetstone. 'Will you at least admit that what you have done to your sister is to push her into a corner? That you used your authority over her to do this?'

'What other choice did I have?'

'That was not my question.'

6.

The lamp above the red-painted hand was not lit. Instead, the sign was like a dark, bloody print outside the brothel, a warning not to enter the large building. Ayae thought its advice well given.

She stood silently beside Lady Wagan while Caeli talked quietly to the driver. She had asked more questions after it had been revealed that Benan Le'ta would be inside, but little more could be said by either. The Lady of the Ghosts had spent the aftermath of the trial organizing the freedom of the Mireean people from Wila and, though Muriel had not said so, Ayae believed that Lady Wagan had made a large concession to ensure that the deal was reached swiftly. *She has sent a letter to Eilona in Zoum*, she thought as she gazed up at the dark shape of the building. *Lady Wagan would only do that if what she asked of the bankers was so unusual that it required a family representative. Even an estranged one.*

Caeli's return stopped Ayae's thoughts. Behind her, the carriage had begun to move and, after it had gone down the street, the guard directed them to a narrow alley. As the three entered, a cold wind blew, and Ayae felt the first hint of it — but not as much, she noted, as both Caeli and Lady Wagan, who pulled their cloaks tight.

At the back of Sin's Hand there was an empty stable and from it, a stillness swept over the well-trodden yard, a quiet that was broken only when Caeli knocked heavily on the back door.

Inside, a large black man led them down a narrow hallway. A pair of lamps had been tied to the ceiling, and from them, light shone; but the lack of movement that Ayae had felt from the stables was also present here, displayed in the unlit candles that lined the sides of the hall, the solid drippings of wax caught in cruel representations of sexual desire. At the end of the hall, a large floor opened up, most of it in darkness, though it was not dim enough to hide the stage or tables that filled it. A long bar that Ayae walked past was, likewise, a series of still shadows, and she could not help but think of it as a prop in an elaborate stage show, one that was performed with a stale regularity each night for men who struggled with reality.

The stairs creaked dangerously under her step – a reminder that, for all she had felt the hint of a chill, her skin was still heavy – but the man who led them to the floor did not stop until he reached the open-curtained doorway.

Inside were five people: four men and one woman. The woman had long, pale blonde hair and sat alone on one of the long black sofas at the back of the room, her leather-clad legs stretched out in front of her, and a long red jacket wrapped around her body. She gave the briefest of glances to Ayae and the other two women when they entered, then folded her legs beneath her, ensuring that her lack of interest was made clear. The four men, however, turned to Lady Wagan, and a young and attractive man approached her first. She greeted him by the name of Sinae, but Ayae did not linger on the two, for she saw Lian Alahn rise from the couch where he had been sitting. After greeting Lady Wagan, he made his way towards her. Behind him, Benan Le'ta wedged himself into the corner of the couch he sat on, beyond him, a young white guard remained in place.

'Ayae.' Illaan's father took her numb hands into his. 'Finally. I have tried to gain a meeting with you since your arrival.'

'You know where I have been.' She pulled her hands back. 'You could have knocked on that door.'

His face took on a frozen politeness and Ayae continued past him, to where Le'ta sat.

The fat merchant shifted uncomfortably beneath her gaze and Ayae was aware of the silence and stillness that was rising behind her, as if what she had felt outside had crept up the stairs and into the room. Chains had been fastened around Le'ta's wrists and Ayae could see red marks from where he had tried without success to pull his hands free. That was not the only place where he had suffered: his face and neck had a series of ugly yellow bruises down the right side and he had lost weight, leaving his skin to sag in a sick, ugly pull down his neck.

'Yes,' he said, finally meeting her gaze. 'Get a good look. I am a murderer's reward.'

Ayae did not turn from him, but directed her question to Lian Alahn. 'Why is he here?'

'Justice is found in many places, even a brothel.' The Traders' Union leader stood beside her, but not close. 'Tonight's meeting is about organizing the transport of the Mireean people across

570

Yeflam, but it is also about the final pieces of the puzzles: the books that were printed, the hotels that priests lived in, and the deal that was made to return the sale of flesh to our city. It took me a long time and a lot of money to dig this man up so that I could have all the answers. He had made it all the way to Wilate on his stubby little legs. But the answers are here and I thought we could hear them now.'

Le'ta raised his manacled hands up and pointed at him. 'Only luck saved you,' he said.

'Before we discuss luck,' Sinae Al'tor said, interrupting the conversation and clapping his hands together as he did. 'Why don't I first do something about the cold in this room?'

'That,' a woman's voice said from outside the room, from the dark of the hallway, 'will not be necessary.'

7.

'It is not an attractive picture of me that you paint.'

'Should it be?' Jae'le's whetstone ran down the edge of his sword in an easy stroke. 'The exercise of power has many faces. At times, it is subtle, at times it is elegant, but more often than not, it is ugly. It has been ugly here, but it has not been Asila.'

Zaifyr heard the whisper of a haunt, and he saw the faint hint of another as it walked around his brother. Jae'le could not see it, any more than anyone else could, but Zaifyr used it to anchor his thoughts, to remind him of why he had come to Yeflam. His brother's words had surprised him, though they were not atypical for him: he was not a man given to speaking of sentimentality, though he could be found to act on it regularly, especially in relation to his family. After all, he had not left his home to take up arms against the child. But Zaifyr thought that the plight of the dead – of the young man who stood near his chair, watching the whetstone run along the blade – and the very real importance it had to him had been what convinced Jae'le that the trial was correct, that the child was a threat unlike any other they had seen.

'I do not doubt that, but it is not the sum of what I have

done,' Zaifyr said finally. 'Aelyn has made her choices as well, and there are other concerns at stake with the child. Very real concerns.'

'I am not trying to claim that you do not have reason,' he said. 'I am only using it to show how we have not changed completely over the years—'

A shudder ran through the ground.

'Eidan,' Jae'le whispered.

A second followed, and this one, longer than the first, felt as if the stone ground of Nale had begun to break apart.

Jae'le vaulted over the back of his chair, but he was two steps behind Zaifyr, who had raced through the doorway unarmed. When he reached the door, another shudder ran through the rock, and the door twisted open to his touch, the hinges breaking to reveal the long dark outside.

For a moment, Zaifyr saw nothing unusual. The sky had cleared of its clouds, and a cold wind had picked up, as if drawn out of the naked scatter of stars and moon; the gate of the estate remained closed, and the road beyond it was empty. Then, in a faint echo that grew louder, he heard the drums of the Yeflam Navy begin to sound. Voices followed. He could not make out the words, but they were sharp, loud, as if orders were being shouted to soldiers, to sailors, and then the ground again shook, but this time it was weaker than the first two.

A dark shadow began to appear on the horizon. It was huge, as if the night sky had twinned to a darker sky, but as it drew closer, the ground shook again, even louder than the previous shocks. It broke the gate in half and, in that wreckage, Eidan emerged. He took a handful of steps before he stumbled and fell to the ground.

As Zaifyr and Jae'le drew closer they could see that Eidan was severely injured but not dead. The side of his face was caked with blood, caused by a trio of hard slashes from the cheek to his ear, and which had torn most of the lobe away. Likewise, the leather shirt he had worn had been shredded on his left side, and blood ran freely from wounds across his stout chest. As Zaifyr reached him, Eidan tried to stand, pushing himself up with his right hand, which in turn revealed that his left was bent at an odd angle, his fingers broken badly, as if he had thought to catch a spiked object. He stumbled as he rose and it was then, as the charm-laced man caught him, that he saw the damage done to Eidan's left leg, and the bone that poked through the leather and flesh.

'She . . .' Eidan muttered thickly, falling into his arms. 'She has brought them here.'

'Them?' Jae'le repeated.

But Zaifyr had not needed to ask who he meant.

He felt the first before it came through the ruined gate, felt the cold burning hatred that, for a moment, reminded him of Lor Jix, before it landed on the top of the broken rubble.

It was not right to call it a man, though Zaifyr knew that it had once been such. It had been a large man, close to six foot three, and he could still see the shape of that man in his haunt, a haunt splayed out in the muscle and bone of the creature that dropped from the wall and entered the yard. He looked very much like a butterfly that had been laid out in a case, but rather than being pinned to wood in a collection, here the collector had fastened the haunt into flesh, into arms and legs. Zaifyr could still see that he had been a young man, that he had been a Leeran soldier, despite the horrific lengths that his arms now stretched and the hideous swelling of his legs, and the hump of his back – and he could also see, on the haunt's face, a frozen horror. Yet, for all the horror, the emotion that washed over Zaifyr was one of a burning hatred, and he could see the second presence, not a haunt like the soldier, but an ancient dead, much like Lor Jix, wrapped through the creature of the Leeran's spirit so that it could wear the flesh of the dead soldier as he might have worn armour in life.

In its hands, the creature held a huge spiked mace. It was the weapon that had torn through Eidan, but the creature had not done that without suffering itself. Its arm – the right arm – hung uselessly from its socket.

When it saw Zaifyr and Jae'le, it let a roar tear from its throat and through the night sky. In a matter of moments, two new creatures leapt onto the rubble of the fence. One was long and lean with bone spikes piercing its skin, the other appeared to be a huge, distorted beast.

Neither was what the first creature had called to, however. The darkness in the sky, the darkness that was so very much like a second skin to the world, began to flow like an ocean towards the three. It was not until it had cleared the gate that Zaifyr glimpsed the blunted face, the misshapen form, but as he saw it, he knew also that it was not quite of this world, that it existed truly as a shadow, just outside the one he stood in.

As he realized that, the child walked through the broken gate.

8.

Bueralan boosted Samuel Orlan to the window before he pulled himself up. In the small frame, he gazed down at a narrow ledge wide enough for the toes of his boots and the ends of his fingers. The drop after that was large, but not dangerous, and he watched Orlan release his grip as he dangled from the ledge and land hard, but otherwise fine. Bueralan was on the edge of beginning his descent when a part of the tree-lined horizon cracked and shifted, as if a part of a mirror had suddenly broken off to reveal smoke behind.

'Orlan,' he shouted.

'Ignore it!' The cartographer was crouched on the ground, examining it intently. He turned and cried, 'I found her tracks!'

Another piece of the night sky cracked and, on instinct, the saboteur glanced back. The narrow room had begun to fill with smoke, the thin fingers that had reached ahead of him and Orlan now dragging a misshapen body, and the building's frame groaned, as if the passage of it was too much weight.

Taela's tracks were not difficult to find when he reached the ground. She had landed near where he had, and the heels of her boots had dug deep into the ground. However, unlike his, her boots were surrounded by half a dozen heavier steps that began to multiply into a rushed trail towards the stables. The entire skyline behind the building had taken on a shattered appearance and the reflection of flames began to show on it as the smoke discoloured the night sky higher.

Bueralan did not need to follow the tracks. It was clear that, as the catapults had released the stones and fire that had crashed through Yoala Fe's mansion, the First Queen had organized Taela's rescue, and it was obvious that she had not bothered with him or Samuel Orlan. The two of them could head in a different direction, take their own chances. They had no obligation to pursue because they had no responsibility for anyone but themselves and their own safety. Yet Bueralan continued across the yard with Orlan beside him.

Halfway to the stables, he turned to look behind him and came to a halt.

There, spread out across the front lawns of the mansion, across the long gravel driveway that he, Taela and the First Queen had travelled to the party, was a scene of such slaughter that Bueralan could not move. He heard Orlan call his name, but as the old cartographer turned to follow his gaze and saw the scene behind them, he did not finish the second half of his name.

The two stared at the scarred land silently. The grass had been torn up and burnt, and it was wreathed in such smoke and fire that, for a moment, he thought a demon from his childhood had been conjured, a creature from a netherworld whose very step left a burnt print in its wake. He imagined it a huge figure, towering over the landscape, a face of unspeakable horror. He could see its hands reaching down to tear at the earth, to leave the huge divots in the land that he could see, as it broke the bodies of men and women and horses.

But no such horror existed.

Instead, Bueralan saw a single mount in the centre of the field. It was riderless and covered in dirt and blood and it was so still that it could have been cast from dark, tarnished bronze.

It was through that one beast that Bueralan envisaged the horror that had befallen the soldiers who rode on Yoala Fe's mansion. He heard the order that had been given, heard the words that swept through the ranks surrounding the mansion grounds, heard it repeated by the units hidden by the women who sat in circles of blood. He saw the first kick of the horse's rider, saw the gentle nudge that began the movement of the cavalry, saw the first break from the illusion, a gentle shimmer over the body, a warping of the night sky. The catapults groaned from behind and the slow walk continued as the machines of wood and steel were dragged out. A shout halted the riders. He heard the sound of the siege engines being wound back. He heard a sword being drawn. The horse sidled in anticipation. Spurs tapped its flanks. Finally, it began to move in freedom, to pick up speed. Its rider gave a loud shout. A second shout rang out. A third followed, but it was not until the fifth or sixth that the shouts turned into screams. Not until then that the ground began to break apart before the horse, that the heat was exposed. Then a violent stream of flame burst from the ground to the horse's left, then the right. It halted. In front of it the ground began to break. The shells of butterflies rose only to burn. Spurs dug into its flanks but the horse refused to go further as all but the ground it stood on began to break apart, as the long-dormant streams of lava began to break their shackles beneath the First Province and spew upwards.

'They're here,' Samuel Orlan said softly. 'Aela Ren's soldiers are here.'

The horse began to sink to the ground, its forelegs giving way first.

'Bueralan,' the cartographer began.

'I heard you.'

He turned from the sight before him and chased the trail of Zi Taela to the stables.

He burst through the doors just as the back of the stables were being opened and the sixteen horses that had been within prepared to ride out into the broken skyline. Ce Pueral stood at the gate, one hand pushing it open, while the other held her drawn sword. He could almost not see her for her soldiers, who wore the black and red of the First Queen and held their own weapons in their hands, including heavy crossbows. 'No!' he shouted to the latter, raising his hands, for the six soldiers who sat double on the mounts held the loaded weapons and they turned immediately to him, lifting the devastating weapons.

But none fired.

Bueralan heard Taela cry out his name from the back of his grey, the surly beast pawing the ground as if it knew with more intimacy than the others what horror awaited it outside. 'Bueralan,' she said again, her hand extended. 'We have to leave! This is *our* chance.'

'Such words.' Above her, from the shadows of the first floor, where Bueralan had found the Saan Prince, Aela Ren emerged. In his hands, he held both sword and dagger. 'They are naught but lies.'

9.

The woman turned to the door of the siege tower and shouted – but only a moment before Heast's sword hacked into her skull.

He dismounted roughly, afraid that he was too slow, too awkward with the stirrups, but made it through the door before a young man finished scaling the wooden ladder. A quick glance revealed the inside of the tower to have three levels, each reached by a long ladder. Already, the Leeran soldier was pulling himself through the first onto the next level. There, the weak orange light revealed the youth of the man's face, the dark hair, the stubble and his look of determination. Heast passed a scattering of iron bolts on the floor in his heavy-footed pursuit; if the woman's crossbow had not fallen hard to the ground when he killed her, he would have turned for the weapon, but since he could not trust it, he hauled himself up the ladder with his sword in one hand.

A pair of bedrolls lay in the corner of the first floor, a lantern in front of them, but Heast's gaze only grazed it, focusing instead on the boots of the young man, now disappearing onto the next level.

He heard a desperate slide and scurrying and, as he was

halfway up the ladder, a solid thump. Quickly, he hauled himself up and at the lip, he saw the young man, his foot jammed into the leather stirrup of a crossbow. He had a bolt grasped in his hand and was struggling to attach the bow's string to his belt to begin pulling it tight. He looked up only moments before Heast crashed into him.

It was not an elegant charge, but it drove the young man onto his back and gave the Captain of the Ghosts time to spin his blade around and drive it downwards. The man screamed and Heast leant on it more, while his steel foot rose and fell on the soldier's face until he went still.

A low breath escaped Heast. 'If you had not panicked,' he said to the dead man below him. 'If you'd had a different crossbow.'

Releasing his sword, he limped over to the tower's drawbridge. A long rope held it in place, and Heast sliced through it with his ugly dagger and let it clatter open.

A cold wind blew into the siege tower. Outside, the ravine lay in darkness, and he could see the torches of the Maosans, riding hard towards them, drawn by the sounds of battle. Heast turned and walked back to the dead Leeran and freed the crossbow's tangled string before he picked up the heavy weapon. The leather quiver that the soldier had pulled the bolt from lay on the floor and Heast bent down to pick it up as he returned to the end of the drawbridge. There, he clipped the string to his belt, thrust his foot into the strap and loaded it with professional ease. When he had finished, he walked to the edge of the bridge, the crossbow pointed upwards in his right hand, and his left hand touching the fresh wet ring where his flesh and steel met.

At the edge of the bridge, he saw that the darkness of the ravine had broken beneath a pale white light, a light that came from both Kye Taaira and the large, misshapen form of Nsyan.

The latter was less human in appearance than his brother, Myone. A mass of muscle had grown across Nsyan's back, and it wrapped around his torso and neck, leaving it impossible for him to wear armour. It made the twisting, swirling whiteness in his chest easier to see and Heast was left with the impression of a parasite, squirming and turning in anguish. By that light, he saw a small, withered third arm extending from the right side of Nsyan's chest, beneath the two muscular arms that wielded two giant axes. They whirled and struck at the man before him with a furious speed, and it was from that man that the white light came: the two-handed sword that had appeared so dull and old now glowed with its own light. Yet, there was nothing pure in that light, nothing that suggested a holy or blessed air, and the light cast itself like old bones, like something long buried and best forgotten, and it was beneath *that* light that the parasite within Nsyan's chest—Nsyan himself, Heast believed — so rebelled.

Heast had never seen a Hollow fight before, but he had not expected the savage joy he saw in Kye Taaira's face, as if a deep, primal part of him had finally found release. Heast had seen both men and women fight with such intensity before — had seen, in truth, such emotions displayed on numerous occasions — but he had never thought to see it on the face of one born to the Plateau. Nor did he expect to see four bodies of Leeran soldiers through the ravine, each one a violent stone to mark the path the tribesman had taken to Nsyan, ending where Taaira now stood, both hands on the hilt of his sword as he feinted and slashed, blocked and turned, the length of his blade catching the creature's skin repeatedly, always drawing blood, and always pushing him backwards.

In the scrub, Heast saw a Leeran soldier move, circling around the pair.

It was a difficult shot, yet he lifted the crossbow to his shoulder, ready for when he saw the soldier again; but Taaira, who leapt over a low slash from Nsyan, and ducked under an ugly chop that followed, took three steps towards the soldier before his heavy sword lashed out and crashed through the raised defence. As if he were nothing more than a nuisance, Taaira turned quickly and blocked both of Nsyan's axes.

Heast's bolt punched into the ancestor's side.

He roared, the sound bursting over the ravine, but in that moment of pain, the ancestor's axes fell from their defence, and the tribesman drove his sword forward.

It punched into the creature's stomach, deep and hard. Leaning on it, Taaira pushed the blade further into his ancestor. In doing so, the tribesman was exposed to Nsyan's axes, but as they crashed towards him, Taaira released the blade and drove his fist into Nsyan's right arm. The speed of it broke the momentum of the swing and broke the arm, and he darted away from the other axe by moving to the ancestor's right. Yet, when he was almost out of reach, almost free, the sickly arm Heast had thought lame snagged his clothes.

Nsyan roared as he lifted the axe in his left arm up high . . . but that roar turned into a scream and he dropped the axe, grabbing at the sword in his stomach, only for a second roar of pain to burst from him as he released the hilt.

Heast had expected Taaira to move out of range of his

ancestor, but the tribesman surprised him and grabbed the hilt of his sword with both hands. There, he began to lift the blade, drawing it up through the mass of muscle and twisted bone and, in doing so, lifted the larger figure of his ancestor off the ground. In the chest of Nsyan, the highlighted parasite mirrored the agony that his scream announced to all of those in and around the ravine, and for a moment, Heast saw it transformed into the figure of a man, a large, bearded man – and then, as the light and the revealed figure began to fade, it started to disappear. Taaira continued to raise the sword until, a moment before the darkness of the ravine was restored, the body parted as if it were nothing but old, rotted meat.

10.

The Eyes of the Queen had seen too much. The assault on Yoala Fe's mansion had turned into an unmitigated disaster. The sky outside the stables was smothered with smoke, the ground beneath it lit with fire. Earlier, she had stood at the back of the mansion and watched in horror as the illusion that her witches had used to hide the First Queen's forces had begun to splinter. She felt the gazes of her soldiers turn to her, the question of what to do unspoken and, in response, she had tightened her hand around the Voice's arm. The young woman had been in the middle of telling Pueral that she could not leave Samuel Orlan or Bueralan Le, that they had to find both men, but her voice — speaking her own desires, not the Queen's — had fallen silent. She watched the sky begin to break and did not resist Pueral's heavy lurch into a run.

A run that began as the assault on the front of the mansion did, as the first catapult was fired, and the horses began to charge.

With each step she took, Pueral felt her control of the situation stripped away, felt her sphere of influence reduced to the soldiers around her, and to the safety of the Queen's Voice.

By the time she reached the stables, the young woman who had been but a small part of the operation had become the centre of it, a figure whose freedom would, at the very least, be an act of denial against the man who now stepped onto the edge of the first floor of the stables.

She did not need to give the order to fire.

Yet, as the crossbows emptied, Aela Ren jumped onto one of the horses and all but one of the bolts missed him.

The one that hit did so in the lower half of his chest, but the Innocent, his sword held much like an axe, tore into the neck of the man who had shot it. The chain mesh broke apart as if it were naught but paper, and the scarred man flung the body from the horse before his swords snapped out in a series of blocks and parries from where he sat.

'*Out!*' Pueral shouted. 'Get him *outside!*'

It was Lanos who reacted to the command first: the old tracker shouted and pulled on the reins of his horse before driving his heels deep into its flanks. As he came in closer, he ducked low and wrapped his old, hard arms around Aela Ren's waist as his mount ploughed out of the stables.

The charge did not last much longer and Pueral, standing in the open gate as her soldiers tore out after him, saw Lanos topple to the ground. Yet the tracker had taken Ren far enough that the other soldiers around her had enough time to reach a heavy charging gallop that forced the small, scarred man to twist and turn out of their way.

Pueral turned to the stables. There, the tall grey stood with the Queen's Voice in the saddle and Bueralan and Orlan shielded by its body.

'Captain Le,' she said to the saboteur, the title falling easily from her lips. 'She is your charge now. Do you understand that?'

'Yeah,' he replied reluctantly.

'Ride hard, Captain. With any luck, you will find soldiers to stand by you.'

She left the stables without waiting for an answer. Ahead, her soldiers and Aela Ren fought, and already three had been dismounted, and one horse would never rise again. Still, Pueral had one plan left, and she held to it. After that, she would deal with Aela Ren's army, later she would take his head to the steel boxes, and parade it before those who had been hidden from her. Lanos lay on his back, his stomach torn open viciously. Next to him knelt Tanith, but when she rose, her face was hard, and in her hand she held her ugly knife and her cracked jar.

'What we do now was once outlawed,' she had said to Pueral a week earlier. 'Even here, in the heart of Ooila, few witches will do this, but for Aela Ren, I will. During the Five Kingdoms, the man known as Qian said that the cruellest thing we did to the dead was to use them as if they were but fuel. He said you had to honour them. It is from here that all our practices of rebirth have come. But in this jar is another form of magic, one that goes much more to the heart of Qian's own home and the horrors that happened there. In this jar are parts of the dead themselves. Parts I have tied to the blood that Aela Ren wrote his letter in, parts that will wish to devour him, and that I can control to do so.'

The Eyes of the Queen drew her sword, the witch now in step beside her. Ahead, Aela Ren had killed six of her soldiers, and had wounded a seventh.

'*Aela Ren!*' she shouted, the words torn from her throat with all the military training she had, all the authority she knew, and all the anger she felt.

Her soldiers fell back and, in the middle of them, the Innocent turned to face her.

She raised her heavy sword to him.

A small smile parted his scarred lips, and she thought, as her pace began to increase, how his disregard for human life was apparent in that one motion, how it revealed just how little he thought of those he had killed, and those who stood before him – and then her sword blocked his thrust, and the armour on her wrist fell like a shield before his dagger. He was quick in his response, though, and his sword cut out in long slashes that she met with shrugged blocks of sword and armour while she angled herself around him, drew him away from where Tanith stood, and gave her the time she needed to cut into her own hands, and give focus to the dead that she held in her grasp.

The glass jar struck the ground next to him.

Ren stepped back immediately, as if he felt the power flooding from the broken shards, and Pueral herself, though she had thought to press home her advantage, found herself stepping back from it for that reason.

The ghosts that poured from it did so in such a flurry that their fury was undeniable. After a moment, Ren frowned and attempted to take another step back, only to find that he could not move. Around his feet, the fragments of men and women that he had killed grasped at him, clawed deep into the boots he wore, and soon a miniature tornado began to spin around him and lift him from the ground. Soon, Pueral could see faint ghostly hands holding his arms and legs, and the vague outline of a figure, neither male nor female, forming. Across the body hundreds of faces began to appear, each snapping and biting, and puncturing the Innocent's skin. In response, he snarled, and he drove his torn boots into the figure, where he found purchase, enough to break free from its grasp and land on the ground.

Pueral took a step forward as the creature did, closing in on Ren. Yet, he twisted out of the way of her heavy sword, and moved backwards, keeping out of the cold reach of the creature. *You take those steps.* Pueral felt a hard joy run through her, and she saw her remaining soldiers edge in closer, preparing to attack the Innocent. She struck again, forcing him to block, and her return swing was quick, a vicious slash he stepped back from, close to a mounted soldier — but in a swiftness she could not follow, he slammed his sword into the front of the horse's legs, and as it tumbled forward, his dagger jammed into the soldier's eye. But in the last movement, he did not have enough time to avoid the reach of the creature, and its hands latched around his neck before it began to lift him up again.

And Tanith slumped to the ground.

It happened in such a blur that Pueral did not even notice that Ren's dagger had caught her in the neck, had broken her control of the creature and freed him from its grasp.

Pueral charged, but Ren's sword — so fast, so blistering fast — battered aside her thrust with ease. Her armour turned aside two of his return cuts, but she did not relent, she did not fall back. She slammed her sword at him, losing all the finesse that she had once had, hoping to use her size and her armoured weight to overpower him . . . only to feel the hard end of his blade part the steel she wore before it parted her flesh and sank into her stomach. She felt herself torn as the Innocent began to lift his sword, felt herself split, and as the blade ripped through steel and flesh and bone, she gazed at him, at the fury that was deep on his face, and felt a certain satisfaction that he would not forget her, not any time soon.

The Cold Soul
Against Your Heart

The people I spoke with, the stories I recorded, are but a fraction of what I heard. On the slaves' blocks throughout Gogair, more and more blind men and women are being sold, and each of them has a similar story.

It is clear that the child seeks only submission. She does not seek to engage men and women in terms of reason and purpose. Her desire to reclaim the world, to repair the damage, as her priests claim, feels not just hollow, but a terrible falsity, one that hides an awful truth.

—Tinh Tu, *Private Diary*

1.

'She had the better of you for a moment there,' Bueralan said as he walked around Aela Ren. In his hand, he held a sword, the end pointed casually at the ground. 'Her name was Ce Pueral. You'll want to remember it.'

'It will fade,' the Innocent replied harshly, the bestial quality to his voice that Bueralan had heard a week ago returning. 'They all fade.' The scarred man regarded him flatly from above her torn body, a figure whose tattoos of violence now included the wounds left by the ghostly mouths of the creature when they tore through his armour. 'You will fade as well.'

'Do I look like a man who cares about being remembered?' Around the saboteur, eight of Pueral's soldiers remained. All but two had their stolen mounts, and of the latter, one knelt painfully on the ground. 'How about you all?' he said to them. 'You still got some fight left?'

'Don't be a fool.' Ren ignored the soldiers around him and focused on Bueralan. 'You cannot stand against me.'

'I feel fatalistic,' he said and raised his sword.

The saboteur had a realistic expectation of what he would accomplish in the final hours of the night as he paced around the Innocent. Behind him, the horizon was a ruinous line of fire, and when the first sun rose and cast its orange-red haze over the First Province of Ooila, he did not expect to see it. He was the contrast to Pueral: the Eyes of the Queen had been angry, but her loyalty and her service to the First Queen had refused to allow her mind to be overwhelmed by defeat. That was not to say that she could not acknowledge it: she had seen it and that was why she had named him captain in the stables, why she issued him with a command to be obeyed before she began to walk into the broken horizon.

'Get up,' he had said to Samuel Orlan as Ce Pueral approached the witch. He grabbed hold of the grey's reins. 'Get up and hold tight to Taela.'

The cartographer shook his head. 'The horse cannot carry all three of us.'

'He won't.'

'Let me—'

'Get up,' he ordered.

'Bueralan—' Taela began.

'Aela Ren will follow me.' In the poor light of the stables, both had the appearance of being washed out, of being made from old colours. He offered them a smile without humour. 'He wants to hear a name from me. You both know that. You will get nowhere if I am with you.'

'We'll get nowhere without you,' she said. 'Aela Ren's army is out there.'

'The grey will get you through.' He rubbed the horse's nose. 'He's an old soldier. He'll find a way through. He and Orlan.'

'You cannot kill him,' the cartographer said, his voice heavy with resignation. 'You can only make him kill you.'

'All my friends are dead, old man.' Bueralan grabbed the pouch around his neck and pulled it over his head. Gently, he placed it into Taela's hand. 'You take this. You take it and you destroy it. You do what I could never do.'

She began to argue, to decline, and he felt the first push of her hand against his in rejection, but then her fingers curled around it. 'It's cold,' she said quietly.

'It always was.'

He helped Orlan onto the back of the tall grey and, though the cartographer resisted, though he argued that all three of them should go, that they were surrounded, Bueralan saw the pair out of the stable. He stood in the doorway and watched the tall grey canter from the mansion, and out into the burning horizon. Maybe they would make it. He believed that they would. He had to believe that. He remained there until the cries and shouts of Pueral and her soldiers reached him and he turned to face in that direction. He saw Aela Ren lifted from the ground by a figure he could not rightly describe, but he knew it would not be enough.

On the stable floor, where the first of Pueral's soldiers had fallen, a sword was still in its sheath. Bueralan bent down and rolled the corpse over before he pulled the blade free.

The weight was decent, but the cross-guard was a rounded piece of steel that did not cover his entire fist. 'It will do,' he said to the soldier, rising. 'Let's see if you'll be proud.'

He strode out of the stables without armour, wearing the black clothes he had worn to Yoala Fe's engagement party, but that did not concern him. In some way, he believed it was better. Armour blunted a blow. It softened a thrust, it turned a cut, it kept a man alive when he otherwise should not be, and Bueralan had already been alive longer than he should have. He should have died in Ranan. He had, to a degree, died in there. The wound had been struck when he had found Kae. He had been struck again when he found Ruk and Liaya, and then her sister, Aerala. He could see them clearly, still, on the floor. But it had been when he found Zean, his body covered in what looked to be a thousand wounds, that the final blow had been delivered. His blood brother. His *family*. He should have drawn his sword then. He would have died in that cathedral, Bueralan knew, but he would have died beside the people who mattered to him. He would have been spared the journey of grief to Ooila, the futile attempt to turn back what had happened, the path that ended with him standing before the Innocent, Aela Ren.

Pueral's soldiers were the first to strike.

A rider from the far left charged first. She leant low on the saddle and urged her mount into a gallop while her sword swung free. In her wake, the other five found their footing, and soon the six mounts were charging at the spot where Ren stood, his gaze never leaving Bueralan. When the first sword came close to him, its length holding the smoked horizon in its blade, he merely shifted to his left. He continued to move to his left, turning in a full circle to come into the path of the mounts that had followed, but he did not move as they came closer. Instead, he met their slashes with heavy, angry cuts, each quicker than Bueralan could follow – and within a handful of heartbeats, Ren had pulled himself into the saddle of one, replacing a man by grasping him by the throat.

He had not quite got settled when Bueralan grabbed him, his hand snapping around Ren's arm a moment before he hurled him from the saddle. The Innocent went with the movement and came up from a roll with his sword thrusting at Bueralan, but the saboteur turned it aside. He met the speed with his own, catching each strike before returning in a low cut that allowed him to step inward, grab Ren's leathers, and bring his forehead down to strike the Innocent hard on the head. The blow hurt, but it always hurt, and it left the scarred man open to Bueralan's fist, which released the leather jerkin and jabbed shortly into his throat. He had killed other men with the move, but Ren was quick enough that he caught the punch only on the side of his neck, and stiff-armed Bueralan hard in the chest to get some distance – only to find himself on the back foot as the saboteur quickly closed the space.

2.

'Let me take him.'

The words sounded distant to Zaifyr, as if spoken by a haunt he could no longer see; yet he knew that it was spoken by a man, by Jae'le, just as he knew that in his arms he held his brother, Eidan. The large man's blood was seeping over his right hand and down his arm. But his focus was on the beautiful young woman walking towards him, on the woman whose very presence caused the dead to respond as they did to him: by whispers of words and cold touches, by imitating a sense of closeness that their brittle bodies remembered only in the most primal sense of longing. In their need, they did not know that she was responsible for their situation, that she had kept their remains in the world to give her power. They merely responded to her power.

'Brother,' Jae'le said, his hands drawing the weight of Eidan from him, 'you can let him go.'

'You must beware of those with her.' The large man's voice was a pained whisper. 'She raised them on the Plateau.'

'I know where they are from,' Zaifyr replied.

The large man's hand grasped him. 'Qian—'

'That is not my name.'

'I did not think she would bring them here,' Eidan continued, his breath laboured. 'I thought she had entered Yeflam only in the company of myself. I held no suspicion. I thought she left them in Faaisha. But they are here. They came upon me before I reached the edge of Nale. There were seven of them. They were wet, as if they had been in the ocean, as if they had been hidden beneath the black water for all this time. When they saw me, they let out a roar and attacked. I crushed their bones. I broke their limbs. But they would not die. I threw four back into Leviathan's Blood, but I fear there are more. I fear they are all here.'

As he spoke, Zaifyr heard shouts from outside the gates, while the drums from the ocean were lost beneath breaking waves.

'Eidan,' the child said, stopping a dozen paces before the three men. The white robe that she wore was unstained, either by dirt or by blood. 'You must be stronger for me. I want the first of my betrayers to rage against my justice. I want him to test my power before he fails. Only then will you be an inspiration to my faithful.'

'In other words,' Zaifyr said, stepping in front of his injured brother, 'you want to rely upon fear.'

Her laughter still held its sweet lie of innocence. 'I will claim you as well as my betrayer, all the brothers together.'

Zaifyr had begun to let his power flow into the dead around him, but he paused. Something in her words had caught a hold in him, had allowed for a moment of uncertainty to find a perch in his mind. 'Where is Aelyn?'

'I had a vision.' The child ignored him, the smile on her face fading as her lips straightened. 'It was after your trial that it came to me, a thread of fate revealed. I saw you, Qian, standing on the deck of a Yeflam ship. The sight of it brought me a great sense of foreboding. Behind you were the Floating Cities, but they lay wrecked, and yet were complete. My vision would shift between the broken pillars and sunken cities and that of an intact and whole country. Yet, as I drew closer, it became clear to me that Yeflam was in ruins. A sense of dread started to overcome me and I was drawn to the very centre of the wreckage. Drawn here, in fact, to where Nale once sat. But once here I was drawn beneath the water, but when I tried to enter it, I could not. In the reflection of the water, however, I could see myself. I stared at it for some time until I began to hear a name spoken from the depths of the ocean, a name spoken by my image. I could not hear it properly, but I know that it is mine.'

'You did not answer his question,' Jae'le said from behind him. 'Where is Aelyn?'

'Not here,' the child said simply.

It was the creature who held the huge spiked mace who attacked first.

He let out a bellow, and Zaifyr saw the ancient dead within curl throughout the body, giving it a strength that it would not otherwise have had as it leapt into the air, lifting the ugly weapon high . . . but Zaifyr, his power flooding into the bodies of a pair of haunts, saw two cold, barely formed figures emerge in the air next to the creature. Their cold hands wrapped around his arms and tore the mace from his grasp, before the creature was thrown into the ground.

'Lor Jix,' he said, flooding his power through the words,

reaching down through the dark ocean quickly and sharply, 'it is time.'

He received no answer but for the brittle coldness that flooded through him, a chill that, he saw with a grim pleasure, went through the child as well. Anger straightened out the lines of her face and, above them, he saw the sky bulge as the dark mass pressed against the reality that it was not part of. But as it did, the first of five tall mastheads began to rise beneath the feet of the child. It forced her to take a step backwards to avoid being impaled, just as it forced Zaifyr and his brothers to do the same. Slowly, the masts continued to rise, outlined by a pale, broken light. From each, long pieces of rope led down to the thick rails that edged a massive deck. There a large, square cabin rested at the stern, behind a wheel that was easily the size of two men. At it stood a solitary figure, a short, ugly man who radiated a cold fury similar to the three creatures who stood around the child. Yet his feet appeared to rise from the ship's deck and, as it continued to lift into the night sky, as more and more of the mammoth vessel was revealed, as a ship greater than some icebergs rose, more and more men and women appeared on its decks. Finally, the last of the hull lifted through the stone of Nale and the ship that Zaifyr had glimpsed in broken halves on the bottom of the ocean rose full and complete into the night sky.

It rose into a sky that was cracking apart, a sky that was giving way to the darkness behind it. As it did, Lor Jix appeared beside Zaifyr.

It was from his awful voice that the order to attack the child was given.

3.

Bueralan pressed forward, his sword leading in a series of quick jabs that forced the Innocent into a pattern of defence until, finally, a slippery parry allowed Ren to gain an opportunity to thrust in return and stop momentum, but the bottom of Bueralan's sword caught the blade and flipped it up before battering it to the side with a wide slash that caused Ren to move backwards. It was a small victory, but against a warrior of the Innocent's skill, small victories began the path to victory, and Bueralan, stepping up the speed of his own attacks, felt the moment seep into his muscles, into his movements, and the rhythm of violence that he had not felt for such a long time returned to him. A low thrust forced Ren into a block, and a cut at his waist saw him move to the right, but it was Bueralan's charge that caught the Innocent by surprise, and the saboteur's blade sliced across the side of Ren's face as he dropped beneath a slash that would have easily crashed into another man's skull. Bueralan followed with a series of controlled cuts, but as Ren came to his feet, a solid block turned to a powerful thrust and Bueralan was forced to step back, moments before a riderless horse thundered past.

'We are not alone, not any more,' Aela Ren said, his sword held low as he continued to move to his right. 'We can end this now.'

'I'm just starting to hit my stride.' Bueralan held his sword behind him as he moved to his right. 'Maybe I'll take an ear next.'

'We have come a long way to hear you speak.'

'Maybe a tongue.'

Ren did not step back from his charge, but rather met each blow. Each block and parry he made picked up speed, as if he had been learning from Bueralan, mirroring the Saan who had stood around the Innocent a week ago and watched his battle with one of their own. Bueralan met his speed, however, and when he could not raise his weapon in defence, he moved to dodge the attacks that the Innocent made. At one point, he dropped low to cut in a wide circle at the shins of the other man. Aela Ren leapt over the sword and Bueralan caught his sword in a block on the way down and drove his fist into Ren's chest, beneath the crossbow bolt. The Innocent grunted in pain and Bueralan punched him again, and then a third time, before the Innocent grabbed his shirt and dropped him in an ugly flip over his back. Ren's foot came crashing down onto his chest and his breath burst from him. A second blow cracked his ribs, but Bueralan knocked the other foot out from under the other man and came to his feet, his sword parrying a thrust. In desperation, he tried to turn it into more, tried to turn the parry into a thrust, and instead, the sharp edge of Ren's sword cut deep into the side of his chest.

Bueralan's left hand tightened on Ren's sword arm, trapping the blade in place. With a shift of his weight, he crashed his head down again, but Ren, ready for it, shifted and the left side of his face and eye hit awkwardly and bloodily on his skull. With a grunt, Bueralan released Ren's trapped arm and spun around, his sword arcing through the air to slash down on the Innocent, only to find that he had moved through him. Bueralan felt the man's boot crash into the back of his calf, trying to shatter the bone, and his foot twisted as he moved out of the blow. Stumbling, he left Ren's reach and came upon the body of Pueral, who lay on her back, her armour and stomach sliced open, revealing a dark, bloody mess.

'You holding back?' Bueralan turned back to the Innocent, his left hand going to the wound on his chest, his leg protesting the weight he put on it. 'You sliced her open. You shouldn't find it a problem to do the same for me.'

'You are making it difficult.' Aela Ren spat a mouthful of blood on the grass and grasped the bolt in his chest. With a grunt, he pulled it free and tossed it onto the ground. 'But as I said, we have come a long way to hear what you will say.'

Though one eye was blurred with blood, Bueralan could see men and women standing on the edges of the field. They emerged from the smoke and fire of the horizon but were little more than shadows. He could see the silhouettes of riderless horses both behind and in front and he assumed that the soldiers who had begun the fight with him were now dead. But one — one of them drew his eye, a horse whose silhouette gave way to a smoky grey, and who had, he knew, carried Taela and Orlan.

'What is her name?' Ren asked.

'I don't know,' he replied, a familiar sadness filling him. 'I've never known.'

'You are lying.'

His charge was a slow, lumbering run and it did not surprise Ren. The Innocent battered aside his thrust and cut high in response; Bueralan's block tore at the skin on his right side and he pulled back from pressing the blow from the pain. It was all the opportunity that Ren needed, and he pushed Bueralan, whose slow blows and parries saw cuts and nicks appear on his arms, lining his tattoos. Yet, he did not step back. He knew that he had lost, but he kept pushing. He knew that the Innocent could have killed him twice. He could have thrust into his stomach or cut through the front of his throat, and the realization saw Bueralan begin to hammer his sword with both hands holding the hilt, reduced to a novice through his pain, through the futility.

He should never have left the cathedral, never left the side of his blood brother, never left his friends. He should *not* be here! His sword sweeps became wild and reckless and he knew that he was exposed, that Aela Ren was stepping to his left and right and beneath, his gaze holding to Bueralan as if he was seeing a truth buried beneath his flesh and bone. Finally, a wild swing forced Ren to bring his sword up in a block and, quicker than Bueralan could react to, Ren rolled his blade and trapped the saboteur's sword arm.

Then, in a swift, hard set of movements, Aela Ren broke Bueralan's forearm, drove the end of his elbow into his face and swept him off his feet.

A moment later, the Innocent's sword speared into the ground next to his head.

'Enough,' the scarred man said, releasing it. 'I have waited long enough, Bueralan Le. You will tell me her name.'

4.

Eira entered the room slowly, a chilled air preceding her.

She no longer dressed in the pale, elegant gowns that Ayae had seen her wear in the Enclave, but leather armour that had been dyed white and stitched together by thick dark-grey thread. On her left hip sat a white leather sheath with grey straps holding the hilt of her sword in place. The length of the blade disappeared under a dark-grey cloak lined with white fur that fell over her shoulders, and her hair had been tied back, giving Eira the appearance of a woman younger than she normally seemed. But the look she gave to everyone in the room as she walked through the open door was anything but that of an insolent youth.

'It has felt like dozens of years to reach this moment,' the Cold Witch said, speaking to Ayae as she approached. 'It is grief that allows time to slow, don't you think?'

. 'No,' she replied.

'Perhaps you have never truly grieved, then?'

Ayae shrugged off the insult. For a brief moment, she had thought that the Keeper had been invited, but none in the room had reacted well to her presence – she saw Lady Wagan's hand fall to Sinae's arm to silence him before he spoke, heard Lian Alahn's bodyguard straighten from the wall he leant against — and the tension rose with each step that Eira made towards her. In response, Ayae remained where she was, even as the brief chill sank into her skin and forced Lian Alahn to step away from her.

'Would you believe I did not even know that Benan Le'ta would be here tonight?' While the Keeper spoke, Ayae saw Caeli step into the empty doorway, but as she returned to the room, the guard shook her head slightly, revealing that she had seen neither the man who had led the three of them up to the room, nor another of the Keepers. 'I was given one task, but I would be remiss to pass up this one. Our little Traders' Union official who ran. He has been quite the asset to us — or at least he was until he fled with the money we gave him.'

'I never — I have been accused of many things,' the fat merchant began.

'Oh, hush, Benan,' Eira replied, her gaze holding Ayae's. 'A despicable man will do a lot for power, if it is within his reach. He will betray his ideals and he'll sell out his friends. He will do it so quickly you will wonder if he ever had friends. But it is when he loses his spine for it, when he runs away, that I quickly lose interest in him. Though I suppose since you tore through Bnid Gaerl and his soldiers, some people might almost forgive him.'

'But not you,' Ayae said. 'Right?'

'What good is a puppet if it runs away?' The woman smiled faintly. 'Still, it is my own fault, really. I had pushed my hand to the top of my puppet and felt the rotten cotton. I discovered it when I convinced him that Lady Wagan was simply too dangerous to be free in Yeflam.'

Ayae felt the floorboards creak beneath her weight. 'You probably didn't even need Kaqua for that,' she said.

'I simply promised to support his interests.' Eira turned towards Le'ta. He had pushed himself into the corner of the couch, his bruised face a mask of terror, his chained hands raised in defence before him. He began to whisper as the Keeper approached him, but Ayae could not make out his words, and soon she could not see his face. 'You may find this hard to believe, but the Enclave has been paralysed in debate about Qian and Jae'le for nearly a hundred years. It began after a cart bearing a young child came to one of our ports. It was of no real interest to us, except for the sensation that was reported by Kaqua when he came upon her. It was he who reported the child to us, describing what it is you feel when you stand beside the child now. It was to him that the first of her delegates came to see when they arrived in Yeflam, but he was a lone voice when it came to her divinity, for the child had done nothing to compare to the Five Kingdoms. Aelyn and her brothers had done more that spoke to the rule of gods, and many of us thought it was only a matter of time until Jae'le and Qian began to assert themselves again. A lot of the Enclave thought we would fall in with them, when they did. Aelyn did not favour that. Neither did Kaqua. Aelyn said that they simply would not return to power. After a while, he began to suggest that there was another power. It was hard to support at first. The child's delegates did not help: they were nothing more than witches and warlocks and ignorant of much in the world. Fo and Bau believed that the lack of education was the most obvious flaw in the child's divinity. They argued very strongly about that. It was not until Qian killed them in Mireea that it began to change for me. Some of the others had already come around to it, but for me, it was their deaths. It was Fo's in particular. It broke my heart and I saw in it something I had not seen since I was a child. I saw my mortality. Many of us did.'

'All men and women must die,' said Muriel Wagan. She, like the others in the room, had been forced to take a step back from the Keeper's cold. 'Surely it was not that surprising that it would happen to you as well?'

'You know as well as I do what happens to the dead.' Eira did not turn to address the other woman. 'Do you truly accept it so kindly?'

'You said you no longer believed that you could become a god,' Lian Alahn said, his skin looking goose-bumped and pale. 'Why the trial, then? Why the alliance with Le'ta?'

'The first because it was offered. The second – well, Lady Wagan, perhaps you could explain it to him?'

'Fear,' the Lady of the Ghosts said flatly.

Eira laughed. 'Would you believe it was about hope?' She shushed Benan Le'ta quietly as his pleaded whispers became fainter and fainter as the cold increased. Ayae caught Caeli's eye and glanced down at the floor. The other woman nodded, but it was the look that Sinae Al'tor shot over her shoulder and the quick shake of his head that caused Ayae a moment of panic. 'A god recreates the world,' the Keeper continued. 'All that is broken, she remakes. Aelyn understood that. Kaqua did as well. Both have seen so much, and both knew that it would be the responsibility of a god to repair the world. Both had long ago accepted the responsibility themselves. That is why they made the treaty. It was not just for Yeflam: it was for all of us. It was Kaqua who said that if we were not gods, then we were part of the wreckage, part of the destruction caused by the gods. He said that we could be remade as well.'

The blonde girl on the couch remained still, appearing to betray no interest in what was taking place around her.

'Then what point did the trial serve?' Alahn demanded.

'To break Aelyn Meah,' Ayae said, a hollow sense of despair opening beneath her.

'No,' Eira said, rising. 'That was Qian's plan, but not ours. Your mistake – like his – was to believe that Aelyn leads the Enclave. That Aelyn is somehow the most important figure of it. But that is not true. The Enclave is all of us. The trial was simply the last part of our debate in what we should do with Aelyn's two brothers.'

When the Keeper turned back to her, Ayae finally saw Benan Le'ta. The fat merchant sat at the end of the couch, his hands held before him as if he were seeking supplication. A hardness had entered his skin, but it was only after a moment that Ayae realized that the definition she saw was not a trick of the light in the room. Rather, he had been frozen. Ice had worked its way over his body, creating a tomb through which she could see his panicked eyes, and the suffocation that was taking place.

Eira smiled at her, but before the Keeper could speak – before she could continue to freeze the room behind her words – Ayae's hand shot out and grabbed her leather vest.

Then she brought her foot down heavily on the wooden floorboards.

5.

The crew of *Wayfair* did not stand on the deck of the ship as normal sailors might. Zaifyr had seen that their legs rose from it, suggesting a more intimate relationship with the ship than a mortal crew, but after the order to attack was given, he was proved right in a startling fashion.

Before his gaze, the ship began to break apart. It began at the top of the masts, where the bodies of men and women started to materialize and spring into the night sky. They leapt high, and they leapt for the darkness that was breaking into the night sky, their bright bodies lighting it up to reveal the unformed nature of it as they landed against it. As more and more of *Wayfair* began to crumble into its crew, Yeflam grew brighter and brighter, as if the stars had begun to fall.

Zaifyr turned his gaze to the child. Some of the crew had left the emerging darkness and had landed on the ground, but the child did not retreat from them. The first of the crew to attack her were a pair of women whose features were sharp and verging on bone; but as they came within contact of the child, their bodies began to break apart, the centre of their chests dissolving, while their shoulders sagged inwards. It reminded Zaifyr of what had happened to Anguish on the Mountains of Ger and he flushed his own power through the two women. If he had not, he was sure that their bodies would have continued to break apart. Yet, as he pushed his power into their forms, he discovered that the child's power had attacked them in the same way as he was acting to defend them, and he found himself reacting against the sensation of consumption by hardening their bodies. In the span of two heartbeats, he rebuilt their chests and drove out the child's rot. Moments later, she responded with a thrust of power that hit him so hard that the two women disintegrated and he fell to his knees, the taste of blood from his nose in his mouth.

The child could not press her advantage, however. In the sky, the darkness was roaring, and its bellows drew her attention to it. As she turned, the crew of *Wayfair* rushed her. The three creatures that had attacked Eidan leapt to her defence, but the crew swarmed over them. The huge weapons that the child's creatures carried could not hit the dead, and their attempts to hurl away the ghostly bodies that tore into their skin were futile. When the first of the crew reached the child, she was forced to retreat, and as she did, the ghosts that were near her lit up brightly like flames as they began to fall apart. Shortly after, the child's power returned to the three dead men who protected her, and it flushed through their bodies and their weapons with such a fury that the crew of *Wayfair* began to fall.

Yet, there was one who did not.

Lor Jix stalked towards the child while his crew fell around him, his cold, colourless form a startling purity of anger before the child.

Zaifyr heard Jae'le call his name, but the sound was distant.

It was as if it was spoken from thousands of miles away. It was not until he spoke a second time that his urgency reached Zaifyr.

'Eidan cannot stay here,' Jae'le said. At his feet, the torn body of his brother lay on his good side, Jae'le's cloak of feathers laid across the other, blood soaking through it already. 'Bones must be set, wounds must be stitched. It cannot be done here – not in this.'

Zaifyr met his brother's gaze. In it, he saw the fury that had burned for the last weeks, but for the first time he saw that it was not an anger that responded to the child's presence. Rather, he saw that it was a response to the threat she had issued to his family, to the duty that he had given himself over to after the Five Kingdoms.

'If I lose control,' Zaifyr began.

'I will not allow it,' Jae'le finished.

Around Zaifyr, the dead began to slowly appear. At first, the haunts began to take shape from a leg, or a shoulder, the faint outline of their incorporeal body that they had recently gained with the loss of their mortal one. They were the recent dead who had been drawn to him, who had thought to seek him in the quiet moments of the night, or the day, and ask to be released from their hunger and their cold. But soon, the older dead emerged beside them, the broken shapes of their bodies also given a solidity, a definition equal that of *Wayfair*'s crew. Yet, while the crew numbered no more than a hundred, the haunts that were taking shape around Zaifyr were endless. They were drawn from the generations of men and women who had been born into the world and died since the War of the Gods.

They began to overtake Lor Jix, rushing ahead of his slow stalk towards the child, allowing him to heal from the injuries the child's power had done to him. His left arm, Zaifyr saw, was but a pale strip, the substance of it almost gone. As the swarm of the dead drew closer to the child, the charm-laced man began to invest in them the horror of the years he had spent listening to their whispered pleas. He remembered how he had listened to them asking for simple warmth, to be sated from a hunger that could not be satisfied. He felt their demand that he give more of his power to them, that he open himself entirely, that he give them the life that they had lost. They lit the sky up, not like stars, but like a bright white sun, as the dead in Asila had. But unlike then, Zaifyr tightened his control of them. He forced them towards the child. He focused their desire. He made it so that all they could see was the beautiful young woman. He had them ignore the dark shape that loomed high above them in the sky – the terrible shape that began to descend downwards, that was attacked by the crew of *Wayfair*, that tried desperately to push through them to the child.

He heard Lor Jix's laugh, and it was a terrible thing, but the cold chill that ran down Zaifyr's spine was one of anticipation as the ancient dead's colourless hands closed around the child's throat.

6.

The floor gave way in a splintering crack and Ayae's weight pulled Eira down with her.

It was, therefore, Ayae who crashed through the bottles and glasses of the bar first, she who hit the benches they sat on, she who felt it give before it shattered beneath her weight. She worried that a piece of wood would dig through her legs, or plunge deep into her thighs and cut hard into her arteries; but the edges of both wood and glass that tore through her trousers could only scratch against her, could only hint at drawing blood, and surrounded by the wreckage that she had landed in, Ayae slammed Eira into the back wall. Her hard fingers dug into the white leather of the vest she wore, gouged deep for a handhold, and used it to lift her forward and back again as she slammed Eira into the broken racks of alcohol.

A sudden burst of cold sprayed across Ayae's eyes, blinding her. Instinctively, she lifted her hand — but the heavy, hard punch that followed hit the centre of her chest, forcing her to release her hold on Eira.

A second punch slammed her over the bar, where she hit the ground in a hard, tangled mess.

Ayae's sight came back slowly as her fingers tore away steaming ice from her face and she rose to her feet. In the dim shadows of her returning sight, she saw a shape rushing towards her, and she began to turn away from it; but she could not move fast enough and it hit hard against her shoulder, rocking her backwards as the object that hit her exploded in a heavy odour of alcohol. A second slammed into her chest, and a third, but it was not until the fourth that she realized that what was hitting her was hard spikes of ice, flung by Eira and drawn from the bottle she held in her bloody hand.

She braced herself for a fifth, but instead the Keeper fell sideways as a pair of booted feet swung out of the hole and into her face.

Caeli followed elegantly, dropping from the hole in the ceiling to the broken remains of the bar. Ayae's heart lurched at the sight of her and she began to call out, to tell her to flee, but the guard swayed to her left as a heavy burst of brown-coloured spikes shot out, and her shout was lost in the sound of the hard ice hitting the ceiling. Ayae could not see Eira, but Caeli continued to move to her left, the spikes following her as she lifted herself over the edge of the bar and landed behind it only seconds before a large lance pierced where she had been standing. Another tore through the wood of the bar, but the guard, moving swiftly in a low crouch, came around the front of the bar. There was a pause and Ayae saw Eira regain her feet, but before she could shout out to Caeli, the guard grabbed the broken edge of the bar and vaulted back over it.

Ayae drew her sword and began to rush forward on her heavy legs, but just as she came to the edge of the bar, Caeli landed in front of Eira, and the latter spat.

The guard reeled backwards and Ayae realized that the cold blindness that had afflicted her before had now affected Caeli. But by then, she was at the bar. '*Down!*' she shouted, her voice a bark that she did not know if Caeli would understand. But the guard dropped suddenly, leaving a space for Ayae's heavy body to land as she cleared the bench of the bar, her sword lancing into Eira's neck. The Cold Witch had been so focused on the woman before her that she had little time to react, but even as the blow landed, Ayae saw the thin layer of ice around her neck crack, deflecting the blow.

Despite it, Eira cried out in pain, but it wasn't until Ayae glanced down that she saw Caeli's dagger through the white leather of Eira's right boot.

A moment later, sharp and hard ice burst out over them and Ayae dropped over Caeli, using her body as a shield while the Keeper retreated in a bloody limp.

'You were supposed to kill her,' the guard muttered.

'You were supposed to leave with the others,' she shot back, feeling the ice against her skin, feeling it rip through her shirt. 'Can you see?'

'Yeah, she missed.' Suddenly, the ice stopped falling. 'Caught me just below my eye. Burns like you wouldn't believe.'

Ayae could see the cold red mark beneath her eye, like a smudged tear. 'It'll leave a mark,' she said, pushing herself up. 'Good thing you're so ug—'

The blast of ice that caught her as she stood was the hardest that Ayae had felt. It tore apart the top end of the bar and burst through the remaining bottles behind her, showering both her and Caeli in alcohol. Her body went numb, but Ayae also felt a surge of fear when she saw the fluid begin to freeze on her as the blast of ice stopped. In panic, she found Eira before her, her face a mask of rage and anger, but her eyes focused on Ayae, on the liquid that was freezing not just around her but on Caeli, who lay on the ground unable to rise.

Caeli's danger was of more immediate concern to Ayae than the risk to herself. She felt a break of the hardness of the skin that had encased her since she had killed Faise and Zineer. The warmth that she had come to associate with her power — a portion of her power, she understood now — now began to flood through her. Her anger returned with it and threatened to overwhelm her, even as the alcohol stopped its swift freezing, even as Caeli began to crawl further along the bar floor, out of the puddles of alcohol that lay around her. Ayae saw in the tall guard Faise, saw her again on the first floor of the building, held beside Commander Bnid Gaerl. She heard his voice. She saw the look on Faise's face. Ayae's fury returned, but rather than it being aimed at Eira, at the woman who had finally drawn her sword, Ayae's anger was for herself, for losing such control, and for a moment, in the bar of Sin's Hand, Ayae desperately wanted to stop the warmth that was rising through her, that was breaking the hardness of her skin and revealing flames beneath.

But to do so would be to let Caeli die, she knew. To deny her power, to deny both the heat in her and the hardness that could encase her, would be just as bad as letting it sweep through her without control. To give into her fear of how she had killed Faise was to kill Caeli. She could not allow that. Not again. She would not allow the power in her to kill because she did not have the discipline to control it. Before Ayae, the edges of Eira's hair began to catch alight, and her cloak began to burn suddenly and violently. Eira dropped her sword, but the fire found life easily in the alcohol-soaked clothing of the Cold Witch and soon the woman was screaming as the flames covered her entire body, as they remained confined to her, even after her cloak fell to the ground.

Ayae watched as Eira ran towards the front doors of Sin's Hand and flung them open to reveal the night. The night's darkness was not thrown back by the flames that clung to the Keeper, but by a sky that had been lost beneath the broken white light of the dead.

7.

'What you need,' Aela Ren said, 'what you have always needed, Bueralan, is a clear motivation.'

Slowly, the saboteur pushed himself off the ground. Halfway up, he stumbled and fell to his knees, but his good hand circled around the hilt of the Innocent's sword, and he used that to pull himself upright. His head swam, and he could barely see the scarred man ahead of him: gummed with blood and swelling shut with pain, his left eye could not focus properly, and the pain had begun to extend to his right eye. He took a deep breath to steady himself and it hurt enough that he was sure he had broken ribs. But the worst of his pain was in his right arm and he cradled it tight against his chest, unsure if the white he saw was his tattoos or his bone. Yet he took a step, and as he did, his left hand dragged Ren's sword from the dirt, and he began to struggle after him, aware that the men and women who had watched him and Ren fight had come closer and formed a dark, faceless circle around them.

Bueralan slowly closed the gap between himself and the Innocent, who stood before the dark shadow of the stables.

'Let her go,' he said in a cracked voice when he was finally in reach of the scarred man. 'Let them both go.'

'I could not care less about Samuel Orlan. If I was confident that the next would be a better man, I might kill him myself, but history has proved that they are rarely anything but an annoyance. But the Queen's Voice — *but Taela*. She is simply mortal.' He drove the young woman to the ground in front of Bueralan, his hand wrapped tightly around the hair at the base of her skull. The right side of her face was bloodied, and a long cut ran into her hairline, but the fear in her eyes, he saw, was not for herself. 'Isn't that right, Taela?'

The saboteur raised the sword, even as the Queen's Voice mouthed *no*. 'I'll say it again,' he said. 'Let her go. Let them both go.'

'I do not fear my own sword.'

Slowly, Bueralan turned the blade around and pressed it against his stomach. 'Nothing gets said if I die, remember.'

A thin smile cut a new scar on Ren's face. 'Do you honestly think you'll die?' He tightened his grip on Taela's hair, causing her back to arch in pain. 'Look at yourself, Bueralan. If you were but a mortal man, you would be dead, but you are not. You are god-touched and you cannot die. Not until a god allows you to.'

'I die like everyone else,' he snarled.

'No, *she* dies like everyone else.'

A strong hand took the sword from him, a hand belonging to one of the shadows around him. He saw a woman's white face and in her dark eyes he saw a sadness that his weak hand made no attempt to hold tightly onto the hilt.

'Bueralan.'

His hand curled into a fist.

'You know her name,' Aela Ren continued. 'I will hear it. We will all hear it. If you do not say it, only an innocent will die.'

It was the repeat of the word innocent that caused a broken laugh to escape him. His leg gave way and he slumped to the ground, his laugh turning bitter. *Only when what is at stake is innocence.* Bueralan heard the child's voice again and met Taela's gaze. 'I'm so sorry,' he said, though he knew, even as he said it, that he had nothing to apologize for. But he could think of no other way to respond to the sympathy he saw in her eyes. 'I just don't know any name.'

'She will not die easily.' A dagger appeared in the Innocent's hand and he pressed it hard against her neck, breaking the skin, and letting a line of blood appear. 'I will take parts of her with this dagger. I will take her mind and her beauty with her limbs. I will take all that is her before I allow the eternal suffering that is death to reach her, Bueralan.' As he talked, the saboteur's blurred gaze remained on Taela. He could see her determination and her strength, both of which she would use against Ren. He saw around her neck the strap of leather that he had tied around the pouch that held Zean's soul, the pouch that came to rest down in the centre of her chest, not over the heart, not directly, but close. As Aela Ren spoke his litany of horrors that he would bring on the woman before him, he wanted to tell her to throw the stone away, to take it from around her neck; he wanted to tell her about the man who had been his blood brother, the man who had followed him into exile, who had stood beside him through so much, and who he had ultimately left to die alone.

Slowly, his gaze left Taela and found the Innocent. 'I keep telling you, she doesn't have a name,' he said. 'She's nothing but a piece of evil, a thing to dominate us, she . . . she . . .'

Ren threw Taela to one side and grabbed Bueralan's blood-soaked shirt. 'What is her name?' he demanded.

'You're a fool,' Bueralan said roughly. 'She won't give you what you want.'

'Her name?' His voice roared with his need and, as the words washed over him, the saboteur felt himself dwarfed by the magnitude of it, the lifetime of pain. '*Tell me her name!*'

'Se'Saera,' he whispered, once.

8.

It was spoken without words, pushed into his mind like a brand, burnt upon the consciousness, and he heard nothing and thought nothing but the name Se'Saera.

It was accompanied by a wave of pure force that rushed over Zaifyr. He felt himself lifted by it, and as he rose into the air, he felt his connection with the dead stretch thin. It was as if he was suddenly limited to them by a tether that kept him within their reach and felt it go taut. He felt his body strain. His joints began to ache and he thought that he would snap, that he would be severed . . . only for the connection he had to the dead to do exactly that. He felt their need leave him for the first time in ten thousand years, felt an emptiness inside him grow. He felt a singular bliss that he had not felt since he had been but a young man sleeping beneath the furs in his parents' tent. He would tie the charms of protection to the covers before he went to sleep. As he floated, he thought of those that he still wore, one for each god who would die. Who was dead. He longed to reach out to touch the copper and silver, to assure himself that the bliss he had begun to feel was real, to know that it was not his imagination or a dream, but as he thought that, as he felt his hands move, the feeling of emptiness began to dissolve, and he heard Lor Jix's bellow, his cry of sheer outrage—

And then Zaifyr slammed into the stone ground.

'Se'Saera,' he murmured. *A name.*

Her name.

Hands shook him, dragged him along the stone, and he heard his name called. But it was not until he heard a sword being drawn that his vision began to return, that the world returned to him in a startling, painful rush.

Jae'le stood above him. He held his sword in his right hand, but it was what Zaifyr could not see that disturbed him. All his senses were open, all his power, but he could not see the dead that he had given form too, could not see those who had swarmed over the child, or those who did not. He could not see the crew of *Wayfair* and he could not see the darkness that had spread out in the sky. He could not see Lor Jix and he could not see Se'Saera. Where but moments before the ancient dead had stood with his colourless hands around Se'Saera's beautiful neck, there was nothing, not even marks against the stone ground to suggest that she or the ancient dead had stood there.

The three creatures that had stood with Se'Saera remained, however. It was their bloody forms that had begun to circle around him and Eidan that had prompted Jae'le to draw his sword.

Slowly, painfully, Zaifyr began to push himself to his feet. As he did, a growing awareness of the dead around him began to filter back, as if they were lamps relit after being blown out. As their strength increased, he began gradually to filter his awareness of them from his sight. 'Why do they not attack?' he asked, indicating the three creatures.

'Our sister approaches,' Jae'le said quietly. 'I fear the suggestion of betrayal we heard from the child is no longer that.'

It was not until Aelyn and the Keepers were lit by the moon's light that Zaifyr began to sense them by their power. The sadness he had felt earlier returned with it, only now it had a depthless quality to it, and it threatened to combine with the bitterness he felt over Se'Saera's escape. He knew that the god had been taken to whoever had said her name and that a part of her had been solidified because of it. Zaifyr could not explain how he knew the latter, but he had the strong sense of a part of his world being made permanent, and the sensation left him with the urge to sink back to the ground in frustration.

Instead, he greeted his sister.

'It was inevitable from the day you arrived in Yeflam,' Aelyn said, ignoring his greeting. She no longer wore her blue, but was dressed instead in a mixture of leather and chain, and a cloak he had not seen her wear since she had begun to build Maewe. As in the wars they had waged before then, Aelyn did not wear a sword. 'I asked you not to begin this. I pleaded with you from the moment you walked into Yeflam not to destroy all that I had worked for.'

'Are we to have a conversation, then?' Jae'le asked evenly. 'One in which your betrayal is given legitimacy?'

'Does Eidan still live?' A strained thread entered her voice. 'Tell me that there is that still, at least.'

Out of the corner of his eye, Zaifyr saw his brother shift beneath the cloak of feathers, a bloodied hand emerging. 'He lives,' he said.

'Allow me to take him.' Aelyn took a step forward. 'He can be healed here.'

'And after?' He looked at Jae'le. 'What do you think will happen after?'

'The rest of her betrayal,' he replied.

'*My betrayal?* Only you two could believe that.' While she spoke, the Keepers began to spread out. The order, Zaifyr saw, was given by Kaqua, who stood just behind Aelyn. Yet, as they began to form a ring around him and his brothers, he noticed that not all the Keepers were present. He was not familiar enough with all to name those who were missing, but he thought that it was three in number. 'Neither of you have looked upon the world in the last hundred years,' Aelyn said. 'You have been hidden for so long that you cannot see that the world no longer needs men like you. It no longer needs destroyers or conquerors. It needs healers. That is what the people want. That is our responsibility, now. The pair of you cannot see that because you create nations without compromise. You make them by razing the ground beneath any who do not agree with you. I know, because I have seen it. Just as Eidan and Tinh Tu have seen it. It is why neither of you could make a country like Yeflam. Why you could never champion education, peace or prosperity as all three of us have. You could never have built what we have and you could never have governed it.'

'I do not see Tinh Tu here.' Jae'le lifted his sword as he had done earlier. 'And our brother is at our feet dying.'

'It was not meant to be this way.'

'That is the child's fault. She is no more than you describe us to be. She is merely an echo of what began long ago.'

'We are all echoes, brother. Will you give me Eidan?'

Before either Zaifyr or Jae'le could reply, the ground shook. It began beneath Zaifyr's feet and rolled out through the Keepers and the child's creatures, forcing some of the former to their knees. But it was the loud crack nearest to him that caught Zaifyr's attention, and he turned in time to see Eidan's hand rise a second time before it fell again.

In the aftershock, the pillar that held Nale aloft began to split.

9.

Bueralan was not aware of everything that followed. He had spoken her name and, in the aftermath, he felt as if it had been torn from him. He felt the absence of it, though he had not known it was there, and he wondered how it was that he had not recognized it. He had no answers and, above him, the sky began to break apart. It no longer resembled broken glass, but was instead made from smoked air and burnt soil, and for a moment, he thought that a darkness had formed, that it had ruptured the sky and come to loom over him. He feared that he was going to be lifted up, and for a moment, he felt himself rising . . . but soon he realized that what lifted him were hands, a woman's hands, and that Taela had pulled him into her lap. She came into his vision, but his blood-blurred eye had trouble focusing on her. Against the dark, dark sky, he saw her in two forms, her bruised and cut face overlaid with that of a woman of wealth, a woman older than she was now but one of an undeniable grace. He could not escape the impression that these two versions were trying to combine, to return to a single vision of the future, but the longer he looked at her, the further the two seemed to drift apart. She spoke, at first to him, though the words were dim, and then over her shoulder. Bueralan could no longer see the shadowed shapes of the god-touched men and women who stood beside Aela Ren. As Taela began to speak again, he reached for her with his good hand, to tell her to flee, but she merely took his hand and held it, as one might someone who was dying, and she spoke again. This time, he heard Samuel Orlan reply. His voice sounded as if it came from a great distance, and it had in it an undeniable sadness.

A girl came to stand over him, then. She looked to be no older than sixteen, her white body slim and still hinting at the child she once was. But, with her wave of blonde hair and green eyes, there was a beauty about her that suggested very strongly that, within a few years, she would be a truly magnificent woman.

She lowered herself to her haunches beside him.

'Se'Saera,' Bueralan murmured.

Above her stood Aela Ren, but the saboteur could not make out his face clearly.

'It is a beautiful name,' the girl said, finally. 'I knew you would speak it tonight. I saw you say the words. I saw you change the world.'

'You could have spoken it.'

'It must be said by a mortal first.'

He laughed weakly. 'I was just told I would live for ever.'

'That depends on my father.' Se'Saera turned her gaze on Taela. 'You have not used the gift I gave you, Bueralan.'

'You know as well as I do that it was no gift.' Samuel Orlan appeared next to them, his grey beard streaked with soot and blood. 'Now, let us stop this, Se'Saera. You have punished him more than enough. It is time to show mercy. Allow him to walk from here and out of history. Let him be forgotten like all the men and women who first spoke the names of the gods.'

'Mercy.' The newly named god drew out the word, as if she found the sound of it strange. 'I can do that, if I so desire.'

'Your first acts after being named are always remembered.'

'But even as he spoke my name, he worked against me,' she continued softly, ignoring Orlan. 'He left my enemies alive. He left the words that shamed me spoken.'

The cartographer began to speak again, but Se'Saera's hand rose, and he was lifted from the ground and thrown backwards. Bueralan, barely able to move, dropped his good hand from Taela's and began to search for a sword or a dagger. He could find none and he felt panic set in. Worse, he could not move quickly enough to free Taela from his weight, to give her a chance to run, and the woman who held him understood too late that the green-eyed gaze was on her and on the leather pouch around her neck.

Bueralan landed heavily on the ground, his body jarring with pain as Se'Saera grabbed the other woman and raised her to a standing position.

'The Mother's Gift,' she said, her hand curling, touching the pouch. 'That is what they call it here, is it not?'

'Yes,' Taela whispered.

Bueralan's good hand reached out for Se'Saera's leg, but a boot landed heavily on it and ground down hard until bones splintered.

'I have heard much about the witches in Ooila,' the god continued. 'They make an elaborate ritual of their skills. They draw the soul from its small piece of glass or stone like a dog

631

lured by a piece of meat. They trap it in a cold bottle to sit and wait for the blood of a pregnant woman to be dropped into it. Then it is drunk, and it finds the little vessel in the womb, and it takes hold with such violence that it kills the child waiting to be born. But do you know that none of that ritual is needed?'

She snapped the leather cord.

'Please, I—' Taela's voice faltered into a whisper. 'I'm not pregnant.'

'You don't need that, either.'

And as Bueralan cried out, as his note of objection tore from him more painfully than her name had, Se'Saera took the crystal from the pouch and crushed it in her hand. She raised it to Taela's mouth and, with deliberate slowness, forced her fingers between the other woman's lips. She pushed open Taela's jaw, using a strength that no person could hope to match. Then she pushed her hand deeper into Taela. She did it in such a way that the violation was not just about the cruelty, but the enjoyment of that brutality. It was an act of pleasure and power and dominion over a human being who could not respond equally. Bueralan tried to raise himself off the ground to stop it, but Aela Ren's boot left his hand and planted firmly on his chest. He could do nothing but watch as Taela resisted swallowing. As she held her breath. As tears streaked down her face. He watched as Se'Saera's other hand closed over her nose to suffocate her, to force her body to accept the soul of his blood brother.

She held it there until Taela gasped desperately for breath. At that moment, Se'Saera's palm fell flat against Taela's mouth, and she forced the broken shards of the crystal down her throat.

Bueralan turned away, unable to watch the violation further. His bloody eye focused on the scarred face of the Innocent and saw the immortal man, the man who had known the gods of old so intimately, watch the new god intently.

The Inevitability
of Responsibility

Her question, 'Do you know who is lying to you?' —
the question that is phrased through her priests — is
more insightful than she realizes.

—Tinh Tu, *Private Diary*

1.

Nale began to crack as the pillar beneath it started to splinter into Leviathan's Blood.

Zaifyr watched as, in a mixture of pain and anger, Eidan climbed to his feet while the ground shook. Jae'le's cloak fell from his shoulders, revealing the horrific wounds that were across the left side of his body. He began to say something to Aelyn – 'You *know* he . . . This not the way . . .' – but the words were slurred and Zaifyr was not sure what he said. When it became clear that he could not stand, when Aelyn, her face beginning to crumple in sorrow, moved towards him, Eidan curled his right hand into a fist and punched into the stone at his feet. The ground shuddered again, but this time splits began to emerge beneath Zaifyr's feet. As if they were the shadows of birds passing above, they rushed past him and widened into fissures that opened under the Keepers. The fault lines went beyond them too: they tore down the wall and gate of Aelyn's house and ran into the streets beyond.

As the ground shook again, Aelyn rose into the air. She lifted her Keepers with her, just before the northern half of Nale sagged. The stone beneath Zaifyr took on sudden and deliberate tilt. Frantically, he reached the lip of the break, intent on jumping across the gap emerging between him and Jae'le and Eidan, when a sudden wind knocked him off his feet.

Zaifyr fell backwards. He slid down the steepening incline, but regained his footing by angling his body flat and using his feet and hands to brake. He achieved that without any injury, but he knew that Aelyn's attack had not meant to injure him. It had only been intended to throw him away from his brothers and in that, he knew, she had succeeded. Ahead, he saw Jae'le's cloak rise into the air as the wind began to form a series of dark funnels around where he and Eidan stood.

Zaifyr began to move. He knew that once Aelyn had grabbed Eidan — as she would, even if his brother had rejected what she said — she would turn on Jae'le.

Behind him, he heard Aelyn's house groan and, a moment later, stones scattered across the ground as one of the towers toppled. Yet, when he turned towards it, to make sure that the distance between him and it was adequate, it was not the splitting house that caused him concern, but the sight of two of Se'Saera's creatures making their way towards him. The first held the large two-handed mace that had done so much damage to Eidan.

He still could not sense the dead properly. His power was returning, but not enough that he could have the dead catch the ugly mace that was hurled at him. Instead, he ducked beneath it, but the tilt of the ground took him off balance, and he slid across the stone, closer to the pair. It was the second of the two, the lean creature with bone spikes on its shoulders, that rushed him as he tried to regain his balance. The bones, Zaifyr saw, were taken from humans and had been nailed into place against the creature's shoulders; similarly the chains that had been wrapped around its hands had been attached with long spikes that pierced wickedly through its skin. He saw that *very* closely as the hands came within millimetres of landing on him, and would have done on a second attack, had not an albatross ploughed head-first into the creature's back.

The giant dark-winged bird was the first of a dozen that came in low and fast along the tilting land of Nale. Their long sword-like beaks were levelled like spears and their sharp claws followed.

They did not stop to aid Zaifyr, but instead continued up the growing incline of stone, before disappearing over the ledge in answer to Jae'le. The sight of them did not reassure Zaifyr: they were nothing more than a token of what his brother could have once summoned. Yet it was also true that the sheer size of the birds and the violence that could be rendered by their beaks and claws would provide some distraction. Already, Zaifyr could hear shouts from the Keepers.

Before him, the lean creature tore the broken-necked albatross from its back and casually tossed it aside. Behind it, the larger one picked its ugly mace up from the ground.

On instinct, Zaifyr reached out to the haunt of the albatross. The dead bird appeared before him, clearly in confusion, and its thoughts were so alien, so strange, that for a moment Zaifyr felt his control of it slip; but as the two creatures closed in, the ghost of the bird erupted into the air in a sudden burst of broken white colouring and began tearing into the skin of the lean creature, ripping at the wounds it had already made. Roaring, the creature dropped to the ground, but Zaifyr could not watch its attempts to stop the bird's attack.

He ducked under the heavy swing of the large creature's mace. In a snatching motion, Zaifyr reached out at the creature's chest and snagged the cold haunt within. He was trying for the Leeran soldier, but with his power still struggling to return after the feedback from the child's naming, he had to rely upon a physical motion to help direct his attack, and he caught the ancient dead within. The cold thing snarled and pulled back, the strength it had threatening to break his hold—

Which it would have done, had not the ground finally broken.

Its sudden plunge into Leviathan's Blood thrust Zaifyr into the creature as they both hit the water. In a fury of churned ocean, he lost sight of the stone floor plunging downwards and could not see the creature he still gripped. He could taste the bitter salt and felt the harshness of the water against his skin, scalding it. He tried to quell his panic, but he did not know how deep he was being dragged, only that he was indeed going deeper, caught in the wake as half of Nale plunged. In desperation, Zaifyr put his feet against the creature's chest and pushed – only to feel its hand grab his calf and latch tightly onto it.

Afraid that he would be dragged down to the ocean's floor, Zaifyr snapped hold of the ancient dead with his power. Its form twisted beneath him, and the physical hand tightened, looking now to break the leg it held. Zaifyr tore the ancient dead towards him, trying to rip it not just from the body it was in, but from the blood ties that secured it to the Leeran soldier. The ties held the two of them in strained conflict as they sank deeper and deeper, the black water rushing past in a depthless oblivion. The creature did not want to give way: to do so would leave it in the landscape dominated by Leviathan's Blood, and while one of the ancient killers from the Plateau might well wish for but a drop of blood to hit his or her prison in the dirt, the blood of the Leviathan was not what it desired. The remains of the god treated no human with kindness. It was in that black prison that Zaifyr left the ancient dead after he tore it in bursts of white from the body of the Leeran soldier. Its cold hate raged at him as he kicked free of its chest, but it could do nothing to stop Zaifyr's desperate rush to the surface.

His legs ached with the strength it took to challenge the pull that the sinking parts of Nale left in its wake. He could see very little, but was dimly aware of more stone plunging into the water. The echo of it in the water left him concerned that another piece of land might be falling above him. He almost changed direction when the downward drag of the water lessened. Had he become disorientated and started to swim in the wake of the destruction? That fear exploded through him when he felt stone, and if his hand had not broken the surface a moment later he would have stopped his ascent.

Instead, he pulled himself out of the water at the feet of Kaqua, the Pauper.

2.

'You should take him with you,' Caeli said quietly.

'No,' Ayae replied, her voice also hushed, as if she believed that they might be overheard, among the sound of voices, the cries for help, the demands to know what was going on. 'Let him help with the evacuation.'

Behind her, the shattered smile of Sin's Hand leaked light onto the road. Inside, a handful of men and women pored over a map of Yeflam, while the blue-armoured Yeflam Guards stood in a circle outside, responding to individuals and directing crowds. It was not what Ayae had expected to happen when she and Caeli stepped out of the brothel, intent on chasing down the still-burning figure of Eira; but after a handful of steps both had staggered beneath a rushing wave of raw power, and in its wake, Ayae and Caeli had felt the name Se'Saera thrust upon them. Ayae had vomited on the ground, harder hit by the wave than the blonde woman, and when she raised her head, Xrie was standing before her.

He watched her intently without saying a word. At his side, his sword remained in its sheath, but Ayae became slowly aware of the fact that his armour was scratched and gouged, that the blue in his clothes was torn and stained, just as the lower half of his face was, leaving him with the appearance of having feasted on another. Beside her, Caeli had begun to draw her sword, but Ayae's hand had fallen on her shoulder. 'No,' she said, even as, from the darkness behind him, two dozen Yeflam Guards emerged. 'He's not here to fight.'

'You really want to take that risk?' the guard asked.

'You're not here to fight, are you?' she said to him.

'No,' Xrie replied roughly. 'I am not here to fight you.'

Her hand had tightened on Caeli's.

'I will not abandon my soldiers,' he continued, taking a step forward. As he drew closer, he revealed an ugly bandage around his throat. 'I will not see them killed by Se'Saera's beasts. I will not see them sacrificed, just as I will not see their families killed. I will not betray their trust.'

'Betrayal of your peers, but not your country.' From behind her, Lian Alahn emerged from the narrow alley next to the brothel. He was covered in dust and cobwebs, having taken a passageway that Sinae told Ayae later was rarely used, even by politicians who wanted to keep their reputations unsullied. Sinae followed Alahn and his guard, standing on one side of Lady Wagan, with the blonde woman whom Ayae believed was Sinae's own guard, on her right. Alahn scowled. 'I could almost applaud you,' he added, 'if I did not believe that you knew full well of the attempt on my life.'

'Spare me your indignation, Mister Alahn.' The Soldier turned and indicated for one of his soldiers to come forward. In his hand, he held a cloth sack, its end stained darkly even in the night. 'You are a man of opportunism and I have never had time for such men. However, what is taking place on

Yeflam now goes far beyond you and the petty politics you peddle. If you doubt me, you need only ask a friend of mine for his opinion on the matter.'

The red-bearded head of Fiel, the Feral, rolled out of the sack.

A moment later, the first of three quakes shook Yeflam. The head shifted and rolled past Alahn. The Traders' Union official ignored it as he tried to keep his balance, only to fall when the second quake moved the ground. Finally, the head came to rest at the feet of Lady Wagan.

She picked it up by its red hair a moment before the third and strongest quake shook Yeflam. Without so much as a false step, the Lady of the Ghosts held the head and walked past Alahn and Ayae. 'You do as I say,' she said to Xrie, 'and we will save as many people as we can. After that, we will march on Se'Saera and take our retribution for all that she has done.'

Xrie did not reply immediately and Ayae, her hand dropping to her sword, believed that he would deny her.

'Agreed,' he said in his damaged voice.

Ignoring Lian Alahn's loud protests, Lady Wagan led the Soldier into Sin's Hand. In the wreckage of the bar, she had a map of the artificial country laid out and began to plan the evacuation. Ayae lit the candles and lamps in the room, and once she had finished, she saw that Alahn had entered. He was not lending his voice to the plans and did not until Ayae stood in the doorway, preparing to leave. Now the Yeflam people had begun to flood the dark streets: their cries for help filtered through the conversation and planning of movements. In the distance, Ayae could hear shouts and screams – worse, she heard the sound of stone breaking, as if the whole of Yeflam was groaning in pain. Her gaze turned in the direction of Nale, and she thought of Zaifyr.

The night had been bright when she first stepped out of the door in pursuit of Eira, but the light had come from the bodies of the dead. She had seen that light in Mireea after Fo and Bau died and she could still remember the chill when one brushed against her. If she closed her eyes on the step of Sin's Hand, she could picture the ghosts of Mireea along the cobbled roads. She could see the haunted look that they gave her as they passed, a look that mixed envy with desire. The darkness that she stared at now was far more troubling. In it, she saw only tragedy, and her mind conjured images of Zaifyr lying dead beside Jae'le and Eidan.

'You don't have to go,' Caeli said, her voice still soft. 'He would not expect it.'

'But he would do it for me,' she replied.

The guard grunted, but she had seen the same bright sky Ayae had. 'Try to stay safe,' Caeli said to her. 'I don't want to have to come looking for you.'

3.

'After you were released from your prison, I asked your sister why she accepted your freedom.' The Pauper spoke casually from the broken piece of stone he sat upon, his faded robes drawn about him in a mash of sodden colour. 'You had destroyed her home just as you had destroyed mine, after all. Do you know what she said?'

Zaifyr rose slowly to his feet. He ached: his skin felt as if it had been scalded, and the effort of swimming up had left his muscles burning. His clothes were heavy with water that irritated his skin, but they had been torn as well. The ancient dead had done that, and it had ripped handfuls of charms off him as it did. No doubt they drifted through the ocean, where they would come to rest on the floor of Leviathan's Blood. But what he had lost was replaceable.

As a light rain began to fall, he gazed at the ruins around him and admitted that what he saw might not be so easily replaced either.

Nale was split in half.

The northern half of it had fallen into the black ocean. Eidan's punch through the ground had broken the huge pillar that held it. It had also spread destruction to the cities that surrounded Nale. The bridges had gone first, it appeared. Even in the night, Zaifyr could see how a tremendous weight had been put on them, as they struggled to hold Nale aloft. When the bridges had given way, the force by which they were wrenched into Leviathan's Blood, the strength that tore them out of the stone fittings, was so powerful that the pillars that held up the other cities had cracked. He could see that the edges of Fiys and Maala had already begun to sag, and he could hear the grating of stone, as if it were the groan of the living, as it struggled to remain upright. Voices – in shouts and screams – filled the night to accompany it. They joined the cries that came from the churning waves of Leviathan's Blood, from the people who clung to pieces of wreckage and who were terrified by the water that they were in.

'She said,' Kaqua continued, after it became clear that Zaifyr would not reply, 'that she did not resent a dog its nature.'

Behind the Keeper, the Enclave slumped, half its walls broken to reveal furniture like the innards of a giant, while its end pointed towards the Mountains of Ger.

'You're not listening,' the other man said.

'You haven't said anything worthwhile yet.'

'You have never listened to me, Qian.'

He could not see Jae'le, Eidan, or even Aelyn. 'Where are the others?' he asked.

'You have never had time for a man like me. Your family is just the same. I could not speak to the dead or change the very nature of life. I could not grab the sky or the earth in my hands.'

The rain began to fall harder. On the remains of Nale, on

the wreckage that lay in the black water, Zaifyr saw the Keepers emerge. They were dull impressions, but they grew stronger as they pulled themselves from the water. The strongest sensations he had were of damp forests and a person who did not register as one, but as many.

Zaifyr finally turned to the Pauper. 'You forgot Tinh Tu,' he said.

'No, I did not forget her.' Now that Kaqua had his attention, he rose from his seated position. 'She would have understood what was happening here long before now. She would have felt my pushes. She would have seen my influence.'

'The Enclave is not one person,' he said, feeling as if a final piece had slotted into place for him. He saw now how Kaqua had hidden behind that line, how he had used it to shield himself as he manoeuvred the Keepers to where he wanted. Including, perhaps, his sister. 'That makes it easier, doesn't it?'

'It does, yes. It makes it easier to nudge, to suggest and to prompt. You must understand: I do not tell people to do anything, I do not make them act against their nature. That is what Tinh Tu does. Her voice is her power. That is why she stitches her lips together. That is why she does not speak. But I am not like that. I must see the problem first. I must be able to work with it. Then it is true: the more people you have, the more chance you have to see a problem. The more voices you have to speak it, the more debate you have. It is like a web you spin. After a while, everyone sees how the problem is theirs. How it is our shared responsibility. Of course, not everyone will be like that. Take you, for example, Qian. You understand the pain the dead experience, but you do not see it for the living. You do not see the struggle mortals have in this world. You do not see that this is as important as their death, as well.'

'I see a lot of people suffering right now. You don't seem too concerned that there are people drowning. That your navy appears to have been destroyed.'

'It breaks my heart.' Behind Kaqua, more Keepers began to appear. They came to the edge of Nale, to where the buildings fell into the ocean, where the broken stone of the city lay upon other pieces of stone. 'We worked so hard to not bring it to this point. We had tried to convince Se'Saera that the embarrassment she endured in the trial was not widespread across Yeflam. But she would hear nothing of it. She demanded that the words die here.'

'And you agreed?'

'Look at this world, Qian. Look at these broken suns and poisoned oceans. Madness, war, plague — this is the end of times. One day soon the suns will extinguish and we will die in the darkness. If a nation must be sacrificed for that to be stopped, then that is a fair trade.' He sighed. 'I wish it were not true, but it is.'

Delicately, Zaifyr began to reach out with his power. He could feel the dead, but their cold, their whispered desires, were no worse than the words of the man before him. 'I find it hard to believe that my sister agreed with you,' he said.

'I have had over a thousand years to weave my web around Aelyn.' The Pauper smiled. 'But to be honest, it was you who finally pushed her into supporting Se'Saera. It was you who convinced her that the responsibility of the world was one that we could not shoulder. After Asila, she took that upon herself. She saw how fragile this world was. She and Eidan both saw that. But it was only once you were here, once you ignored all her power, that she realized she could not keep the burden she had taken upon herself.'

The haunts appeared as, from the water behind him, Zaifyr felt his sister rise from Leviathan's Blood. The two haunts he had animated, a young man and woman who had fallen and drowned in the splitting of Nale, streamed into the hard, white-lit ghosts to kill Kaqua . . . but before they could, he felt himself lifted by a swirl of wind, felt hands grab him, and he was dragged into the surging storm that he knew, even before he saw his sister, came from deep within Aelyn.

4.

Ayae made her way with difficulty through the crowded streets of Ghaam. Each step away from Sin's Hand took her further beyond the order that the Yeflam Guard had established. Each step took her closer to a growing wind, to a cold rain, and to where the sky had begun to swirl above Nale in an ugly, bruised coloration. Yet, she made progress towards it, pushing her way through streets that were filling with hastily loaded wagons, occasionally pushed by men and women, but mostly pulled by oxen and horses. Other men and women ran past her, carrying children and possessions on their backs or in their hands. She had thought that she would see carriages ferrying people, but she had already passed one of the long ones, overturned, its horses stolen. She did not linger to learn what had happened, but continued to push further into the city. Around her, she heard snatches of conversation. 'The Leerans?' said one man; another spoke in a near hysterical voice, 'The pillar in Nale is broken, we're all—' 'We're fine, we're fine,' a woman cooed to her children, running away from him. '—it is the Keepers, they have betrayed—' said an elderly man, his cane thrust out before him. 'For the priests—' '—the Keepers would not—' one couple argued darkly. 'There was a fire—' '—at the start, I saw—' 'Ran down an alley—' A man, a woman, and a woman again, caught Ayae's attention, and she slowed to a walk to hear their words. 'She was alive. I could hear her cry, I could.'

Despite herself, Ayae stopped. 'Where exactly is she?'

The woman she had spoken to was perhaps a year or two older than her, but narrow and tall, her dark hair slick with rain. 'Two blocks south,' she said, finally. 'Near the road that leads to the docks. You will see two houses with red doors and a third with orange. The alley there. But I do not think you should bother. She is likely dead already.'

Ayae thanked her and began to run along the stone road. Ahead, the bruised sky darkened further, and she heard the violent rushing of the wind rise above the crash of the ocean. To her horror, she thought that the wind had begun to take on a shape, a definite human shape. It loomed above Nale, undefined in its face and in its body, but the shape was unmissable. She was also sure that there was a buzzing sound, as if hundreds of voices were speaking softly, but she could not make out a single word. Still, it was enough that Ayae told herself that she ought to follow part of the woman's advice, that she should not bother looking for the woman who had been on fire and continue onwards to Zaifyr. But when the lane that led to the docks appeared, she took it, and soon found the houses that the woman had mentioned.

In the middle of the alley she found Eira.

The Cold Witch lay against a fence, her body soaked by the rain and curled against the wooden pales. At first glance, Ayae thought she was dead, but she could feel the sensation of cold coming from the body.

With her foot, she nudged the Keeper onto her back, and

blanched. Eira's skin was a mess, a heavy blackened melt that the wet had gone some way to solidifying. Her hair had been burnt away, and she had torn her armour off as she ran, leaving little to cover the rest of her body. There was hardly anything that Ayae could identify as human, but the hatred that broke apart the loose flesh of Eira's face when she bared her teeth at the sight of Ayae left her in no doubt that the Keeper was still very much alive.

'You'll heal from this,' she said quietly.

Eira made a guttural noise in reply, unable to speak.

'You probably think I'm going to leave you because of that,' she continued. 'You think I'm going to leave you be because I feel pity.' Her hand fell to the hilt of her sword. 'But Aelyn was right about one thing: you cannot put aside the burden of your actions.'

The Keeper's burnt fingers began to push at the ground, began to try desperately to put distance between her and Ayae.

Ayae's foot settled on Eira's leg and she felt the flesh give way as she pushed down. A small whimper escaped the woman. Ayae could see in her eyes a terrible panic and fear that replaced the hatred. Her foot did not rise, however. Once, she might have responded, but it would have been because she did not know that Eira would follow her for years, that she would do so to enact a revenge that would be targeted at the people in her life as well as her. She knew now that Eira would pursue her. Bnid Gaerl had taught her the folly of believing otherwise.

Yet, thrusting her sword into the badly burnt woman was hard, harder than she had thought, and before the end, she questioned herself.

'Well done,' a deep, male voice said once she had finished. 'Very well done.'

She found Anguish on the shadowed ends of the fence that Eira had lain against, its ink-black skin a darker shadow.

'Jae'le and Eidan need your help,' the creature said.

'You smell of Leviathan's Blood,' Ayae said as she wiped her sword clean along her pant leg. 'I thought you were hiding on top of the Enclave.'

'The ocean.' He moved out of the shadows and along the edge of the fence like a cat. 'Beneath the waves her voice was dull to me. I could ignore her there. I could hide from her as she searched Yeflam for me. But she was strong and each day I was forced to sink deep into the ocean to hide from her. It was on the last days that I found the first pair of her creatures, waiting beneath the docks of Yeflam to rise out of the water. When they rose, I rose with them.'

Her sword slipped into its sheath. 'That sounds a lot as if you answered her call.'

'She is gone.' He hissed the last word with joy. 'Gone to the poor soul who spoke her name. By another god, he might have been rewarded, but from her — from her there will be only suffering.'

'And now here you are to beg for help?'

'They will die without you.'

'You'll forgive me if I don't believe you.' Ayae began to walk out of the alley. After a moment, she heard Anguish scramble after her.

'Please, *please*.' He landed deftly on her shoulder, but before he could settle, she caught him. Beneath her fingers, she could feel no bone, no muscle, just a faint chill. 'Don't ignore me, please,' he said, a thin wheedle entering his voice. 'Eidan and Jae'le are in need of your help. I know you go to help Qian, but you cannot get between him and Aelyn. That battle is not for the likes of you and me. But Eidan – Eidan *will* die, if you do not help. That is a fact. He was set upon by her creatures and hurt, but his true danger comes from Leviathan's Blood. He has fallen into it and his wounds have been tainted by her poison. Jae'le does not have the power to save him from that and from the creatures.'

'You disappear,' she said. 'You reappear. Your eyes are closed, but I hear Se'Saera's voice in all of your words.'

The creature squirmed in her grip, but could not break free. 'Do you not think it would be an easy thing for me to speak her words?' he asked angrily. 'I could be a pet, a prized creation by her side, if I could but find my faith in her yet again. She created me. She owns me. And yet here I am, begging you to save a man whom she has tried to kill tonight. You might think of that for a moment.'

The rain began to fall harder. Ayae contemplated ignoring Anguish, considered throwing him down the end of the alley and walking away. She did not trust him, but his words had rung true enough to her, and that stilled her hand. If Jae'le and Eidan were in danger, Zaifyr would want her to go to them first, would want her to do everything she could for them, before she entered Aelyn's storm – though, as the density of that tempest grew, as the giant above Nale became more and more defined, Ayae was increasingly concerned that she would be unable to push through it.

'They are not far from here,' Anguish pressed. 'Please.'

'Okay,' she said, finally. 'But if this is a lie, look behind you at Eira before we leave.'

5.

Standing before the burning siege tower, the grey-haired woman introduced herself as Qiyala, but offered no rank.

Heast had not planned to set fire to the tower, but before he began to descend through its guts, before the Maosans rode into the ravine, he had fallen to his knees as the name of the child god forced itself upon him. *Se'Saera.* He repeated it aloud, and again as he rose, regathering the crossbow as he did. *Se'Saera.* The intrusion angered him. The very nature of it, the force-fulness of it — it was an invasion of his self. But he did not kick the lamps over inside the siege tower because of his anger. No, he kicked them over because neither he nor Taaira had killed all the Leeran soldiers who had lain in wait in the ravine. At least two had fled, but with the name of their god revealed, he believed that those two would return quickly with more soldiers. They would find the nearest outpost and then they would come back. Heast and the others needed to be gone before then. At the door of the siege tower, he lit the fire that now burned strongly, and said exactly that to the nominated leader of the Maosans. He — a young, olive-skinned man by the name of Isaap — had cast his eyes to Qiyala, revealing what

Heast had suspected since he had first seen them approach in the dark.

'There are not many of us left,' the woman said to him now, as they rode through the night away from the ravine. 'Desertions, death — Iata has squandered most of his veterans.'

'Talon?' he asked.

'Second rank,' she admitted.

The equivalent to a sergeant, then. 'Why have you stayed?'

'Family.' Qiyala pointed along the line of horses which rode in single file without light. 'I have a grandson. He's not too smart, but at least he didn't carry a torch.'

'That wasn't your idea?'

She grimaced. 'Isaap is First Talon.'

'I see war has changed little in Faaisha,' Heast said drily. 'You can lead if you have the right blood, the right family and the right money.'

'It is no different anywhere in the world.'

'You have not seen the world, then.'

Qiyala offered him a lopsided smile that revealed a missing tooth. 'Iata will be happy to see you, won't he?'

Heast did not reply and she did not press him. She certainly knew who he was now, for when he had turned to her before the burning siege tower, she had saluted him and addressed him as the Captain of the Spine. If that was all she knew of him, then she would know, at the very least, what he had said to Kotan Iata a decade earlier, when he had ridden up to Mireea.

'He still calls himself Warden,' Qiyala said. 'If you are curious.'

'I am not.' Gently, Heast pulled on the reins of his mount. It fell behind the woman's and into the darkness. 'But thank you.'

As she continued onwards, two young men passed him,

both giving him nervous glances, and then, after a longer pause, the tribesman Kye Taaira appeared. The Maosans had not been happy to see him in the ravine, and they had kept their distance from him like children who feared a monster under their bed. There was more truth in that than he cared for, Heast knew, for the Hollow of the Pacifist Tribes of the Plateau had become a fabled nightmare in the Kingdoms of Faaisha. For his part, the tribesman bore the looks cast his way with quiet patience, and he had slung his sword over his back wordlessly before he mounted and fell into a slow walk at the end of their line.

'You and I must talk,' Heast said to him quietly. 'If you want to continue with me to Maosa, that is.'

'I will not apologize for what I did, Captain,' Taaira replied without pause. 'My ancestors are my responsibility.'

'Is it your responsibility to be reckless and stupid?'

'I was not—'

'You were.' Heast's voice allowed for no disagreement. 'You could have got both of us killed and it is unacceptable for you to act like that. You cannot disobey orders. You cannot disobey _me_. I am aware that you have your responsibilities, but I have mine too, and I cannot be true to them if you keep battlefield secrets from me. It will serve neither of us if you continue to do that. You cannot win a war by doing that. You do not keep your fellow soldiers alive by doing that. You risk not just yourself, but those around you, and I will not allow you to bring such foolishness into this endeavour if you cannot understand this.'

'I know all my ancestors,' he replied evenly. 'I know the horrors that each of them is responsible for. I know their flaws and their weaknesses. The risk is mine alone.'

Heast's hand reached out for the reins of Taaira's horse and pulled it to a stop. 'Understand me,' he said, 'very clearly.'

Taaira began to speak.

'No, you will listen to me, for I will say this only once. In the war that is before us, I will ensure that you retrieve your ancestors, but you must obey me on the field for that to happen. If you cannot do that, then you are of no use to me, and I will leave you dead on the ground here for scavengers in the morning. I will send your sword back to the Plateau with a note of apology to the shamans who gave it to you. I will tell them what I have told you: that your reckless behaviour put in danger not just me, but the soldiers who fought by my side and the people who relied upon me. Then I will tell them that I will deliver the remains of their ancestors in the weeks and months and that they need not bother to send another poorly disciplined warrior to be in my presence. Do I make myself very clear, tribesman?'

The Hollow's brown eyes held Heast's and the Captain of the Ghosts did not flinch. Finally, Kye Taaira nodded, and said, 'My apologies. It will not happen again.'

6.

Anguish directed her to the Ghaam docks. It was not a true dock, not like the long, multi-lane stone constructions that spread like fingers across the black water at the edges of Yeflam. Instead, it was a single stone dock that enabled small skiffs to draw against it, with a launch ramp alongside. It was one of the ways that merchants shifted their produce from city to city without using the streets.

It was at the southern edge of the city and, as Ayae made her way to it along a road that was awash in heavy rain, she had her first glimpse of the wreckage around Nale.

Fiys, the city that lay between Ghaam and Nale, had begun to slide into Leviathan's Blood. The bridge that had lain between it and Nale was gone, as was half of Nale itself. It had fallen into the churning sea, which was littered with the debris of buildings as well as the bodies of men and women, and of children and animals. Most lay surrounded by clothes and small pieces of furniture, such as chairs and tables and splintered doors. There were, however, still some people alive in the poisoned water, and they were swimming and pushing towards Fiys as if they would find safety there. They would not, because Ayae could see that the city was damaged. The four stone pillars that had held it reached up like broken fingers from the water, the damaged platform clear to her even through the driving rain.

Then she saw Jae'le at the end of Ghaam's stone dock.

He stood on the far edge, his hair and beard flattened by water against his skin, giving him the appearance of being so emaciated that he could only be a victim of a terrible starvation. Yet, he stood without flinching before his enemy, his sword drawn to protect Eidan, who lay in the shallow water beneath his feet. He was so still that Ayae could not tell if the large man was alive or not, but on her shoulder, she felt Anguish tense.

At first glance, the creature that paced around Jae'le appeared to be an animal, for it moved on its feet and hands much like an ape would. But what she took to be a body of brown-and-white fur, she realized, was no more than pelts that it wore. Yet, no matter that it might be human by birth, it made feints and lunges like a predator, skittering out of Jae'le's sword, never in range, but always a danger. Its behaviour was like a hunting pack animal's, for its attacks were intended to divert its prey from another attacker. In this case, a large, lean figure with bones emerging from its shoulders that had begun to emerge from Leviathan's Blood behind Jae'le. Ayae did not know if she could reach him before the creature was upon him. Her right foot fell on the stone platform, followed by her left.

'You cannot kill the two Jae'le stands before.' Anguish was forced to shout into her ear to be heard over the wind and rain. 'Leave him to fight them and take Eidan away from there!'

She had lost most of the heaviness she had felt since Faise's death and her feet finally felt as if they were moving at a natural speed.

'Few can kill these creatures!' He screamed desperately into her ear. 'You are not one of them!'

'Are you?' Ayae shouted back.

'No!'

She drew her sword as she left the ramp; her feet splashed through the shallow water of the dock; and before the creature could turn from Jae'le, she used its hunched back to vault into the air. If she could have, Ayae would have called out to Jae'le, would have warned him, but as the roar of the wind increased, and the rain became harder, she let flames run down the blade of her sword instead. Her body grew warmer with the action, and her hand felt as if it was on fire, as if the flames were igniting from her blood, but the pain did not linger. Clearing Jae'le's head, she brought her burning blade sweeping down on the lean creature . . . only for the sword to be caught in metal-wrapped hands. From her shoulder, Anguish leapt free of her soaked shirt and launched his ink-black body at the creature's face, causing it to flinch, releasing one hand to grab at the dark shape, and in that moment, Ayae's sword slid free and she slashed deeply across its chest.

Forgetting Anguish, the tall creature turned to her, its hands lashing out. With Jae'le at her back, she could not retreat from them, so she met the blows, turning each aside, feeling her opponent's strength in each strike, but relying on her own speed to keep her ahead. After a series of sweeping slashes, Ayae realized that although the flames on her sword began to wear out, washed away by the storm, the world had begun to slow around her. She could see the grimace in the creature's face contort into snarls and shouts, and she could see the torn skin around its left eye flap, just as she could see Anguish scamper through the water to Eidan. The control she had gathered to herself in Sin's Hand remained, and the frantic, burning rush that had been in her body weeks ago, the gnaw of anxiety that had been building in her ever since Samuel Orlan's shop had caught fire in Mireea, was absent.

Yet Anguish's words were proving to be correct. No wound that her burning blade caused on the creature saw it slow. Indeed, the long wound across its chest — a mortal wound on another — had not bled. She could see bone, and beneath it a darkness that hinted at still organs. She could even see now that it had been wounded from behind, its leather vest torn as if an animal had attacked it, but there was no blood, just as no gore spilled over the hands that had been wrapped in spiked chains. Dropping beneath a series of wild punches, Ayae knew that sooner or later she would mistime her reactions and the creature would catch her skin and draw blood from her. And, as she thought that, she felt Jae'le's right shoulder lean against her left, and she turned on instinct, her sword came around in an arc without fire to find the second creature barrelling past in a vicious charge that, even though it tried to stop, saw it skid in the water, only halting beside the taller creature before it turned to face both of them.

7.

In the heart of the storm, Zaifyr could hear Aelyn.

'I cannot blame you for this, brother. Not entirely.' He could not see her: the wind was filled with debris, with stone and wood, as well as hard, pelting rain. Her voice offered him no help. He could hear it over the wind around him, but that was only because what he heard was not one voice, but a hundred whispers. The wind that held him, the element that she had crafted hands from, and that grew in size and shape as it lifted him, was covered in faces. None of them was fully formed, but each had blind eyes and mouths, from which she spoke. 'We were to become gods. We were the Keepers of the Divine. The world was our responsibility.'

He could not move. He tried, but the hands on him tightened, and he felt himself lifted higher into the storming sky. He was rising with such a speed that he found it difficult to breathe: it felt as if he was beneath the water again, but this time he had to push himself downwards rather than up to find safety. Around him the splintered parts of houses and stone from Nale moved like swords and lances, some massive, but all lifted by the storming giant that Aelyn had formed over the remains of the city.

'But you are not free of blame, either.'

A shattered beam lanced suddenly towards him. A haunt wrapped itself around it, just briefly. The wind tore at its body harshly, ripping through Zaifyr's power, but not before the wood was diverted above him.

'When we agreed to support Se'Saera, I thought, *This will be my Asila*,' Aelyn said through the mouths of her storm giant, giving no hint that she saw what he did. 'This will be the horror that will follow me into divinity. This will be what I will spend thousands of years atoning for.'

Zaifyr could feel most of his power, now. When he opened all his senses, he could see in the night sky the souls of birds, both large and small ones, of those who hunted over Leviathan's Blood and those who did not. He could see, too, men and women, but they were fewer now. They had a limit that the storm giant was lifting him past. He would need to make both stronger, give both a new density if he wanted them to help him.

He focused on the human haunt that had deflected the beam, a young man who had died on the top floor of a hotel, a rich young man who had overdosed, and he had him slam into the wind-made fist.

A section of blind faces broke apart, but the storm giant, now clearly formed, did not release him.

'But there will be some things I will not be able to forgive myself for,' Aelyn said in hundreds of voices.

A storm petrel followed the ghost, and another followed it. Zaifyr grasped them both so they appeared in the sky like sharp knives that drove them into the hand of the storm giant, destroying more faces. After the petrels his power flowed into a dozen cormorants, then came gannets and, as the grip began to weaken, a flock of pelicans sliced downwards like swords, severing the winds from each other and dropping Zaifyr.

In free fall, he reached for the haunt of the albatross that Jae'le had summoned earlier. It was familiar to him, not as alien as the birds he had infused, and so it was easier for him to grab the big bird and force his power into it, giving it shape and form. A second later, he hit its spectral body hard, so hard that he felt a rib snap. The speed of his fall almost punched him through the body and onto the stones and churning water below.

The wind rushed at him angrily. Aelyn's storm giant had another hand and it swept down for him, forcing the albatross to bank away. In doing so, he saw a more definite shape in the monster that his sister had made. It had no legs, but was instead a torso that sat in the sky, its face defined by the angry storm clouds and lightning that crowned it. It was not the first time that he had seen such a creation from her, but he had not seen one marked by so many mouths, or heard her use it to speak as she did now.

'I will not be able to forgive myself for killing my family,' her thousand voices said. 'I will not be able to forgive the failure of my love. I had dreamed of making universes with Eidan. Our love was to define who we would be in divinity. The loss of that will be the greatest regret that I keep with me.'

You do not have to, Zaifyr wanted to tell her, as the albatross rose before the storm giant, as it moved around its grasps, as it slid between the debris that it hurled. *You can end this. You can save the people of Yeflam. You can stand with us.*

But he knew that she would have to break Kaqua's control first.

That would not happen, not here, not above the ruins of Nale. The Pauper had had thousands of years to set his words in her, doing so without her knowledge. Even now, he could remember how he had felt after he killed the two priests, how easily he had agreed with Kaqua. Zaifyr had thought that they were his own thoughts at the time, that he knew exactly what Kaqua did with his power when he made that clumsy thrust of suggestion in their first meeting. But now, he was not sure. He could not be. He remembered how quickly he had agreed, how it had been something that he wanted to do, but now he could see how the Pauper worked, how he had made Zaifyr's own thoughts stronger, how he had taken his doubts, his hopes, and strengthened them.

Aelyn floated in the centre of the storm giant's head, its form an extension of her. Her eyes were closed when he came upon her, but they opened now.

He said her name, once.

From the giant's mouth, a roar burst. The wind that came from it was like a volley of arrows. Zaifyr could not avoid them, could not see them clearly, and they tore at his clothes, sliced open the skin of his arms and back, and forced him to press hard against the ghostly body of the albatross. He reached frantically out for the haunt of another bird, for anything that he could hurl against her, to stop her attack, to force her to talk to him, but even as he reconnected with the flock of pelicans that had broken the giant's grip, he knew it would not be enough.

He had but one option if he did not wish to be destroyed.

8.

The steel edge of Ayae's blade caught the spiked punch of the lean creature, right before her hand thrust out, slamming heel-first into its chest.

She hit hard, intent on pushing it out into Leviathan's Blood. She knew that any fire she could ignite on the leather vest of the creature would not last, and so she focused on the force she struck with, on her strength. For all that she was sure that she heard ribs break in response, the creature took but half a step backwards beneath her strike. Shocked, she lingered in the aftermath of the blow longer than she should have, and would have been hit hard had Jae'le's sword not come up to block the creature's other hand. With both its hands held at bay, Ayae stepped back, intending to strike again with her hand, but as her foot moved backwards, she let her sword fall from its position and turned, stepping around Jae'le and bringing her sword down in a sweeping slash at the bestial creature. It jerked from the path of her blow and, instead of tearing through flesh, her blade hit chain and she realized that beneath the heavy furs the creature wore, its body had been wrapped protectively. But it left the creature heavy and slow and she pressed forward as she felt Jae'le move in the opposite direction, his blade catching a blow from the lean creature that followed her movement, while in front of Ayae, the bestial creature reared back and revealed a white face heavily tattooed into a snarling bear beneath its heavy fur hood.

Swiftly, her sword darted out and tore through its left eye.

It roared, but before she could press forward, she felt Jae'le hit her back, and heard a grunt from him. She moved out of his way as he fell backwards, long scratches from the spikes on the lean creature's hands leaving their marks across his chest. Ignoring the bestial creature, Ayae brought her sword around in a circle and hammered into the second slash of the creature, the one that aimed to tear further into Jae'le's chest. Her blow came down heavily across its wrist. It dug deep into the chains, parting them, parting the skin beneath until it hit and lodged in the bone there.

The creature ripped its arm away, and in doing so, tore Ayae's sword out of her grasp. She let it go, dropping flat in the shallow water as Jae'le's sword swung heavily through where she had stood. The blade tore deeply through the mid-section of the creature. Jae'le followed the attack, moving with a sudden speed that Ayae, for all her swiftness, for all her accelerated perception, had difficulty following. Briefly, she wondered why it had taken until now for Zaifyr's brother to show it, but as the thought passed through her, Ayae saw Anguish, who had crawled on to the back of Eidan, turn his closed eyes to Jae'le.

'*No!*' Anguish shouted as the large man's body shuddered, and Ayae realized that whatever power Jae'le had tapped into to attack the creature had been taken from the threads that he had bound around Eidan to keep him alive. But as he attacked the lean creature, as his sword struck out in a series of fast and hard blows, as she saw the damaged arm come clean off and land on the ground, black water came from Eidan's mouth in a shuddering cough.

A second followed as the bestial creature loomed over the large man.

Ayae darted forward without thinking, her body ploughing into the creature, the force of her lunge folding it onto its back, while her hands dug angrily into its chest.

The chain yielded beneath her hot hands and the creature tried to rip itself away. It slammed its heavy arms into her in desperation. She dug deeper into its mail, reaching for its skin, but she was rocked by a blow to her head by the tattooed face of the creature slamming down, and she fell backwards. Even as she did, she saw the hilt of her sword slide along the ground to her and, as the creature raised its mail-heavy arms, Ayae scooped the blade up and brought it powerfully into the right arm of the creature.

There was no finesse to her blow, no elegance. She drew the blade back and swung it again as if it were an axe. She felt flesh and bone give way, and as she drew the blade back again, as she hurried to her feet, she swung the blade through the creature's breaking arm and into its head.

The steel edge caved the tattooed face in as if it were hollow and when she ripped her sword out, half the skull tore apart like old, gristly meat, before the creature's body slumped to the ground.

'Throw it into Leviathan's Blood.' She heard Jae'le shout from her right, from where he had pushed the lean creature into the ocean. 'We cannot kill it, but there is something down there to make it wish it was dead.'

Behind him, a long, dark tentacle pawed at the stone dock. The bestial creature was still alive as she dragged it to the edge. It struggled weakly against her when she first grabbed its furs, but by the time she reached the edge, it had become stronger, as if the damage to its head, to its brain, had merely been a shock to it, and whatever lurked inside it needed only time to rework the controls of the body it inhabited. But she pushed it into the tentacle's grasp, and from beneath the black water, she saw a dozen – thicker, the size of her legs, and coloured a dark, ugly red – rise to take it and drag it down into its depths.

When she turned, Ayae discovered that an ox and cart had come down to the dock. It stood there patiently as Jae'le, now holding Eidan, carried his brother to the back of it.

Closer, she saw that the ox had wounds over its back and neck. In the cart, pushed to the side from where Eidan was laid, the bedding and clothes were soaking wet. But it was the voices she could hear once again that caught her attention.

'Can you hear that?' she asked.

'It is Aelyn,' Jae'le said. He pointed to the storm and, with a shock, she saw the fully formed storm giant. It towered over Nale, its body rippling with lightning, as if the energy was its veins and blood. Yet, its face did not look like anyone she knew, and remained curiously featureless, without eyes or a mouth. 'The words are her own.'

She tried to focus on what was being said, but it sounded too much like the wind.

'Without you, I would not have been able to keep both of us alive,' Jae'le said. His hand fell to her shoulder. 'I thank you.'

'What is she saying?' Ayae asked.

'She is asking for forgiveness.' He turned back to the cart. 'She is asking it of the people of Yeflam, though many will not know that. But she is asking it of us too.'

'Why would she ask it of us?'

Lightning lit up the storm, and Ayae thought that she saw flocks of birds illuminated, but only briefly.

'Because Zaifyr is going to kill her,' Jae'le said, a terrible sadness in his voice. 'Once she is dead, he will be our responsibility.'

9.

The first of the birds to hit Aelyn was a storm petrel.

It hit her from behind. It had pierced through the back of the storm giant's blunt head while Zaifyr drove the dead pelicans into the wind that poured from its mouth. It was a move of desperation: he could feel the skin beneath his fingers breaking, could feel his clothes splitting, feel the remaining charms in his hair tearing free, but mostly, he could sense the pelicans breaking apart. The endless roar of the giant smashed into the bodies he strengthened. The sheer primal force was too much for the dead birds, and so he reached for the small petrel and drove it into her like a dagger. It caused the wind to break, for just a moment, and his power returned to the haunts of the pelicans, and the large birds surged towards Aelyn.

Within moments, the ghosts had swarmed over her just as the ghosts of Asila had.

She had arrived with Jae'le and Tinh Tu and Eidan, a week after he had made his last walk down the long road, a week after he had finally given the dead what they had asked from him. His memory of that time was not perfect: he could recall flashes of images, could remember some scenes, but he had lost himself. By the time his brothers and sisters arrived in Asila, they found not just a city in ruins, but a nation caught in the grips of a mad horror, and a brother who stood in the centre of it. Later, in the years that followed his release from the tower, Zaifyr had not asked Jae'le what he had seen that day. He had not asked him what they had done. How long they had fought. He did not ask because he wanted to put as much distance as he could between himself and the event. He was not that man. He would not be that man again. But he knew that, before Aelyn's hands reached for his neck, before the ground beneath her began to break as Eidan's construction came to life, that she had talked to him. All four of them had talked to him. They had pleaded with him to stop, but he had heard only the words of the dead.

Zaifyr wanted to speak to Aelyn. He owed it to her. He wanted to pull the birds away from her to do it, but he knew that he could not. He did not have the words to undo what Kaqua had done. Nor, as the giant's head began to web with lightning, did he have the words to undo what he himself had said. He could not take back the words he had used earlier, in the quiet rooms of her house and in the trial on Nale. For all that the Pauper had done, Jae'le was right: Aelyn was also a victim of the power he had, of his response to any who opposed him.

He wanted to tell Aelyn that. He wanted her to know that he understood what he had done. He felt the urge keenly as his power flowed into the birds that tore at her skin. He wanted to tell her that he had not been trying to destroy her, that he had set out to destroy Se'Saera, to free the dead, to bring an end to the horror that he saw each day.

But to what point?

Around Aelyn, the winds burst out against the ghosts of the birds.

Did he hope to stop her with these words, to somehow diffuse the situation that was before him?

No.

He knew better than that.

Inside the storm giant's skull, thunder crashed and, suddenly, its head burst apart.

The wind slashed out towards him, the strength of it punching into his chest, cracking more ribs. His breath was stolen and his bloodied hands loosened their grip on the albatross. As if sensing his weakness, a second and third burst from the headless giant and hit him in the chest. It ripped at his clothes, tore away more charms, and bit into his skin. Trying desperately to focus through the pain and the short gasps of breath that he could manage, Zaifyr's power surged into three of the pelicans that he could find. He gave them density and size – he turned their thick bodies solid like steel, made their heavy beaks like axes – and gave them as much life as he dared before he forced them into Aelyn's fury.

The birds struggled towards her. Their white bodies changed beyond the normal constraints that life gave them as more of Zaifyr's power surged into them. They grew larger, more imposing, and he knew that he was making them into monsters. Monsters that he would use to break through her defences.

Aelyn began to reform the head of the storm giant, to use it as a shield, but Zaifyr knew that she was too late. He tightened his hold of the monsters he had made, kept his control, for they were his responsibility, just as Asila had been the responsibility of his brothers and sisters.

That was why they had come then, he knew. When it had

become clear that he could no longer be responsible for his own actions, they had taken responsibility for him. They did it not because they were gods, or because they were the rulers of the Five Kingdoms: they did it because there was no one else to whom the duty could fall. They had stood before him for the same reasons that he had when he went to Yeflam in chains.

The first of the monstrous birds reached out to strike Aelyn, but Zaifyr stilled it.

He could not hold it for long. He was exhausted, both mentally and physically. He needed to strike now, but he could not. Faced with the moment when he had to plunge his undead creations into Aelyn's skin, into her body, he could not do it. He could not kill her. Yet not to kill her was to accept his own death. He saw that clearly. He saw her frustration and her loss, and even though he knew that Kaqua had woven his arguments into her, woven his fears and desires into all of the Keepers of the Divine, he could not kill her. He had to take responsibility for his own part in it, as well. He did not believe that what he had done was wrong, but he also knew that he had not done it correctly. He stilled his second and third birds. His emotions tore at him. He knew that he wanted to free the dead, knew that the horror they existed in could not continue. But the price — the price was not just the woman who was his sister, it was to give up his family, and it was to give up himself. To kill Aelyn was to give up the man he had crawled back to in the tower. It would be to return to the man he had once been.

And he was not the man he had once been.

A moment later, the wind took him.

Epilogue

Not so long ago, I received a letter from one of my
brothers. I replied to it, but my reply was dismissive,
angry for what he and another of my brothers planned
to do to my sister. I had not yet arrived in Gogair. I
was still in Salar, in my dark, warm corridors. Yet, as
I sat at my desk to work, I could not escape his words.
I read them again. And again. And eventually, I began
to walk in the cities of Gogair, to follow the threads
that were there, to see the tapestry that was being
sewn before us all.

In Yeflam, I imagine that I will have to apologize
to him.

—Tinh Tu, *Private Diary*

1.

The Captain of the Ghosts arrived at the gates of Maosa in the rain.

Huddled in his cloak, Heast sat next to Kye Taaira and watched the gate slowly open. It was part of a large, solid wall made from stone and wood which encircled the town like a shackle around a wrist. A fool's fortune had been spent on the wall sixteen years ago when Kotan Iata had first claimed the title of Warden and the people of Maosa had never broken free of it. It was not that the wall was poorly constructed, for it would not be easy to breach, but it had halted the expansion of a town on one of the least desirable tracts of flat land that Heast had seen. As the Kingdoms of Faaisha grew in wealth and size, many believed that Maosa had been in a good position to turn itself into a major city at the eastern edge of the nation, building political and economic bridges with the Plateau and Mireea. Under another leader, it might well have done so, but under Kotan Iata, a man who saw prosperity only through the sword and who was consumed by his ambition to be a Marshal of Faaisha, no such expansion was possible. It condemned the small town of Maosa to despair, a situation that was all-too apparent when Heast and Taaira rode through the gate.

Isaap and his soldiers rode ahead of the two men as they made their way through the narrow streets of the town. To Heast, an inn that dominated the first street best symbolized the conditions that he saw as their horses made the slow, muddy trek to its centre. Made of thick cuts of wood, it was a low, long building, half of it closed off by a roof that had collapsed inwards. A pair of wet crows sat at the top of the rubble, and a half-starved dog eyed them from a dangerous piece of dry cover that it lay under, reluctant to leave. The half of the inn that had not been repaired was the half that used to offer lodging, but the other half, the half that held the bar, was still open. It was empty but for one elderly barkeep who stared out of the large door with a flat expression as Heast rode towards the small castle in Maosa's centre.

The castle had been built at the same time as the wall, and it bore strong similarities to it in the stone and wood used to construct it. Its halls were cold and dark when Heast entered, and the echo of the group's footsteps preceded them. At the two large doors that led to the throne room, the guards admitted them without collecting the swords that they carried.

Behind the doors, Kotan Iata waited. He was a tall olive-skinned man who had long ago gone bald, but maintained his height and air of gravitas as he aged. In his late sixties now, he wore heavy robes of red and black and carried in his hand a large silver sceptre. He used the ceremonial piece to point to various wooden soldiers that had been placed around him and on top of a coloured chalk map of the Kingdoms of Faaisha. As Heast watched, young pages hastily picked up the figures at his orders, moving pieces that wore green and brown for Leera and red and silver of Faaisha across the floor.

'Aned Heast,' Iata said without raising his head. 'You have cost me a tower.'

'I saved your soldiers,' he replied.

'A tower is worth two score of men. You know that as well as I.'

A fool's statement, made by a fool, Heast knew. The soldiers around him – from the veteran Qiyala to the newly appointed First Talon Isaap – shifted uncomfortably.

After the silence stretched out longer than was socially acceptable, Iata looked up and met Heast's gaze. 'I have heard that Lord Tuael has requested you,' he said, finally. 'Please know that I do not agree that you are needed.'

'I will only be here briefly.'

'See to it that you are,' he said, dismissing him.

Outside the castle, he and Taaira parted from Isaap and his soldiers, except Qiyala. The veteran planned to direct them to an inn, but after travelling a block, Heast dismounted and told her and the tribesman that he had another person to see first. Kye Taaira gave him a curious look, but Heast merely handed him the reins of his own horse in answer to the unspoken question. 'I'll find you in The Eel later,' he said. 'See that the horses are fed and watered.'

'Of course,' Taaira replied, taking the reins. 'May your friend remember you kindly, Captain.'

Maosa unravelled before Heast in a nest of poverty and quiet despair, very different from when he had last walked its muddy roads. Then, it had been an angry town, on the verge of revolt against Iata, and it had taken Lord Tuael himself to calm them.

Heast had been the Captain of the Spine then, and he had advised Tuael otherwise, words that he knew had reached Iata later. But, as he made his slow, uneven walk down the streets, as he passed men and women who met his gaze with dull, flat eyes, and saw into houses that were empty tombs, he did not reconsider his advice. As the rain began to fall harder, he began to hope that he was wrong and that the old witch Anemone no longer lived in the tangled sprawl of houses at the back of Maosa.

Sadly, her house remained. It stood buried in a warren of narrow streets among a collection of small, poorly built houses that leant against each other. With his hand pressed against the joint where flesh and steel met, Heast made his way up the path to her front door. He passed a rangy cat and a pair of muddy chickens, but it was the fold of the curtains in the windows and the potted plants outside the house that assured him that it was still occupied.

The door was opened by a young, olive-skinned woman. She was thin to the point of being underfed, emphasized by the oversized leather trousers and shirt that she wore. She had dyed her hair a dark, unnatural red and it was pulled back into a ponytail, revealing the edges of dark tattoos that wound around the base of her neck. She could not have been much older that seventeen, Heast thought.

'You are late, Captain,' she said. 'My grandmother wishes you to know that.'

'I did not know I was on a schedule.'

'You were on her schedule. She died a month ago.'

'Does she still wait for me?'

'Yes, Captain, she does.'

2.

Bueralan awoke to the sound of a horse being led through the stables. He had not expected to fall asleep, certainly not as heavily as he had, and he was surprised to find that a blanket had been laid across him. Groggily, he turned his head and, through swollen eyes, watched Samuel Orlan lead a grey horse past him and into the stable next to Bueralan's tall grey. Grunting, the saboteur pushed himself to his feet slowly, his splinted arm held across his chest and his broken hand cradled above it. Finally, he struggled out of the stall where he had lain and came to stand next to the older man, saying, 'That's your horse, isn't it?'

'She has done better than either of us.' Orlan was running a brush along the back of the grey, picking out burrs and leaves, while also checking her for wounds. 'I can only imagine the horror she had to come through to reach us.'

'You have only to look out of the door to see it.'

'She was stabled at my shop,' he said. 'Aela Ren and Se'Saera have gone to Cynama.'

Bueralan then realized that the two were alone in the stables. With a heavy step, he made his way to the open door and gazed at the empty but broken land outside, the land that was still littered with the bodies of men and women and horses, and where a faint sulphuric odour hung in the air from the lava that had burst through the ground.

'Se'Saera took Taela with her.' Orlan came up to stand beside him. 'I tried to stop it from happening, but I was ignored. I tried to tell them that Taela was in great pain, and great distress, but . . . You could still see the scratches around her mouth and the despair in her eyes when Se'Saera took her arm . . .'

Bueralan did not close his eyes, for fear that he would be able to see it. 'You could leave,' he said. 'You could get on your horse and ride away, ride far away.'

'Before I came here, I said I would see this to the end,' the cartographer replied. 'Even if I could, I would not step away now.'

'The end?' A hollow laugh escaped him. 'I will tell you the end, old man. They'll burn Ooila to the ground and they'll torture Taela every day until she gives birth.'

'No,' Orlan corrected him softly. 'No, I am sorry to say that they will not do all of that. Se'Saera has issued an order to Ren and his soldiers. She has ordered them to leave the country. She has demanded that Aela Ren and his soldiers destroy Cynama so that the path to Dyanos is clear. *Glafanr* will meet us there. After that, we are to head to Leera — and you and I are to be part of that journey, I am afraid. There may be no guards around us, Bueralan, but we are prisoners who are to be loaded onto that ship before it sails into her war against the Kingdoms of Faaisha, against Yeflam, and against the remains of Mireea.'

'Why the rush?'

'She has seen the future,' he said, as a single butterfly rose into the burnt sky before them. 'General Waalstan will not survive the year.'

3.

The girl led him into the small, warm house. It had only two bedrooms, a kitchen that led into a tiny backyard, and a small living room filled with jars and books and boxes. In the last, Heast knew, the bones of the witch, Anemone, were packed beside the bones of her daughter, her sister, her mother, and the two generations of women who had come before her. They had bound themselves to their daughters in servitude and, Heast suspected, the old witch had done the same to the girl who he followed.

'Have you taken her name?' he asked.

'It is an old name,' the girl replied. 'One with power, one without.'

'It is also a flower.'

'Yes.' She smiled. 'My grandmother bids you hello.'

He sat on an old lounge, the fabric torn around the edges of the arms, and stretched his steel leg out. 'I am sorry I missed the funeral.'

'She knows you are not, Captain,' the young Anemone replied. 'The rituals that bound her to me are nothing you would find pleasant. In fact, if I were to be honest, my grandmother's opinion is that you do not like witches at all.'

'I liked her,' he said. 'But she and I have had that conversation before. If she is to haunt me with it, she can begin another day. What else does she have to say?'

The girl laughed, and in her laugh, Heast heard echoes of the old woman he had known. 'She wants you to know that she is sorry to hear about Baeh Lok,' Anemone said, sitting on a chair opposite him. 'She wished that she could have spared him that fate. However, it is her opinion that he was right to take the letter to you. The war is going poorly for the Lords of Faaisha. The rumours of defections in the smaller kingdoms are true, just as the defeats in others are. But she says that is not the reason she agrees with the calling of Refuge. Kingdoms rise and fall, she says. But now there is a god. Se'Saera has been named. She has been revealed. She says that you have seen the soldiers she has made and you have heard about the slave routes to Gogair. Grandmother says that is enough for Refuge. She says it was enough for the soldiers, it is enough for the witch, and it should be enough for the captain.'

'Should it?'

'She also wants you to know that your friend, the one who accompanied you long ago, the one who frightened her.' The girl paused. 'Zaifyr,' she said. 'Grandmother says that he has died.'

'And Muriel Wagan?' he asked.

'She still lives.'

Heast pushed himself slowly from the couch and thanked the girl.

'My grandmother,' Anemone said, as he reached the front door of the house, 'wants to know what you think.'

He met the girl's dark eyes. 'It is enough,' he said.

'She wants me to accompany you when you leave.'

'And what do you want?'

'There is no future for me here,' she said truthfully. 'I wish to continue my grandmother's legacy. It is mine, as well.'

'Gather your things,' Heast said. 'We won't be here long.'

It was the news about Zaifyr that sat uncomfortably in him as he left the girl and made his way to The Eel. It surprised Heast and he wanted to question it, but he could not imagine that the old witch would have lied to him: he could no more doubt her loyalty in death than in life. Still, a part of him had relied on Zaifyr to kill Se'Saera, to leave the Leeran Army without its figurehead, to leave him a simple, if messy, job.

Inside The Eel, Kye Taaira was waiting silently at a table surrounded by Maosan veterans. Only Qiyala engaged him in conversation, but even she, when Heast pushed through the door, raised her hand with the others to call him over. In the discussion that followed, the veterans voiced their discontent, their fear and their anger, but Heast found himself returning to the death of Zaifyr, to the failure of the charm-laced man's gambit. He had placed everything on convincing the Keepers to side with him. He had allowed shackles to be put around his hands. He had let the house he had sat in become a prison. He had been so sure and so confident that Heast could imagine that he had only failed if both the Enclave and Se'Saera had fought against him. He would have to know for sure, of course, but if such an alliance had occurred . . . well, Heast had to admit, the complaints that he was hearing might soon become calls for peace.

Eventually, he left the veterans and fell asleep on the narrow bed. In the morning, he awoke to find that the rain still fell.

Heast did not eat breakfast that morning. Instead, he belted his sword around his waist and, with the tribesman beside him, walked into the stables. There, Anemone waited for him. She had an old, thick cloak over the clothes she wore the day before, and around her waist were a dagger and a collection of pouches. She had neither a pony, nor a horse, and he made a mental note to buy her both before the day was out. Kye Taaira greeted her respectfully, but it was onto the back of Heast's horse that the young witch climbed, and the three of them rode silently through the muddy streets, turning not in the direction of the gates of Maosa, but towards the castle.

Veterans began to emerge onto the streets as the three of them made their way in the rain. At first, they came singly and in pairs, but a large group, led by Qiyala, waited for them before the castle. He felt Anemone's warm, excited breath against his neck as he and Taaira rode up the path, and he glanced at the tribesman once, to find that he regarded everything taking place with a calm acceptance. The guards outside the castle took the reins of Heast's and Taaira's mounts as they drew up to the heavy doors of the building.

Inside, he made his way to the centre of the castle. On his right stood Kye Taaira, on his left, Anemone, and behind him followed Qiyala and the veterans. The doors of the throne room opened at his approach and the tall, robed figure of Kotan Iata was revealed. He stood in the chalk outline of the Kingdoms of Faaisha, a silver goblet of wine in his hand, and a young page with chalk-stained hands crouched over the map, recolouring the blemishes that had been made by the wooden figures and their movements. At the sight of Heast, Iata frowned, but his scowl deepened into outrage when he realized that behind him were his own soldiers.

'You were not invited here,' Iata said, throwing the goblet where, a moment ago, the page had knelt. 'Guards—'

Heast's hand clamped over his mouth and his dagger plunged into Iata's stomach.

The self-proclaimed Warden of Maosa struggled, but soon his body dropped to the floor. In the silence that followed, Heast turned to the men and women who stood behind him and regarded each of them. 'My name,' he said, 'is Aned Heast. I am the Captain of Refuge.'

extracts reading groups
competitions books new
discounts extracts
extracts
competitions
books
new
events books
extracts
new reading groups
interviews
discounts
new books events
events new
discounts extracts discounts

www.panmacmillan.com

extracts events reading groups
competitions books extracts new

reading groups
events
reading groups
extracts
discounts
title
interviews
events
books
new
interviews
new books
extracts
books